Ma[illegible] e and can't imagine a better job. A seven-time finalist for [illegible] prestigious Romance Writers of [illegible] *RITA*® A[illegible] author of more than one hundred romance novels. Her books regularly appear on best-seller lists and have won several awards, including a Prism Award, a National Readers' Choice Award, a Colorado Romance Writers Award of Excellence and a Golden Quill Award. She is a native Californian but has recently moved to the mountains of Utah.

Reese Ryan writes sexy, emotional romance with captivating family drama, surprising secrets and complicated characters. A panelist at the 2017 Los Angeles Times Festival of Books and recipient of the 2020 Donna Hill Breakout Author Award, Reese is an advocate for the romance genre and diversity in fiction. Connect with Reese via Facebook, Twitter, Instagram or reeseryan.com. Join her VIP Readers Lounge at bit.ly/VIPReadersLounge. Check out her YouTube show, where romance readers and authors connect at bit.ly/ReeseRyanChannel.

Also by Maureen Child

Tempt Me in Vegas
Bombshell for the Boss
Red Hot Rancher
Jet Set Confessions
Temptation at Christmas
Six Nights of Seduction

Also by Reese Ryan

Savannah's Secret
The Billionaire's Legacy
Engaging the Enemy
A Reunion of Rivals
Waking Up Married

THE EX UPSTAIRS

MAUREEN CHILD

JUST A LITTLE MARRIED

REESE RYAN

MILLS & BOON

First Published in Great Britain 2021
by Mills & Boon, an imprint of HarperCollins*Publishers* Ltd
1 London Bridge Street, London, SE1 9GF

www.harpercollins.co.uk

HarperCollins*Publishers*
1st Floor, Watermarque Building,
Ringsend Road, Dublin 4, Ireland

ISBN: 978-0-263-28305-1

0921

THE EX UPSTAIRS

MAUREEN CHILD

To my kids, Jason and Sarah,
for every hug, every laugh, every tear.
You make my life amazing.

One

Henry Porter smiled.

"She's here, boss. And she doesn't look happy."

His assistant's news made his smile widen into a damn grin. "That's fine by me, Donna. I'm not in business to make the Carey family happy."

"Right." The older woman lowered her voice. "Well, mission accomplished. Do you want me to send her in? She doesn't have an appointment," she added unnecessarily.

"Make her wait five minutes," he said, pushing up from his chair. "Then send her in."

He disconnected from the call, then slowly walked to the bank of windows affording him an impressive view of Los Angeles and the suburbs that stretched out beyond it. He'd miss the view when he moved the company headquarters to Orange County, but he'd have an ocean view then and that would take the sting out of the move.

But for now, he took those five minutes to settle by staring out at the bustling city beneath him. He needed to prepare to face the woman he still thought about far too often.

He'd known that either Amanda Carey or her older brother, Bennett, would show up at his office soon. Hell, he'd done everything he could to ensure it. He considered it his lucky day that it was Amanda currently cooling her heels in the outer office with Donna.

Over the years, Henry had had a few opportunities to throw the proverbial monkey wrench into Carey plans. Convincing people to cancel mergers. Underbidding the Careys on different contracts. And on those occasions, he'd kept his name out of it, so he could anonymously stand by and enjoy their frustrations.

Well, *Bennett's* frustrations. That's what this was all about. Showing his one-time friend that times had changed. *Henry* had changed and he hadn't forgotten.

This time though, Henry was taking a damn bow. He'd let word get out that it was Porter Enterprises that'd bought the piece of property right out from under the Careys. He'd known they wanted it—then he'd made sure they didn't get it.

And, since Amanda Carey had come to see him personally, he knew he'd made an impact. Henry hadn't spoken directly to the woman since a charity fundraiser in San Diego a year ago. At the memory, his mind instantly filled with the image of her that night. Her long, dark blond hair twisted up into a knot at the top of her head, she had worn a one-shoulder, white, floor-length gown that made her look both ethereal and like a sex goddess at the same time.

She'd simply taken his breath away—though he hadn't

let her see it. They'd literally bumped into each other at the bar and the look in her eyes should have killed him on the spot. Instead, she'd set him on fire in a way that no other woman ever had.

Henry didn't much care for the fact that Amanda could still hold so much power over him. But there was no point lying to himself—though he'd deny the truth to anyone else.

The two of them had spoken briefly, keeping it all business because there were too many prying eyes and perked ears surrounding them for anything else. But she hadn't been able to hide the knives in her eyes as she looked at him. Was it perverse of him to enjoy that side of her? To know that as much as she tried to pretend that he had no effect on her, her temper spiked just being close to him?

And damned if that temper didn't tug at him in a way a simpering smile never would have. He wondered what that said about him, but didn't really think too much about it. After all, since the moment he'd met her, back when he was in college and Bennett Carey was still a friend, Henry had been drawn to her, Bennett's younger sister. He'd met her when she was eighteen and by the time she was twenty, Henry had fallen hard. She was pretty and smart and funny and everything he'd wanted.

He'd never met anyone like her. The more time he'd spent with her, the more he'd felt that hard, irresistible draw. And finally, over the course of a two-week Italian vacation he'd spent with the Careys, he'd only wanted her more. Just before that vacation ended, he'd had her. Finally. In the boathouse at the Carey lakeside mansion, Henry and Amanda had had sex and he'd discovered she was a virgin, when it was far too late to stop. She hadn't wanted to stop anyway, he remembered. They'd been wild for each other and when that passion finally exploded, neither one of them had known what to do with the aftermath.

As it turned out, though, they hadn't had to worry about it.

Scowling to himself, he pushed those memories aside, leaned back against his desk, folded his arms across his chest and waited. When his office door opened, a stray slash of sunlight spotlighted her on the threshold as if she were a Broadway star claiming the stage and only awaiting a round of applause to continue.

He damn near gave it to her.

She wore a vivid scarlet jacket with a white shirt and black skirt that ended a couple of inches above her knees. The red stilettos added an extra three inches to her height and did amazing things for a pair of already great legs. Her long blond hair fell loose around her shoulders in a tumble of waves that made him want to bury his hands in them.

"Amanda..."

She took a breath, quietly closed the door behind her, then whirled on him with those oh-so-familiar knives in her eyes again. Only this time, they were aflame, as well.

"You did it on purpose."

He gave her a smile that he knew would only irritate her further. "Good to see you, too."

"Oh," she warned, "don't try for charm, Henry."

"You think I'm charming? Good to know."

"No, I don't," she said, but he didn't believe her.

She crossed the room to him in several long, quick steps. Her heels were muffled against the thick, muted jewel-tone rug, but nothing had quieted the temper bristling around her.

"What I want to know is *why* you did it."

"You want to be more specific?" He knew exactly what she was talking about, but why not hear it from her?

"The old hall. Near the Carey Center. You bought it."

He gave a chuckle he wasn't feeling. "That's illegal, now?"

"No, just despicable." She dropped her black leather bag onto one of his guest chairs, set both hands on those lusciously curved hips and said, "You knew we wanted that building."

Yes, he had. "Now, how would I know that?"

Throwing both hands up, she said, "Spies?"

He laughed, genuinely enjoying himself. Seeing Amanda in a temper was even better than he remembered. In the ten years since their one and only night together, she'd only gotten more beautiful. More intriguing. And more desirable.

"Seriously, Amanda? You think I hired spies?"

"Why not? Wouldn't that be in line with your long-term game plan of making the Careys pay?"

His easy tone dropped away. "Pay for what?" They both knew what she was talking about, but damn it, he wanted to hear her admit it.

Rather than that, though, all she said was, "It was ten years ago, Henry."

"Time flies and all that."

"And you're still looking for what? Revenge?"

He forced a laugh he didn't feel. "Revenge? A little melodramatic, don't you think?"

She swung her hair back over her shoulders. "What else should I call it?"

"Karma?" he offered. Of course this went back ten years. To one particular night. The night with Amanda and the aftermath that had defined Henry's ambitions and plans and set him on the path he'd been traveling ever since.

Her mouth briefly went tight, then she turned around and took two fast steps away before turning and marching right back. "Is it really so important to you to submarine us that you deliberately bought that building out from under us?"

"Yeah. I guess it is. You want to hear me admit it?" He locked his gaze with hers. "Fine. I admit it. I found out you wanted the building, so I made a better offer."

She inhaled sharply. "Just like that."

"Exactly."

Her expression tightened and her eyes narrowed on him. "And what are you going to do with the building?"

"How is that your business?" Damn, she looked good. Everything in him wanted to touch her, but with her temper flashing white hot, that seemed like a dangerous move. Still, no one said he couldn't enjoy the view.

"Damn it, Henry." Now that temper was fading into frustration.

"Why are you so worked up over one of Bennett's ideas getting shot to hell?"

She shot him a hard look. "What makes you think it was Bennett's plan?" she demanded and he had to admit he hadn't thought about that. Hadn't considered much of anything beyond outscoring Bennett.

"Damn it, Henry," she muttered darkly, "you screwed it all up."

If she'd just sounded angry, he could have fired back. But she also sounded…defeated and he didn't like it. He might not have seen much of Amanda over the last decade, but he'd kept up. He knew she'd gotten a degree in business, that she'd been promoted to vice president of the Carey Corporation and that she was as driven as he himself was. So hearing that tinge of disappointment in her voice bothered him. "What are you talking about?"

As if she suddenly realized that she'd said too much, Amanda closed up. He watched shutters drop over her eyes and her expression smooth out into one of blank indifference. "Nothing. Doesn't matter. I shouldn't have come here."

"I'm glad you did," he said.

"I'll bet you are." She reached down and grabbed her bag.

"Amanda," he said abruptly, "believe it or not, this wasn't about you."

Slinging her bag over her shoulder, Amanda looked at him for a long minute, then said, "I don't believe that, Henry. I wish I could, but I just don't." She looked at him. "I don't know what else you're up to, but stay away, Henry."

"Is that coming from you? Or from the Carey family?"

"Same thing," she said tightly.

Years ago, he might have argued with her. But somewhere along the line, she'd fallen into step with her powerful family and now she was right. It was the same thing. So he'd stop worrying about why Amanda was taking this so personally. He was going to make the Careys pay and if that included Amanda, then…

He watched her leave and enjoyed the view. She always did have a great butt. Those legs of hers were long and tanned and made him want to take a longer, lazier look. But that wasn't going to happen anytime soon.

So Henry told himself he'd just have to indulge himself with his memories of their long-ago night together. Of Amanda beneath him, rising up over him, of the taste of her mouth and the feel of her heat drawing him in.

Ten years and it was like yesterday in his mind. Not just the magic of being with Amanda, but the way it had ended. And then facing off with Bennett.

All of it.

That night and the aftermath had been driving him forward. Pushing him to take chances, risks, to build a company that could rival the Careys' in every way. And now that he was nearing the completion of his plans, he wasn't about to pull back—or "stay away" as Amanda said.

Henry Porter wasn't finished.

Amanda made it past his assistant, out of the luxuriously appointed office of Porter Enterprises and into the elevator before she slumped against the wall and took a deep breath in an effort to calm her racing heartbeat. But it would take more than breathing to calm her.

Her anger had driven her here, but it wasn't fury she'd felt facing Henry again. As crazy as it sounded, even to her, desire had pulsed inside her with one look into his dark, forest green eyes. His black hair was a little longer than he used to wear it—curling over his collar—and at six foot two, he was tall enough that even in heels, she'd been forced to tip her head back to meet his eyes. And that's when she'd had trouble. It had always been his eyes that had drawn her in, though God knew he was the whole package. Tall, lanky, dressed in an excellent black suit, he'd looked good enough that any sane woman would have drooled a little.

Amanda wasn't immune to it, even knowing what she did.

Why it had to be Henry Porter who affected her on every level, Amanda had no idea. But it had been that way between them from the moment they first met, when she was eighteen and Bennett had first brought his college roommate home over a long weekend. Then a year and a half later, Henry had gone with them on the annual family trip to Italy and it was there that she'd taken that long, luscious tumble into love.

Of course, that tumble had ended with a spectacular crash, she reminded herself, and straightened up as the elevator hit the ground floor of the chrome-and-glass office building. She walked through the lobby, across the polished, white granite floor and out the doors that opened onto a busy LA street. The rush of traffic and the people hurrying up and down the sidewalks were all enough to push thoughts of Henry out of her mind.

However temporarily. She had a long drive back to Orange County and she knew that her brain was going to replay that scene with Henry over and over.

Muted sunlight poured into the boardroom through the wide windows that displayed a view of Irvine, California. Tall, mostly glass-and-chrome office buildings rose up from green belts that looked like spools of green velvet ribbon set free to wind past the buildings like gift wrap. On the 405 freeway, cars were stacked up in the inevitable traffic jam, and in the far distance, Amanda picked out the smudge of blue that was the Pacific Ocean.

The Careys had settled their corporate offices in the same city where the Carey Center spread across several acres of former ranchland. The center hosted their Summer Sensations every year, with performances—everything from ballet to symphonies to musical theater—scheduled every weekend throughout the summer.

After the day she'd had, the last thing Amanda wanted to do was sit through a family meeting. But there was just no way out of it. If Henry hadn't interfered, she would have been able to announce her plans for the hall located just a quarter mile from the Carey Center. That building had been there forever and the Careys had pretty much ignored its presence. But oh, once it went up for sale, Amanda had had so many ideas for how they could use it and expand and improve the center at the same time.

It would have been the chance to prove to her family just how much she could bring to the Carey Corporation. Amanda was in charge of the schedule for the performances and she'd hoped to build on that.

"Now that's shot to hell," she muttered.

"What?" Her older sister, Serena, leaned in closer. "Something you want to talk about?"

Amanda looked at her. At thirty-two, Serena was two years older than Amanda. Her hair was two shades lighter than Amanda's dark blond and her blue eyes were somehow softer. But then, Serena had always pretty much lived up to her name. *Serene.* Divorced now, she had a three-year-old daughter, Alli, and was finding her way back into the family business.

With a quick glance around at the conference table, where most of her family was gathered, Amanda saw that no one was paying attention to her and her sister at the moment, so she lowered her voice to keep it that way. "I drove into LA this morning."

"Well," Serena said with a muffled laugh, "that explains it. The traffic would put anyone in a bad mood."

She could take that excuse and run with it, but she didn't. "Yeah, it wasn't the traffic. It was Henry Porter."

"Seriously?" Serena's expression displayed her surprise. "You went to see Henry?"

Shooting a quick look to the end of the table, Amanda turned back to Serena. "Shh. Yes, I did. I had to." Well, no she hadn't and probably shouldn't have, but the deed was done now and she could only kick herself for giving in to the urge to face him down in person.

"How is he?"

"Same as ever," she said, thinking again of how he'd looked, posed against his desk as he waited for her to enter his office. A short, sharp jab of heat whipped through her before she could squash it. How she could still feel anything for a man who had practically declared himself the enemy of the Carey family was the mystery of the ages, but there it was.

"Did you know he's moving?"

Amanda straightened up and looked at her sister. "Moving? Where?"

Serena started to say something but was interrupted when Bennett spoke up loudly. Forced to pay attention, Amanda promised herself to get Serena alone as soon as she could. How did her sister know anything about Henry's plans?

"Okay, everyone," Bennett announced, "let's get this rolling. I've got an appointment with the head of Merchandising in—" he checked the gold Rolex on his wrist "—forty minutes." Then he looked at Amanda. "How's the lineup for the Summer Sensations coming?"

She smiled in spite of the turmoil in her mind.

"Pretty great. We've got the Chinese Ballet back this year and tickets are already moving well. They're scheduled to perform in July," she said, opening her tablet and scrolling through the performers already listed. "Before then, we've got a production of *Sweeney Todd*, and a chorale made up of three local high schools."

Bennett groaned, and Amanda ignored it.

"They're really excellent and it's good for us because it showcases local talent—and I've got more on that in a minute." She looked back at her tablet. "We also have the Los Angeles Philharmonic set down for three shows sprinkled through the summer and several other options to explore." Looking at Bennett, she added, "It's only April so we have plenty of time and most of the performers from last year's pageant are eager to come back."

"Still not sure about the chorale, but otherwise, good news." Bennett nodded, then looked at Serena. "How's marketing coming?"

"Slow," Serena admitted, her voice clear, but soft. "I'm finding my way. I'll have a full report for you at the end of the month."

Amanda hated seeing her sister doubting her abilities. Serena had never been as invested in the family corporation as the rest of them. All she'd ever wanted was a family of her own. She'd once planned to have six kids. When she fell in love it seemed everything would go as she wanted, then he walked out because he just wasn't ready. Which left Serena heartbroken and all too vulnerable when Robert had come around. She'd been swept into a marriage that made her miserable, had a daughter she adored, then got a divorce that left her free and happy again.

Now she was back at the company, leaving three-year-old Alli at the company day care downstairs and finding her way back into the Carey Corporation.

"Okay, Serena's being modest," Amanda said abruptly and had Bennett's gaze focusing on her again. "She's handling setting up the auditions for the Summer Stars program and getting the website up and ready. Her team's ready to calibrate the voting when it starts and she's working with our ad company to get a couple of commercials ready to run on local channels."

Serena spoke up quickly. "Nothing's ready to go yet—"

Bennett held up one hand. "Sounds like you're on it, though, so good news, Serena. I think the Summer Stars idea is going to be big."

"It's exciting, isn't it?" Their mother, Candace Carey, caught their attention. "Giving people the chance to audition live for a spot in the Summer Sensations performance schedule? Wonderful. I'm glad I don't have to understand how the online voting will be tallied, but I'm looking forward to the contest itself."

"It was a good idea," their father, Martin, agreed and smiled at his wife, but Candace gave him a cool look. At sixty-four, Martin's dark blond hair was liberally sprinkled with gray, but his blue eyes were as sharp as ever. He'd given his tall, muscular build to both of his sons, and even now the older man was a presence.

Which was, Amanda admitted silently, sort of the problem. He'd been "retiring" for the last year, insisting his children could now take over the day-to-day of running the company his own father had built. But retiring meant actually staying away and doing other things. That, Martin was having trouble with, and his wife was at the end of her rope.

"Serena," Martin said, "if the Summer Stars website is ready to go, why isn't it live yet?"

Bennett, oldest son and CEO, shoved both hands into his slacks pockets as their father took over the meeting. He gritted his teeth hard to keep from speaking; Amanda could see the muscles in his jaw twitch. His dark blond hair was cut stylishly short, and his sea-blue eyes were now focused on the window across the room. Amanda thought her older brother looked as if he'd been born in a well-tailored suit. At thirty-four, he was the designated head of the family business—but Martin simply couldn't let go.

Serena cleared her throat, looked from Bennett to their father and said, "The website is almost ready. We're tweaking some of the information and I want the team to be able to update the vote tallies and the pictures almost instantly, so Chad Davis is working on making the site easier for everyone to navigate. We should go live in a week or two."

"Make it a week," Martin said, tapping his fingertips against the wide, mahogany table.

"Two is fine," Bennett interrupted and shot his father a quelling glance. "We'll have it up and running in plenty of time, Dad."

Candace sighed heavily and Martin winced. Nodding, he said, "Fine. You're in charge, Bennett."

Bennett went on, determined to finish everything before their father jumped in again. "Has anyone heard from Justin?"

"No," Serena said with a quick look at Amanda to see if she had spoken to their youngest brother. At a shake of her head, Serena looked down the table at their parents. "I tried to call him last week, but only got his voice mail. I'm sure he's fine, Mom. You know Justin."

Candace Carey was nearly sixty and, thanks to excellent genes and the most intricate moisturizing routine in the world, looked fifty. Her short hair had recently been dyed a rich chestnut, with red highlights that made her blue eyes shine. The few wrinkles she did have were all from smiling and Amanda thought that was the mark of a life well lived.

"I do and you're right, Serena. He's fine. I spoke to him yesterday and he's in Santa Monica."

"He should be here," Martin grumbled. "He's a Carey. His place is in this meeting."

Candace shifted in her seat and narrowed her eyes on her husband. "He's working on something that's important to him and—"

"What's more important than the Carey Corporation?" Martin demanded.

Amanda's turn to wince when her father blurted out exactly the wrong thing. She could actually *see* her mother's temper spike and wondered silently why the woman's husband completely missed it.

"That's a very telling question coming from you, Martin," Candace said and Amanda winced again. When everything was fine, Candace called her husband "Marty." Things were not fine.

Martin caught on finally and obviously realized—too late—that he'd stepped in it. "Now, Candy, that's not what I meant."

"It's exactly what you meant," Candace said, giving her husband the hard glare all her kids would recognize. "Honestly, Martin, we've been over this a hundred times. You said you were retiring. We made plans."

"I know we did, sweetie," Martin said. "And we're going to do everything we planned."

"When?" She tipped her head to one side, tapped her manicured nails on the table and waited.

"Well," Martin hedged, "we've got the Summer Sensations coming up and—"

"And Amanda's in charge of that and doing a wonderful job." She smiled and nodded her way and Amanda's lips curved slightly. "What else?"

"There's the new merger with the Macintosh hotel line—"

"Bennett is on top of it all," she assured him.

"What about Justin?" Martin asked, obviously playing what he thought of as a trump card.

"Justin will be fine without your supervision, Martin," Candace said, leaning toward him. "We've raised our kids." She swept out a hand to include three of them. "Honestly, Martin, I'm starting to think you don't want to spend time with me."

Amanda winced and shared a worried look with her sister.

"You know that's not true, honey," Martin said, reaching for her hand.

Candace pulled away, though, and shook her head. "Oh," she said, rising and grabbing up her black leather bag, "I think it is. You've been very clear where your loyalties lie."

"Mom…" Bennett's voice cut into the tension mounting in the room.

She held up one finger and instantly got the silence she was signaling for. "I'm going to meet your aunt Viv for lunch—"

"I thought we were going to lunch," Martin said.

"And I thought we would be in Palm Springs for the week, so we're both disappointed," Candace retorted.

Amanda glanced at Serena again and her sister winced in sympathy with their mom. They both knew that Candace Carey had been looking forward to her and her husband seeing some of the world, spending time together during his retirement, and now it looked as though Martin was trying to avoid just that. This was not good.

"Now, honey, I wanted to make sure everything here was going fine before we left for a week is all…"

Candace's eyebrows lifted. "No, that's not all. The problem is, you can't let go. You trained Bennett. You turned the company over to him and promised me you would retire and we'd start traveling."

"And we're going to," he argued.

"How are we going to Europe if you can't even go to Palm Springs?" Shaking her head, Candace tucked her bag under her arm, lifted her chin and said, "No. You don't want to travel beyond company headquarters. That's clear." She looked at Bennett briefly. "Good luck to you, sweetie."

"Now, just hold on a minute," Martin said, rising to meet his wife's irate gaze.

"I've been holding on, Martin. Now I'm done." She looked at each of her children. "You all have a lovely day. Not you, Martin."

"Honey—"

Candace didn't even glance at her husband as she swept out of the room, and Amanda could only think how odd it was that she and her mother were both having man trouble.

Two

Henry stood in the living room of the Tudor-style mansion in Beverly Hills and, not for the first time, heard that nagging internal voice telling him to get out. Well, he was. Finally. Not that it was a bad house. He gave a quick look around at the sun-washed living room where his mother's beloved antique furniture stood, like monuments to the past. It was pretty, if uncomfortable, and seemed more suited for—well, he told himself, *anyone* other than him.

Idly, he looked up at the portrait hanging above the blue-tiled fireplace. Happier times, he thought as he stared at the smiling family that had been frozen in time by a talented artist. His parents, of course, looking young and eager for the future, and himself, at ten, with a stiff smile to indicate he didn't much care for the suit he'd been forced to wear.

Two years after that painting, his mother was dead

and his father had become a shadow of the proud man in the painting. He'd never been happy in this house since. Which explained why he'd finally moved back to Texas five years ago. Not that he was any happier, but at least he wasn't surrounded by memories he'd rather forget.

Frowning to himself, Henry hit speed dial and listened to the ringing before his father picked up.

"Hi, Dad."

"Henry. What's going on?"

Right to the point. That was his father. No time for just talking, catching up. Even retired, Michael Porter was brusque and stingy with his attention.

"Yeah, you know I'm selling the house."

"About time," Michael threw in and Henry shook his head. Clearly his father still hated this place, even from a couple of states away. Once Henry's mother died—or *abandoned them* as Michael Porter put it—the man had spent as little time in this house as humanly possible. He hadn't sold it because whatever his personal feelings about the place, Michael knew a good investment when he saw it. And he hadn't been wrong about that.

A 1920s estate, the Tudor house came with nearly five acres of property—almost unheard of in Beverly Hills since most of the bigger estates had been broken up and sold at a profit decades ago. So he'd held on to the place even while resenting every square inch of the house that had once been so happy and was now almost a mockery of what had been.

As for Henry, after his father moved to Texas, Henry had stayed on because it was easiest. He didn't spend much time there anyway, except for sleeping, and the house itself was close enough to the Porter offices that traffic wasn't an issue. Now that he'd decided to move the company headquarters farther south, the house had to go.

"Right." Henry asked, "I wanted to know if you want me to ship the portrait to Texas."

There was silence for a couple of telling seconds before Michael answered, "No. I don't want it."

He'd known the answer before he'd asked the question and still, he'd had to make sure. When Henry's mother died, Michael shut away her memory as if she hadn't existed. He'd taken down the portrait and stored it and it wasn't until Michael had moved to Texas permanently that Henry had rehung the painting. He still wasn't sure exactly why he had. Maybe it was just what his father would have called orneriness. His father took it down, so Henry hung it back up.

Could be that simple. But either way, he didn't have time to figure it out now. Since Michael didn't want it, Henry would take the portrait with him.

"All right, then. What about the rest of the stuff?"

"What I wanted I brought with me to Texas," his father said. "You get rid of the rest however you decide."

He couldn't help but glance around the room again. Hell, every room in that house had been decorated by Evelyn Porter and her husband didn't want a single stick of furniture. But then, neither did her son. And he wondered what his mother would think of that. "Everything all right in San Antonio?"

"It's good. In fact," Michael said, "I want you to take a look at this new tech company down here that's making a name for itself in gaming."

Okay, then, family stuff finished and moving on to business—right where Michael liked it. Henry shook his head and walked across the hardwood floor to the front window. Staring out at the tidy lawn and picture-perfect gardens, he just listened.

"They've got a new programmer who's kicking ass in his department. Word is, they're looking for investors to grow fast."

"The word?" Henry said with another shake of his head. "Meaning, you've got a spy in the company and have some inside information."

"*Spy* is a harsh word."

"But accurate?"

Michael chuckled. "Let's just say we've got the jump on this by a week or two. You move on this fast and we'll have our competitors gnashing their teeth."

The old man had always had a nose for business. And however his father had gotten the information, it wasn't something Henry would ignore. Hell, he himself used informants to keep tabs on his competitors and—he thought about the Careys—enemies. Amanda hadn't been wrong about that. He'd found out about that hall near the Carey Center going up for sale before they'd had a chance to make a bid and he'd jumped on that, too. Just like he would this gaming company.

Turning his back on the view, he stalked from the room and down the hall to the study, where he sat behind what had been his father's desk and drew out paper and pen. "Okay, Dad. Let's have it. Tell me everything you know."

Another chuckle and his father's voice saying, "Glad to see you turning out just like the old man, Henry."

Well, that gave him pause. Even as his father spoke and he took careful notes, Henry had to ask himself if he really wanted to be that chip off the old block.

* * *

After the interminable family meeting, Amanda grabbed Serena and the two of them had lunch at La Ferrovia, an upscale Italian restaurant not far from work. Over excellent eggplant parmigiana, they talked family, what to do about their parents' feud and how to convince Justin to come back into the fold. Though they didn't come up with any solutions, it always helped Amanda to talk things out with her sister.

"Lunch was great," Serena said and gave Amanda a quick glance.

"After that meeting, we should have had wine with lunch," Amanda mused.

Her sister laughed and shook her head. "If we did that every time the Carey family had a contentious meeting, we'd be half-drunk all the time."

Not necessarily a bad plan, Amanda thought but didn't say. As not only the two girls in the family, but the two middle children, they'd been close since they were kids—except for the year or so that Serena was married to Robert O'Dare. She'd pulled away from the whole family then and Amanda had been hurt that her sister could cut her off so easily. Then later, of course, she'd found out that Serena was so miserable in her marriage that she hadn't wanted anyone to know what a mistake she'd made.

For a long time, Amanda had felt guilty for somehow not seeing what her sister was going through. Now, though, she was just grateful to have that closeness back.

Now, they sat on a bright red couch in the company day care center so Serena could check on Alli. Truthfully, Amanda enjoyed these little visits, too. Her niece was adorable and watching the three-year-old play with her friends was a good way to let her brain take a mini-vacation of sorts.

But today, she was happy to have the extra time for more than the usual reason of Alli-watching. Amanda had had an idea percolating in the back of her mind all day and this little interlude before they went back to work gave her the perfect opportunity to broach the subject. For her little plan to work, she'd need Serena to help.

At least a dozen children, five and under, were shrieking and crying and laughing, and the women who worked there, Amanda thought, should have medals pinned to their chests. She loved kids, but a whole roomful could be intimidating as well as deafening. Some children were having books read to them, some played with a train set, and Alli and her "boyfriend" were playing with baby dolls in the corner.

"Isn't that sweet?" Serena smiled at her daughter. "Alli talks about Carter all the time."

Amanda shot a look at her niece and felt a little tug at her heart. Alli was the shining star of the Carey family. The only grandchild, she was completely adored by all of them. But right now, Amanda had other things on her mind.

"Serena," she said, turning back to her sister, "you said Henry's moving. How did you know?"

Serena looked at her in mild amusement. "He told me. Obviously."

Stunned, Amanda just stared at her for a second or two. "How is that obvious? No one in the family talks to Henry. Haven't for years."

"Well, I do," her older sister said with a shrug.

"And you never said anything? To anyone?"

"Come on." Serena gave her a wry smile. "Why would I do that? Bennett would have had a cow. And there's no telling how you would have reacted."

"What's that supposed to mean?" Stupid question, she told herself.

"Please." Serena gave her an incredulous look before shifting her gaze back to Alli. "You haven't exactly been a fan of Henry's, but I always thought it was ridiculous to completely cut the man out."

"But—"

Serena sighed. "I mean, if I stopped talking to everyone Bennett has a feud with, I'd only speak to family—" She paused. "Correction. I wouldn't be able to talk to my little brother, either."

Good point, Amanda thought. Bennett was no happier with their brother, Justin, than he was with Henry Porter. So you had to make your own call there, and Amanda wasn't willing to give up talking to Justin, either.

Still, this wasn't about their brother. "But it didn't bother you? What happened between Henry and me?"

"Of course it did," her sister said, pausing for a sip of her Coke. "It was terrible. But you had us. Henry didn't have anyone on his side."

"You're on his side?" Amanda couldn't believe it.

"Wrong way to put it." Serena held up one hand. "I only meant that I wasn't going to pile on, giving him grief, and I called him one day to say so, and… Well, we started talking more regularly."

"Regularly," she repeated. "For how long now?"

"Oh, a couple of years, I guess."

What had happened between her and Henry was ten

years ago, so it wasn't as if Serena had run right to him to offer consolation. But still…

"Okay, but how did this start up? You just called him out of the blue?"

Serena sighed, leaned back against the couch and took a sip of her Coke. "No. I bumped into him accidentally. It was right after my divorce and I went to that spa in Santa Monica, you remember?"

"Sure." Now Amanda felt a little guilty, unknowingly prodding Serena into talking about what had been a very painful time in her sister's life.

Serena had never really been into the family business like the rest of them. All she'd ever really wanted was to be a wife and mom—as strange as that sounded these days. Although, wasn't it the height of feminism to make your own choices? To have the life you wanted in spite of anyone else's expectations?

Off subject, she told herself. Serena had married Robert with stars in her eyes and found out only when Alli was a few months old that Robert was less Prince Charming and more Cheating Slug. So Serena had gotten her divorce and full custody of the daughter Robert didn't care about anyway, and had rejoined the family business.

"You stayed at that resort on the beach while Mom and Dad took care of Alli. You said you had a great time."

"I did," she said on a heartfelt sigh. "That place is just magical. In fact, it might be time for another long weekend there. I wonder if Mom would watch Alli again."

Now, Amanda said aloud, "Of course she would. But you're veering off target. How did your spa weekend turn into meeting up with Henry?"

"Did you think I was the only guest staying at the hotel?" Serena asked.

"No, but—"

"I'm just teasing." Serena reached out and patted Amanda's hand. "You know, it's not technically a spa. I mean they have treatments—wonderful treatments—but it's a hotel as well and Henry happened to be staying there that weekend."

"Happened to be?" There was no way Amanda was willing to believe that Henry just happened to be at the same hotel that Serena was staying at on the same damn weekend. That "coincidence" was so farfetched it couldn't be believed.

"Yes. He was having his house repainted, so he was staying at the hotel for a week."

"Uh-huh." Her brain started racing with the implications. Why would he have been there to "bump" into Serena? Was he using her? Was Serena an unwitting spy for Henry? Was it *she* who'd let it slip about the hall Amanda had had such plans for?

"Oh, stop it." Serena frowned at her and took another sip of her Coke. "I can see you spinning theories in your head. Not everything is a conspiracy. Sometimes people just actually do bump into someone they know. You're getting as bad as Bennett, Mandy, and that's not a good thing."

Surprised, she asked, "What's that supposed to mean?"

"I mean you're becoming suspicious and distrusting and if you keep spending so much time at the company, with Bennett, it's only going to get worse."

"I'm not suspicious," she argued, "I'm just…careful."

"Sure. You know, going through life expecting people to betray you isn't exactly healthy."

"Neither is walking through a minefield blindfolded."

Serena smiled, glanced at her daughter, then back to Amanda. "I don't do that. Let's just say that I'm willing to trust people until they give me a reason not to."

Neither one of them said Robert O'Dare's name, but they both knew he was whom she was talking about. And for a second or two, Amanda felt guilty for giving her sister such a hard time. After all, Serena's husband had betrayed her—big-time—and she wasn't the one sitting here being, as she said, suspicious and distrusting.

"Anyway," Serena went on, "that first night at the hotel, I went downstairs for dinner, and saw Henry in the bar. We were both alone, so we had dinner together."

Envy pricked at the edges of her heart, but Amanda really didn't want to admit to that. "Just that easily?"

She shrugged. "Why wouldn't it be?"

Amanda just stared at her for a second. Did she really not get it? "Well, let's think about it. Porter Enterprises has pretty much been at war with the Carey Corporation for the last five years."

"I'm not the corporation, Mandy," Serena reminded her. "And neither are you."

"But we are Careys. And Henry is Henry. Why was he so friendly? Did he try to get information out of you?" As she asked the question, she fought down a flare of anger at the man who would use her sister against her own family.

"Why wouldn't he be friendly to me?" Serena's calm tone was dissolving into impatience. "I'm not Bennett. Or you, for that matter. He had no reason to avoid me. And no, before you ask, he did not pump me for information. For God's sake, Mandy, we're not in a soap opera. Stop looking for motive here."

"No, not a soap opera," Amanda agreed. "More like a corporate thriller. Come on, Serena. You know as well as I do that Henry has outbid us on a number of properties in the last few years. Not to mention that he's gone out of his way to steal some of our best employees—"

"By offering them better pay and benefits?" Serena shook her head. "That's not stealing. It's making them a better offer—that Bennett could have matched if he'd been willing."

"That makes it okay?"

"That makes it business."

"No it's not. That's war." And Serena was being deliberately blind to it. Would she even have noticed if Henry had dug information out of her by asking leading questions?

"Wow." Serena laughed. "I had no idea you had this love of drama."

"It's not funny." Her own sister didn't see that Henry Porter would do whatever he could to sink the Carey Corporation? How was that even possible?

"Oh, sweetie, of course it is. Henry's not Dr. Evil, planning world domination…"

"No," Amanda snapped. "Just Carey domination."

"And," Serena added as if her sister hadn't spoken up, "Bennett's surely not a saint."

"True, but—"

"No *buts*." Serena drew her head back and studied Amanda as if seeing her for the first time. "I'm starting to think that this isn't really about Henry swooping in on properties or employees at all. I think it's more about what happened between the two of you."

"You're wrong," Amanda said firmly. Okay, maybe there was a tiny thread of that in there somewhere, but mostly this was about Henry going out of his way to make *her* family pay. Wasn't *that* what had happened?

Serena shook her head and her butterscotch-colored hair swung out gently and fell into perfectly trimmed curls. "Look, Mandy, we all know exactly what went on between you and Henry ten years ago…"

Amanda squirmed uneasily in her seat and took a long drink of her now-cold coffee. Yes, everyone knew. Because Bennett had caught her and Henry naked together in the boathouse at their home in Italy. God, she could still remember the flush of embarrassment when her big brother had walked in on them right after—

"But it was ten years ago, Mandy. When do you let it go?"

"Me?" she countered, just a little offended that her sister didn't understand the humiliation of being found with her first lover right after she'd had an orgasm that had left her shaken to her bones. Then there was the fight between Bennett and Henry. The fists. The vicious words. Henry leaving and the family meeting to "discuss" what had happened as if Amanda were just an interested outsider.

"When does Henry let it go?" Her voice was pitched low, but demanding. "Do you think he picked the Carey family as his target out of the air? Is he trying to destroy us little by little just on a whim? Or does it all go back to—" She broke off, swallowed hard and then said, "And if we're talking about me, how can I let it go? Henry's not letting me, is he? It's not like I lay awake at night, thinking of him." Not often, anyway. "But with him trying to submarine us all the time and Bennett in a constant state of irritation, it's really hard to just tuck it away into the memory file."

"You're right." Serena laid one hand on Amanda's arm and said, "I get that. But what is it you want from me?"

"Help," she admitted. Amanda had been thinking about this since the family meeting ended. "I need to know what Henry knows about us."

Serena frowned. "I don't know how I can help with that. We don't talk business, Mandy."

"Yeah." She shook her head, dismissing that. Mostly because she had the feeling they *did* discuss business, but Serena just hadn't noticed. "I don't expect you to give me answers. I need you to help me *get* those answers."

"How?"

"You said you talk to Henry."

"Yeeesss…" Wariness put about fifteen syllables into that one word.

"I need you to get me into his house."

For a second or two, no one spoke and Amanda knew what her sister was thinking by the stunned expression on her face. Well, who could blame her? Amanda never talked about Henry and the day she did, she asked for help to infiltrate the man's house. Okay, that would sound strange to anyone.

"You can't be serious." Serena pulled her head back and looked at her as if she'd lost her mind. "If you want to talk to Henry, go to his house yourself."

"I don't want to talk to him. I want to spy on him."

Serena laughed, then noticed her sister wasn't laughing with her. Slowly the smile faded. "Aren't you taking this a little far?"

"I don't think so," Amanda argued, lowering her voice as she started talking. "I've been thinking about this ever since I saw him at his office this morning."

"Thinking about *what*, exactly?"

She threw a quick glance over her shoulder to make sure all of the kids and the caregivers were too far away to hear her, before she turned back to Serena. "I figure that there are only two ways to find out what he's up to. Either hire a spy in his house…or become one."

"Oh, boy." She rolled her eyes. "Mandy, are you listening to yourself?"

"Absolutely," she said, smiling now at the brilliance of her plan. "If you can get me into his house, I can find out what he's up to. What he knows about us and how he's getting information."

"So, what? You're Amanda Bond, now?"

"With a little luck, why not? But maybe more like Mata Hari." She sat back against the couch and let her mind wander to all the possibilities stretching out in front of her. And since she didn't have to admit it to anyone else, she could at least acknowledge to herself that part of the appeal of being in Henry's house was being close to Henry. If she was around him for a while, maybe she could get him out of her head.

Ten years since their night together and she'd never been able to completely forget it. God knew, she'd tried. She'd had several lovers and even a few one-night stands, looking for the same explosion of lust and pleasure and excitement that she'd once felt with Henry. But no matter whom she'd been with, that night remained unrepeatable.

And that just irritated Amanda. Why was it Henry Porter who pushed every button and lit every fuse? She had to think that she was remembering that night with him as more than it had been. Maybe she'd been too in love to notice that the sex wasn't all that great. A comforting, if not really likely, thought.

"Spies." Serena choked out a laugh. "Okay, and how do you plan to do that?"

Amanda snapped out of her thoughts in a blink and focused again on her sister. "I haven't really worked out all the bugs yet," she admitted, chewing at her bottom lip as she tried to shuffle through the ideas racing though her mind. "But you said he's moving, right? Well, he'll need extra help, won't he?"

"I suppose."

She shrugged. "So tell him you've got someone who can help out temporarily."

"You. Working for Henry. As a maid."

"Maid, packer, gardener, I don't care," she said, warming to the idea even more than she had when the thought had first struck her. "I just need to get close to him for a while."

Frowning thoughtfully, Serena sighed a little. "He did say last week that Martha, his housekeeper, was going to be hiring some temporary people to help with the move."

"Perfect!" God, she could already see how smoothly this would go. She'd need a good disguise, but that was no problem. Amanda had always had a good hand with makeup. Add a wig and maybe hunch a little to make herself look shorter. She could do this.

"Not really," Serena reminded her. "Even if I give Martha your name and she hires you… Henry will recognize you."

"No, he won't." Amanda waved that away. She wasn't worried. Much.

"This is a bad idea," Serena mused.

"No way. This is going to be great." If she had any doubts, Amanda ignored them.

Maybe a disguise sounded silly, but it was the only thing she could think of that would get her into Henry's house. The plan would work because she would make it work. She wanted to get information on Henry. It had nothing to do with the fact that she'd felt a blast of heat when they'd faced each other only that morning. Nothing to do with the dreams of him that occasionally haunted her sleep. This was all about how he'd gone behind her back and snatched her one chance to prove to her family that she was more than capable of expanding their dynasty.

Oh, she knew Bennett trusted her to do her job, but she also knew that he had tucked her into a nice little box so he didn't have to think about her. It was respect with a caveat. Well, she wanted out of the box and this was the way to make that happen.

"Can you do it?" she asked. "Can you get me into Henry's house?"

Serena thought about it for a long minute, then nodded. Amanda sighed in satisfaction, but it was cut short when her sister spoke again.

"I'll do it for you on one condition."

"What?" Suspicion colored her tone and she had to wonder if Serena had been right earlier when she'd accused Amanda of becoming as suspicious as Bennett.

"You said earlier that you couldn't just tuck away the memories of ten years ago."

Scowling, she shifted her position on the couch. She really didn't want to talk about that. "Yeah?"

"Is that really the reason you haven't let it go?" Serena asked, her voice soft and low. "Or is it that you didn't want to forget it?"

Amanda narrowed her eyes. "Are you psychoanalyzing me now?"

Her sister grinned. "Should I be?"

Amanda expelled a long breath. Amazing. With everything going on in the Carey family, it was *her* Serena wanted to analyze?

"Seriously? You're worried about me?" Stunned, Amanda stared at her. "When Bennett is wound so tight he snaps at anything that moves? When Justin can't be bothered to check in for the same meetings that we're all forced to attend? What about Mom and Dad and the retirement wars? Then there's *you*."

"Me?" Now it was Serena's turn to look shocked.

But Amanda had been holding this in for a long time, so she let loose. "You've been divorced two years, Serena. Have you even looked at a man? Or are you going to use Robert as a shield for the rest of your life?"

Serena scowled at her. "Low blow."

"Maybe, but that wasn't an answer, either."

"You're projecting, Mandy."

"Now you even sound like a therapist."

She ignored that. "Instead of answering the question about you, you try to shift the subject to everyone else. And besides, I haven't seen you out with a man lately. Like in forever. So you're not as sanguine as you pretend to be, are you?"

"Oh, yeah," Amanda said nodding. What she said hit a little closer to home than she was willing to admit, but at the same time, she noticed that Serena hadn't exactly argued Amanda's point. "Big words now, too. You missed your calling. You should have been an actual psychologist. You've got their routine down pat. Answer a question with a question."

"Uh-huh," Serena said. "And I notice that's not an answer, either."

God, she was right. Fine, she hadn't been dating much. Or ever. But she was busy. She had a life. The one she wanted. And she didn't need Serena pointing out the cracks in her walls. Especially when her own walls were looking a little shabby, too.

Sighing, Amanda looked around the room. Primary colors on the walls, cushioned carpet that made it feel as if you were walking on a trampoline. Shelves filled with books and toys and several small tables and chairs where a few of the kids sat coloring. Strange place to be having this in-depth conversation. But it was so long overdue for both of them, maybe it had just been time.

"How did we get into what I think of Henry when I was supposed to be finding out how *you* know so much about him?"

Serena laughed, shot a quick glance at her little girl, then looked back to Amanda, still smiling. "Because I'm a Carey, too. I know how to deflect as well as you do."

"Great." Amanda snatched her sister's bottle of Coke, took a sip and handed it back. "Still deflecting too, Serena. You want to know what I think of Henry, but you're not willing to tell me why you're avoiding men.

"And fine, I'll let that one go for the moment and just ask why you're friends with the man who's made it his mission to ruin us."

"He's not trying to ruin anything," Serena said with a shake of her head. "He's just taking care of business. Like Bennett does. So it's okay if we do something but traitorous if Henry does it?"

"Well…"

Serena stabbed her index finger at her. "Ha. Got you there, didn't I?"

"No." *Yes.*

"It's no big deal, Amanda. We don't talk every day and pass notes to each other." She shrugged. "Every once in a while we have lunch and we talk."

"But why?" That's what Amanda couldn't figure out.

Serena shrugged. "I like him. Plus, the family can't tell me who to be friends with."

Okay, she could understand that. Amanda didn't take orders any better than her sister did. "I want to say good for you, but it's hard for me because I'm so mad at him."

Serena patted her hand again. "Furious doesn't get you anywhere, honey. Believe me, I know."

Amanda instantly knew that Serena was talking about her divorce and she felt bad for letting this conversation slide in that direction. And for the cheap shot she'd taken earlier. "I'm sorry. I didn't mean—"

Serena waved her apology off. "Don't worry about it. I'm not mad about my marriage dissolving anymore. Not even really sad." She took a breath, looked at her daughter again and said, "I'm actually grateful to Robert. He signed away paternal rights to Alli and she's worth everything."

Amanda's gaze shifted to the little girl, too. Hair the color of her mother's was pulled high into two pigtails, with bright red ribbons. She wore a tiny pair of jeans and a white shirt with red flowers on it, and a pair of impossibly small red sneakers. Serena was the only one of the Carey kids to have a child and a part of Amanda worried that she might never have kids of her own. Not the way her love life was going, anyway.

"You're right. She's completely worth it."

Serena grinned at her. "Sad doesn't last any longer than a good mad does. But some things are forever."

"Wow. Psychologist. Poet. Any other secrets you're hiding?"

Turning her head slightly, Serena gazed out the window and murmured, "So many..."

Her sister suddenly felt miles away and Amanda wasn't sure how to reach her. Before she could ask if there was something she could do, if there was something specific bothering Serena, the other woman turned back and gave Amanda a smile that didn't quite reach her eyes. But the message was clear. She didn't want questions. Didn't want to talk about whatever it was that had put such a wistful expression on her face, and Amanda couldn't really say much to that because she had plenty of secrets herself.

Not the least of which was, after all these years, she still spent far too much time thinking about Henry.

Three

The next day, Henry took three meetings before lunch and considered it a damn good day. He had taken over a vineyard in Napa, struck a deal with the new game designer in Austin and formed a merger with a medical supply company.

"Dad was right," he muttered, slipping his suit coat on. "Diversification is key." Hell, Porter Enterprises had so many different interests, he could live three lifetimes and never get bored. Not that business bored him anyway, but Henry couldn't imagine running a company that dealt with only one product. How the hell did you get yourself motivated when you were looking at another day of the same old thing?

"Which is just another reason to move the company headquarters," he told himself, with a hard look around his office.

This place still carried the stamp of his father, and while he didn't begrudge it, Henry wanted to do some "stamping" of his own. Michael Porter had retired and turned over the reins to Henry four years ago and since then, Henry had been more interested in building the company than in redecorating. But it was time. Hell. Past time.

With Michael in Texas, playing golf and going fishing on the bass boat that had been his first purchase, the company and its physical home were Henry's business alone. Time to start doing things his way.

He turned for a look out the windows displaying that view of Los Angeles and the distant smudge of the Pacific and knew he was doing the right thing. He wanted to look out at more than buildings. He wanted to see the ocean. He wanted new views, and if that new headquarters brought him closer to the Carey family—and Amanda—well, that was all right with him, too.

Just thinking her name had her image rising up in his mind and his blood stirring into a simmer. Seeing her yesterday had given him a new image to focus on, and just remembering the snap and fire in her eyes made him want to see her again. He didn't even question that continual burn he felt for her anymore. What would be the point? What he *did* about it was the more interesting question, anyway. One he didn't have an answer to…yet.

When his assistant buzzed in, he answered. "What is it, Donna?"

"Mr. Haley's here."

"Great, send him in."

The door opened a moment later and Henry's best friend walked in. Mick Haley was tall, with a hard jaw, sharp green eyes and muscles you would expect from a former Navy SEAL. These days, Mick owned and operated the world's top security company. Which was how they'd met several years ago.

Mick had been hired as a bodyguard by the actress Henry was dating. Well, the affair with the actress hadn't lasted, but his friendship with Mick had. A few years ago, Mick's company had expanded to include cybersecurity and Henry had wasted no time hiring Mick's company to secure Porter Enterprises.

Mick said, "If you want to beat traffic, we'd better get moving."

"There's no beating the traffic no matter what time of the day."

"Yeah," Mick said with a grin, "but I'm driving."

"Fine." Henry sighed. Mick had the habit of driving as he once had, dodging bullets or land mines or enemy troops. He called it *defensive driving.* Whatever you called it, it made for a terrifying ride. He didn't much care for cars on the best of days, but riding with Mick was a damn adventure. "My life insurance is paid up."

"That's the spirit." Mick grinned again and turned for the door. "If you'd let me take you to the track and teach you how to drive defensively, it wouldn't bother you as much."

"Pass," Henry said. Bad enough to ride with Mick. No way did he want to increase the risk by doing it himself, too.

"About time you got out of LA," he was saying as they walked out of the office together.

"Yeah, so you keep saying."

"Must be true, then."

Henry laughed shortly and stopped at his assistant's

desk. "Donna, once you finish that correspondence, you can take the rest of the day."

"Are you serious?"

Henry shrugged. "I am. Let's call it a holiday."

"For all of us?" someone two desks over called out.

"Is that you, Jeff?"

A young guy with a half-assed goatee pushed his chair back in a fast roll. "Yep. Did I hear 'day off'?"

The other three employees in the big office were all watching him now, waiting for an answer to Jeff's question. Henry thought about how hard everyone had worked to put a recent merger together. And how much work they'd be doing handling the move. He glanced at Mick, who was quietly chuckling, before turning back to Jeff and the rest of the crew.

"All right. It means all of you. When Donna's finished and checks out, so can the rest of you."

"Woot!" Jeff threw both hands in the air and some applause came from the others.

"Fine. Enjoy. Tomorrow we're all working on the move." Shaking his head, Henry walked through reception and down the hall to the elevators, with Mick right behind him.

They stepped into the small area and as the doors swished shut, Mick looked at Henry and asked, "Bucking for Boss of the Year?"

"Yeah, I'm making space on my trophy case."

"The size of your new house," Mick mused, "you've got plenty of room for it."

"Not to mention the view," Henry said, leaning back against the elevator wall and watching the floor lights blink on and off.

"Yeah, it's a good one." Mick stood almost at attention, facing the elevator doors as if expecting attack at any moment. He'd spent so much time over the years as a warrior, Henry suspected his friend couldn't—or didn't want to—turn it off.

"From the roof especially," Henry said, thinking about the rooftop patio that had pretty much sold him on the house. From up there, he could see for miles in every direction. The wind blew hard, unimpeded by other houses or office buildings, and the previous owner had set up shady spots and tubs filled with flowers that he hoped a gardener could keep alive, and damn it, he liked the space. In Beverly Hills, even with the acreage surrounding the house, he was still in the middle of the city. In South Irvine, it was definitely suburban. Surprised the hell out of him just how much he liked it.

The conversation died off until they were in Mick's Range Rover sliding in and out of traffic. It was enough to make anyone seasick.

"So you're moving into the house tomorrow?"

"Starting to, anyway." He winced when Mick slid past a Prius and bulleted on. "The movers will get it all done in Beverly Hills, then drive it down here. Martha's got help to supervise the unpacking, so it should go smoothly."

"Never could see you in BH," Mick said, casually steering through the slowing traffic, never slowing down himself.

Yeah, it really wasn't for him. Maybe things would have been different if the Porter house had more good memories than bad. But for Henry there was just too much misery wrapped up in those beautiful walls.

"It's a good house," Henry argued. "It's just not mine."

"I get that." Mick darted over two lanes, then back

again, managing a kind of flow that no one else was able to devise.

Henry grabbed the door and just managed to avoid hitting the invisible brake when Mick squeaked between two cars with less than a whisper to spare. "You do know there are no IEDs to avoid on the 405, right?"

Mick tossed him a grin. "Better to be prepared."

"Right. I'll go with 'better to be alive.'" Henry tore his gaze away from the cars flashing past as Mick showcased more of his "defensive driving." The man had been a bodyguard to princes, celebrities and heads of corporations, so he prided himself on being able to drive himself and his passengers out of tight situations.

So instead of watching the approach of possible imminent death, Henry looked at his friend and said, "Have you got your cyber guys meeting us at the house?"

"No, not today." Mick whipped past a minivan driven by a woman who looked horrified at how closely the Range Rover came to her. "I'm going to give the place a good look over and we'll have Teddy and the team come out tomorrow. I want an idea of what we're going to need."

Nodding, Henry thought it was good to go with the experts. He wanted as good of an alarm system on the new house as he'd had on the Beverly Hills property.

"You ought to think about getting a dog, too."

"I'm not home enough to have a dog," Henry said automatically. He'd considered it, of course, because he'd had a dog as a kid and sometimes missed having a pet. "Wouldn't be fair to an animal to leave it on its own all day."

"You have a housekeeper," Mick reminded him.

"Housekeeper, not dog keeper," Henry countered. "Not fair to Martha to ask her to not only move, but to housetrain and care for a dog along with it."

"So go to a shelter," Mick said, weaving in and out of traffic like a ballet dancer on steroids. "Get an older dog. You don't have to start with a puppy. Get a dog that needs you, too."

He hadn't considered that, but now wasn't the time. "Just handle the alarm system, will you?"

Mick grinned. "We will, but it's going to cost you."

Since Mick's company had installed the system on his current house, which was half the size of his new house, Henry already knew the bill would be staggering. But hell, that's what happened when you insisted on the best.

"We ran basic background checks on the movers you've hired."

"A little overkill, don't you think?"

Mick shrugged. "They'll have access to the house, no matter how briefly. Doesn't hurt."

"Fine, but you don't need to check out the household staff. That's been done."

"Anyone new?"

Henry thought about it. "Housekeeper's hired the sister of a friend to come in and help with packing and setup in the new house."

"Do you know her?" Mick asked.

"No, but I know Martha, so don't worry about it." Henry snorted a laugh. "I'm not one of your projects, Mick. Just set up the new alarm system and new locks on the doors and we're good."

"All right. You're the boss."

Mick steered out of the diamond lane and headed for an exit. Henry glanced up, surprised they'd already made it to Irvine. Terrifying or not, Mick's driving cut a good half hour off the trip, even with traffic.

Henry wasn't going to be sorry to see that drive to the office end. He'd been living in a hotel in Newport Beach for the last couple of years and making that trek into LA every day along with thousands of others.

He hadn't wanted to live in the Beverly Hills house. Too many memories, most of them not great. Should have sold it years ago, but at the same time, on those nights when he worked late, he stayed there, rather than face the drive.

Soon, that wouldn't be an issue. With the new house only a few miles from the company headquarters, fewer headaches. Plus, there was the knowledge that his being in Irvine would drive Amanda and the rest of the Careys nuts.

And, he knew it was time to build something of his own outside the company. Time to think of making a life. Or pretending to.

He'd tried it once, eight years ago. He'd met and married a socialite and within three months, he'd known it for the mistake it had been. Lauren had wanted more from him than Henry could give and it hadn't taken long for her to figure that out. After a huge settlement and a divorce, Henry had steered clear of relationships. He preferred the one-night-stand kind of woman because they both knew going in that there were no expectations on the table.

There had been only one woman in his life who had ever made him want more. Amanda. Hard to be married to one woman while still thinking about another. He'd thought at the time that marrying a nice woman with whom he shared good sex would be enough to wipe

Amanda out of his mind. But all it had done was define just how much Lauren wasn't Amanda.

Not that he was still in love with Amanda or anything. It was only that whenever he saw her, his blood buzzed and his body burned. Lust he could deal with. It was love he wasn't interested in.

What did that say about him?

And did he really want to know?

Being a spy wasn't easy.

Especially when it involved packing crystal glassware the housekeeper didn't trust professional movers to pack correctly.

Amanda still wasn't sure exactly how Serena had managed it, but her sister had gotten her into Henry's house—that he had sold. He was moving to Irvine, which was way too close to her own home in Laguna. And practically on top of the Carey Corporation building. He'd done that on purpose, she just knew it. But that was a worry for another day. God knew she didn't have the time to worry about it at the moment.

Since she'd arrived that morning, she'd been too busy to get any snooping done, so unless she was going to find some information in the butler's pantry, she was out of luck.

Amanda wore what she thought of as her disguise pretty well. A short, chin-length black wig, a pair of wire-rimmed glasses and her shoulders hunched to make herself look shorter. Her black slacks and no-longer-completely white shirt were so plain, even she wouldn't look twice at her. She wore simple black flats and kept her head down as she worked. Martha, the housekeeper, was a nice woman but a tough taskmaster.

"When you finish with those goblets," the older woman said to her, "you can start on the wineglasses. You'll find them in the butler's pantry."

"Right." Nodding, Amanda kept working while Martha scrubbed out the insides of the now mostly empty cabinets. Since she couldn't snoop, maybe she could get some information another way. "So, I have to ask, why would anyone want to leave this beautiful house?"

Martha glanced at her and gave a sharp look at the half-dozen goblets sitting on the island, unwrapped. Dutifully, Amanda took a sheet of brown packing paper and carefully wrapped one of the heavy water goblets.

"Well," the woman said while she worked, "Henry's never really liked this house much."

"What's not to like?" Amanda loved it. A Tudor-style mansion, it had window seats, leaded-glass panes, dark wood floors and rich, dark colors on the walls. "It's like a fairy castle."

Martha paused, looked at her and smiled. "I agree." Glancing around the room, she sighed a little. "I'm going to miss it, I'll admit. But Henry will be happier with the move."

"You've known him a long time?" Finally, some information.

"Since he was eleven," Martha said. "I came to work for the Porters right after they moved here from Texas. The house was different then."

"How?" Curious now, she could silently admit that she wanted the information for herself rather than for her self-appointed spying mission. After all, knowing what Henry's life was like when he was a boy wouldn't help her any now.

"They were a good family," Martha said and moved on to the next cabinet. "Mrs. Porter, she was a sweetheart. Kind. Funny. Henry and his father adored her."

She'd known that Henry's mother had died when he was a boy, but she didn't know much more than that since he hadn't wanted to talk about it. This wasn't why she was here, in the house Henry was about to leave, but learning more about the man she'd never been able to forget was irresistible.

"What happened?"

Martha turned to look at her and lifted one eyebrow, and Amanda reached for another goblet to wrap. *Uh-huh. Taskmaster.* Nodding, the older woman went back to her own work, but she kept talking.

"It was heartbreaking to see, I can tell you that. Mrs. Porter was out, picking up Henry's birthday present. She was two blocks from home when a drunk ran a stop sign and hit her car." Martha turned, memories of pain in her eyes as she added, "Poor woman died instantly."

Everything in Amanda fisted. Her heart ached and a swell of sympathy for the boy Henry had been rose up inside her, thick enough to choke off her voice. He had never told her any of that, but then, who would want to talk about it? Looking back, she remembered that Henry had never been interested in road trips. He'd never talked about cars as if the perfect one was the holy grail—as Bennett and every other guy she knew had. And this explained it. Horribly.

But Martha didn't wait for her reaction. She simply rinsed out the cloth she was using and bent to her task again. "Mr. Porter was devastated, of course. That man doted on his wife." She shook her head and sighed. "She was the center of his universe and when she died...well.

I've never seen a man so broken and hope to never see it again."

"And Henry?" Amanda finally managed to ask.

Sighing at the memory, Martha said, "Naturally, the poor boy was just lost. Plain and simple. It was so quick. So impossible—and yet very real." Another sigh. "When that first awful grief passed, Henry's father closed himself up tight, letting the anger of her loss just burn inside him. He closed Henry off, too. The man acted as if his wife had died on purpose. Used to mutter about betrayal and how she'd left him. He was constantly torn between grief and fury and poor Henry had to navigate some hard water there."

Amanda was discovering more about Henry than she'd planned to. She didn't want to feel sympathy, yet couldn't help it. She couldn't even imagine what it had been like for him. Her own mother, Candace, had always been the rock in the family. And while she and Martin were currently doing battle over the retirement thing, they had always been a team. Candace was like the sun and the rest of the family sort of revolved around her. Amanda realized that without her steady presence, she and her siblings would have had very different lives.

Because now that she thought about it, her father would have reacted to her mother's loss much as Henry's father had. And Henry was an only child. He didn't have siblings to help him through the pain. He'd had only his father and it sounded to her as though Mr. Porter had been so devoted to his own agony that he'd missed his son's.

But even as her heart ached for Henry, her mind insisted that tragedy and pain in childhood didn't explain being a hard-ass in adulthood. Didn't excuse his calculated attempts to take down the Carey family. Deliberately, Amanda set aside the pity she felt for the boy Henry had been and remembered that she was here because the Henry *she* knew was busily trying to ruin her and her family.

"Do you need me to do anything else besides the glassware?" she asked, changing the subject because she had to put aside her feelings for Henry's past. Not to mention the fact that she wouldn't find out much about what he was up to by wrapping glassware in the kitchen.

Martha glanced at her, then at the box where only a half-dozen glasses rested. Her eyebrows lifted. "Maybe the kitchen isn't the best place for you. Just…finish up what's in front of you, then you can join Ellie in Henry's study. Most of it will be packed up by the movers in a day or two but there are some things he wants us to take care of."

His study. Now things could be getting interesting. She hid a smile and said, "I'll finish up, then, and join Ellie."

Martha laughed a little. "Oh, to be young enough to have that much energy."

It wasn't youth. It was excitement. Amanda was close now. With a little luck, she'd find out how Henry was getting information on the Carey family.

By the time Henry got back to the Beverly Hills house, he was ready for a beer on the patio. Just a chance to sit still without Mick trying to kill him on the freeway. Besides, in two days he'd be out of this house, so there wasn't much time left to enjoy the patio beneath a pergola blooming now with the wisteria his mother had planted so long ago.

But he stopped by his study first. He just wanted to get a couple of files to read while he relaxed. He hadn't meant to scare the crap out of the women working in the room.

"Mr. Henry!" Ellie, about forty, with short red hair and bright green eyes, turned, one hand clapped to her chest as if holding her heart in place. "I swear, you move as quiet as a ghost."

Made sense, he thought idly, since there were plenty of ghosts in this house. The memory of his mother. The memory of what they'd been as a family before she left. The memory of his father before he'd become so...different.

But all he said was, "Sorry, Ellie. I didn't mean to sneak up on you. I won't bother you for long. I just need a few things." She'd been packing his first editions and Henry was grateful she hadn't fallen off the library ladder.

"You go ahead," she said on a choked laugh. "Once my heart starts again, I'll finish up in here."

He grinned and shot a look at the other woman, packing his desk drawers into a box set on the blotter. She had to be one of the new people Martha had taken on. "I don't know you, do I?"

She was tall, in spite of her hunched shoulders, with short black hair and bright blue eyes behind a pair of glasses she was currently squinting through. "No, we haven't met. I'm Amelia. I'm just here to help in the move."

Henry frowned when she ducked her head, avoiding his gaze. Her voice was familiar, somehow, though the speech pattern wasn't. She had the top drawer open and was gathering up pens, notebooks and more rubber bands than he'd realized he'd tucked inside. She was going slowly, though. Methodically. As if she were looking for something in particular, but if she were, she was doomed to disappointment. He wasn't worried about her packing his desk. There was nothing to interest anyone but him.

"Well, you go ahead with what you're doing," he said, walking toward the desk and the file cabinet behind it. Amelia scuttled out of his way as if afraid to get too close. He frowned to himself again as he caught her scent on the still air and something familiar raced through him. Henry shot her a quick glance and wondered. More than one woman in the world used that scent, he knew. But there was something…

"Is there anything you don't want us to pack?" she asked and gathered his thoughts for him.

"All I need you to do is pack the desk and," he added with a nod to Ellie, "the first editions. The movers can handle the rest."

She nodded, still keeping her head down, and now he wanted to see her eyes again. To feed his own curiosity. But she wasn't going to give him that. He had to wonder why.

Turning back to the cherrywood files, he flipped through them. Yes, all of his files were digitized, but he still kept some in hard copy. Reading on computer screens all day gave him a headache so it was practically a vacation to read paper. Which was also the reason he preferred *actual* books to ebooks.

Amelia moved around him and he couldn't dismiss the slight buzz of recognition he felt when she did. Her scent wafted in her wake and he breathed deeply of it. The fragrance reminded him of summer nights, with its hints of coconut and lime, and the last time he'd been surrounded by that scent, he'd been with Amanda. Frowning more deeply, he drew out the files he wanted. When he straightened, he looked at Amelia again, but she was still avoiding looking at him. Interesting. No one was that shy. So why be so blatantly secretive? The very fact she was trying to hide made him wonder.

So much for a beer on the patio. He was going to stay right there in his study and spend a few minutes figuring out why Amelia was both familiar and a mystery.

Quick footsteps sounded out from the hall as Martha entered the room and called, "Ellie?" Then she noticed him and gave him a warm smile. "I didn't know you were home, Henry."

"Just got here," he said, carrying the stack of files to a dark maroon leather club chair. He sat down, stretched his legs out in front of him and then reached up to turn on the standing brass lamp just behind him.

Funny. This room held more memories than the rest of the house, and most of them weren't pleasant. If he closed his eyes, he was pretty sure he could hear his father's voice and see him, sitting behind that ornate, way-too-big desk, burying himself in the work that had consumed him once Henry's mother had left them.

Maybe that's why Henry himself never spent much time here. His father had decorated this room and Henry had never bothered to change anything, because again, he avoided it, usually. He did like the chairs and the hand-knotted Persian rugs, so they'd be going with him to the new house. But the overwhelming antique desk, the boring paintings and most of the tables and lamps would be going into storage.

Henry was getting a fresh start and he was going to

have a new look in his own damn study. But for now, he glanced at Martha and asked, "Is there a problem?"

"Not at all, but I could use Ellie's help for a bit." She looked to Amelia and said, "You stay here, finish up with packing the desk and whatever else Mr. Porter needs you to do."

Head still ducked, Amelia nodded and Henry frowned. Was her neck permanently bowed? He studied her busily packing as Martha and Ellie left for the kitchen or wherever. She was ignoring his presence and that shouldn't bother him, since it gave him quiet to go over the files.

But there was an undercurrent to Amelia's silence and that *did* bother him. More, it intrigued him. She wouldn't look at him. Her perfume drifted to him and stirred up memories he usually fought into submission.

Annoyed now, Henry was determined to figure out what was happening. He needed to see her eyes.

Pushing up from the chair, he walked toward the desk, where Amelia was busily and purposely looking down, focused solely on packing. He walked to within a foot of her, then simply said, "Amelia?"

She lifted her head and stared into his eyes, and Henry felt the jolt. It amazed him he hadn't recognized her immediately. How he could have missed it was beyond him. She might be hiding behind unnecessary glasses. Wearing a black wig to hide her honey-blond hair. But now he knew who she was.

The last woman he would have expected to find, here, in his house.

Amanda Carey.

Four

Though Amanda had really surprised him, Henry hid that along with the smile curving his mouth. He wasn't going to call her out on her ridiculous disguise. He didn't know what she was up to, but he was willing to go along with her charade. For now. "When you pack the desk, make a note of which drawers have been put into which box."

She ducked her head again, silently telling him she had no idea it was too late to hide her identity. "I will."

"Okay," he said, backing away, because he liked her being nervous, but he didn't want to scare her off entirely. So he walked to his chair, and watched her.

Why was Amanda here? Why was she in disguise? Never mind. That second question had an answer. She was incognito. But why? What did she hope to gain by this?

He sat down, gathered up the files, but rather than

reading them, he watched her. She bent over to reach into the middle drawer and he did a quick mental inventory of the contents. Nothing there she shouldn't see. Nothing that would interest anyone, in fact. So he relaxed enough to enjoy the view.

Amanda always did have a great butt. He smiled to himself as his gaze swept over the curve of her behind and the long legs currently covered by modest black slacks. Now that he knew it was her, he decided he'd have a little fun. Push her and see how far she was willing to take her deception.

"So, *Amelia*. How long will you be working for me?" he asked.

She went still for an instant and he could only imagine that she wasn't happy he was talking to her. "Just a few days. I'm only here to help with the packing."

"And the unpacking? At the new house?" He smiled to himself when she went still again.

"I don't really know, Mr. Porter. I suppose that's up to Martha." Her voice shook a bit and he was glad. She really was nervous. Good. She was here, in his house, probably trying to be a super spy or something. And whatever her plan was, it wouldn't work.

"Oh, I'm sure Martha will need the extra help," he said. "You should probably count on sticking around for a while."

She ducked her head and made a big production out of stacking the desk's contents into a moving box. But it was far too late to hide from him.

Did she really believe a pair of fake glasses would be enough to disguise her eyes? From him? No. Those blue eyes had stayed with him all these years. They'd haunted his dreams, muddled his thoughts and basically been with him for the last ten years.

Hell, everything he'd done and accomplished over the last several years had been because of the Careys. Because of *her*. He'd been driven to prove them wrong. To show them all that he didn't need *them* or their powerful family to succeed. And he'd won, hadn't he? He'd taken his father's company and made it one of the top five in the country. Hell, the world.

So how could he possibly forget anything about her?

"I'm almost finished with your desk. Is there something else you need?"

He pushed up from the chair and walked toward her. "That's an interesting question."

She went still, then instantly moved to close the first box and move on to another.

"Not really," she said, still not looking at him.

Henry considered flirting. Just to see how far she was willing to take the charade, but he decided against it. No matter that he knew the truth, he wasn't coming on to a maid in his house. Didn't mean, though, that he couldn't enjoy making her uncomfortable.

He eased one hip down onto the desk and watched as she packed up the bottom drawer. Her hands were small and delicate, but her movements were quick, as if she couldn't wait to finish the task and get away from him. Still nervous, then. Maybe the best thing he could do was back off, let her regroup and gather her nerves.

"Actually," he said, "once you finish the desk, there's nothing more I need help with. You can talk to Martha about where she needs help."

She shot him a glance, then nodded.

Meanwhile, he walked back to the chair where he'd

been sitting, picked up the files and began talking as he pretended to read them. "Have you ever known someone you would do anything to best?"

"I'm sorry?" She looked at him briefly and now that he had her attention, he layered it on a little thicker.

"Not really an enemy," he mused aloud, "but someone who deserves some payback."

"I...suppose. Maybe," she said.

"Oh there's never a *maybe*," Henry told her, beginning to enjoy himself. "You'll know if it happens to you. You won't have a doubt and you'll go out of your way to make that person—or people—regret messing with you."

She took out boxes of envelopes, the extra boxes of pens he kept in there and a ream of paper for his personal printer and tucked them all into the packing box. "Then no, I've never had that happen to me. Have you?"

He smiled. "Oh, yes. And I've been dealing with them for ten years now."

"Isn't that a long time to carry a grudge?"

She was crouched behind the desk now, keeping him from seeing her. But he'd heard the genuine curiosity in her voice, so he answered honestly.

"It's not a grudge," he said, thinking about the personal mission he'd been on for ten years. "It's... *Justice* is a strong word, but the closest I can get."

"Justice? For what?"

Now she just wanted to make him say it, so he accommodated her. The Carey family had had their way for far too long. It was time he started giving it back and letting them know why. But in particular, it was Amanda's turn to squirm. He gave her the truth that had been pushing him for ten years. He wanted to make Amanda

Carey stand up and call him out. Because as amusing at this was, he thought, having her in his house with no subterfuge between them would be better.

"A woman I was involved with set me up with her family." He gritted his teeth at the statement and the fresh flood of old memories that raced through his mind. "Her family then tried to ruin me, so I'm returning the favor."

She slammed the desk drawer and he smiled, waiting for her to jump to her feet and deny everything. But it didn't happen. He wouldn't have thought Amanda could surprise him, but she had. The girl he remembered had been short on patience, self-control. Looked like things had changed.

"How do you know she set you up?"

"Pretty obvious," he said tightly. Hell, what else would have brought Bennett to the boathouse in Italy in the middle of the night, if she hadn't either let it slip that she was meeting Henry or flat out told Bennett. What Henry had never really been able to figure out was *why* she'd done it.

If she had wanted him to leave her alone, why not just say so? Tell him to get lost. She'd never had a hard time speaking her mind. But she hadn't. Amanda had been as crazy for him as he was for her—either that or she was a hell of an actress.

Before they were together on that night, he'd known Amanda for two years, off and on. He spent a lot of holidays with Bennett and his family and Henry had watched Amanda grow and change, from eighteen to twenty. They laughed together, swam together, and the heat between them built slowly, inexorably until finally, they'd had each other one night in Italy. And

Henry remembered feeling his future open up in front of him. All he could see was Amanda. All he wanted was Amanda, and for a couple of hours, he knew that his world was right. That he'd found the one woman in the world for him.

Then Bennett had shown up and blown it all to hell. But the question remained, what had brought Amanda's older brother—and, at the time, Henry's best friend—to the boathouse that night? How had he found them?

Answers never came, but the memories never left.

The memory of him and Bennett, shouting at each other, fiercely throwing punches while Amanda screamed at both of them to stop. He remembered moonlight streaming out of a cloudless sky, the water of Lake Como slapping against the dock, and the slam of Bennett's fist into his jaw. A friendship he'd depended on had ended that night, along with what he'd thought he had with Amanda.

"When her older brother walked in on us right after we had sex—I figured he knew something was going on. Otherwise, why would he be there at all?"

"So you don't *know* she turned on you, you're just guessing."

He scowled at the top of her head, since that's all he could see. Was it easier, he wondered, for her to lie to him if she wasn't looking at him?

"It's not a guess."

"I hope not," she said. "If you've been trying to deliver karma on the strength of a guess, that would be a sad way to live your life."

Irritation rose up from his gut and flooded his chest. "Sad? I don't live a sad life." He was fine. Always had been. "I do what I want, when I want. How is that sad?"

"Well, if it's so great to be you, why are you so bent on payback?"

He scrubbed one hand across his face and wished to hell she'd stand up and look at him. But she just kept packing as if she were having this weird conversation with a stranger.

"Because this family went out of their way to brush me aside." And even after all these years, Henry could feel the stab of betrayal. He hadn't had many friends until college. He'd been too focused on fulfilling his father's goals and plans. But as his roommate, Bennett had drawn Henry into his circle of friends. He'd taken him to Carey family vacations and holiday celebrations. He'd included Henry at poker games and parties at school. Bennett Carey had been Henry's first true friend. And his betrayal had been the driving force behind everything Henry had done since.

He'd worked night and day, devoted himself to success and had built Porter Enterprises into the kind of company his father had only dreamed of having.

But with that success, he'd paid the price. There were no close friends. Only acquaintances, business connections, and Henry always…*always*…was on guard for the next knife in the back. Bennett had taught him well.

That long-ago night had both fueled and shattered his future.

She looked up briefly. "Another guess?"

"No guessing," he said flatly, meeting her gaze until she ducked down again. "They set out to destroy me."

"You look all right to me," she pointed out.

"That's because they failed." A good thing to remind himself of. Their failure. His success. And he would continue to keep that record shining. Oh, the Carey

Corporation was strong. There was no way he could undermine their foundations, but he was able to make sure they didn't grow as they wanted to. By throwing roadblocks in their way—such as buying that stupid hall because he'd discovered Amanda wanted it—he could make their progression much slower and more difficult than they would like.

"And you're sure of that, too?"

He laughed now, hearing the slight edge of anger in her so carefully controlled voice. "Oh, yeah. They haven't been able to stop me or destroy my company, so yes. They failed."

"And they've stopped trying?"

"No. I wouldn't be surprised," he added wryly, "if they tried to slip a spy into my own damn house just to keep tabs on me."

She went completely still and Henry had to hide a smile. There was a long pause before she said, "That sounds ridiculous."

"It does, doesn't it?" he agreed and walked back toward his desk. When he came around the edge, he stood there, looking down at her. "Wouldn't it be pitiful for someone to wear a disguise and try to sneak into my house?"

"Well, maybe not pitiful," she said, shooting one glance up at him. "Daring, though."

"Sneaky, not daring." He kept his features blank even though he wanted to laugh at the sudden stiffness in her shoulders and the lifting of her chin. She was insulted.

He'd pushed her hard enough for today, he told himself, though he was looking forward to having her around for however long this masquerade was going to continue. Whatever the reason for her game, she wasn't going to win. But that only made the game more fun for Henry.

"Anyway," he said abruptly, "I'll get out of your way, so you can get back to work."

"Thanks," she muttered and he heard the masked anger in her tone.

"Sure. I assume," he said as he stepped back, "you'll be at the new house tomorrow helping Martha organize."

There was a pause and Henry knew Amanda was considering just how far she wanted to take this.

Finally, though, she said, "Like I said. I'm...not sure."

"Well, I think Martha will still need the help, so I'll expect to see you." He turned and headed out of the room, stopping only long enough to pick up the discarded files he'd left on the club chair. As he walked out of the room, he smiled to himself and realized he was going to enjoy this move even more than he'd anticipated.

Amanda finished up in the study and muttered, "Damn it. All of that for nothing."

Not only had she had to deal with Henry, but she also hadn't found a thing that might give her a hint as to how he was getting information on her family. Frustrating. Even more frustrating was the fact that whenever he came close to her, she felt a blast of heat whip through her like a stray lightning bolt. For one unsettling moment, Amanda had been sure he'd recognized her. The way he looked into her eyes. The puzzled expression on his face. But then that moment passed and she'd felt safe again in the disguise that was uncomfortable but, apparently, convincing.

But beneath everything, she was irritated. Amanda looked around the room. The space was huge, but it was dark and somehow claustrophobic, with its heavy, dark green drapes at the windows, the dark leather chairs and the burgundy-colored walls. There were framed paintings and photographs of different businesses that Porter Enterprises encompassed and a pendulum clock on one wall, loudly ticking off the seconds. It sounded like a heartbeat in the stillness and sort of creeped her out.

The room didn't look like Henry at all. At least, not the Henry she'd once known. Had he, along with becoming a corporate pirate of sorts, also become staid and…boring?

"No," she assured herself. "The man who had been in here bugging me wasn't boring. Annoying, yes, but not boring."

More likely he'd simply never made changes to the room after his father left. And she wondered why. Wasn't this his home, too? Why hadn't he laid a claim to it, stamped it with his own personality? Was he too involved in trying to destroy the Careys to bother thinking about his surroundings?

"Are you finished in here?"

Amanda spun around to face Martha, standing in the open doorway. "Oh. Yes."

"Well, then, don't just stand there. You can come on back and help me in the kitchen again."

"I'll be right there."

"Good. We've got a cleaning crew coming in after the movers finish tomorrow—not that *my* house needs cleaning," she added as if insulted at the very thought of a cleaning crew coming in. "But *my* kitchen will be cleaned *my* way," she said with a sharp jerk of her head. "We're cleaning that room, top to bottom, until it shines."

Oh, God. Amanda really wanted to just walk out of that house and forget she'd ever come up with this stupid plan in the first place. But on the other hand, she and Henry had just had the longest conversation they'd had in ten years. It hadn't exactly been friendly, but it had been…illuminating. And if she could just keep from hitting him over the head with something when he irritated her, she might get some answers. All she had to do, she told herself firmly, was survive being a maid.

When this was all over, the first thing she was going to do was give her own maid a *huge* raise.

Martha swirled around and headed down the long hall, her footsteps hammering out a beat that matched the relentless ticking of that awful clock on the wall in the study. Amanda threw a hard look at it, gold pendulum swinging back and forth. While she walked to follow Martha to the kitchen, she wondered how anyone could stand the sound of seconds being ticked off their life.

Two hours later, Amanda had broken three nails and scraped the back of her hand, and the throbbing in her knees matched the damn ticking of that stupid clock. She was exhausted, hungry and oh, yes, *dirty*. Honestly, a raise wasn't enough for her own maid, Rose. She deserved a two-week vacation somewhere amazing. Or a car. Or both.

"Okay," Martha announced and waited for Amanda and the two other women helping out to turn and face her. “I think we’ve earned a break. You can all take a half hour and then we’ll tackle the butler’s pantry and the laundry room.”

“Sure thing,” the other two women chirped and Amanda only stared at them all. She’d once thought that she worked hard every day. Working on her computer, making calls, taking meetings, she’d gone home to her condo tired enough to order dinner and have a glass or two of wine with her feet up.

Now? She was too tired to chew and felt as if she didn’t have the strength to pick up a wineglass. And she wasn’t finished. Still, she took advantage of the “break” and almost crawled into the beautifully tended backyard.

It felt good to have the sun on her face and the soft breeze sliding in off the ocean, which ruffled the leaves as well as tousled the hair of her black wig, tossing it into her eyes. She shook it back, dug her phone out of her pocket and kept walking until she reached the stone bench situated beneath a tree covered in pink blooms. She dropped onto it and half wondered if she’d be able to get up again. Then she shrugged off that worry, hit speed dial and waited for her sister to answer.

“Amanda! I tried to call you earlier and you didn’t answer.” Serena’s voice was fast and pitched low.

“I had it turned off,” Amanda admitted, tipping her head back to stare up at patches of blue sky through the cloud of pink flowers. “Sorry, couldn’t talk before. The general in charge of the maids gave me a break. Which is not going to be long enough.” She sighed, planted her right hand on the bench and leaned back. If it wouldn’t look too pitiful from the house, she’d stretch out right there and take a nap.

"Well, hope you're having a great time, because here in the office, things are not good."

Frowning, she dismissed the beautiful tree, the landscaped grounds and her own fatigue long enough to ask, "What's happening?"

"What isn't? Bennett's a crazy person, looking for you because the Oregon Choir has to postpone their performance by two weeks."

She straightened up. "They can't do that."

"So Bennett told them, with a lot less diplomacy."

"Oh, God." Amanda pushed up from the bench and almost stabbed her fingers through her hair, but she would have pulled that stupid wig off. Walking aimlessly across the grass, she asked, "Why are they postponing?"

"I'm not really sure, something about their primary singer straining her throat and she needs time to recover and…"

"No, no, no," Amanda argued, shaking her head. "That's their marketing, publicity guy. He tried this two years ago, too. It's as if he wants us to prove how badly we want the choir. Last time, he tried to get me to increase the publicity for their tour. They're very popular and he knows it so he's always angling for better pay or more promotion."

"Well, Bennett didn't know that."

"Oh, damn it." She should have been there to handle things, Amanda thought in disgust. "Tell Bennett I'll take care of it."

"Yeah, that's not going to work because if you check your phone, you'll probably see a half-dozen calls from him on it." Serena's voice went even lower as she added,

"He's not going to be happy to know I talked to you and he didn't."

"Why are you whispering? Aren't you in your office?"

"Yes, but Bennett's popped in here four times today, looking for you." Serena paused. "I don't know if he thinks I've hidden you under my desk or something, but—"

"Fine. Tell Bennett I'll call him tonight."

"Good luck talking to him. He's even more irascible than usual."

"Great." Amanda glanced back at the house, wondering if Bennett and Henry were on the same wavelength because they were *both* driving her nuts today. "Don't worry about it. I'll call the Oregon guy and get this straightened out."

"Do you have the number?"

"In my phone." Amanda blew out a sigh. "Look, just cover for me with Bennett and I'll talk to him tonight."

"Where are you, then?"

"What do you mean where am I?" Amanda frowned at the phone. "You know where I am."

"Yes. But I can't tell Bennett that, can I?" Her voice dropped even lower. "He would completely lose it."

Yes, he would. "Um, then tell him I'm trying to land another performer for this summer. *And*, tell him I wouldn't tell you who it is."

"Fine." Serena huffed out a breath. "But this pretend-maid thing better be worth all of this."

"I think it will be," she said. At least she hoped so.

"And don't forget, we have the first audition taping for the Summer Stars contest tonight and you have to be there."

"Crap. I forgot about that." Must be all the fumes from the cleaning products. "Fine. What time?"

"Seven thirty. Be there, Amanda, because I promise you, Bennett will be."

Why did that sound more like a threat than a promise?

She hung up a moment later, scrolled through her contacts list and hit Dial. Ten minutes of wrangling with the Oregon Choir marketing director, Cory Davis, got things straightened out and they were back on schedule.

"But you can tell your brother that I didn't appreciate the threats."

"Bennett threatened you?"

"With a lawsuit!" Cory was outraged.

"Well, of course we're not going to sue," Amanda soothed. "Just as, of course, you're going to be performing at the center as scheduled."

"Naturally," Cory said, mollified at least until next summer, "I'm pleased to see that at least one member of the Carey family is reasonable."

Right. "Okay, thanks, Cory. We'll see you at the beginning of June."

When she was finished, Amanda wanted nothing more than to sit down under that tree again. She had plenty to think about. Bennett over the edge. Serena in the middle of everything. Her mother and father at war. Martha the taskmaster.

But mostly, she was rethinking absolutely every word that had come out of Henry's mouth. Did he really believe she had set him up? That she'd somehow worked it so that Bennett would find them after that amazing bout of sex? Why would she have done that? She'd never been so mortified as the night her brother had walked into the boathouse in Italy and saw her naked.

But if Henry really did believe that, it would explain why he'd never called her. Why he'd disappeared from her life completely until he'd begun his *take-the-Careys-down* campaign.

"Of course he could have *said* something," she mumbled. "Even if it was to yell at me. Then I could have told him that I had nothing to do with Bennett showing up."

She'd spent the last ten years believing that Bennett had been right about Henry. Back then, her brother had accused his best friend of using Amanda to wedge his way into the Carey family and fortune.

When Henry disappeared and never contacted her, Amanda began to believe the same thing.

Had they both been wrong all this time? She stopped walking beneath a lemon tree and the scent of the white blossoms surrounded her, flavoring every breath. As she thought it through, she came to one obvious conclusion.

"It doesn't matter. If we were both wrong all this time, what does it change?" Henry had still spent the last several years trying to sink her family. He'd gone out of his way to undermine them whenever he could. Up to and including buying the hall that she'd had such plans for.

He'd taken his father's company and built it into a powerhouse that rivaled the biggest corporations in the country. And he had used his newfound power to go against everything she was and believed in. Everything *she* had been working toward for years.

So why was it so hard for her to put that one night with him behind her? And why was she even more attracted to him now than she had been in the past? Was it that slightly ruthless streak? His determination? His image rushed into her mind and left her more than a little breathless. For just a moment, she remembered how it had felt to have him standing so close to her in the study. The buzz of…recognition. Attraction. Heat had swamped her even as she fought to keep her gaze from straying up to meet his. He hadn't recognized her, she was sure of that.

Because Henry never would have been able to keep from calling her out on it if he had. So while she'd been doing a slow burn that close to him, he'd simply been venting, or whatever, to an employee he no doubt had figured couldn't have cared less what he had to say. Well, he'd told her more than he would have wanted her to hear. Now she simply had to decide what to do about it. They'd started years ago as a simmering flame that had burst into a wildfire that consumed both of them. Then it was gone and they were both left in the cold.

She still felt the chill of it and had to wonder if he did, too.

"So even if this all started with a misunderstanding," she whispered, looking at the house where Henry was, "it's done now. No going back. Only forward. And there's no common ground for that." Frowning, she lifted her gaze to the second floor, where she knew Henry's bedroom was, and wondered if he was currently planning his next foray against the Carey family.

"If he is," she vowed, "it will fail. I'll make sure of it."

The Carey Center was a palace to the performing arts.

Three levels of seating, fronted by glass railings

that rippled like waves on the ocean. Those rails were wrapped around an oak stage where the honey-colored wood was polished to a gleam that rivaled a mirror. The stage was seventy feet wide and fifty deep, perfect for a complete orchestra, a huge choir or an intricate ballet.

Every red velvet seat in the house had a wonderful view of the performance and the ceiling was studded with crystals that looked, with the reflected lighting, like stars in a black sky.

The hall itself sat two thousand, not counting the five private boxes and other VIP seating. Backstage, there were several dressing rooms and a luxuriously appointed performer's lounge.

The lobby of the center was elegant, with miles of Spanish tiles and acres of glass and chrome. There was a café for refreshments, a gift shop and a first aid station, just in case.

For now, though, the center was mostly empty, but for the front row, where their first contestant's family sat nervously waiting for the show to begin.

Halfway up the center aisle, Amanda sat between Bennett on one side and their mother on the other. While Bennett mumbled to himself and repeatedly checked his email, their mother tapped the toe of her shoe against the floor and reminded Amanda of that awful clock in Henry's house.

"Are they going to start tonight some time?" Bennett demanded, checking his watch for the fifth time in the last few minutes.

"They'll start soon. Look." She pointed to the stage where the pianist from the home symphony was taking his seat at a gleaming black Steinway grand piano. Accompaniment was provided for the contestants if they required it and Jacob Baranca was one of the best pianists in the world. "Jacob's getting set."

"Finally."

Amanda looked at Bennett in time to see his scowl. "You don't have to be here, you know. The contest is my deal and I can handle it."

"Like you handled the problem with that Cory from Oregon?"

"I did handle it," she countered, "no thanks to you. Why would you threaten to sue him?"

A little shamefaced, Bennett said, "He wouldn't listen to reason."

"Yes, I'm sure you were the very soul of reason," Amanda said.

"Fine. I shouldn't have and you fixed it." Frowning, he asked, "Who was this new performer you were talking to?"

Amanda took a breath and held it. She really should have come up with an explanation, but by the time she got home from Henry's, exhausted, she'd had time only to change and rush to the center. "It's a surprise."

He shot her a dubious look. "Fine. Whatever. Anyway, this is the first night of the auditions and I wanted to be here. Make sure the technicians have the logistics down."

"You know, Bennett," their mother said, interrupting both of them, "you don't have to do *everything* in the company yourself. Honestly, you're becoming more and more like your father."

"Thank you," he said.

Amanda rolled her eyes. "Speaking of Dad," she said, "where is he?"

Candace smoothed the skirt of the sleek plum-colored

suit she wore. “I have no idea. All I’m sure of is that neither of us is in Palm Springs.”

“Mom,” Bennett said, “stop being so hard on him.”

“Of course you’re on his side. You’re turning out just like him,” Candace shot back.

“There are no sides,” Amanda said on a sigh.

Candace patted her hand. “You poor thing. You just don’t see it.”

Eyes rolling again, Amanda tried to shift the conversation back to what she and Bennett had been talking about. Half turning in her seat, she spotted the cameramen, ready and waiting for the audition to begin. “Don’t worry about it, Bennett. We’ve got two different camera angles to work with. Behind us, and there—” she pointed “—stage left for close-ups. Then we’ll get the recording edited to showcase it.”

Every contestant’s audition would be displayed on the Carey Center website, with some background information on the performer beside their performance recording. Once all twenty of the contestants were online, the Careys would open the voting—with their tech wizards making sure that no one could stuff the ballot box, so to speak.

The winner of the competition would be the star of their own show one night during the Summer Sensations concert series.

“Fine, and the techs will get it to the website wizards?” Bennett looked at Amanda, eyebrows arched in question.

“No, Bennett,” she said, sarcasm dripping. “We’re going to take the recording out and burn it when it’s finished being edited.”

“Little snippy aren’t we?”

"Because I'm a woman, I'm snippy?" she demanded, sitting back to glare at him. "But you're a man so you're just frustrated?"

"Don't pull that feminism crap on me, Mandy. It's not going to fly. You're in charge here, so what're you complaining about?"

"Oh, gee, that maybe the brother who says I'm in charge keeps checking up on me?"

He gritted his teeth briefly and jerked her a nod. "Fine. I get it. Now can you hurry this along?"

"For heaven's sake, Bennett, if you can't take the time to enjoy yourself, then go away." Candacc leaned past Amanda to give her son what they used to call the "Mean Mom" stare. Whatever it was called, it worked. Bennett sat back and returned to checking his phone.

"Mandy, who's the first contestant?" her mother asked.

Amanda turned to look at her and smiled. "Jackie Carson," she said, checking her notes again to make sure she had that right. "She's singing a selection from *La Bohème*."

"Oh, God, opera," Bennett muttered.

"I love you, my son, but all of your taste is in your mouth," Candace said, leaning forward again to give her oldest child another glare.

Amanda snorted, then everyone quieted as the lights died away and a spotlight blossomed onstage. Checking that the camera crew was on it, Amanda sat back to give Jackie Carson her complete attention.

A few moments later, a young woman with long red hair tumbling over her shoulders walked into the light, lifted her chin and began singing. Her absolutely pure, lovely voice soared through the center and reverberated, due to the excellent acoustics.

Beside Amanda, Candace Carey leaned forward, a dreamy look in her eyes and a soft smile curving her mouth. Even Bennett, Amanda realized when she sneaked a look at her brother, was captivated by the woman pouring her heart and soul into a song of love and loss.

When the music trailed off and the last, haunting note of Jackie's voice drifted into the rafters, Amanda sat back while the woman's family jumped to their feet, applauding.

"Okay," Bennett grudgingly admitted, "that was really something."

"She was *wonderful.*" Candace dipped into her black leather bag and pulled out a handkerchief that she used to dab at her eyes. "Honestly, Amanda, if all of our contestants are of her caliber, it's going to be an amazing contest."

Amanda had to agree. For a few shining moments, Jackie Carson had taken her mind off everything but the moment. "You're right, Mom," she said on a sigh, "that was a *great* start to this contest."

"She's got my vote," Henry Porter spoke up from behind them.

Five

"What the hell?" Bennett jumped to his feet and spun around to face the man.

Amanda took a breath and held it.

"Keep your voice down," Candace ordered as she, too, stood.

Down below, Jackie Carson was surrounded by her family hugging and laughing together, celebrating a magnificent audition. Here…the family situation was a little different. But just as inescapable.

Amanda gritted her teeth and stood up. She braced herself before turning to look at the man who continued to haunt her life. She'd seen him only a few hours ago and here he was again. Henry was wearing a beautiful black suit with a dark blue shirt and a black tie. His too-long black hair curled over his collar and his green eyes seemed almost to glow in the dim lighting.

He looked both elegant and dangerous, and a curl of

fire swept into life inside her. His eyes were locked on hers, as if the rest of the world had slipped away into nothingness. Tension spiked and she could acknowledge, at least silently, that her tension wasn't coming from anger.

Bennett was practically humming with banked fury and Candace, true to her kind nature, emanated a sort of calm acceptance. Amanda was somewhere in between with a whole lot of lust wrapped up in it, too.

"Henry," Candace said, holding out her right hand. "It's good to see you."

"Is it?" Bennett demanded, turning a stunned expression on his mother.

"Mrs. Carey." Henry ignored his old friend, shook Candace's hand and gave her what looked like a grateful smile.

His gaze shifted once more to Amanda's and she wondered what he was thinking because his eyes flashed with…something she couldn't read.

"Exactly why are you here?"

Henry looked briefly at Bennett, before turning back to Amanda. The heat in his eyes made her want to squirm, so she kept deliberately still. It wasn't easy.

Though he answered Bennett, he was looking only at Amanda when he said, "Your website claimed the auditions were open." He shrugged and glanced around the concert hall. "Not many people taking you up on the invitation, are they?"

Bennett stiffened, clearly insulted. "They will. This is just the first one."

"Which is why I came," Henry said. "Mostly."

His gaze was still fixed on Amanda, and Bennett

didn't miss it. "Yeah, well, audition's over so maybe you should go."

"You'll have to excuse my son," Candace spoke up again. "I gave his father too much room in raising him."

"Seriously?" Bennett asked. "You're taking his side in this?"

"There is no 'side,' Bennett. And holding on to anger for ten years is just ridiculous. Along with exhausting."

Henry nodded at her, but Amanda wanted to point out that Henry was as guilty of that as the Careys. Still, she was surprised by her mother's reaction. No one in the family really talked about what had happened ten years before and Amanda had always been grateful for that. But at the same time, she'd been oblivious to the fact that it seemed only she and Bennett were still harboring anger over it.

Interesting.

"Martin and I were supposed to be in Palm Springs this week," Candace said.

"Mom…" Bennett's chin dropped to his chest.

She ignored Bennett and took a quick look over her shoulder at the young woman and her family before turning back to say, "But I have to admit, I'm glad I was here to see our first contestant in person." She looked at Bennett. "Don't tell your father I said that."

"Don't put me in the middle of the war," Bennett countered.

Too late for that, Amanda thought. All of the Carey kids were in the middle. Well, except for Justin, who had the good sense to spend most of his time out of range. But she focused on the conversation again when her mother looked to Henry.

"What did you think of our first amateur performer?" Candace asked.

He smiled and said easily, "She was amazing. I think you're going to really have something special with this contest."

Amanda blinked. This had been her idea. Her baby, so to speak, and having Henry applaud it gave her a small rush that she really didn't want to think about.

"I think so, too," Candace said, then dropped one arm around her daughter's shoulders and gave her a brief hug. "It was Amanda's idea, you know."

"Is that right?" Appreciation shone in his eyes and that little rush Amanda felt gleamed brighter. "Well, it was a brilliant move."

"Thanks." Why was he being nice? And why did she care what he thought of her? Heck, yesterday she'd been ready to pummel him for thwarting her plan and here she was now, basking in his appreciation? Made no sense whatsoever and yet…

"Why not invite him to the house for a drink?" Bennett muttered.

"You've done well for yourself, Henry. Congratulations," Candace said, ignoring her son's blustering.

"Well, hell, Mom, why don't we throw him a party?"

Amanda nudged Bennett and got a dirty look for her trouble.

Henry grinned, then said, "Thank you, Mrs. Carey. That means a lot."

"I bet it does," Bennett grumbled.

"Bennett," his mother said, "I love you dearly, but you're being tiresome."

Bennett threw both hands up, and glanced at Henry in time to see a small smile. Amanda could have sworn she'd almost glimpsed a matching one on her brother's face. But that had to be a mistake.

"Henry, if you want to come to the auditions, we can't stop you," Amanda said, keeping her voice far steadier than she was feeling.

"Agreed," he said with a smile.

"I just don't understand why you want to be here."

He shrugged again and the carefree move really seemed to bother Bennett. Probably why he did it. "Since I'm moving to Irvine, I thought I'd get acquainted with the center. I'll probably be spending a lot of time here."

"You're moving—" Bennett broke off midsentence. "Why here?"

"Why not?" Henry countered.

"Never pictured you as one to enjoy opera."

Henry smiled. "Good to expand your horizons, Bennett. You should try it."

Candace's lips twitched and Amanda wondered if the real reason Henry had come was just to give her brother a hard time. Then Henry's gaze shifted back to her and she rethought that. He'd come to see her. Why? Had he figured out that *she* was the maid, Amelia? If he had, he wasn't showing it or, thank God, mentioning it.

A taut silence strung out then until it was broken by Martin Carey's shout. "There you are!" He hurried down the center aisle, focusing his attention on his wife, who merely glanced at him.

"You're late," Candace said. "You missed the performance."

"I had a call—"

"Of course you did." Candace nodded at Henry, then gave Amanda a one-armed hug and blew a kiss to Bennett. "Well, I have to be going. Amanda, sweetie, that was a wonderful start to your contest. Congratulations."

"Thanks, Mom."

Martin brushed past his children to follow Candace and screeched to a stop when he noticed Henry. "Porter? What are you doing here?"

"We've already covered that, Mr. Carey," Henry said amiably. "You can ask your wife."

"My wife—" Martin seemed to suddenly remember that he should be going after Candace. He gave Henry another questioning stare, then hurried after the woman who was almost to the exit already.

Amanda watched him go and wished Bennett would go, as well. But it was as if her brother was rooted to the spot. He and Henry were having a staring contest now and neither of them was going to give in. It was up to her to call an end to it. "Bennett, would you go and remind the cameramen to get the audition recording to Clark in tech as soon as possible?"

"They know that," he muttered, still glaring at Henry.

"Please," she said and gave him an imploring look when he turned his gaze on her.

"Fine." He stepped out into the aisle, but paused for another shot at Henry. "But I won't be far. And, we're not done, you know."

"Going on ten years now," Henry pointed out. "I'm aware."

Grumbling under his breath, Bennett stalked up the aisle and Henry gave him a big smile as he went. Turning back to Amanda, he asked, "So is he afraid I'm going to rip your clothes off and toss you on the floor?"

Whoa. Her body responded to that even while her

brain was reminding her that was pretty much what had happened ten years ago.

"He knows that's not going to happen," she said with a lot more surety than she was feeling at the moment.

"Could be interesting," he said.

"Could be a disaster. Like before."

His smile faded. "Ended as a disaster," he said. "Didn't start out that way."

No, it hadn't. And if she allowed herself to, she could bring back every moment of that night with Henry. How her heart had raced, her body humming beneath his, the feel of his hands on her skin and the taste of him filling her. *Yep, every minute.* So she didn't let herself remember.

When Bennett was far enough away that he wouldn't overhear her, she said, "Henry, why make things harder?"

He shrugged. "Hey, Bennett's the one looking for trouble. I just came to see the audition."

"You could have seen it on the website," she pointed out. "It will be up within the hour."

"Not the same," he said and glanced up and around at the interior of the center. "You were here."

"You haven't dropped in to see me at any time before tonight. What's different?"

He shrugged and every muscle in his chest rippled beneath that dark shirt. "Maybe I just thought it was time."

"Uh-huh. Time for what, exactly?"

"Interesting question, isn't it?" He smiled at her and her stomach did a slow roll and spin, then he started talking again. "I haven't been here in a long time. It's an amazing place," he admitted, almost reluctantly. Turning his gaze back to her, he said, "Beautiful."

He wasn't talking about the center now and that thread of heat inside her seemed to spread in reaction to the gleam in his eyes as much as his words. "Henry, nothing's changed. You moving closer won't change things."

"Who's trying to change anything?" He brushed the sides of his jacket back and tucked both hands into his pockets. "But like your mother said, ten years of warfare is ridiculous."

She didn't believe that for a minute. If *he* believed that, he wouldn't have swooped in and bought the hall that Amanda had wanted. He'd done it to make a point. That the war was still raging. "And one sentence from my mom is enough to make you change your mind?"

He only smiled. Irritating.

"So you're a big fan of the Carey family now? Is that it?"

"Some of them," he admitted. "Your mom for one. I always liked Candace."

Hard to argue with that. Her mother really was the best, so she could hardly blame him for being fond of her. And as she thought about it, she remembered how her mother had always welcomed Henry as if he were another of her children. Knowing what she knew now about the loss of his own mother made her realize how much he must have appreciated that.

But that still didn't change what he'd been doing for years. What he'd *just* done to her and her plans.

"My mom brought you here."

"No, you did," he admitted.

"Why?"

"Still working that out." And he didn't look happy about it.

"Henry, what is it you want?"

"Satisfaction," he said quickly. "What about you, Mandy? What do you want?"

His use of her nickname unlocked secret places in her heart and she really wished they'd remained closed off. She didn't want to remember the other Henry. The man she'd loved and lost ten years ago. The man she'd pinned hopes and dreams on only to watch them all disappear when he did.

What did she want? To prove herself to her family. To dream without the longing that still dogged her. To find the kind of joy she'd once had when she'd believed Henry loved her.

All of that and more.

But she didn't tell him that. Instead she said only, "I'll let you know. Right now, I have to go and congratulate our first contestant. I'm assuming you can find your own way out."

One corner of his mouth tipped into a half smile and she wished she didn't find that expression so…tempting.

Amanda steeled herself against her own feelings and left him standing there to walk down the aisle toward the stage. She plastered a bright smile on her face for Jackie Carson's benefit and tried not to feel Henry's gaze on her as surely as she would have a touch.

It didn't work. But she tried.

Henry didn't have to worry about a damn thing.

The movers swept in the following morning and took everything that was going with him to the new house in Irvine. The rest—the antiques and what he thought of as his mother's favorite "girlie" furniture would be stored. He didn't want to use it, but hadn't been able to bring himself to get rid of it, either. So he would tuck it away where he didn't have to think about it.

Which, he had to admit, was exactly how he had treated memories of Amanda.

She'd been pushed into a corner of his mind where she couldn't easily torture him. Yet still, she managed to sneak out when he least expected it to dance in his mind with a torturous regularity he hadn't been able to defeat.

Seeing her last night had hit him harder than he'd expected it would. The image of her rose up in his mind and he took a second just to enjoy the memory. Her hair had been long and loose and she'd worn a sapphire-blue dress with a scooped neckline, long sleeves and a skirt that looked as if it would swirl around her legs with every movement. It wasn't particularly *sexy*, yet, clinging to that body of hers, it had radiated sex.

Hell, he'd gone to the center only to shake her a little. He hadn't thought it would do the same to him. Still, he was glad he'd gone because having Candace Carey treat him as she had before everything had blown up that long-ago summer had been…good. Hell, great. And Bennett had hated it, so that was a plus.

Henry walked through the new house, avoiding movers and Martha and her crew. Henry had spent a couple of hours at the new office, making sure Donna and the movers had the situation in hand, then he'd driven home, really appreciating that it was a five-mile commute on city streets. He watched as movers shuffled in furniture and mountains of boxes and was grateful he didn't have to deal with anything but his own study.

Heading upstairs, he planned to go up on the roof. Get some air, enjoy that incredible view and get out of the way of the dozens of people trooping through his house. He caught Amanda's scent and frowned to himself. In disguise or not, she was imprinting herself on his place and it was going to make it even harder to ignore her. He knew that long after she'd gone, he would be remembering that scent and he would picture her here, in his home. He would be tasting that memory, dragging it into his lungs and filling him with mental images that would torment him. No way to avoid it, either.

Even if she left his house today, he would know she'd been there. And he would see her. In every damn room. That stupid disguise of hers—did she really think he could be fooled by it? Didn't matter a damn. He knew who she was. Could see beneath that black wig and faux glasses. And his mind did the rest for him, showing him Amanda as she really was, with her long, honey-blond hair and bright blue eyes that saw more than she should and gave away little.

She hadn't always been so guarded. He remembered those eyes being open and alive with laughter and shining with a love that was as young as she. But somewhere along the line, she'd put up walls between herself and the rest of the world. Was it after the boathouse? Or was she a part of setting up that scene as he'd long believed?

He didn't know. But it didn't really matter, either. He didn't trust people easily now because he'd learned early on just how devastating it could be to have that trust turn and bite you in the ass.

Henry pushed her out of his mind and took the wide

stairs at a jog. He wanted his laptop and a good furniture website. The rooms in this house were expansive and had a sort of flow to them that gave an open feeling from the moment you came through the front door. It felt even more expansive with so little furniture in it. Hell, it practically echoed.

Pausing at the landing, he looked down at the wide hallway and the open great room that spilled off it. Spanish style, this house was as far from the Beverly Hills Tudor as he could get and Henry admitted silently that he much preferred this style of home. Red tile lined the hallway, but the rooms arrowing off the hall boasted wide-plank oak floors. There were so many windows, it was as if the outdoors was inside.

The house itself was built in an open square with a center patio that was accessible from every room on the ground floor. He turned to glance at the empty loft at the head of the curved, wide staircase and the two halls that stretched from that space, offering access to both wings of the house. Watching the parade of movers below, he thought that Martha, showing them the way, was like a drum major at the head of a marching band. Smiling to himself, he walked down the hall to the master and stepped inside only to be stopped at the sight of Amanda, bent in half over his king-size bed, putting fresh sheets on the mattress.

So much for avoiding her.

His gaze locked on the curve of her butt and as she reached out, smoothing sheets, the pull of her shirt against her breasts. His hands itched to touch her again. It had been ten years, since the last time he'd been with her, but damned if he didn't remember the soft slide of her skin beneath his palms. He hated that wig she wore and wanted instead to see her long blond hair slipping over her shoulders again.

"Stupid bed," she muttered and crawled onto the mattress to tug at the sheets, wrinkling them beneath her knees as she went.

He almost laughed. How had she thought she could pretend to be a maid? Since it was clear to him she had never changed her *own* sheets.

"Having trouble?" he asked.

She went completely still on her hands and knees and slowly swiveled her head to look at him. Henry's body went hard as stone in a blink. His casual pose, leaning one shoulder against the doorjamb, belied the tension inside him.

Amanda, on all fours. On his bed. Looking back at him over her shoulder. Oh, yeah. His brain completed the fantasy, stripping her clothes off, providing moonlight rather than the bright sun pouring through the French doors leading to a wide balcony and that long blond hair of hers that he wanted to thread his fingers through. Then the illusion dissolved as she gave a startled yelp and shimmied back off the bed.

"You surprised me."

"Same," he said, pushing off the doorway and strolling casually into the room. He wasn't *feeling* casual, though, and Henry told himself that of the two of them, he was by far the better actor. Hell, it was a wonder he could walk at the moment.

"Martha asked me to make up your bed and I was just—"

"Calling the bed names?"

Her lips thinned out and her eyes narrowed. "How long were you standing there?"

"Long enough to enjoy the show."

Pushing those ridiculous glasses back up her nose when they slid down, she took a quick, sharp breath and frowned at him. "Once I get the bed made, I'll be out of your way."

"You're not *in* my way," he said, walking across the huge room. He took it all in with a glance. Wide-screen TV over a kiva-style fireplace, dresser and chest along one wall and two overstuffed chairs drawn up in front of a now cold hearth. The French doors opened onto the balcony that had drawn him from the first time he'd seen the house. He could see the ocean through those doors, though it was too far away for him to be lulled by the slap and pound of the waves. He needed furniture out there, too, he supposed and told himself to get his laptop and start shopping. Walk away from Amanda. Stop putting himself through the pain of want.

"It's a beautiful house," Amanda said, catching his attention so that he turned to look at her.

"Thanks. I think so."

"You'll need some chairs on that balcony, though, if you really want to enjoy the view."

"I was just thinking that," he admitted.

"You have the internet, don't you?"

He drew his head back and gave her a grin. "Yeah, I do. Came upstairs to get my laptop and get started on that."

"You should get a chaise or two, along with the chairs and a table. You have plenty of room."

He looked back at the balcony and thought she had a point. Hell, he could almost see it. "Not a bad idea."

"It's been known to happen," she mused, then picked up the top sheet and started unfolding it.

"Let me help you with that," he said abruptly, surprising both of them.

"That's not necessary," she argued.

"If it was, I probably wouldn't have offered," he admitted. Walking to the bed, he took one edge of the dark blue sheet and helped Amanda shake it open enough to drop over the mattress.

She looked nervous and he was glad to see it. He liked having her on edge around him. Let him know she wasn't as unaffected as she pretended to be.

She pulled the sheet down, tucked in the bottom edge and then watched as he pulled it free a bit.

"Don't like my sheets tied down," he said with a shrug.

"Okay." Turning, she lifted the forest green duvet off a nearby chair and swung it out to come down over the mattress like a parachute. "You know, I can do the rest by myself if there's something you should be doing..."

"Trying to get rid of me?"

"It's your house," she reminded him.

"True, but it's full of strangers at the moment."

"We'll all be gone soon enough," she said and slipped first one, then another pillow into the cases. Plumping them, she set them against the heavy, dark wood headboard, then grabbed a half-dozen other throw pillows and tossed them onto the bed, as well. When she was finished, Henry waited for her to turn to face him.

"Eager to be done with the job and get out, is that it?"

"It's a temporary job, Mr. Porter," she said and moved toward the master bath. "Once we have you settled, my work is done."

When she said it, Henry realized he didn't want her

job to be over. He wanted her there. In his house. Ideally, in his bed.

He glanced at the freshly made sheets and that's when he noticed that the bedside table drawer was partially open. He glanced back at the adjoining bath, then walked to the table. He opened the drawer, saw that the few things hc kept there had been rifled, but whatever she was here looking for, she hadn't found it in that drawer. He looked down at the box of condoms, chuckled and told himself that at least she knew he was ready to roll.

Walking back to the bathroom, he watched as she unpacked a box of towels, then stacked them neatly on the shelves. "So what do you do when you're not a temporary maid?"

She looked back at him. "I, um, work in the family business."

"Is that right?" Smiling to himself, he folded his arms over his chest and asked, "What kind of business?"

"Oh," she hedged, "a little of this, a little of that, really. We're very diversified."

You could say that again, he thought. The Careys had a hand in a million different pies, much as he did. But their main focus was the center, real estate holdings and the five-star restaurant they owned in Laguna.

"Diversified, huh? What part do you work on?" He was trying to trip her up. Since she wasn't much of an actress, he hoped she might accidentally spill something she didn't want to.

"That depends, really. Wherever I'm needed, I guess."

"That's vague enough," he said.

She looked back at him. "Are you writing a book?"

"If I were," he said with a quick grin, "I'd need more information."

"And a more interesting subject." She finished with the towels, picked up the empty box and turned toward him.

"Oh, I'm interested." Henry smiled when he saw the flash of nerves in her eyes.

This day just kept getting better.

Six

While he looked at her, seeing past the clumsy disguise, Henry had an idea. "Do you want to see the reason I bought this house?"

Her eyes held questions and a little doubt, but he knew she wouldn't be able to resist.

"I guess so."

"I'll take that answer," he said. "Follow me."

He walked out of his bedroom and down the hall to a closed door that he opened to reveal a staircase lit from above, with the sun shining down through a heavy pane of glass.

"I was expecting another bedroom behind that door," she admitted, looking up the stairs to the closed door above.

"So was I when I first saw this place," he admitted, and started up, with Amanda close on his heels. He opened the door to a wash of sunlight and the wide scope of a deep blue sky studded with white clouds. Stepping back, he made way for her to join him and when she had, he closed the door behind them.

"This is—" she did a slow turn, taking it all in "—fantastic."

"Just my reaction," he agreed and looked at the rooftop patio, seeing it again as if for the first time.

Cool blue tiles on the floor that almost made it seem as though you were walking on water. A pergola covered by flowering jasmine vines that grew from terracotta pots at the base of all four posts and filled the air with an almost too-sweet fragrance. A hot tub, covered now, but ready for relaxing beneath a star-splashed sky some evening soon. There were raised beds filled with more flowers that spilled bright colors over the edges and waved in the breeze sliding in from the ocean. There were chairs drawn up to a round chrome-and-glass table and a small wet bar, complete with refrigerator.

Amanda walked toward a gathering of chaises left behind by the former owner. There were thick navy blue cushions with white piping on several chairs as well as the chaises, and the whole setting looked like an oasis.

"This really is amazing," she said, walking around the gathered furniture to look out at the view over the vinyl railing.

"Yeah," Henry agreed, though he wasn't admiring the same view she was. Having her here, he knew, was asking for yet more memories to taunt him, but it would be worth it.

"You can see for miles from up here," she whispered as if more to herself than him.

"Yeah, it was the selling point," he admitted, joining

her at the rail. "After leaving LA, I realized I wanted something less…closed in, I guess. When I stepped out onto this roof, I knew I'd found it."

"Understandable."

"Have you ever had a moment like that?" he asked. "Seeing something. Knowing you had to have it?"

It took her a moment to answer. "Yes. Once."

"How'd that work out for you?"

She tipped her head up to look at him and swept some of that fake black hair out of her eyes at the same time. "Not well. Just because you *have* something you want, doesn't mean you get to keep it."

He knew she was talking about the two of them. Because he'd damn well felt the same when he first met Amanda. The moment he saw her, when she was just eighteen and more beautiful than anything he'd ever seen before, Henry had wanted her. Even the thought of her had become everything to him. Not just the woman who made him want, but almost a symbol of everything that had been lacking in his life.

After his mother died, he'd been alone more often than not. And even when his father was there, Henry had been on his own because Michael Porter had been more mentor than father.

Then suddenly, there was a gorgeous, funny, kind woman looking at him as if he were all she could see and Henry had felt his world shift. Settle.

"Well," he said, his voice firm as he pushed away the memories, "I'm planning on keeping this."

"Don't blame you," she said, pushing away from the rail. "I'd better get back to work."

"Sure." He watched her walk toward the door but

he couldn't let her leave. Not yet. "I like you with your own blond hair better, Amanda."

She stopped dead.

The sun streamed down onto the roof, glancing off the sapphire tiles and dazzling Amanda in a glow that made Henry's heart clutch in his chest. He couldn't look away from her as she slowly turned to face him. There was irritation and acceptance stamped on her features and he enjoyed knowing he'd caught her off guard.

She sighed. "How long have you known?"

"You think you fooled me?" he countered and took a few steps closer to her. "I knew right away. That wig and the glasses? Not much of a disguise."

She actually looked embarrassed. "Fooled everyone else."

"Not me," he said and closed the last of the distance between them. Locking his gaze on hers, he shook his head. "You think I wouldn't know your eyes? Wouldn't see past the short black hair to *you*?"

"Honestly?" Her mouth twisted. "I didn't expect you to be around as much as you were."

He laughed shortly, but he believed her. "So you were planning what? To sneak around and look for information on me?"

She bristled. "Strange to hear you sound so insulted. Isn't that what you do, Henry?"

Confused, he asked, "What're you talking about?"

She folded her arms over her chest and hitched one hip higher than the other. Tipping her head to one side, she studied him. "Somehow, you're getting inside info on me, on my family and what we're doing."

He had been. He wouldn't deny it. But he hadn't had to don a disguise and sneak around to do it. "I'm not admitting to anything, but if I were, could you blame me? Ten years ago, your brother accused me of all kinds of crap, then set out to destroy my father's company."

"How?"

"By doing just what you're accusing me of," Henry said. "He paid for information, undercut offers, snatched up real estate that we were after. Sound familiar?"

She shifted uncomfortably and he had the satisfaction of knowing that at least he'd given her something to think about. Hell, Bennett had gotten this ball rolling. All Henry had done was keep it going. "Is it really so surprising that I'd do the same?"

"No," she said after thinking about it for a moment. "I suppose not. So it shouldn't surprise you any to find me here, doing what I thought I had to."

"No, I'm not surprised." In fact, he'd enjoyed it. "So you're here for what? Payback?"

She pushed one hand through the hair of her wig and scowled as if the motion wasn't satisfying at all. "Can you blame me?"

"Answer my question first," he said, never taking his gaze from hers.

"Fine," she blurted out, throwing both hands high in exasperation. "Yes, I came here for a reason. I want to know how you're getting your information, Henry." She set her hands on her hips. "Happy now?"

"Sure," he countered wryly. "Nothing like finding out your ex is snooping through your house to put a smile on your face."

She ignored that statement. "I need to know who's talking to you."

"Why would I tell you that, Amanda?"

"Uh-huh," she said, nodding sharply. "And *that* is

why I'm wearing this ridiculous wig and the glasses. I knew if I confronted you and just asked outright, you'd never tell me." She pulled the glasses off while she talked and he was looking into her summer-blue eyes.

"I'll say it again. It was *your* family that came after mine ten years ago, Amanda. Did you think I'd forget about that?"

She laughed and turned her face into the wind. "No."

"At least you know me that well."

"Damn it, Henry…"

"Did it work?" he asked aloud. "Did you find what you were looking for?"

"I did not. And you know it." Disgusted, she twirled the glasses in her right hand. "Do you keep everything in your mind, or just on your computer? Not a single piece of paper or a Post-it note with any clues. Nothing. It's been a frustrating couple of days."

"Yeah, I can see that," he said, amused in spite of himself.

"You don't have to enjoy it so much," she snapped.

What did it say about him that he enjoyed even the bristle of her temper? "Can't help myself. You've been working as my maid for two days. How'd it feel?"

"Like a misery," she admitted, huffing out a breath. "You'll be happy to know that Martha should have been a drill sergeant or a general or something. The woman has no off switch. Work, work, work."

He had to admit, he almost felt sorry for Amanda because he did know what a stickler for work Martha was. They'd had more than one maid quit because they simply couldn't perform up to the older woman's standards. "You must have kept up or she would have gotten rid of you."

"I'm so proud," she mumbled.

Henry wanted to reach for her. His hands burned to touch her, but he knew she'd pull away, so he controlled that urge.

"Well," she said, "the upside to being discovered is that I can lose this wig. Hold these for me." She handed him the pair of glasses, then reached up to pull off the black wig. "God, that feels good," she whispered, running her fingers through her own hair as it tumbled down to hang free around her shoulders. She shook her head and the wind lifted that golden-blond mass into a glorious tangle that only made him want to spear his fingers through it.

She was the most beautiful woman he'd ever seen. But even more than that beauty, he admired the quickness of her mind, the stubborn streak that pushed her into doing things like being a maid/spy, and her ability to laugh at herself. As she was now.

"If I'd thought you'd be at the house so much, I never would have tried this," she admitted, holding up the wig and glaring at it as if it were a misbehaving pet. "Who knew you weren't chained to your company as Bennett and my dad are to ours?"

"I used to be," he said, handing her back the pair of glasses. "When I was scrambling to keep Bennett from killing us off, I spent most of my time at the office, listening to my father rage about 'those damn Careys.'"

"Charming," she said. "But my father and Bennett were no fonder of the Porters."

"I can see that." Hell, their families had been in an undeclared war for years. Both sides had battled blindly, neither of them willing to quit, scattering the wounded along the sidelines as they went. Until it had become, as

Candace Carey said only the night before, *ridiculous.* He hadn't been able to admit that to himself before, but he could see it now.

Henry's company had long ago passed Bennett and the Careys. Porter Enterprises was bigger than he'd ever imagined it would be. And the need to prove himself—to anyone—well, Henry had grown out of that years ago.

So he'd continued this mutual-destruction pact merely out of habit. And maybe for the amusement it brought him to know that he was driving Bennett insane. Also part of it, though, was knowing that even if they were at war, it meant that Amanda was thinking about him, too.

How was it possible that he wanted her more than he had ten years ago? Back then, she'd been all he could see. All he could think about. Now, his world was much bigger, but so was his desire for *her.*

She folded and unfolded the glasses in her hands and blew out a breath. "Since I'm leaving without the information I came for, the least you can do is tell me something else."

Henry laughed shortly. "The least I can do? Who's the spy here?"

She waved that away and he thought that, at the moment, he might have been tempted to tell her everything.

"Fine," he said. "Ask."

"Okay, then." She pushed her hair back with one hand, and took a deep breath before speaking. "Why did you really come to the audition last night?"

He looked deeply into her eyes and said the simple truth. Henry didn't bother with the glib answer—annoying Bennett, or trying to interrupt whatever the Carey family had going. Instead, he told her the real reason. The *only* reason he'd been there.

"To see you. The real you." Her eyes widened just a bit and if he hadn't been watching her so closely, he might not have noticed the tiny reaction.

"And it was worth it. You were beautiful. You always are," he amended, "but last night, you seemed…more. And I really liked that dress."

Just thinking of how she'd looked in the sapphire dress, with that luscious hair falling around her shoulders, brushing against her neck, made him want to reach for her. And he wondered if she'd allow it. If she'd slide against him like she used to. If she'd welcome his touch as he craved hers.

To answer his own questions, Henry reached out for her, took her upper arms in a firm but gentle hold and pulled her in close.

Her head tipped back, her eyes locked on his. She didn't say no. Didn't pull away. He took that as an invitation that he was going to accept. Keeping his eyes open, on hers, he bent his head to claim her lips in a kiss that started off tender. Damn near hesitant. But she leaned into him, and Henry deepened that kiss, tasting her as he'd wanted to for far too long.

He pulled her in close, pinning her to his body, and he felt her hook her arms around his neck, and he heard the wig and glasses hit the floor behind him. She opened her mouth under his, and the first sweep of his tongue sent both of them over the edge of hunger into quickening desire.

She moaned, tangled her tongue with his, and Henry fought to breathe. Stars burst behind his now-closed eyes as the feel, the scent, the taste of her filled him.

She was everything. She was *all*. Always had been. He'd tried to forget her. Tried to lose the memory of her in other women. Had even married someone in a vain attempt to move the hell on. None of it had worked.

He craved her now more than he ever had before. Had to have her. He broke the kiss and stared down at her as he struggled for air, fought to speak past the pain of need clutching at him.

"Over here," he said and took her hand, tugging her toward one of the thick cushioned chaises on the roof.

"No." She dug in her heels and pulled back when he would have drawn her closer. A harsh laugh shot from her throat as she shook her head. "Wow. I'm saying no, Henry. I'm not sleeping with you. Not now, especially."

He gave her a quick half smile. "Who said anything about sleeping?"

"Point," she acknowledged wryly, but pulled her hand from his.

Amazing, Henry thought, how empty he could feel at the simple loss of her touch.

"But I'm not a pushover anymore, Henry."

"You never were," he corrected and remembered the time when they were together. "There was nothing easy about you, Amanda."

Nodding slightly, she shifted her gaze to the view beyond the roof where they stood in the wash of sunlight. They were so close, he thought, and yet they might as well have been miles apart. He could still taste her. His heartbeat was hammering in his chest and his body ached for more—even knowing he wasn't going to get it. Maybe *because*.

"I've been without you for ten years, Henry," she finally said, her voice hardly more than a whisper.

"Now you don't have to be," he said.

She turned her head to look at him and her eyes were almost wistful. Was she wishing things were different? And if she was, why didn't she make them so?

"Sex wouldn't solve anything."

"Maybe it doesn't have to."

"There's a male reaction," she said on a short laugh.

"Guilty," he admitted, holding one hand up as if taking a pledge. Then he moved closer, ran one hand up and down her arm just to watch a flash of desire spark in her eyes. "I want you."

"I know," she said softly. "I want you, too."

"Then…"

"Sex with you complicates things that are already so muddled and twisted up, I'm not sure I could navigate those waters." It cost her to admit that; he could see it in her eyes.

"Besides," she added, lightening her tone as if she felt as cool and casual as she was sounding, "sex on a chaise on the roof in broad daylight with a houseful of movers and workers just two floors below us?"

"Could be exciting," he murmured and she shivered, letting him know without words that she was feeling the same no matter what she was saying.

"Yeah, thanks for the offer," she said, but shook her head. "Now. Since my subterfuge is outed, I'm leaving. You can tell Martha that 'Amelia' quit."

"Too scared to stay?" Would that challenge push her into changing her mind?

"Scared? No. Too tired to try to please your drill sergeant housekeeper for another day? Yes." Still, she smiled at him, though it was too brief to Henry's mind.

"She's tough. You're tougher," he said.

"Maybe I'm not feeling so tough right now," she said. "So it's definitely time to go."

"If you're going to leave, then let's say goodbye properly." Henry swooped in on her, pulled her up close again and, just for a minute, luxuriated in the feel of her body pressed to his. He'd missed just this, Henry thought. Having her heart beat against his, her breath dusting his face, her eyes staring up at him with so many questions written deep inside.

Having this moment wasn't enough, though. He didn't know what the hell was going on between them now any more than he had ten years ago. All he was sure of was that he had to touch her, taste her, have her or he wasn't sure he'd live through the torment of doing without much longer.

He kissed her then and poured more into it than he had the first time. He took and gave and allowed the sensations crowding inside him to take him over. Just the touch of her mouth to his sent him racing toward a completion he needed more than his next breath. And though he couldn't have that… Yet, he still showed her in that kiss what it meant to have her in his arms again.

She went limp against him even as her mouth fused to his. Her tongue took what he offered and he knew she felt what he did. Wanted what he did. Needed, as he did.

And because he was so sure of that simple fact, he was able to let her go, though it cost him, tearing at his guts, twisting his heart.

He lifted his head and looked down at her features, softened and blissful, and he wondered if his face carried the same stamp. Rubbing his hands up and down her arms, he set her back from him and struggled to find his balance. Hell, struggled to *breathe*.

He watched her slowly gather herself, and when she was steady, Henry bent down and picked up the ugly black wig and discarded glasses. Holding them out to her, he felt the brush of her hand when she took them from him.

She whipped her now-wind-tossed blond hair back behind her shoulder, then tipped her head back to look up at him. "I'm not going to try to lie and say I didn't enjoy that because what would be the point?"

He only nodded.

"But Henry," she said, "it doesn't change anything that happened ten years ago. Doesn't make the war going on between you and my family suddenly end."

"What will?" he blurted out before he could stop himself.

She blew out a breath. "Honestly, I don't know if anything can. Goodbye, Henry."

He watched her leave and didn't follow. As she said, what would be the point? And when the door closed behind her, Henry moved to the railing and looked out at that expansive view. Alone.

After a long, dream-filled night, Amanda was tired, crabby and so churned up, she could hardly concentrate. Late morning, she was at her assistant's desk, when her youngest brother strode in. She heard the reaction first, then watched as a ripple of awareness spread from desk to desk as he walked through. Like waves on the ocean, whispers followed him, women pushed their chairs out into the aisle to get a better look and Amanda could only smile as he got closer.

Justin Carey was six feet two inches tall, with light brown hair that fell across his collar and managed to look rebellious without being tacky. His square jaw carried a perpetual shadow of whiskers and his sharp blue eyes missed nothing. As the youngest, he'd spent most of his life observing his siblings and parents and the world around him while managing to keep himself apart.

Even today, in the Carey world, men wore custom-made suits and power ties—but Justin gravitated to black jeans, Doc Martens and a black leather Armani jacket. And women practically drooled when he walked by.

To Amanda's eyes, he looked just what he was: the rebel in the family and he was damned proud of it. She'd come to understand that Justin enjoyed the role of outsider in the family and played it up whenever possible.

He walked right up to her, grinned, then hooked one arm around her shoulders and dropped a kiss on top of her head. Amanda laughed, then gave him a playful shove that didn't move him back an inch.

"To what do we owe the honor of a visit?" she asked wryly. "And first, let me say that I notice you showed up on a day a family meeting is *not* scheduled."

"Not an accident," he replied, still grinning. "Actually, I came to talk to you, Mandy. Got a minute?"

Curiosity roared to life inside her as she looked at her younger brother. "For you? Sure."

She led him into her office and, instead of taking the chair behind her desk, sat down on the forest green couch. Patting the cushion beside her, she said, "Take a seat. Or do you want something to drink?" She waved one hand at the small fridge against the wall behind her desk. "I've got some sodas, water and juices..."

He laughed. "Yeah, no thanks. Now, if you had a beer…"

"Sit down, Justin," she said with another shake of her head. "And tell me what's going on."

He shrugged out of his jacket and tossed it at the end of the couch. He wore a black T-shirt beneath that jacket, and though it felt weird to notice, Amanda had to admit that her baby brother was ripped. Of course, if he didn't want people to notice, the T-shirt wouldn't be so tight.

"Okay, here's the deal." Justin propped one booted foot on his knee. "I've been avoiding coming back here—"

"Yeah, not earth-shattering news," she said.

He shrugged. "Not really in the mood to have Dad tell me that I should be taking my place in the family dynasty again."

Amanda winced. True. Their father had never understood Justin's reluctance to fall in line with the other Careys. It wasn't so much that he was angry about the situation. More like Justin completely befuddled Martin. Their father simply didn't understand his youngest son. Bennett had been the perfect Hereditary Corporate King, she thought, capitalizing the title even in her mind.

The difference was, Bennett actually *enjoyed* the ins and outs of running a hugely diversified company. He was excited by the challenges and always looking for ways to expand the family's holdings. Serena hadn't wanted the business world, but when her marriage dissolved, she came in and gave it her best anyway.

As for Amanda? Well, she'd always wanted to be a part of things. On her own terms, of course. She wasn't interested in burying herself in business as Bennett did. Or in only doing enough to get by, like Serena. Amanda relished the organizational nightmare of scheduling performers for the center. And she'd had a plan to build on the center's reputation—but that had ended when Henry snatched the hall right out from under her.

Funny, but when she was talking to him the day before, when he was kissing her, she'd forgotten all about how he'd submarined her. Now though, it came back to niggle at her even while she tried to focus on her brother.

Justin had never fit in at the company. He'd avoided interning there by getting a job at a local surf shop when he was sixteen. He had gotten a master's in business like the rest of them, but he'd also taken classes that had baffled their father. He couldn't understand studying something that wasn't going to benefit the family. The legacy he had built and wanted to leave to his children.

Amanda shifted on the couch, kicked off her high-heeled sandals and curled one leg up beneath her. Smoothing her slacks with the palms of her hands, she looked at Justin and asked, "What's going on? You never just show up out of nowhere unless something's wrong, so spill it."

He laughed shortly, but it didn't reach his eyes. "Hey, not nice."

"But accurate," she countered, smiling. "So talk."

"Fine." He shifted, too, laying one arm along the back of the sofa as he turned to face Amanda. "There is something going on and before I talk about it, I want to know where Dad's standing on the whole retirement thing."

"On shifting sands." Amanda propped her elbow

on the back of the couch and rested one fist against the side of her head. "Mom's irritated because Dad can't let go. And Bennett's wound even tighter than usual for the same reason."

"Great," Justin muttered and scrubbed one hand across his jaw.

"What's this about, Justin?" She watched him and the first tiny curl of worry began to unwind through her. "Do you need help? Are you in trouble?"

He laughed shortly and pushed off the couch. Staring down at her, he said, "You don't have to look so stricken, Mandy. I'm fine." Shaking his head, he stalked across the width of her office before spinning around and heading right back. Looking down at her again, he said, "It's just that I've got some things going on and I'm looking for the right time to lay it all out to the family."

Now her curiosity really kicked up a notch. Justin showing up out of nowhere was a sure sign that something was happening with him. And now he tells her there's something to say but wasn't telling her what it was?

Amanda fought down her frustration because at the moment, her youngest brother looked torn between confessing all and locking his secrets up tight. Hammering at him wouldn't get him to tell her anything. She knew that from experience. He was just hardheaded enough to keep everything to himself even if he wanted to tell her. Instead, she'd have to finesse it out of him.

"Well, okay," she admitted, "now's not the best time to spring something on Bennett or Dad. But when is?"

"You've got me there," he admitted and shoved both hands into his jeans pockets. He shifted his gaze to the wide windows displaying a view of the green spaces and the other office buildings spearing up nearby.

"So really, you don't have much to lose by doing it now, since the timing will *never* be perfect."

He glanced at her and she could see him considering his options. "Yeah, but if I wait until Dad officially retires and actually leaves the building, then I only deal with Bennett."

"If Mom can't get him to—and she can't—no one can." Amanda stood up and walked barefoot to stand in front of him. She still couldn't get over how tall he was. Younger than her by two years, Justin was no longer just her little brother. He was a man who obviously had his own plans and designs that he was keeping entirely to himself. Very *un*-Carey-like. Although, she told herself, she'd kept the hall and her plans for it a secret. Or so she'd thought.

She still wanted to know how Henry had found out about it in time to steal it from her.

But today's problem was Justin and the frustration in his eyes.

"Can you at least tell *me*?" she asked.

Looking down at her, he gave her a wry smile. "Of course I could tell you," he said. "but I'm not going to."

"Well, why the hell not?" *So much for finessing, Amanda.*

He laughed, leaned in and planted a kiss on her forehead. "Because I'd rather do it all at once. If I can't tell everyone yet, then I'll just hold on to it for a while longer."

She slapped his chest with the back of her hand and he pretended to be hurt. "That's not fair. First you tell me there's something to know and then you say you're not telling me what it is. Why did you come here today again? Just to torture me?"

"Would I do that?" He grinned at her. "Just thought I'd come see my favorite sister."

Scowling a bit, she muttered, "I'm going to tell Serena you said that."

"I'll call you a liar," he said on a laugh, then pulled her in for a quick hug. "Now, put your shoes on and I'll buy you lunch."

Amanda sighed, slipped her shoes on and poked one finger at her brother. "Okay, but for this, it's going to be a very expensive lunch."

"I expected no less." They walked out together, Justin's arm around her shoulders, her arm around his waist. Whatever reason had brought him back to Carey country, Amanda was glad to have him.

If nothing else, he'd almost managed to take her mind off Henry.

Seven

Henry liked working at home. Who would have guessed? Sure there would be some days he'd have to go into the office, but since it was now less than five miles from his house, that didn't bother him, either.

"Working or planning on working?"

The voice had Henry's head snapping up and his gaze spearing to where Mick Haley stood in the open doorway to the study.

"Working," Henry said, "but just finished up with something. What's up?"

"Thought you might want a walk-through of the new security setup." Mick wore a dark red polo shirt with jeans that were worn and faded and his heavy work boots looked as if they'd traveled miles. And probably had.

"Sure." Henry stood up and Mick laughed. "What?"

"I'm not used to seeing you without the suit I'm pretty sure you were born in."

"Work at home," Henry said. His jeans were black, his boots much newer, and he wore a blue dress shirt with the sleeves rolled back to the elbow. "The uniform's easier."

"Yeah, it would be. Gotta say, you got a great house here. The view's not bad, either," Mick said with a shrug. "I was up on the roof checking the satellite connection."

"View's the best part." Until yesterday, he thought, when Amanda had been there. Then, having her to look at was far better than the sweeping 360 view.

Mick headed back into the hall and waited for Henry to catch up. "We've got your cybersecurity all wired in. Every computer, including your tablets and phones, are covered."

"Good." He sometimes did business on his phone, so it was good to have that secure, as well. Henry followed his friend down the long hall and nodded to Martha as he passed her and one of the maids she'd hired. Of course, Amanda/Amelia wasn't there today and damned if he wasn't disappointed.

He'd spent most of the night thinking about her, reliving their time together on the roof, and he'd come to the conclusion that he didn't mind that she'd come to spy on him. Hell, he would have done the same thing, probably. And she didn't get the answers she wanted, so it didn't matter anyway. What he did mind was that he missed seeing her *now*. He'd gone ten years with only occasional sightings of her, and now in the span of a couple of days, he'd become accustomed to having her near. To catching the scent of her on the air. To listening for the sound of her voice.

And… Since yesterday, he missed the taste of her in his mouth. All night, that memory had plagued him. He'd gotten only snatches of sleep and even then, she rose up in fitful dreams to torment him. Mostly, he lay awake, recalling in exquisite detail the feel of her against his body, her breath on his face, her mouth fused to his.

"You might want to tune in," Mick said wryly and Henry dragged himself up and out of his tangled thoughts.

"What?"

"I'm showing you how to turn the damn alarm system on and off, so thought you might want to listen up." Mick grinned as he studied him. "I know that look."

Frowning, Henry replied, "I don't know what you're talking about."

"Right. There's a woman on your brain."

Damned if he'd admit to *that.* Snorting a laugh, Henry said, "You're confusing me with yourself again. Who is it now? Amber? Diana?"

"Wendy," Mick said with a grin. "But I'm not thinking about *my* current woman. I'm wondering who yours is."

Sunlight speared through the transom window over the wide front door, to spill across the red-tiled floor. There was a round pedestal table in the entryway and a heavy ceramic bowl sat atop it, boasting a spray of yellow and white flowers. From the kitchen, music streamed quietly, and from upstairs, the hum of a vacuum purred into the otherwise stillness.

"You're stalling."

"Nothing to stall about," Henry countered. "There is no woman."

Mick shrugged. "If that's the story you want to go with, fine by me. Just so you know I'm not buying it."

"So noted," Henry grumbled, then said, "Show me the stupid alarm system without all the commentary."

Laughing, Mick said, "Fine. Listen up." He went through the whole explanation, then said, "Input a password, then I'll show you the other setups throughout the house."

Henry did as he said, then stepped back.

"Tell me you didn't use your birth date."

"I'm not a complete idiot," Henry muttered. He'd used Amanda's birthday so now he'd be reminded of her every damn time he came and went through the door.

Probably a bad idea.

"Okay, then. I'll take you around. One of my guys is still wiring up the third floor, but he'll be finished within the hour."

"That's great, Mick. Appreciate it." Henry followed when Mick started into the great room.

Looking back over his shoulder, Mick grinned. "You're not going to appreciate the bill—even with the friend discount."

"Yeah, yeah," Henry said. "If you want the best, you have to pay for it."

And since he still wanted Amanda, he wondered what price fate would demand.

"Well," Amanda said on a sigh, "I guess they can't all be brilliant."

Her mother sat beside her at the center and reached to pat her hand. "Admittedly, the woman isn't the best singer in the world, but I have to give her credit, too. She had the courage to audition. I don't think I would have."

Amanda looked at her mom and smiled. “Neither would I. But then, I already know I can’t sing.”

After a really long day and the disappointment of not being able to pry Justin’s secrets out of him, it was good to be there, working on her Summer Stars program. To remember what was important. To push Henry out of her mind for however long she could manage it. Although so far, that meant not very long at all.

“And to give the poor woman her due,” Candace murmured, “‘I Will Always Love You’ is not the easiest song to sing.”

“True,” Amanda agreed, watching the young woman run grinning off the stage into the arms of her proud husband. “Unless you’re Whitney Houston or Dolly Parton.” Sadly, their contestant had been neither. Still, her audition tape would go up on the website and people would be able to see it and vote for her if they wanted to.

“You saw Justin today, didn’t you?”

Amanda glanced at her mother and felt a little guilty for not saying anything earlier. “You know he was here?”

“Oh, yes.” She waved one elegant hand and her diamond wedding band glinted in the dim light. “He came to the house to see me. Your father doesn’t know he was in town, though, so…”

“Got it,” Amanda said with a nod. Martin would not be happy that Justin had blown in and out of town in a couple of hours. But she was pleased to know that her little brother had stopped in to see their mother anyway.

“He wouldn’t talk about what he was up to,” Candace said and Amanda heard the worry in her mother’s voice. Apparently, motherhood lasted forever. It didn’t matter how old your children were—they remained your kids.

"But," Candace continued, "he seems…happy. Excited, really, so I was glad to see that."

"If you're wondering, he didn't tell me anything, either," Amanda said.

"Well," Candace said on a sigh, "that's disappointing."

"I know. I did my best to pry it out of him, but he's a Sphinx when he wants to be. Sorry, Mom. But I do agree that he looked good. Less tense."

Candace frowned slightly. "He worries about disappointing your father, though he shouldn't and I told him so. We raised all four of you to think for yourselves. To find your own happiness and to do what drives you."

"You did, and thank you." Amanda gave her mom's hand a quick squeeze.

"And speaking of that," Candace said softly, spearing Amanda with a knowing look, "it was nice seeing Henry the other night, wasn't it?"

"Hmm? Nice?" Okay, this conversation had taken an unexpected turn.

"I always liked Henry," her mother mused, "and so, baby girl, did *you*."

"Mom…"

"For heaven's sake, it's been ten years," Candace said, leaning in closer and lowering her voice. "You can't talk about this yet?"

"I don't want to talk about it with my *mother*." She shivered dramatically.

"I've actually had sex, you know," Candace said, her lips twitching. "And I can promise it was more than the four times required to produce you kids."

Amanda laughed, covered her ears and shook her head. "I really don't want to hear that."

"Your father and I loved each other. Of course we had a good sex life."

"Loved?" Amanda picked up on that one word. "Past tense? Should I be worried about coming from a broken home?"

Candace laughed and it was a bawdy, loud sound that you simply did not expect from a sophisticated, refined woman like her. It was a rare moment that sparked her signature laugh, and usually Amanda enjoyed it. When her mom was laughing at her, however, it was different. Several people in the contestant's audience turned to look toward them at the sound and Amanda's chin hit her chest. When her mother's laughter finally faded away, Candace spoke again.

"Oh, thanks, sweetie. I haven't laughed like that in too long." She grinned and said, "I notice you didn't remark on the *had* a good sex life statement."

"Really don't want to know."

"Well, that's a shame, because it's always been good," Candace said, sighing. "Still is, when I can get the man away from his blasted company."

"How did we get onto your sex life?" Amanda asked. "And how do we get off it?"

"Fine. I'm done."

"Thank you. So I don't have to worry about you two getting divorced?"

"No, but you could worry about me hitting your father over the head with something heavy," Candace admitted. "The man is completely devoted to his damn work."

Trying to remain in neutral territory wasn't easy, but Amanda gave it a shot. "Well, he did build up Grandpa's business into something incredible..."

"And must he babysit it for eternity now?" Candace

shook her head. "No. He promised to retire and by God, I'm going to get him out of that business if I have to drag him out."

"You might have to."

"Absolutely. Do you know where he is tonight?" She didn't wait for Amanda to answer. "We were having an early dinner and he took a call from an old investor and immediately left the table to go lock himself in his study. When I left home, he'd been on the phone for forty-five minutes already.

"I'm tired of playing second fiddle to the company, Mandy."

"I don't blame you."

"And what are you tired of?" Candace asked bluntly.

"What? Nothing."

Her mother gave her a knowing look. "You can't fool me, Mandy." She gave a little sigh. Shifting her gaze to the stage area. Still lit for the performance that had ended minutes ago, it gleamed like a jewel in the otherwise dim hall. "I see how you are, always pushing at work for more responsibility, more assignments, more of everything. You never see your friends anymore—"

"I see them," Amanda argued. "I just took a ski weekend in Montana with Liz."

"Sweetie, that was in February. We're in April now."

Amanda huffed out a breath. "Well, I've been busy."

"That's my point," Candace said. "If you're not careful, you'll end up like your dad. Just where Bennett's heading."

"That's not such a bad thing, is it?" she wondered, but as she thought about what her mom was saying, she started to worry.

"It is, if that's all you think about." Candace reached

to the seat beside her and picked up her black bag. "When you kids were little, Martin and I spent time with you. Not just training you to take over the company, but actual time."

"I remember," Amanda said. Most weekends, they'd all piled into the car and taken a drive, stopping at historical markers, or whenever her parents saw something interesting. Her father *never* passed up a historical marker.

"Now, Martin's forgotten how to simply *be*. How to have *fun*. And apparently, it's up to me to remind him."

"If anyone can," Amanda said, "it's you, Mom."

"Thank you." Candace patted her daughter's hand. "And, since we're being so honest, I'm going to say that I saw the gleam in Henry's eyes when he looked at you."

"Mom..."

"More importantly, I saw *your* eyes." She waited for Amanda to look at her before adding, "Ten years ago, you found each other and then it all blew up."

"I know. I was there." And she really didn't want to relive it all with her mother.

"You've both grown and changed and maybe it's time to take another look. Give yourself permission, Amanda." She stood up and looked down at her daughter. "Do yourself a favor, honey, and don't forget how to enjoy your life." Leaning over, she kissed Amanda's forehead and turned to go.

Her crowded mind, racing with everything her mother had just said, managed to focus long enough for her to ask, "Are you headed home?"

"Nope," Candace said. "I think I'll pick up your aunt Viv and go out for a drink."

"A drink?"

"Is there a Chippendale's around here?" Candace wondered aloud. "Or are they out of business? I'll have to Google it."

As she walked away, Amanda stared after her, and blinked in surprise. Her mother at a male strip club? Just one more thing she didn't want to think about.

Instead, she went over everything else the woman had said. Was her mother right? Was Amanda forgetting to have a life in her rush to prove herself at the company? Her world had become her home and the office. The last time she'd actually done something *outside* of work was dressing up as a maid and going to Henry's house. What did that say about her?

She sighed. "What it says is, you're thinking about Henry again." And not just Henry. But that kiss. He'd picked up a few new moves since the last time she'd kissed him. But the heat, the magic, the pure, stunning thrill of him, was still there.

Amanda hadn't felt anything like that with anyone else. Ever.

Her mother was right about one thing for sure. In ten years, she and Henry had both grown and changed. But was that enough? A curl of warmth settled deep inside her, then began to spread, like thread sliding off a spool. She shifted uncomfortably in her chair and told herself to forget it. Her spy game was over. She had zero reason to go see Henry.

There was nothing between them anymore. One kiss didn't mean anything. So just… "Get over it already."

Twenty minutes later, Henry turned off the alarm, opened the door and stared at the woman looking back at him.

"What are you doing here, Amanda?"

"Stop talking," she said, then wrapped her arms around his neck, pulled his head down to hers and kissed him until he had to remind himself to breathe.

He wasn't stupid enough to ignore the gift being handed him, so he grabbed her tightly against him, swung her into the house and slammed the door. Pressing her back to the door, he tore his mouth free and muttered, "Just a second. Wait. Wait." Nearly blind with the need pumping through him, Henry punched in the alarm code, then turned back to Amanda.

He didn't care why she was there. Didn't want to know what had prompted this visit. All he wanted was *her.*

Her eyes burned with the same desire throbbing inside him. Whatever had brought her to him, Henry blessed it. He caught her face between his palms and then took her mouth with the same fierce need she had shown him. She ran her fingers through his hair, then down across his shoulders, and he felt every touch all the way down to his bones.

Her hands dived beneath his shirt, ran up and down his back, as far as she could reach, and the slide of her palms stoked the fire in his blood. He hadn't expected her, but now, holding her, he couldn't live without her another minute. Hunger that had crouched inside him for ten years lunged off the leash and fed.

He tore his mouth from hers, then trailed his lips and tongue and teeth down the line of her throat. She tipped her head back to give him room and breathed fast and heavy as the fire between them burned.

"Too many clothes," she whispered and moved to tear at the buttons on his shirt.

"Right," he muttered thickly. "Let's fix that."

While her fingers flew down the line of buttons on his shirt, he tore at her silk shirt and vaguely heard the soft "ping" of buttons hitting the tile floor and skittering down the hall. He pulled the tail of her shirt free of her skirt, then hungrily flipped the front catch on her blue lace bra. Then her breasts were bare and open to his touch and Henry didn't miss a moment.

He filled his hands with them and she tipped her head back against the door he had her propped against. When his mouth followed his fingers, she shrieked and used one hand to hold his head in place. "Just like that," she said drunkenly. "More. More."

"There's always more," he muttered and dropped his hands to the hem of her black skirt. He shoved it up high on her hips, then ripped off her blue lace panties. "Thanks for wearing a skirt," he muttered.

"You're welcome. Also, you're wasting time."

"Right." He reached down, freed himself and in a heartbeat, he was driving into her heat. On that first stroke, the top of his head flew off and he only half heard her shout of triumph. Again and again, he pushed into her, and with every withdrawal, he felt the loss of her and those feelings tangled inside him until Henry couldn't see past the bright lights flashing in front of his eyes.

To be with her, in her, again was more than he would have expected. More than he remembered. As she said, just *more.*

Her hands clung to him. She hooked her ankles at the small of his back and pulled him in deeper, harder. Her head rapped against the door but she didn't seem to care. He was blind to everything but the need clawing at him. He heard her groans, felt her body fist around him, and when she jumped over the edge, she screamed and he experienced her pleasure with the convulsing of her body around his.

Then she stabbed her fingers through his hair, tipped his head back and kissed him mercilessly, and while their mouths were fused, he raced off that cliff right behind her.

Shaken, breathless, he held her tightly against the front door and knew he'd never come and go out of the house again without remembering this moment. Her birthday as the alarm code. Now this. Yeah, Amanda was seared onto his house as well as she was onto him. When he knew he was steady enough, he looked into her eyes and said the only thing he could think of. "So nice of you to drop in."

She laughed, really laughed, and since he was still inside her, he felt the laughter as well as heard it. "Yeah, glad you were home."

"Oh, me, too." Gently, he disengaged their bodies, then let her slide to her feet. Amazingly, she still had her black high heels on. Henry didn't know why that hit him so hard, but there was no denying it. While they each tried to straighten out their clothes, Henry managed to say, "If Martha were here, we'd have given her a heart attack."

Amanda stopped tugging the edges of her shirt together—pointless, since there were no buttons to hold it—and gasped. "Martha. I forgot about the little general completely."

"Yeah, she's gone for the week," he said and didn't acknowledge even to himself that his hands shook as he pulled up his jeans zipper. "After the move, I thought she could use a few days so I sent her and her sister to a hotel in La Jolla for a week."

"Thank God." Amanda's shoulders relaxed and she reached up to push both hands through her hair, scraping it back from her face.

Her shirt hung open again and the bra, though hooked, was such a fragile piece of lace, he knew it wouldn't take much to rid her of it. Her black skirt was in place, and as she bent over to pick up her discarded panties, Henry rubbed one hand over her behind.

She went still and tossed him a look over her shoulder. As she had as "Amelia," crawling over his bed. And now, as then, his body went hard as stone and his mouth went dry.

"I'm not finished," he admitted hoarsely.

"Me, either," she said and straightened up only to leap at him. "It's been a long time, Henry, and being with you is stirring everything up inside me."

"I know how you feel. Let's try horizontal this time, though, all right?"

She glanced at the staircase, then back to him. "It's a long way to your bedroom. What if we don't make it?"

"We will," he told her. "Eventually."

He grabbed her hand and Amanda let him tug her along behind him. Her knees were still a little wobbly and the stairs suddenly looked a lot more intimidating than they had from the entryway. Her body was buzzing, her heart pounding and everything in her tingled in anticipation of another hot-and-sweaty round with Henry. But as she watched him, pulling her along the staircase, she knew she couldn't make it up the rest of the stairs. Not yet, anyway.

"Here."

"Here what?" He kept going until she stopped and pulled back on his hand. Turning to look at her, he studied her face for a long second or two, then smiled. *"Here?"*

"Why not?" She dropped his hand, shrugged out of her ruined shirt and slipped her bra off her shoulders and down her arms to drop on the staircase. "I don't want to wait for horizontal."

His eyes fired and she knew she had him right where she wanted him. "We're alone in the house and these stairs are just taking too long…"

"Agreed," he said and turned to capture one of her breasts in the palm of his hand. His thumb rubbed across her hardened nipple and everything in Amanda curled up and whimpered.

"This is horizontal enough. Vertically horizontal," she amended.

"Works for me," he muttered. "Just so long as we don't fall down the damn things."

"We won't," she said and pushed at him until he sat down on the step. Planting her legs on either side of him, she slowly went down to her knees and his eyes flashed bright and hot. She felt exactly the same, Amanda thought wildly.

Coming here had been impulse, driven by a need she was done ignoring. For ten years she'd thought of him. Not one single man had ever lived up to the night she'd had with Henry so long ago. And tonight, she'd told herself that there was no reason to stay away from him anymore. They'd talked. They'd kissed. And the hunger between them, unfed, only kept growing. Time to feed it.

She unzipped his jeans and freed him, wrapping one

hand around the hard length of him until he groaned and let his head fall back against the staircase. Then Amanda shifted, taking him inside her body inch by slow, torturous inch. She'd just had an amazing orgasm, and yet now a new one was building within her with such force, such fury, she raced to meet it.

Only Henry had been able to do this to her. Only *he* had the power to make her blood boil and her mind completely blank out to everything but what was happening to her body. She'd tried to convince herself that she'd built that memory of the night with him into something that was more fantasy than reality. Now she knew for sure she hadn't. Not only was it still amazing with him, it was even more so than it had been ten years before.

Groaning aloud, she took him all the way in, then ground her hips against him, increasing the incredible friction buzzing in her body. His hands clamped down on her hips and his gaze fixed on her as she began to move. Rising, falling, she set a rhythm that pushed at both of them, forcing them to chase the release that waited, just out of reach.

He lifted his hands and cupped her breasts, fingers and thumbs tweaking, pulling as she continued to move. She arched her back, pushing herself into his touch, then lifted her hands high, riding a sweeping tide of celebration, triumph. A moment later, though, she dropped her hands to his muscled, sculpted chest and felt the pounding of his heartbeat beneath her palms.

Amanda felt that first starburst of release and rode him wildly until he joined her at the slippery edge of oblivion, and together, they made the leap.

Eight

Amanda lay sprawled across him, their bodies still locked together, and heard her own breath whistling in and out of her lungs. The clawing need inside her had eased back, thank God, because she didn't know if she could take another bout of sex with Henry at the moment. She felt, Amanda realized, alive with pleasure, loose and completely and thoroughly ravished. Life was good.

"You alive?" he mumbled.

"Yes, but I don't think I can move." She put in the effort to lift her head, brace her chin on his chest and look at him.

"Good." A crooked smile curved his mouth. "If you were able to run up these stairs right now, that would make me look really bad."

She laughed a little, then shook her head. "No worries, then."

"Yeah?" He rubbed his hands up and down her back and over her butt until she squirmed a little. He looked into her eyes. "How would my masculinity stack up if I whimpered a little?"

"Trust me," she assured him, "your masculinity is not in question."

He groaned. "Good to know." After a moment, he asked, "Not that I'm complaining, but why are you here, Amanda?"

She frowned thoughtfully. "I think that's fairly obvious."

"Yeah, but why?"

"I don't really know." Her fingers tapped against his chest as she tried to corral the thoughts that had brought her to his house tonight. "I was at the audition…"

"How'd it go?"

She rolled her eyes. "Nice woman. Tried to sing a Whitney Houston song. It didn't go well."

"Ouch."

"Exactly." She took a breath, looked at his chest and almost bent her head to lick that wide expanse of gorgeous flesh, but she restrained herself. "I was talking to my mom and—"

"Your *mom* sent you here?" Astonished, he laughed shortly. "I'm going to have to send her flowers."

"Funny. No, she didn't send me." Amanda had to wonder, though. Her mom had made a point of pretty much telling her to move on. "She just made me do some thinking."

"And?"

"And, I thought about what I wanted." She shrugged. "Turns out I wanted *you*."

"Consider me glad to hear it."

Her lips twitched as she rolled off him to sit beside him on the stairs. Once again, they tugged their clothes back into place and when she was finished, Amanda looked into his eyes. "I'm not saying I'm good with everything. Or that I've forgotten what happened ten years ago—"

"Me, either," he threw in and she nodded.

"And I still want to know who you're getting your information from."

"Naturally."

"But, all that said," she added with a shrug, "I guess I missed you."

He reached out and tucked her hair behind her ear, then let his fingertips trail along her jaw and down the length of her throat. "I missed you, too."

Amanda drew a deep breath, then sighed. "What does that make us, I wonder."

"Crazy?" he asked.

She laughed under her breath. "I think I can live with that."

"Looks like we're going to have to." On a groan, Henry pushed himself to his feet and held out one hand to her. She took it and he pulled her to her feet. "I still want to try horizontal," he said and cupped her face, dropping a quick, light kiss on her mouth. "But I need food first. How about you?"

Amanda threaded her fingers through his. "Food. Great idea. Have any wine?"

He started slowly back down the stairs. "I think I've got you covered."

Her hand in his, the two of them staggered down the long hall like survivors of a shipwreck. Just outside the kitchen, Amanda noticed something on the tile floor, glinting in the light. One of her buttons.

It had really gone a long way. But then, so had she.

They made sandwiches, grabbed a bag of chips out of the pantry and drank cold white wine the color of sunlight. Amanda was so hungry, their impromptu picnic on the kitchen floor—since the new table had not been delivered yet—tasted like a five-star meal in the Carey restaurant.

Going to Henry had been impulse—or so she'd thought at the time. But the truth was, she'd been headed toward him for what felt like most of her life. For years, she'd buried every thought of him because what was to be gained by remembering? Now, he was here, with her again, and it was as if those years apart were nothing.

"You're thinking," Henry said softly. "Having regrets?"

"No." Shaking her head, Amanda took another sip of wine and admitted, "It would probably be easier to say yes. I regret it. This was all a mistake. But I can't because I don't feel that way."

"Good," he said. "Neither do I."

"Which leaves us where?"

"Hell if I know." He laughed, poured them each more wine and then spoke again. "One thing we should talk about, though." He took a drink and looked at her over the rim of the glass. "Everything happened so fast… Well, I haven't carried condoms in my wallet since I was kid, hoping to get lucky."

She laughed because she remembered that night ten years ago, when the two of them were naked in the boathouse and things were intense when Henry had suddenly stopped. He'd rifled through his clothes, throwing them into the air until he'd found his wallet and pulled a condom out.

"This is funny?"

"No," Amanda said. "I was just remembering..."

He paused and smiled. "Yeah. I remember, too."

A shared moment over a past that had ended badly was now somehow...comforting. How very strange life could be.

"You don't have to worry," she said. "I take the shot every three months. And I'm healthy."

"Me, too. Healthy, I mean." He nodded slowly. Still looking at her, he asked, "So does this mean the war's over?"

"That's a bigger question," she said and leaned back against the wall. Stretching out her legs, she crossed her feet at the ankles, and realized she'd lost her heels on the staircase. Looking down at the wine in her glass, she said, "You and Bennett will have to work things out on your own, but, yeah. I think our skirmish is mostly over."

"Mostly." He sat beside her, back against the wall. And Amanda wondered if that was some kind of twisted metaphor for what they were both feeling.

"Well," Amanda mused, glancing at the detritus of their picnic, "there are still questions."

"Yeah, I've got a few, too," he admitted.

Her gaze shifted to him beside her. In the overhead kitchen light, his green eyes shone like emeralds. His dress shirt hung open, displaying that broad, muscled chest that begged to be stroked and petted. But Amanda fought down that urge and went with another.

"One thing I have to know. Was Bennett right? Were

you using me?" she asked. "Back in the day, were you using me to get close to my family?"

He just stared at her and she could see the disbelief in his eyes. "You don't really believe that. That's Bennett talking."

"Yeah, it is. He hammered me with it for months after you left Italy. And me." The old hurt rosc up to take a nibble of her heart and there was nothing she could do to stop it. "You haven't answered me…"

"Fine. You want me to say it? No. I wasn't using you. I was nuts about you."

She watched him and read what she thought was truth in his eyes. Amanda wanted to believe, because if she did, then that meant she hadn't been wrong about him. But if that were true, then it also meant that she'd spent ten years of her life in a simmering, *useless* fury.

"What about you?" he asked.

"What about me?"

"Did you tell Bennett what we were going to be up to in the boathouse?"

A short, sharp bark of laughter shot from her throat. "Why would I do that?"

"How the hell would I know?" he countered.

"Well think about it," she demanded. "Would I really want my big brother to see me *naked*, for God's sake?" Just the memory of that was enough to make her cringe. Not to mention the fistfight between Bennett and Henry that followed. Oh, sure, every woman wanted her first foray into sex to end with fights and accusations.

"Then how did he know?"

"What makes you think he did?" Shaking her head, Amanda took another sip of wine. "I've thought about that over the years, and if you didn't tell him, then I think I know why he was there." Her gaze fixed on his. "We fell asleep, remember? After sex, we both conked out and didn't wake up until Bennett came in and started yelling."

"Yeah." He took a long drink of wine. "The memory's clear, trust me."

Trust him. That was at the heart of this and she just didn't know if she could. Looking at him now, she felt the embers of what had been love stirring inside her and she knew that though those flames had been quiet for too long, they had never really died out. That was more than a little disconcerting.

Though those long years without him seemed unimportant right now, how could she simply put aside the last ten years? The animosity that had torn at her family because of what she and Henry had done. The war that Bennett had raged over for years. How could she forget all of that and admit even to herself that she still loved him?

And how could she not?

Amanda shook her head, focused on right now and said, "Well, Bennett used to take the boat out early when he wanted time to think. If we hadn't fallen asleep, we would have been long gone before Bennett showed up."

"So you think we were just unlucky?" He snorted at the idea.

"If you didn't tell him and I didn't, then yeah," she said. "Probably."

"That's a hell of a thing," he muttered, and drew one knee up, resting his forearm on top of it.

"It really is," she agreed. Amanda couldn't stop looking at him. She'd missed him. A lot. And being with him now was the answer to all the erotic dreams she'd had over the years.

"But nothing's changed, has it?" she said, more to herself than him.

He looked at her and she could see that he was thinking the same convoluted thoughts she was.

When he spoke, his voice was low in the quiet. "I'd say this confuses things even more."

"Who would have thought that was possible?"

"Yeah." His gaze locked on hers. "So tell me. If you didn't tip Bennett off—"

"I didn't."

"—why didn't you reach out to me?" His eyes were hard now, accusatory, and though she was insulted, she couldn't really blame him. "Ten years. And nothing. Why?"

"Why would I?" she demanded and pushed off the floor. Barefoot now, she walked across the kitchen, then whirled around to look at him. "Bennett convinced me you were using me as a way to wedge yourself into the Carey Corporation."

"You shouldn't have believed that, Amanda."

"You were gone—"

"Because good old Ben chased me out of Italy—"

"—and you never contacted me," she finished as if he hadn't spoken. The hurt of that rose up inside her to strangle her air. "Not once, Henry. You never called. You never came to see me." She threw his own words back at him. "Ten years. Nothing. Not even a damn postcard."

He stood and faced her. His dress shirt hung open, his jeans hung low on his hips and everything in her wanted to touch him. Heck, lick every square inch of him. But she held perfectly still and waited.

"Seriously? I thought you were in on it."

"Well, I wasn't."

"I didn't know that."

"You could've asked me," she countered.

"You could've told me without being asked," he shot back.

"And so it goes," she muttered, "the circle of pain just keeps spinning." Amanda turned away from him, curling her fingers over the cold edge of the smoke-gray granite counter. That icy feel seeped into her bones and she wondered if cold would always smother the heat.

"It's not easy, is it?" he asked quietly and she heard the soft footsteps coming up behind her.

She didn't look at him. "No."

"Just like before," he said, laying both hands on her shoulders and turning her around to face him. "Sex just makes things more difficult."

She tipped her head back to look up at him and she could see that he was as torn as she was. When he lifted one hand to smooth his fingers across her cheek, she felt the tenderness down to her soul and it almost broke her.

She'd loved him so much once, and those feelings, in spite of her attempts to hide them or lose them, were still there, inside her. She could continue to ignore what her heart still craved, or she could take this moment, this time, and use it to ease old pains and strengthen her heart against future pain.

She'd been broken once. Amanda couldn't let that happen again. But she couldn't walk away from what she was feeling, either. Not this time.

She reached up to hook her arms around his neck and sighed when she felt him wrap his arms around her middle.

"Complicated, yes," she said, looking into eyes that had haunted her for so long. "But done right…so worth it."

"We're pretty good at it already," Henry said, a half smile curving his mouth. "But maybe we should stop talking and put in a little more practice. Make sure we get it right."

"Practice is good." Maybe they didn't have to solve everything tonight. Maybe they could just be together right now. For tonight, anyway, they didn't have to be enemies. She was smiling when he took her mouth in a gentle caress that poured heat through her body, chasing away the cold—for now.

Nine

Later, in the hot tub on the roof, they sat together staring up at a star-splashed sky. The surface of the water bubbled and frothed around them, and the pulse of the motor, the rush of the water were the only sounds in the quiet night. A soft breeze slipped past them, adding a touch of cool to skin that was warm and wet.

Henry slanted a covert look at her and realized that she was even more beautiful than she had been ten years ago. Back then, he'd been so drawn to her he could see nothing else and tonight he knew that he felt the same, in spite of the passing years. He refilled her glass with the crisp white wine and watched as she took a sip, and then licked lips he couldn't get enough of.

"If you keep watching me," she whispered, "you're going to make me nervous."

"Oh, I don't want you nervous," he said, "but trembling would be good."

"I can probably manage that for you later." Amanda smiled, then looked up at the sky again.

His body stirred, and even Henry was amazed at his hunger for her. Years ago, he'd thought he could never feel more for anyone than what filled him every time he was around Amanda. Tonight, he knew he'd been wrong. Because what he felt for her now, after so many years without her, was so much more.

"This is amazing," she said in a soft whisper, as if reluctant to shatter the silence of the night.

"It is," he answered, still watching her.

She felt his gaze on her and turned, smiling at him. "I would be up here every night, just looking at the view."

He gave her a quick grin. "Right now, I'm pretty fond of the view, too."

Amanda sipped at her wine and sighed a little. "You're more romantic than I remember you being."

"I've had time to appreciate what I have when I have it."

"And do you?" she asked. "Have me, I mean?"

"I do tonight," Henry said softly. Whatever the future might deliver, for tonight, he was happier than he'd been in years.

Still smiling, she admitted, "I've never seen so many stars."

"We're higher here, farther away from the light pollution." He shifted his gaze to the black, diamond-flecked sky above. "The last time I saw so many stars, I was in Ireland."

"I'm envious." She turned her head to look at him. "I've never been."

He wanted to say he'd take her and that surprised him as much as he knew it would surprise her if he actually made the offer. He didn't, because neither of them knew how long this would last between them. But he could imagine it. And Henry had a very good imagination.

"I stayed at a castle in County Mayo," he said, remembering. "It sat in the middle of hundreds of acres, miles from the nearest city or village, and at night, the castle lights were turned off, so you could see all of the sky, stretching out into eternity. Makes you feel..."

Her mouth quirked as she glanced at him. "If you say you felt small and insignificant, I won't believe you."

He grinned. Nice to be with someone who knew you so well. "No, not small," he said. "But it does make you feel a connection to...something. As if anything is possible."

"We're here, together, after too many years apart," Amanda said, turning her face up to the stars again. "So maybe anything *is* possible."

Henry hooked one arm around her, pulling her in close. Side by side, her head on his shoulder, they watched the stars and he wondered—hoped—she was right.

Eventually, during that long night, they managed to get horizontal.

And, Henry had to admit, horizontal worked just fine. Stretched out on his bed, with Amanda beside him, he stared up at the ceiling and watched the shadows of trees dance in the moonlight.

He propped one arm behind his head, leaned back against the pillows piled against the headboard and shifted his gaze to her when she slipped out of bed and began to get dressed.

"You don't have to leave," he said, surprising himself at the offer. Since his extremely brief marriage, no woman had spent the night with him. He avoided the intimacy because it was easier all the way around. But with Amanda, it was…different.

It had always been. He'd put her out of his mind for his own survival because that first year without her had almost killed him. He'd thought at first that of course she'd come to him. They'd figure something out together. But she hadn't called him or tried to see him and after months of silence, he'd hated her for that. And then he clung to the anger until it had finally become a part of him that he could ignore or feed, depending on his mood.

Finally, though, for his own sake, he stopped thinking of her. Tried to stop the dreams. Because memories brought only pain. Now she was here and he didn't know whether to believe or not. Would she stay? Go? He couldn't know, so he shut himself off from possibilities because the line was too fine.

She stopped, looked at him, and in the moonlight, her blue eyes seemed to soften and shine and her smile was wistful. Tucking her shirt in, she drew the two sides across each other since she no longer had buttons. "Thanks for the offer, but I really should go."

Henry got out of bed and tugged his jeans on without bothering to zip them. "All right," he said as he walked toward her. "But you'll be back."

It wasn't a question and they both knew it.

"Yes," she said. "I will come back."

Nodding, he rubbed his hands up and down her arms, reluctant to let her go. He was feeling too much, he told himself, yet couldn't seem to stop it. That line between belief and regret thinned even further.

"You realize I'm not giving up," she said, looking up at him.

He grinned briefly. "I've never known you to. But what are you talking about specifically?"

"The hall, Henry," she said. "I still want to know how you managed to get it before me."

He blew out a breath and stalled. If he told her the truth, this was over just as it was beginning. Maybe that would be best, he thought, though everything in him fought against it. Henry wanted more of her. More nights like this one. If he lived to be a hundred, he would never forget opening the front door to have her leap at him, all passion and fire. To have her suddenly back in his life was almost as hard as living without her had been, but he wouldn't change it. What that said, he didn't know and didn't care.

So he kept his secrets. "What is it about a hardheaded woman I find so appealing?"

"An insult and a compliment in one sentence." She smiled and his heart turned over. "Impressive."

He gave her a brief smile. He'd successfully dodged her question, but he had one that had been plaguing him. "Answer me this. What were you planning on doing with the hall? Why was it so important to you?"

She finger-combed her hair and it didn't help much. He preferred it this way, long and loose and out of control.

"Does it matter now?"

"Indulge me," he said.

Her lips curved. "I thought I already did."

He grinned again because damn, he'd missed more than her body. More than the pleasure they gave each other. He'd missed this. Sparring with her. Laughing.

Talking. She was quick, smart, funny and never gave an inch. “Okay, indulge me again.”

She took a deep breath and shrugged as she stepped into her heels. “Fine. Guess it doesn’t matter now anyway. The hall’s actually pretty close to the center—I mean, straight across the parking lot.”

“Yeah, I know.”

“Well, I wanted to build a concourse, joining the two buildings.”

That he hadn’t imagined at all. Surprised, and intrigued, he asked, “Why?”

Amanda smiled and said, “The center is amazing, but as far as refreshments go, there’s only the café and it’s really too small for a full house.”

“True.” He still didn’t know where she was going with this, but even in the moonlight, Henry could see the excitement on her features. How her eyes shone brighter as she outlined what she had planned—before he put a stop to it.

“Well, in the concourse, I planned to have a few elegant shops, eclectic stuff mainly, and a pub.”

He laughed. She was one surprise after another. The Carey family was all about sophistication and grandeur. He should have known that Amanda would step outside their carefully constructed box. “A *pub*? Alongside the elegance that is the center?”

“Yes, exactly.” She grinned at his disbelief as if she enjoyed surprising him. “Bennett would probably have reacted exactly like you are.”

Well, that gave him pause. He didn’t like knowing that he and Bennett would feel the same about…anything. When they’d met in college, they’d been very different but a friendship had grown anyway. Back then, Henry had seen how devoted Bennett was to the family business, to earn the crown from his father. And Henry hadn't understood at all. He'd been browbeaten by his father into the company and he'd resented nearly all of it back then. Had he really changed so much that his reactions were now like Bennett's?

That was an uncomfortable thought.

"It would have been perfect," Amanda was saying, her enthusiasm spiking with every word. "The pub would give patrons a place to have a drink before or after a performance, simple food and a place where we could foster new talent. Hold open mic nights, maybe..."

He could almost see it from the mental pictures she painted and he knew she was right. It would work. Hell, it might turn into something as popular as the center itself. But it would never happen now, because he'd chosen to buy it just to piss off Bennett Carey.

Frowning now, he focused on Amanda as she kept talking.

"At the end of the concourse would be the hall." She shrugged and said, "The plan was to gut it, expand it and, finally, turn it into a five-star restaurant, big enough to support a lot of the crowd from the center after a performance and separate enough to make its own customer base, as well." She paused, sighed a little and said, "It would have been..."

"Great," he finished for her and felt a stab of guilt that he'd stolen it out from under her.

"Yeah," she agreed softly, "I think it would have been. And then Bennett would have to—"

Amanda stopped talking and reached down to pick up her bag. But now Henry had to hear it all. "Bennett would what?"

"Why not tell you the rest, too?" She took another breath. "My idiot brother would have to admit. Out loud. That I know what I'm doing."

Well, hell. He hadn't realized that she was fighting for recognition within her own family, and whether he'd been aware at the time or not, he'd managed to submarine her. "Now he won't."

"I'll find another way," she said firmly and he didn't doubt her for a minute.

Still, he felt like a complete bastard for stealing what had been her dream out from under her. He hadn't even wanted the damn hall. Still didn't, come to that. He had no plans for it beyond making Bennett furious. Always before, that result had been enough. Now, it didn't feel like it was.

He could apologize, but what would that mean? Too little too late. As if she could read what he was thinking, she said, "I don't want an apology."

"I feel like giving you one anyway."

"No, don't bother."

"Then what do you want?"

"You've already asked me that once before."

"Humor me," he said with a shrug.

"Indulging, humoring… Where does it end?"

"Amanda…"

"Fine." She took a breath, looked into his eyes and said, "I want to know if I'm making a mistake being here."

"You're not," he said instantly. Whatever was happening between them wasn't a mistake. He refused to believe that. So many years apart had made this time with Amanda even sweeter than he'd imagined it could be. But was she feeling the same?

"Well, of course that would be your opinion." She gave him a small smile and shook her head gently.

"Self-serving, I know, but still true."

"I hope so. I'll have to think about it." She lifted one hand to cup his cheek. "Good night, Henry."

He walked her down, let her out and reset the alarm. Her birthday. Then the dark and the quiet fell down around him and Henry had too much time to do too much thinking.

For the next week, Amanda spent more time at Henry's place than at her own. She excused it by telling herself that his new house was so close to her work, it made more sense than having him at her house in Laguna. But it was more than that and she knew it.

Love, old and new, was rising up inside her and she was afraid to trust it. Trust him. How could she?

And he didn't trust her, either. She felt that.

They talked about the past, let each other in on what they'd been doing the last several years. She knew about his brief marriage and had found herself wondering if *she* was the reason it hadn't worked out for him. But if that were true, why had he never contacted her? Why had he kept up the war with Bennett and her family? And was this time with her just another battle? Would he somehow use this against her?

She just didn't know. And though her mind screamed at her to be careful, her heart yearned. Keeping herself centered between the two was becoming a difficult balancing act. If she fell… Amanda didn't know if she'd survive it this time.

Because as much as she'd loved him years ago, she loved him more now. She hadn't expected it. Hadn't really wanted it, but some things went too deep to ignore. He still held her heart and he'd already broken it once. Could she trust him to not do the same now?

There was too much distrust on both sides, though she hated to admit it. Henry was holding back a part of himself just as she was. They talked about business, but neither of them went deep. They didn't share what they were working on, what their plans were. They could talk about the past, but the future was nebulous and never further away than the following day.

She didn't talk to Henry about her ideas, because she couldn't be sure that he wouldn't simply sweep something out from under her again. And apparently, he felt the same way about her.

They were together, with a wall between them. So busy protecting themselves, they couldn't breach that wall and Amanda wasn't sure they should try.

Then there was her family. None of them knew what was going on between her and Henry, and Amanda knew that if Bennett found out, he'd go ballistic and make her life a living hell. So she kept it secret. Hidden. As if she were ashamed of what she was doing. And she had to ask herself…was she?

"What're you thinking?" Henry's voice came soft in the darkness and she stiffened. Was it time, she wondered? Time to take a leap of faith and see if her trust would be protected or destroyed? And if not now, then when? They couldn't go on like this forever.

Taking a chance, she said, "I'm wondering what we're doing here, Henry."

He grinned and in the dim light of the moon pouring through the French doors off the balcony, he looked far too good and a little dangerous on top of it. Which only added to the thrill of expectation that opened up inside her.

"Right now," he said amiably, "we're resting up for round two."

She had to smile in spite of everything. Yet, what she felt when she was with him wasn't enough to dispel what she worried about when they were apart.

Wanting him as she did, Amanda needed answers. "I mean, where's this going?"

He stiffened and sat up against a pillow he tucked behind his back. She could see the expression on his face clearly enough, so she put his mind at ease on that point anyway.

Laughing at that completely male response, she shook her head and assured him, "I'm not looking for a proposal or even a promise, so you can relax there."

"All right," he said, caution clear in his tone. "Then what is it, Amanda?"

She couldn't think in the bed, so close to him, so she scooted off the mattress and began to pace. It was a good sprawling room for pacing. The space was huge and wasn't cluttered with furniture yet. She could have danced across the floor if she'd felt like it.

Keeping time with her thoughts, she walked a little too fast to the now-cold hearth, where she stood and studied it thoughtfully. "There should be a roaring fire and a dog curled up in front of it. Then the room would be perfect."

"A dog." He repeated it and she looked back at him. "That's what you're thinking about?"

"No." She took a breath and walked back to him. Her bare feet made no sound on the soft rug that lay across the wide-planked floor. She didn't bother grabbing her clothes, since there was no point in being embarrassed about chatting naked with him—he'd seen all of her too many times to count now, anyway.

"No one knows about us," she blurted out and came to a stop at the end of the bed. And she only now was realizing how much that bothered her. "We're sneaking around as if we were children, afraid of being caught and grounded or something."

It was the trust, she thought. Or the lack of it, rather, that was driving the secrecy. Staring at him, she admitted, "I haven't told my family we're together this way."

"Why not?"

She swung her hair back behind her shoulders. "Before I answer that, I'll ask you. Does anyone on your side know about us?"

"My 'side'?"

"Oh, don't get all offended." She waved that off. "You know what I mean."

"I do," he said, and after a long moment added, "And no. I haven't told anyone."

She was sorry to hear that. "So I can ask you the same question. Why?"

He studied her. "Because it's no one's business but ours."

"No." Amanda gave him a long look. "That's the easy answer, Henry. For both of us."

He scrubbed one hand across his face and then pushed his hair back as he obviously worked to gather his thoughts.

"Maybe," Henry admitted, then tossed the sheet off and stood up. "What about you? Why don't you want your family to know? Ashamed?"

"No." She answered quickly, so he would understand

that shame had no part in this. But Amanda also said, "I'm not ashamed, Henry. But I'm not…easy with this, either."

He walked toward her and she skipped back a step or two because God help her, when he was close, her brain simply ceased to function.

"I guess, at the heart of everything, I don't trust you," she said flatly and nearly winced when she saw in his eyes the impact her words had on him. "I hate saying it, and I wish I could change it. But if the truth doesn't happen between us, then what's the point?"

He blew out a breath and looked as though he wanted to reach for her again, but he kept his distance. Maybe he, too, didn't trust himself to have clear thoughts when they got close. Small consolation, but she'd take it.

"You're right," he muttered, and shook his head. "I don't like hearing it, but the truth is, I don't trust you, either."

"Well, that's great, isn't it?" Something inside her curled up and whimpered and maybe it was her hope for a future that could never happen without trust.

Deep inside, Amanda had been hoping that this time with him would lead them somewhere…else. Somewhere they could be together and recapture what they'd had and lost so long ago. But if they couldn't let the past go, how could they reach for the future?

"There's a lot still hanging between us, Amanda, and right now, I don't know how to get past it."

"Maybe we can't." And wasn't that a sad statement? They'd both grown and changed, yet at the heart of this mess was one night that had happened ten years ago. Didn't seem right that it would have such a big influence over choices made now. "Henry, I don't even talk to you about work, because I'm never sure if you're going to use that information against me somehow."

"Do you think I'm not doing the same thing? Amanda, if Bennett knew we were together like this..."

"He'd be furious," she said.

"More than that, he'd have you trying to pry information out of me. And damned if I wouldn't be tempted to give it." He stalked off, grabbed up a pair of loose cotton pants and tugged them on. They hung low over his hips and only made him look even sexier than he did when he was naked.

Amanda was in big trouble and she knew it. She was in love with a man she couldn't allow herself to trust. Love was the open door, but trust was the warmth inside. If you didn't have one, how could you have the other?

His body was stiff, shoulders squared. "There are plenty of things going on at work, but I don't bring it up, because the Carey family has tried to destroy me before."

"I'm *not* the Carey family."

"You're one of them," he countered, then continued. "And you just admitted yourself you don't trust me with information, so don't look so insulted."

She was, though, and didn't bother to hide it. "I never betrayed you, Henry," Amanda reminded him hotly. "You can't say the same."

"Maybe not," he admitted shortly. "But answer me this. Did you defend me to your family when it all went to shit?"

"How could I defend you when you walked away?" she demanded. "You *left*. Without a word to me. You were gone and it was as if nothing we'd shared meant anything to you."

"I didn't have a choice," he reminded her, his voice low and tight, filled with a simmering anger that was fast coming to a boil. "It's not as if I willingly left you. I was staying at your family's house. Bennett tossed me out. I went because there was nothing there for me anymore."

"There was *me*," she reminded him and felt her own temper spike. "Do you know what it was like for me? Alone? I didn't have you there with me to face any of it."

"Yeah? I lost my best friend and the woman I loved all at the same time. If you think I was having a great time, you're wrong." He pushed one hand through his hair and grumbled, "Besides, for all I knew, you wanted me gone, too."

"But you didn't bother to find out, did you?" When he didn't say anything, the anger within became disappointment and a to-the-bone kind of sorrow that made her want to turn in on herself. Which she would not be doing in front of him. "Why are we doing this, Henry? Why are we here together now?"

His gaze snapped to hers. "Because, damn it, I've missed you, Amanda."

That was salve to the open wound on her soul, but it didn't mend it. Maybe nothing could.

But she could at least admit that much herself. "I missed you, too, as I've told you. But if all we can share is a past filled with distrust, then there's nothing really here, is there?"

He thought about it for a moment or two before he said softly, "We could find a way to get past it."

"We haven't yet."

"Have we tried?"

He had a point. They'd both been skating through

this relationship or whatever it was. Staying on the surface, never going far enough to where it might matter. Neither of them willing to take the step that might have closed the gap between them.

"No, you're right." Amanda sighed. "Maybe we're not supposed to. We had our shot ten years ago and we lost it. Maybe that's all we get."

"You really believe that? After this last week?" He rushed to her and took hold of her upper arms and gripped tight. "That's it?"

His touch sent bolts of heat flying through her body but it wasn't enough. Never would be. Not without the whole package. Without love. Trust. A future.

"We're good together, Amanda."

"We *were*," she corrected, shaking her head and staring up into his eyes. "Back then, we had a chance. But it slipped away. Now, we have sex."

"Great sex."

"True." She thought it wasn't just great, but earth-shattering. Soul consuming. And yet… "But it's not enough, Henry. For either of us."

She watched shutters drop over his eyes. His features went cool and disinterested, as if she were a stranger standing there in front of him. He was closing himself off so she had to accept that he was leaving. Again.

"You know what?" He let his hands drop, then folded his arms across his chest. "You're right." Looking down into her eyes, he said tightly, "I want all of you, Amanda, but I don't know that I could trust it if I had it. And I can't give you all of me, for the same reason."

Amanda had told him her truth and now he'd done the same for her and the pain was swamping her. Heart aching, stomach sinking, she met his gaze and told herself not to cry. For God's sake, she didn't want to cry in front of him. She could at least spare herself *that* humiliation. Lifting her chin and digging for strength, Amanda told herself that she'd wanted honesty, at least, between them. She just hadn't expected it to hurt so badly.

"Okay, the truth really does hurt," she said, forcing a smile she didn't feel. "But openness, even when it's hard, is easier to live with than lies."

Henry snorted. "Doesn't feel easy."

"No, it doesn't," she agreed. Turning around, she walked to the closest chair, picked up her slacks and stepped into them. Then she shrugged on her shirt and buttoned it up, all without looking at him. Stuffing her bra and panties into her brown bag, she finally straightened and turned to face him. He was standing where she'd left him, his gaze locked on hers as if for the last time. And maybe it was.

"I'm leaving," she said, "but if we're done, if we're really over… I want one more truth from you before I go."

He nodded stiffly.

"The hall," she blurted out. "How did you find out that I wanted to buy it?"

He scrubbed one hand across his face, then around to rub at the back of his neck. His reaction told her she really wasn't going to like his answer, so Amanda braced herself for it. And still, it hit her hard.

"Serena."

"What?" That she hadn't expected. Why, she couldn't have said. She knew her sister had been meeting Henry for lunch, keeping in touch. The problem was Serena believed Henry was her friend. "Were you being nice to her, being her *friend* just to use her? How could you do that? To her, of all people."

"No!" He blew out a breath. "I like your sister. I don't have many friends and she's one of them. I never used her. Never tried to get information out of her. I don't expect you to believe me, but it's the truth. Which is what you said you wanted."

"It is." But she hadn't thought that truth would close off her throat and stab at her heart.

He walked away, then whirled around and came back. "Then the truth is, over lunch one day, Serena mentioned that you were excited about the old hall near the center. You were going to buy it, but you wouldn't tell her what your plan was yet, and the curiosity was killing her."

Pain, sharp and hot, pulsed in the center of her chest. "And you used that. Used her. To hurt me."

"Yes." He met her gaze squarely. Not trying to avoid the confrontation at all. "I'll admit to that, but it wasn't just you. I wanted to get back at Bennett, too."

"Oh, yeah," she said, choking out a harsh laugh. "Can't forget Bennett. Can't forget that I remain, after ten years, the ragged chew toy that you two fight over. That makes me feel way better."

"It was just a deal, Amanda."

"No, it wasn't," she argued, staring at him as if she didn't know him at all. And maybe she didn't. Maybe she'd never known him as she'd thought she did. "You did it deliberately to hurt me. Bennett was a side benefit."

His mouth worked as if chewing on words he was holding back.

"This has been going on forever," she continued. "You and Bennett, tearing at each other and putting me squarely in the middle, like some tattered hunk of rope that you're using in a twisted game of tug-of-war."

"No one's doing that," he argued.

"Really?" She shook her hair back from her face. "Without me, would either of you have kept this stupid war going for ten years?"

He didn't speak and she took that to mean she was right. But then, she'd already known that. This was harder than anything she'd ever lived through. Even that long-ago pain didn't come up to this. She looked at him and saw everything she wanted—and the one man she couldn't trust.

What kind of cosmic joke was that? To have Henry come into her life not once, but twice, and to lose him both times. Her heart aching, she blinked to keep furious tears at bay. God knew she'd have plenty of time for them later.

"I didn't know what you wanted that stupid hall for," he ground out.

"No," she said. "You just knew I wanted it and that was enough for you."

"Damn it, Amanda, see it from my side."

"What is there to see? You did this to hurt me, Henry, in spite of what you tell yourself." Her voice was so cold, she was half-surprised that ice wasn't filling the room. "And you know what's worse? You used Serena to hurt her family. You smiled at her. You were her friend and you used her."

Both hands now scrubbed his face and then went up to scrape his hair back. "I am her friend," he insisted. "I didn't use her. I used information that she freely gave."

"Spin it anyway you want to, Henry. But the bottom line here is you're a bastard."

"That's been said before."

"Then you should probably ask yourself if there's something to it." She had to go because tears were clogging her throat and burning her eyes. Her heart was broken. Again. And she wanted out of there before she somehow let him know it.

"Love shouldn't be this hard, Henry."

"Love?" he repeated. "Who said anything about love?"

"I did. You just weren't listening." God, she shouldn't have told him that. Should have kept that one painful secret to herself.

"Amanda—"

She ignored him, swung her purse over her shoulder and headed for the bedroom door. When she got there, she looked back over her shoulder at him. He hadn't moved. His features were still and tight and his eyes were shuttered, hiding whatever it was he was thinking, feeling.

Amanda wondered why it should be so hard to leave the man.

And why did it hurt so much that he was making no move at all to stop her?

"Goodbye, Henry."

Ten

Over the next few days, the world shifted. At least, Henry thought, *his* world changed.

Love.

Why the hell did she say that? Why would she throw that out there right before she walked away? She loved him? He rubbed the center of his chest with the heel of his hand, but it didn't do a damn thing to ease the pain centered there.

Love.

He'd lived without Amanda for ten years. Being without her now shouldn't be this difficult. But he couldn't focus. Didn't give a damn about new mergers, pending contracts or meetings with the lawyers. None of it mattered.

Having Amanda back in his life, in his bed, was more than he'd ever thought to have. Now that she was gone again, even breathing was hard. And he only now realized that he'd been missing her for years. That's why he'd never felt complete. Why he'd never been satisfied with the life he'd built for himself. Because she wasn't there.

The emptiness he'd survived for so long without her suddenly looked darker and colder than ever.

Love.

And he had only himself to blame. Wasn't that a bitch?

The nights were the worst, he admitted silently. Even with Martha living in her quarters downstairs, the big house echoed with emptiness. He was too used to having Amanda beside him. The dark seemed to magnify the fact that he was alone, and he'd gone so far now to think about what Mick and even Amanda had said. Getting a dog. At least that would be another heartbeat in the house. Force him to care for something besides nurturing the pain that kept him in a tight grip day and night.

"What the hell's going on with you?"

Frowning, Henry glanced at Mick. "What're you talking about?"

"I mean, you've been a complete ass for days now." Mick sat forward in his chair across from Henry's desk. "I've been talking for fifteen minutes and you were on Mars or something. Hell, when I came in, I swear I saw Donna pick up her stapler and consider bashing you over the head with it."

Frowning, he threw a look at his closed office door and pictured his assistant, just on the other side. Donna by nature was cool, unflappable. Or so he'd thought.

Scowling more fiercely, Henry said, "Then maybe you should leave it alone."

"I could," Mick said and kicked back in the guest

chair, stretching his legs out in front of him. "But where's the fun in that?"

"Fun. Sure."

"All right. What happened with the woman?"

Henry glanced at his friend. "Why does it always have to be a woman?"

"Excellent question," Mick mused. "And one men have been asking for centuries."

Henry stood up, shoved his hands into his pockets and bristled with the hot, driving energy that had been in him since the moment Amanda had walked out. He didn't know what to do with it. All he could do, it seemed, was go over and over that last argument with her and wonder if there'd been a chance to pull it all back. Could he have stopped it? Could he have stopped her from leaving? Should he have?

He remembered the betrayal stamped on her face when he'd admitted using information Serena had given him. And no doubt, she'd told her sister all about it and now he'd lost a friend, as well.

Glaring at Mick, he growled, "How the hell am I supposed to trust her? She's a Carey, for God's sake."

"Ah. Amanda. *Your* Amanda."

She wasn't his now. Frowning, Henry regretted ever telling his pal about what had happened between him and Amanda so long ago. On the other hand, he didn't have to waste time bringing the man up to speed now.

"It all blew up," he muttered and turned to look out the window. The view didn't soothe him today. Just as the view from the roof hadn't eased anything the night before. Hell, Amanda was imprinted on his house now. On his heart and soul. Ripping her out was tearing him in two.

"You knew who she was when you went into this," Mick said easily.

"I know that. Not helpful."

"So what happened?"

Henry gave him a brief summary, then finished by saying, "Okay, I did use something Serena told me against their family, but is it my fault she let it slip?"

"Nope."

"Stop agreeing with me." Days since Amanda had walked out of his house in the middle of the damn night and he was still as furious as he'd been at the time. The question was, whom was he angrier with? Her? Or himself?

Then her face rose up in his mind. Again. The look in her eyes when he had admitted to using information Serena had given him. The betrayal. The hurt. And, like he did every time that image haunted him, he fought it down. Fought his way past it, because remembering tore at him in a way that was nearly unbearable. So yeah, he was angrier with himself than with Amanda. For all the good it did him.

"All right," he allowed, "maybe I shouldn't have used the information Serena gave me, but damn it, if the positions were reversed, Bennett would have done the same damn thing."

"Right." Mick cocked his head and asked, "Would Amanda have done it?"

"What?"

Mick shook his head. "You're raging over this breakup with Amanda, but it's Bennett you're blaming for what you did. So I'm asking, would Amanda have used information against you?"

He had to think about that, and honestly, he wasn't

sure. And even as he thought it, he called himself a liar. Yeah, he knew Amanda. She was determined to prove herself to her family, but she wouldn't have used someone else to do it. She wouldn't have gone out of her way to sink his plans as he had hers.

So he guessed that *did* make him the bastard she'd called him. Worse, to his mind, was the knowledge that he actually did trust her. Of course, that realization came too damn late.

"No," he finally said in disgust. "She wouldn't."

"Right." Mick stood up, went to the coffee bar on the far wall and poured himself a cup. "So bottom line is, you're at war with Bennett and Amanda's the casualty."

He frowned at that, but he didn't argue, because damn it, Mick had a good point.

In his own defense, he muttered, "She's still a Carey."

"And you're a Porter. So?" Mick took a sip of his coffee. "You're the one letting this get out of control."

He snorted. "Just me, huh? Not Bennett?"

"You don't control Bennett," Mick said. "Only yourself. So if you want the war to go on, it will. If you don't...if you want Amanda more than you do the battles with her brother...then stop it."

Was it really that simple? Would it be so easy to end something that had become a part of his life for years? Was he ready to?

Love.

He'd done a lot of thinking the last few days. When everything had happened in Italy so long ago, there had been a part of Henry that hadn't been surprised at all. It had taken him a long time to understand why, but he did now and wondered if that reason was still keeping him from what he wanted.

It went back to his childhood, of course. Which sounded pitiful to his own ears. Allowing choices made by a parent to somehow guide your own choices decades later didn't make much sense. But when his mother died, Henry had watched his father blame her for leaving them. He'd treated her death as a personal betrayal. As if the woman had died to spite him or something, and somehow, Henry had absorbed that lesson.

Even as a grown man, there was a small part of him that was standing back, waiting for people to leave him. So when Amanda was torn from him so long ago, it had devastated but not surprised him. And this time was no different. He'd gone into this relationship with one foot out the door. To protect himself? To hide? Whatever the reason, it was self-defeating and not worth hanging on to.

Maybe it was time to put the past to rest. To move the hell on.

"How do I stop a war that's gone on so long?"

"That's for you to figure out, Henry," Mick said. "I think you can manage it."

Henry's brain was racing and he didn't much like what he was thinking. Mick was right. Amanda had been right. He'd been fighting with Bennett for so long, it was second nature. But was it worth it?

Love.

Frowning to himself now, Henry thought about Amanda, and what was between them—or might be between them now—and wondered. Was Candace Carey right when she said that carrying on this war for ten years was ridiculous? Was it time to let it all go?

He'd proved he was as good as or better than Bennett Carey, hadn't he? That thought brought a deeper scowl. Why had he ever thought he had to prove himself to Bennett? Because he'd once been a friend? Because he'd turned on Henry? Well, hell, Henry had turned on Amanda, so was he any better than Bennett?

"Ask yourself one question," Mick said. "Do you love her?"

Henry looked at him.

"Yeah." Mick nodded and hid a smile. "You do. You just haven't faced it yet."

Was his friend right? Was he in love and too much of a coward to admit it? Even to himself? Hell. Obviously he had a lot to think about. To consider. To face. He had to find a way out of this mess he found himself in and he wasn't about to do any of it in front of Mick.

So for the moment, he'd focus on this appointment and get at least that done and finished. Sitting down, Henry tapped one finger on the report Mick had handed him. "Okay, enough. Let's talk about this instead. Bennett Carey's planning to take over a security company? Why would he do that?"

Mick shrugged, took another pull at his coffee cup. "No idea why." He grinned. "But he'll be disappointed."

"Why's that?"

Smiling, Mick said, "Because the company he's considering isn't nearly as good as mine."

Henry smiled. "Of course it's not. Well, let him have it. I don't need a security company when I've already got you on speed dial." He shrugged. With Mick paying informants, keeping tabs on the Careys was easier than it had been before.

When Henry had first started trying to fight the Careys, he hadn't been in a position to hurt them. But as Porter Enterprises grew, he'd found small ways to make inroads. To drive Bennett crazy. There was always someone willing to talk—secretaries, assistants, mailroom clerks. But these days, he had Mick's expertise to count on.

"I'll have the next report for you on Friday," Mick was saying.

It amazed him just how much time, effort and, hell, money he'd put into the war with Bennett. And what had it brought him, really? Henry shook his head as he reconsidered, well…everything. "No. I think we're done."

Mick stared at him. "You're serious?"

"Yeah." Henry pushed back in his chair. "I am, Mick. You're right. If I want to end the war, it's up to me and this is where it starts. It's enough already."

Mick rose and nodded. "Glad to hear it. You've wasted enough time on this."

Henry laughed shortly. "If you thought so, why didn't you say it sooner?"

"Hey, you're my friend." He shrugged. "It was important to you, so I stood with you."

As simple as that, Henry thought. A friend who was there when you needed him. He held out one hand to Mick and when he shook it, Henry said, "Thanks for that."

"Good luck," Mick said as he walked to the door. "And let me know how it all ends."

Yeah, Henry couldn't wait to find that out for himself.

Love.

He remembered her saying it. Remembered the punch of that one word. His heart had taken a direct hit, and it had been safe for so long that one word had nearly knocked him out. And over the last few days, that word had forced him to think. To question himself. To look deep enough to find an answer that had always eluded him before.

Did he love Amanda?

Of course he did. He always had.

It was time, he thought, to finally do something about it.

A few days later, Amanda attended another family meeting and wasn't surprised in the least to see that Justin hadn't bothered to show up. Wherever her little brother was now, she hoped he was having more fun than she was. The others were there, though. Her father, tapping his fingers impatiently. Serena, checking her email and smiling to herself. Bennett glowering as usual. The only one missing now was Candace.

Amanda felt…apart somehow. She was standing back and looking at her family clearly and could see now that she'd spent too much of her life trying to please them all.

Oh, she loved her job and she was good at it. But when had she decided that she needed to impress Bennett? Why had she spent so much time worrying about what her brother thought about her work? She was every bit as much a Carey as he was and had every darn right he did, too. Nobody questioned her older brother's abilities, did they? Well, she deserved the same treatment.

Bennett was stern and rigid, and would roll right over a person if they didn't stand up to him. And that was her problem, she thought. She'd never taken a stand. Not ten years ago and not now.

Well, that was about to change.

Steeling herself for what was to come, Amanda took

a moment to look at Serena. Ever since that last night with Henry, Amanda had been going back and forth on if she should tell her sister what he'd done—or not. Finally, though, she'd decided to say nothing. Serena saw the good in everyone and there was just no reason to shatter her, hurt her, as Amanda had been hurt. No matter what her own feelings were for Henry, she had believed him when he said he'd never meant to use Serena.

She had to ask herself, then, if she could believe him about that, why was it so hard to trust him on anything else? But she'd been in her own home, alone in her own bed, for days now and just like ten years ago, Henry hadn't called. Hadn't come over. Hadn't made the slightest effort to talk to her, to find a way through this. So clearly, she was in love and he was in lust. Right?

"Dad," Bennett was saying, "why are you here?"

Martin looked at his oldest son and reminded him, "Where else would I be?"

"I don't know," Bennett snapped, throwing both hands in the air. "Retired? With *Mom*?"

"I'm here, too," Candace said as she sailed into the room, wearing a hot pink dress and matching heels. She deliberately took a seat away from her husband and Amanda sighed. The retirement war was still going strong. What was it about the Bennett family that they couldn't stop battling people—even each other?

"Fine." Bennett didn't look happy, but when did he? "Serena, you go first. Update."

"Right." Serena started talking, but Amanda wasn't listening.

Instead, she was remembering what Henry had said when he accused her of being ashamed of being with him. Keeping him a secret from her family. She had gone out of her way to keep the relationship under everyone's radar. Why would she do that? She was thirty years old and made her own decisions, so what did she care if the family didn't approve of those choices?

Funny that it had taken another family meeting to underscore that she was not only a *Carey*, she was Amanda. And she'd live how she wanted to. With that thought set firmly in her mind, she interrupted her sister.

"Sorry, Serena, but I've got to say something." And if she didn't do it right away, she might just talk herself out of it.

"Problem with the Summer Stars audition?" Bennett asked.

"There *is* life outside the company, Bennett," Amanda told him and her mother applauded gently. She sent Candace a fast smile, then focused again on her brother. Standing up, she turned to face him head-on. "No. This is about me. And Henry."

"Porter?" Bennett's gaze narrowed on her. "What about him?"

"I've been sleeping with him."

"You *what*?" Bennett.

"Amanda!" Her father.

"That's lovely." Serena.

"Good for you, honey." Her mother, God bless her.

Strange, but now that she'd started, she felt stronger, more sure of what she was doing than ever before. Looking at Bennett, she said, "To be completely clear, we don't get a lot of sleep."

Serena muffled a laugh, but Bennett's glower deepened until he almost looked like one of those awful yard gnomes.

"What are you thinking? He's the damn enemy, Amanda." Bennett looked furious and Amanda just didn't care. Not anymore.

"Your enemy maybe," she said, facing Bennett down the length of the conference table. She was barely aware of the family watching them now. Amanda had things she wanted to say and now was the time.

"You started this war, Bennett," she told him now and ignored the slap of shock on his face. "You found me and Henry together, happy, and you ran him off. You didn't talk to me. To either of us. You just reacted and expected to be right. Like you always do."

"Now just a damn minute—"

"No," she countered quickly. "You wait. This isn't even my war, but I'm the one who always ends up wounded."

"How the hell are you wounded?"

"For heaven's sake, Bennett," their mother said. "You've got eyes. Can't you see your sister loves the man?"

"Who said anything about love?" Martin looked from his wife to his daughter, completely confused.

Amanda paid no attention to any of it. She focused solely on the brother she loved and needed to make understand. "You set out to destroy Henry for what exactly? Having the nerve to touch me? To love me?"

Bennett gritted his teeth. "It wasn't all about you, Amanda. He was my friend and he went behind my back with my baby sister." He pushed the edges of his jacket back and shoved his hands into his pockets.

Amanda read the shine of betrayal in his eyes and she could almost sympathize with him for that.

"What did you expect me to do when I walked into the boathouse and saw—"

"Maybe talk to me?" Amanda argued.

"You were *naked*," he reminded her. "And so was he."

"Then you should have left. Given us a minute. Let things cool off so we could talk. Instead, you went nuts."

"You do have a temper, Bennett," their mother said and he threw her a furious look.

"Everybody should calm down. Take a break, maybe." Serena looked worriedly from one to the other of them.

"No," Amanda said, "we've waited too long to have this out."

"Well said," Candace murmured. "It's past time the air was cleared."

"You're okay with this?" Bennett demanded.

"I'm not," their father said and his eyes were flashing with banked anger.

"I'm sorry to hear that, Dad," Amanda said, "but in case no one here has noticed, I'm a grown woman and who I sleep with is my business."

"You're absolutely right, dear," Candace said, and silenced her husband with one fulminating look. "I'm happy you and Henry have worked things out between you after all these years."

"I am, too," Serena said softly.

"Oh, we haven't," Amanda continued, looking at Bennett. "Thanks to this never-ending war, we have no trust between us. And without trust, there's nothing. So congratulations, Bennett. Another battle won and another wound for your sister."

"I'm not doing any of this to hurt you!" Bennett

stared at her openmouthed as if he couldn't believe that she would think so little of him. But what else could she think?

It felt good, getting all of this out in the open. Every word was painful and a part of her hated throwing all of this at a brother she loved. But she'd been silent too long. And still, even knowing that, Amanda knew she wouldn't say anything to Serena. There was no reason for one more Carey woman to be hurt by Henry Porter.

Turning to her brother again, she said, "You won the war, Bennett. We're not together anymore."

"Then why the hell did you bother saying anything about it?" he bellowed.

"Your temper doesn't intimidate me anymore, so just stop it."

He clamped his lips shut. Surprise? Probably.

So while she had his complete attention, Amanda said, "I told you because I'm serving notice, Bennett." His features were stamped with a mixture of anger and confusion and she reminded herself that he was her brother. He loved her. He was just…wrong.

"Bennett, I love you. But I can't just fall in line anymore. I'm good at my job here. I'm a Carey, just like you. I have as much right to this business as you do. And I love all of you." She looked at each of them in turn. "But I'm done living my life by the Carey rules."

"What's that mean?"

"It means, Bennett, that I'm done being the chew toy you and Henry fight over."

"She said that to me a few days ago. Nice to hear it said to you, too."

Her gaze snapped to the open doorway. Henry stood

there, eyes locked on her, an unreadable expression on his face. Her heart jumped into a gallop at the sight of him. It didn't matter how they'd fought. Didn't matter that she'd walked out and he'd let her. All that mattered right now was that he was there. In what he would consider enemy territory.

Why?

"What the hell are you doing here, Henry?" Bennett demanded. "Get out."

"Bennett, dear," Candace said, "sit down."

"What?"

"Candy," their father started to say.

"We'll hear Henry out," she said flatly.

"Thanks for that, Candace," Henry told her and spared her a quick smile before focusing on Amanda again. "You're absolutely right, Mandy. You never deserved to be caught in the middle." He walked into the room and closed the door behind him.

He'd come to the office to face Amanda because she deserved it. Ten years ago, he'd left without a word. This time was going to be different. And if he wanted that, then he had to face all of the Careys—but first, Amanda.

"Get out," Bennett said tightly and his mother scowled at him.

Henry shifted his gaze to the other man and said, "Not this time. I'm not here to see you, Bennett. Like Amanda, I've got something to say and it's time you heard it."

"We don't need to hear from you," Martin said.

"Martin," Candace ordered, "leave the boy alone."

"You can't be all right with this."

"I am, though," she said, then turned her head to Henry. "Go ahead, Henry."

He smiled, then looked at Amanda because he could feel her watching him. He'd finally come to his senses and he didn't care who the hell knew it. As long as Amanda believed him. He walked around the table until he was standing right in front of her, forcing her to tip her head back to look into his eyes. He hated the shadows he saw there and knew he was the reason for them. Never again, he promised himself. All she had to do was give him one more chance to prove himself. Damned if he'd fail this time.

Dipping into the inner pocket of his jacket, he pulled out a thin sheaf of papers and handed them to her.

"What is this?"

Henry looked at Amanda. Only her, as he said, "That's the deed to the hall. It's signed over to you."

"Henry…" Her mouth dropped open and she glanced down at the papers before lifting her gaze to his again. He saw the look of cautious joy that flashed across her face and that told him he wasn't too late. He hadn't missed the second chance fate had thrown at him.

"Why?" Bennett demanded, shattering the quiet. "Why would you do that?"

Sighing, Henry reluctantly shifted his gaze to the man he'd once called friend. "Because," he said, "it's past time this war was over."

"Just like that." Bennett didn't believe him and Henry found he just didn't care.

"Bennett, for God's sake, just be quiet," Candace muttered.

"Just like that," Henry said. "Bennett, we've both gone out of our ways for years to get at each other. What's the point? We're both here. We're both successful. Let the damn thing go already."

"I'm supposed to believe you, I guess," Bennett said.

"Do or don't," Henry told him. "I don't care. Like I said, I'm not here for you." He turned his gaze on Amanda, ignoring every other Carey there.

"I'm here for *you*, Mandy. Like I should have been ten years ago. Like I swear I always will be from today on."

She took a deep, shuddering breath. "Henry..."

"Don't say anything." Henry took the deed from her, tossed it to the table, then held her hands in his. "Please. Just let me talk first. I have so much to say to you. Then you can tell me to stay or go and I'll do it. Whatever you want, Amanda." Hopefully, she wouldn't tell him to go. Then he added, "Indulge me."

She smiled, at the memory. "Okay. You first."

Neither of them paid any attention at all to the others in the room. It was as if they'd all disappeared, leaving Henry and Amanda alone in the world.

Keeping his gaze locked with hers, Henry willed her to believe him. To trust him as he should have trusted her right from the damn beginning.

"I have to start with I'm sorry, Mandy. It doesn't seem like enough, but it's all I have. I'm sorry I let Bennett chase me off ten years ago—"

"Hey—"

He ignored her brother. "Sorry I didn't call you. Sorry I didn't trust what we had. And I'm sorrier than you know that I never told you I loved you."

Her breath caught and when he tightened his grip on her hands, he felt her tremble. He'd almost lost this, he thought. He'd almost let her get away when she was… everything.

"And I'm sorry about the hall." He turned to look at Serena. "I'm going to apologize to you, too."

Surprised, she laughed and asked, "What for?"

He smiled to himself as he realized that Amanda hadn't said anything to her sister. Of course she would protect her sister from pain. That's who Amanda was. But to have the fresh start they needed, Henry had to tell Serena.

No more lies, no more half-truths.

"When we were at lunch, Serena…"

"*You* went to lunch with him, too?" Bennett demanded. "*Both* of my sisters going behind my back? What the hell, Henry?"

"I swear," Candace said, "if you don't hush, Bennett…"

His mouth snapped closed, but his eyes were saying plenty.

Henry sighed and said, "Serena, you told me about Amanda's plans for that hall and I used that information to buy it out from under her."

Surprise, disappointment and finally acceptance crossed her features before she looked up and said, "You didn't have to tell me, Henry. Amanda didn't. So why would you confess now?"

"It was my story to tell. And I'm done with secrets, Serena. I'm very sorry for it. I want you to know that. You deserved better." It felt good to say it, but he hoped their friendship would survive.

She studied him for a moment or two before smiling up at him. "I forgive you, but our next lunch is on you."

"Deal." Relieved that he hadn't lost a friend, he said softly, "Thank you."

"Oh, sure." Bennett threw both hands up. "Forgiveness all around. Let's all have cookies."

"Sounds good," Henry quipped and grinned at his old enemy before turning back to Amanda. When he saw the shimmer of tears in her eyes, he hoped it was a good sign.

His thumbs moved back and forth over the backs of her hands, and somehow that action both fired his blood and cooled his mind. How had he ever gone without her?

"Forget about everything else but this. I love you, Amanda. I always have." She smiled and he kept going. "I want you to have that hall. Make your plans a reality."

"What plans?" Bennett asked.

"You didn't have to do that, Henry," she said, with a slow shake of her head.

"Yeah, I did." Dropping her hands, he moved to cup her face in his palms. "I believe in you. I trust you. And I love you more than anything in the world. I will always love you, even if you tell me to leave right now."

"I won't do that," she said on a half laugh.

"Thank God," he muttered and gave her a grin before he bent to plant a quick kiss on her lips.

"I've got something for you." Letting go of her, he dipped one hand into his slacks pocket and came up with a small red velvet box. When he opened it to her to display a square-cut sapphire with diamonds on either side of that glittering, dark blue stone, her eyes went even wider.

"Henry?"

"Marry me, Amanda. Stay with me. Live with me in that house, make a family with me."

Serena sighed.

Amanda laughed and gasped and looked up at him in astonishment. He was taking that as a very good sign.

"And let's get a dog, too." Henry grinned at her. "Like you said, the house needs one. To curl up in front of the fireplace."

"A dog?" Bennett muttered.

"Quiet, Bennett," Amanda told him and Henry laughed. "What kind of dog?"

"From the shelter," he said. "We'll find one that needs to be rescued—like you rescued me." He looked into her eyes and whispered for her alone, "Love me. Marry me. And *trust* me, to love you for the rest of my life."

She reached up to cup his cheek and he swore that was the first real warmth he'd felt since she'd walked away from him days ago. He couldn't lose it again. Couldn't lose her. "Love me, Amanda."

Smiling up at him, she said, "I do love you, Henry. I *trust* you. I trust *us* to build a wonderful life together." She kissed him, then eased back down and said, "I warn you now, though… I want it all. Marriage, kids, dog, job."

Her smile eased away every jagged edge in his soul. "Sounds perfect."

"And I want it all with you, Henry. It's always been you. Only you."

He grinned. "So that's a *yes*?"

"Oh, yes." She held out her left hand and he slid the platinum ring onto her finger, where it glittered and shone in the overhead lights.

"I swear you'll never be sorry," he said and kissed her.

And while the family reacted in the background, everything from Serena's applause to Bennett's muttering, Henry and Amanda took that first step into the future, wrapped up in each other.

* * * * *

JUST A LITTLE MARRIED

REESE RYAN

Thank you to Joss Wood, who came up with the idea for this fun trilogy and was gracious enough to invite me and Karen Booth along for the ride. Thank you, Karen, for wrangling the three of us and our ideas and for being a graphics genius who can always pull our disparate visions together.

Thank you to Tasha L. Harrison, K. Sterling, Meka James, Lisa Kessler and the entire Wordmakers group, who cheered me on every step of the way as I wrote and revised this book.

Thank you to the phenomenal readers in my Reese Ryan VIP Readers Lounge on Facebook. I'm ever grateful for your continued support.

A special thank-you to Angela Anderson, Stephanie Perkins and Shavonna Futrell, who were instrumental in helping to make my previous release—*Waking Up Married* (Bourbon Brothers #5)—a better book. Your loyal readership and honest feedback mean the world to me.

One

"Good to see you again, Chef Travis." The valet greeted Travis Holloway with a wide grin and held up a copy of Travis's latest cookbook. "Would you mind signing this for my girlfriend? She *loves* your competitive cooking show."

Travis was tired and groggy after a long night at his restaurant in Atlanta and a nearly four-hour drive to Asheville that morning. But he would always be gracious. He greeted the younger man warmly, signed the cookbook and suggested they take a selfie that would impress the man's girlfriend. Then he handed off the keys to his black Dodge Charger SRT Hellcat Widebody.

Once the valet drove away, Travis turned toward the building in front of him.

Moonlight Ridge.

Whenever he returned to the luxury resort, nestled in the Blue Ridge Mountains, he couldn't help thinking of when he'd first seen it. He was seven. A social worker escorted him here, telling him how lucky he was that this estate would be his new home. And that his new "father" and "brothers" eagerly awaited his arrival.

His stomach tightened in a knot at seeing his brothers again now, just as it had that day twenty-six years ago.

After a long absence, Travis had first returned to Moonlight Ridge a few months earlier, because his adoptive father, Jameson Holloway, the owner of Moonlight Ridge, had suffered a brain episode. He and his adoptive brothers had been forced to come together, despite years of estrangement following a car accident that had changed all of their lives—his especially.

They'd committed to working together to oversee their father's at-home care and to help restore Moonlight Ridge, which had fallen into disrepair over the past decade. Over the past few months, his brothers, Mack and Grey, had taken the lead on overseeing the updates to the resort. They'd made vast improvements, but a lot still needed to be done.

The resort's food services needed an overhaul, and that was his area of expertise.

Travis climbed the stairs and entered the rotunda. Then he made his way up the grand staircase in the lobby. The elegant space still had many of its original architectural features and decor from when it was built in the 1930s. Travis glided his hand along the banister he and his brothers slid down as boys. He grinned, recalling that winter Mack had gotten the bright idea to sled down the stairwell.

It hadn't ended well.

Travis continued to the third floor, where the offices were located. He stood in front of his father's office, the door partially ajar, and sighed.

Travis, Mack and Grey, all former foster kids, had all been a handful. Each of them was dealing with their own brand of family-induced trauma. It'd taken time, but the three of them had become brothers in every sense of the word. It was the Holloway brothers against the world.

Until it wasn't.

The night of the car accident that had changed everything would forever be burned into Travis's brain. It was the night his entire life went to shit. The night he'd lost his family and, for a time, the use of his legs. It was the night he'd lost his football scholarship, his dreams of playing in the NFL and the girl he'd believed he'd loved more than anything in the world.

It was the night he'd been reminded that there were few people he could trust implicitly. But his adoptive father,

Jameson Holloway, sat atop that short list. He'd nursed him back to health, never allowing him to give up or feel sorry for himself. Always believing he would walk again, regardless of the grim initial diagnosis.

Like always, the old man was right. But it had taken him two grueling years to get there.

And though his body was whole again, he'd emerged from the entire ordeal irrevocably broken. He'd pushed his brothers away. Bitter over the loss of his dreams. Resentful that they'd come out of the accident unscathed, moving on with the lives they'd planned for themselves. Devastated over the girl whose betrayal had triggered everything that happened that horrible night. Angry with the world in general.

Through therapy, he'd worked out a lot of that anger. Since their father's illness, Travis had been forced to spend time with Mack and Grey in person and via phone and videoconferences. He'd been reestablishing a tentative relationship with his brothers. Partly out of a sense of obligation to their father. Partly out of his own guilt over how he'd handled the fallout from the accident.

He'd been wrong to blame his brothers, but he couldn't turn back time. Things would never be the same between them, so spending time with Mack and Grey in person still caused a knot in his gut. It was why he'd bailed immediately after Mack's wedding.

An emergency with the show had arisen, and Travis had taken the opportunity to delay his return. But now he was ready to get started. The sooner they got Moonlight Ridge running smoothly again, the sooner he could return to his life.

Travis entered the room and slipped into the seat beside Grey. "Sorry I'm late."

"Thought you'd changed your mind." Mack, who sat behind the desk, raised a brow. "I called. You didn't answer."

"I was on a call with a potential investor for the proposed New York restaurant." Travis imitated Mack's stern tone and cadence, causing Grey to chuckle. "But I'm here now."

Mack didn't find Travis's spot-on imitation amusing. His frown deepened. "Then let's get started. My *wife* is waiting."

"How is Molly?" Travis nodded toward the door between this adjoining office and hers.

He'd always liked Molly Haskell. Her father had worked at the resort, and Molly and Mack had been an item as teenagers. The relationship ended when Mack left, not long after the accident.

Travis was glad his brother and Molly had found their way back to each other. They belonged together. Not that he believed in soul mates or the sunshine-and-rainbows bullshit about love. Personal experience had taught him better than to believe that.

What he did believe in was mutually beneficial alliances. That was the best anyone could hope for in a relationship. And the relationship between Mack and Molly was equally beneficial. Or maybe sixty/forty was more accurate. After all, Mack "Know It All" Holloway could be a lot for anyone to deal with.

"She's doing well." A soft grin curved Mack's mouth.

For all of his alpha male posturing, Mack was a soft, gooey-in-the-center romantic. His brother had fallen in deep. If he didn't look so damn giddy—by Mack Holloway standards—Travis would feel sorry for him.

"She's meeting with our department heads. She'll stop by and give us an update, *if* we're ever done here," Mack groused. "I know you're living the bachelor life and you've got nothing but time, but our significant others have planned a double date for us, so..."

Travis felt a twinge of envy. Mack was newly married. Grey was deeply involved with Moonlight Ridge's wedding coordinator, Autumn Kincaid. When he'd seen his brothers at Mack and Molly's wedding two weeks earlier, both men seemed settled and happy.

But before the uneasy feeling could take hold, he reminded himself *the bachelor life* he was living was a pretty damn good one. One most men would be envious of.

He enjoyed glamorous events, luxury accommodations, extravagant vacations and designer gear—most of it on someone else's dime. And there was no shortage of beautiful women clamoring to be on his arm when he walked the red carpet at the opening of one of his restaurants or some social event. He had no reason to be envious of Mack or Grey.

His life was just fine the way it was.

"Then let's get down to business." Travis opened the document Mack had handed him and scanned the index page. Then he tossed it onto the desk. "I'll read that later while you two are…more pleasantly occupied." Travis smirked. "Let's just hit the highlights and lowlights. Have you discovered who our embezzler is?"

Since their father's illness, they'd discovered that someone on the staff had been stealing from the resort for several years. Uncovering the thief's identity was their top priority.

Mack frowned and folded his hands on the desk. "We're still working on that."

"But our forensic accountant discovered that most of the irregularities can be traced to food and beverage—the area where we need your help most," Grey added.

"So you expect me to revive the menu while working with a subpar chef who might also be the elusive embezzler neither of you nor your expensive forensic accountant could nail down? Well, that's just fucking great."

Travis walked over to the windows behind Mack that overlooked the property and provided a stunning view of the lake. He shoved his hands in his pockets.

Maybe if his brothers hadn't spent all their time pursuing romantic relationships, they would've found the thief by now.

"Let's begin with the obvious. We'll get rid of the mediocre chef and bring on someone with some real talent. Then if the current chef is the thief, we've solved both issues—the fast-food-grade menu and the embezzlement."

"We considered it," Grey acknowledged. "But Dad won't hear of it. You know how loyal he is. Hallie Gregson was Chef Fern's sous chef for years. When Fern up and left, Pops insisted on giving Hallie a shot as the executive chef. He believes she can become a world-class cook. Says she just needs a bit of—"

"Tutoring," Mack offered. "Which is what you do on those cooking shows, right?"

Mack had obviously *never* watched one of his shows.

"No, it isn't," Travis said impatiently. "I'm not a fairy godmother, Mack. I can't sprinkle pixie dust on this woman and make her a real chef. What I do is give self-taught chefs with *actual* talent the tools to achieve their destiny."

"Sounds like it came right out of the brochure." Grey chuckled.

Travis gave him the evil eye, then folded his arms. "Look, I want to help Pops and the resort, of course. But you're tying my hands and strapping a lead weight to my feet here."

"I thought you enjoyed a challenge."

Travis turned toward the sunny voice behind him and grinned.

"Molly. Good to see you." He hugged his sister-in-law. "And I do enjoy a good challenge, but I'm a chef and a mentor—*not* a miracle worker."

"*Yes*, you are," Molly countered confidently. "I've seen every episode of your shows. You've transformed self-taught chefs with raw talent and a complete lack of discipline into culinary superstars."

"That's kind of you to say, Mol." Travis realized that his sister-in-law was stroking his ego, but it was nice to hear anyway.

The chefs he'd mentored were talented but had a lot to learn, as he once had. He'd had a natural gift in the kitchen and had been cooking since he was a kid, after his biological father died and his mother went off the rails. Then at fourteen, he'd decided he could do better than Jameson's suspect cooking. So he'd honed his skills under the tutelage of Moonlight Ridge's former executive chef, French ex-pat Henri Bernard.

Each week, Chef Henri had shown him how to prepare a new meal. Cooking relaxed him. And as he became more confident, he'd enjoyed adding his own flair and turning a basic meal into something spectacular.

Travis had derived immense satisfaction from watching his father and brothers devour the meals he'd made with such great care. But he'd never considered that being a chef was what he was meant to do with his life.

"I'm good," Travis said. "But I can't turn water into wine."

"I realize this may be your greatest challenge yet," Molly said, undeterred. "But our current staff, including the executive chef, are well aware things need to change if Moonlight Ridge is going to survive. They're all big fans and eager to work with you."

That bit of information made Travis feel the slightest bit hopeful. A self-aware chef who recognized the need for improvement was the kind of clay he could work with. Still...

"If you could turn things around here, it'd be quite the accomplishment," Molly added. "It'd make for a great book. And I'd bet one of those producer friends of yours would jump at the chance to document the process for a limited-run show. It'd mean more revenue for you and for Moonlight Ridge."

"Interesting idea, honey." Mack rubbed his chin. *Translation: he hated the idea.* "But should we really advertise that our current fare is…substandard?"

"We'd also need to invest in a serious upgrade of our kitchen and dining areas," Grey griped. "Moonlight Ridge can barely afford the renovations of the main building we're doing now. Let alone the cottages around the lake."

A mutually beneficial alliance that could make Moonlight Ridge better than ever *and* expand his restaurant brand, Traverser. That was a proposal worth considering.

Travis already had eateries in Atlanta—where he lived—and in LA—where they filmed the cooking network shows. Then there was the gastropub in London. His sights were set on opening signature restaurants in New York and perhaps Rome. Molly's idea could garner investors for his restaurant group and for Moonlight Ridge, which would ease the financial burden on the three of them.

"Brilliant idea, Molly," Travis said.

Molly looked pleased. Mack and Grey didn't.

"Didn't you hear anything I just said?" Mack asked.

"Sure. You said, *Bad publicity, wah, wah, wah*. Then Grey said, *We don't have the money, wah, wah, wah*." Travis imitated the trombone-created voice of the adults talking in the Charlie Brown cartoons they'd watched as kids. "But to address your concern—by the time the show airs, the property will be fully renovated. As for the money, I'll run this by a couple of producer friends of mine. If they green-light the idea, I know I'll be able to raise the capital."

"You're talking about bringing in investors?" Mack stood, and Grey looked alarmed.

"Yeah, why?" Travis shrugged.

"You know how the old man feels about this place." Mack paced the floor. "If Pops isn't willing to make changes in staff, do you really think he'll relinquish control to investors?"

"He'd maintain a controlling interest in the place. The short-term investments would give us the money for renovations and the show would give us much-needed publicity. It's a win all the way around."

Travis sank onto his chair again and crossed one ankle over his knee.

"Good luck selling Pops on the idea." Grey chuckled.

"Now, that's a challenge I'll happily accept." Travis pointed at Grey, then sighed. "As for Hallie the Food Killer… I promise to do my best with her. If I succeed, I should be nominated for the culinary equivalent of knighthood."

Even Mack couldn't help laughing at that.

"I can't help you there," he said. "But you'll have Pops's undying gratitude and ours. Moonlight Ridge means everything to him, Travis. So I know you understand why saving this place means so much to all of us."

"Of course I do. The place means a lot to me, too." Travis's gaze drifted to the mahogany wood paneling and brass wall sconces original to the house. "I'll do everything I can to help save this place. I promise. In fact, I already have plans to meet with Chef Henri. Hopefully, he can help shorten the learning curve on some of the best local food suppliers and what diners in the area are looking for right now."

"Brilliant idea." Mack nodded.

Molly sat in on the remaining half hour of their meeting. The three of them brought him up to date on everything he needed to know to begin his monumental task of whipping the kitchen staff and catering operations into shape.

Autumn Kincaid knocked on the door as they were ending the meeting. She greeted Travis then asked if he'd be joining them for dinner.

"Wouldn't want to intrude on your double date. Besides, I need to head down to the kitchen and size up the staff. Then I'm spending the evening with Pops," Travis said.

"You wouldn't be intruding," Autumn assured him. "I made the reservation for the five of us. I assumed you'd be tagging along."

Tagging along? No thanks.

"Maybe some other time." Travis smiled.

Travis said his goodbyes, then watched as his brothers and their love interests walked toward the elevator hand in hand. He turned and headed back down the stairs.

Nope. Not even a little bit envious.

Sure, they all looked happy enough now. But relationships were constant work, and the payoff was usually disappointment, at best; betrayal, at worst.

Those weren't odds he was willing to play.

Unlike his lovestruck brothers, Travis would happily stick to his "bachelor life," get Moonlight Ridge's kitchen and catering services in shape, find the elusive embezzler then get back to his busy life in Atlanta and LA.

It was the least he could do for Jameson Holloway, who'd done so much for him.

Two

Riley George greeted the valet warmly as she exited her luxury SUV and handed the man her keys. It was nice being back in Asheville—the eclectic mountain town where she'd spent most of her summers when she was young.

During her two-hour drive from her home in Charlotte, Riley couldn't help reminiscing over those fun-filled summers at Moonlight Ridge and the boy who'd captured her heart.

But that had been a long time ago.

Riley was in Asheville on George Family Foundation business, not for a stroll down memory lane. So she would focus on the gala she was planning and all of the good it would do for an incredibly worthy charity. Not on the mistakes of her youth.

She stepped inside the enchanting little French restaurant owned and run by Chef Henri Bernard. Henri had been the executive chef at Moonlight Ridge when her family had stayed there. Ten years ago, he'd left to start a restaurant of his own. When the event committee had decided to have the gala in Asheville, Riley jumped at the opportunity to take the lead on it. Because she knew just the man to handle the catering: Chef Henri.

But Henri had called earlier in the week, insisting they needed to meet in person. So here she was with an uneasy feeling in her gut.

Riley followed the hostess through the charming restaurant that reminded her of the little bistros she frequented during her summers in Paris during college. The scent of savory sauces, fresh-baked bread and mouthwatering meats filled her nostrils.

Henri was seated in the private dining room with another man. The two of them were laughing. Chef Henri was still handsome. His salt-and-pepper goatee stood out against his warm brown skin. His shaved head was a good look for the gentle giant.

"It's lovely to see you." Henri's face lit up as he stood and gave her a *faire la bise*—the traditional French cheek kiss. "Thank you for agreeing to meet me here."

"Anything for you." She smiled at the older man who'd often spoiled her as a child with off-menu creations made just for her. "But I can wait until you're done with your meeting."

Riley glanced at his scowling companion, still seated. Her heart leaped into her throat. She'd recognize that face anywhere—even if it wasn't a regular fixture on cooking network shows. The features of his face had been branded into her memory.

"Travis?"

His dark eyes flamed, and she could practically feel the anger radiating off his dark brown skin. "Riley."

The detached tone of the man who'd been her first love sent a chill down her spine. Instantly, she'd reverted from a confident, professional woman to the teenage girl who was torn between the boy she was head over heels for and her disapproving parents.

You're not that girl anymore. Don't let anyone make you feel that way. Not even Travis.

Riley stood taller and offered Henri a warm smile that hopefully conveyed more confidence than she felt. "I'm early. I'll grab a bite at the bar while you two finish up."

She was in no hurry; she'd booked a hotel for the night.

"No need, I was just leaving." Travis pushed his chair back.

"No one is going anywhere." Chef Henri glanced between them sternly. "I invited you both here for a very important reason. All I ask is that you hear me out."

The beloved chef knew full well neither of them would deny his request.

Travis nodded, then hailed the server. He ordered a boulevardier made with King's Finest bourbon. Apparently, a conversation with her required a cocktail.

But how could she blame him after what she'd done?

Riley sat down and folded her hands on the table. She turned her attention toward Chef Henri. "Okay, Henri. What is this about?"

"It's about the gala." There was a pained look on Henri's face.

Riley's pulse quickened. "Is there a problem with the menu?"

"It's much bigger than that," Henri said. "I've been given the opportunity to open a restaurant in Paris. Something I have always dreamed of."

"That's wonderful news, Henri. Congratulations!" Riley squeezed his forearm.

Travis seemed pleased, but not surprised. He apparently already knew.

"Unfortunately, I would be required to go to Paris very soon, and I would be there indefinitely."

Panic tightened Riley's chest. "But that means..."

"That is correct. I cannot accept this opportunity *and* headline your gala."

Riley's head spun with a million little details. Like the stack of postcards she'd had printed with Chef Henri's face on them and the menu they'd created together so painstakingly.

"This event is built on the draw of a high-profile chef who'll mingle with the guests," Henri continued. "So if this will cause irreparable harm to your organization, I will pass on the opportunity."

"No. I'll figure something out." Riley was momentarily shaken from her thoughts about the countless phone calls she'd need to make. They'd need to postpone the event or perhaps cancel it altogether. "I'd never ask you to give up the chance to fulfill a lifelong dream, Henri."

"I appreciate that, Riley." Chef Henri gave her a grateful smile. "But I have a solution that could work out for all three of us."

"Wait…what?" Travis looked up from his phone.

Henri ignored his former protégé's question. His gaze remained firmly on hers. "Travis will be here in Asheville for the next few months."

Travis set his drink on the table with a thud and sat ramrod straight, his back pressed against the wall. "You're volunteering me for this…this charity thing of hers?"

"I'm not *volunteering* you," Henri corrected him, his voice stern. "It is obviously up to you whether you will accept the project. However, the serendipity of you calling to ask for advice on raising Moonlight Ridge's profile when I was just about to tell Riley I could not do her event… Well, that I couldn't ignore. Especially given how close you two once were."

Riley and Travis had hidden their relationship from their parents as teens. But Henri and Travis's brothers had been aware of it. And they'd kept their secret.

"That was a long time ago, Chef H, and you know how things ended," Travis said.

"I do. And it's time you two found a way to let go of what happened that night." Henri's voice was heavy with sadness. "More importantly, you are both smart, professional businesspeople. Therefore, you must see how ideal this collaboration is. Travis is a *true* celebrity chef. Your guests will be thrilled by the upgrade. In fact, I believe you will need a *bigger* venue." Henri looked at Travis pointedly.

Travis's eyes widened, as if he understood but didn't

like whatever message Henri was silently conveying. He didn't meet her gaze. Instead, he spoke directly to Henri.

"The mighty George family has never been fond of me. I doubt they'd want me headlining their event," Travis scoffed.

"Then this is your chance to prove them wrong," Henri said before turning back toward her. "Would your parents object?"

"I run the foundation, so my parents won't be a problem," Riley said firmly. "But even if Travis was amenable to headlining the event, finding a larger venue isn't an option at this late date. Besides, we're locked in a contract with the current venue."

"And between my plans for the next Traverser restaurant, my obligations with the cooking network and helping to manage Moonlight Ridge, my hands are full, Henri. While I'm here, my priorities are making sure Pops is on the mend and that Moonlight Ridge—"

"Jameson isn't well?" Riley had always been fond of Travis's father, the owner of Moonlight Ridge.

Travis gave her his full attention for the first time since she'd arrived. "My father had a serious brain health issue a few months ago. He's much better now, but seeing after Pops and getting Moonlight Ridge back on track are my current priorities."

"*That* is why I am referring this event to you." Henri tapped the table with one of his thick fingers. "It is a high-profile event that will garner press statewide. Is that not so, Riley?"

"Right. Yes." She took Henri's cue. "There will be lots of press coverage leading up to the event."

"And with you headlining, there will be national interest," Henri continued. "What better way to showcase Moonlight Ridge's new menu and the venue itself...if the event is moved?"

Travis rubbed his stubbled chin thoughtfully, and Riley's belly tightened.

The sensory memory of running her palm along his chin and teasing him about his stubble tugged at something in her chest. It cracked the lid on the storehouse of memories she kept locked away there. Sweet moments with her first love whom she could never quite forget. No matter how hard she tried.

The flashback of that fond memory made her smile. But then she recalled the pain and anger in Travis's eyes the last time she'd seen him. He'd looked at her as if she'd stabbed him in the heart and turned the knife. As if she was the cruelest person on the face of the earth.

And maybe she had been.

"Are we talking about changing the menu?" Riley's mind finally caught up to their conversation. Both men stared at her as if it should be obvious that a change in chef would require a change in menu.

"The recipes I create are proprietary, of course, *ma chérie.*" Henri placed a gentle hand on her forearm. "I thought you knew."

She did; she just hadn't expected it to be an issue.

Deep breaths. Working with Travis on one project isn't the end of the world.

More important, she needed his help. *Desperately.*

Given the flare of Travis's nostrils and the arch of his thick brow, he was well aware of this. *If* Travis agreed to help her, it wouldn't be in the spirit of letting bygones be bygones. He was going to make this as difficult as possible.

Riley swallowed her well-honed George pride and her own distaste for needing anything from anyone.

Despite her family's wealth and her healthy bank account, she was beholden to her family in many ways. She was thirty-two years old and the bulk of the money left to her by her obscenely wealthy grandfather came with two conditions. She had to reach the age of thirty *and* be married to a "man of independent means"—a requirement not made of her male counterparts.

Her grandfather and parents were displeased that she'd secretly dated Travis as a teen. Nor did they appreciate her gravitation toward men whose families were of modest means. Most of them had been perfectly wonderful human beings—as Travis had been. But two notable exceptions—one in college and one in grad school—had turned out to be as interested in her family's fortune as her family had predicted.

Her grandfather had lectured her about having too big a heart, which she wore on her sleeve. He'd worried she'd end up with some "worthless cad" who'd drain her bank account. So he'd added the marriage stipulation before she could receive full control of her trust.

Needing something from anyone—especially from a man—set her teeth on edge. But Travis obviously wanted to see her beg. So, for the sake of the charity and the hundreds of people it would benefit, just this once she would.

"Travis, I realize this would be quite an imposition, but this event is important. So if you could step in for Chef Henri, I can't tell you how grateful I'd be."

"Actually, that's *exactly* what I'd like to hear." Travis smirked.

Riley's belly fluttered as his eyes swept over her.

Is Travis implying that—

"Monetarily." Travis rubbed a thumb and two fingers together.

"Oh, yes, of course. Money." Riley's cheeks burned with embarrassment.

How could she have thought, even for a moment, that Travis had been referring to something more…*personal*?

Riley pulled a pad and pen from her handbag. She jotted

down the same generous figure she and Henri had agreed to. Then she slid it across the table.

Travis glanced at the number, then slid it back.

"Try again, RG. That isn't enough to make me get out of bed, let alone take on a last-minute project that I'd be revamping from scratch." He shifted his gaze to his mentor, who chuckled and shook his head. "No offense, Chef H."

"None taken, son. I taught you to know your worth and charge accordingly," Henri said. "But keep in mind that Riley is an old friend, and you would be doing this as a favor to me." He turned to her and smiled. "I must prepare your meal. Your usual?"

"Please." The tension in her shoulders eased. Riley loved that Henri took great delight in preparing his delicious coq au champagne for her himself.

"I will leave you two to work out the details. Thank you for being so understanding, *ma chérie*."

Travis drained the last of his boulevardier. "Okay, let's talk money."

Riley ordered a drink of her own, rattled not by the impending negotiations but by the man seated on the opposite side of the table who thought her a cruel, unfeeling monster. She hated that, after all these years, what Travis Holloway thought of her still mattered.

Three

"You want *twice* what we were going to pay Chef Henri?" Riley's eyes widened.

She kept her tone neutral, but her aggravation was evident in the stiffening of her narrow shoulders and the way her warm brown skin glowed red across her nose and cheeks. The same cheeks he'd once peppered with soft, slow kisses before he'd eventually kissed her full lips.

Travis fought off the visceral memory of Riley's heavenly scent and the warmth of her skin as he'd held her in his arms one summer evening when they'd met in the woods near the pond at the rear of the property. His back had been pressed against the rough bark of a red maple tree as she'd stared up at him and told him she loved him.

He'd wanted to believe that a girl as sweet and beautiful as Riley George had a thing for him. And he'd fallen hard, fast and deep. But it had all been an act. A rich kid slumming it with the help for a couple of summers. Until it had stopped being fun for her. Then she'd been ready to move on to a guy whose family had even more money than hers.

When she'd ended it abruptly, Travis had been gutted. He'd reacted badly.

"This is a charity gala, Travis." Riley's strictly business demeanor shook him from his daze.

"That's why I'm not charging my usual appearance fee."

"Right." Riley crumpled the piece of paper and raised her eyes to his. "Still, it's a considerable increase in our planned expenses."

"True, but if you go with a larger venue, you can capitalize on a considerable bump in ticket sales." He wasn't being cocky; just stating the obvious.

"I'd love to go bigger to take advantage of your *celebrity chef* status." Riley uttered the term as if it was distasteful. "But we're locked in a contract with our current venue."

"Where and when is the event booked?" When she told him, Travis nodded. "Popular wedding venue. They keep a list of couples on standby, so they can easily rebook the space, if needed."

Chef Henri had set him up with the alley-oop. Now it was time for the slam dunk.

"Alice, the coordinator there, owes my father a favor. I can get her to release you from the contract with a minimal cancellation fee."

"Even if that's true, it would be impossible to find another venue at this late date. My event is in seven weeks," Riley said.

"I just checked." Travis gestured to his phone. "Our grand ballroom is available on that date, so we can accommodate about twice as many guests as your current venue. I'll do whatever I can to help sell out the event and bring in additional sponsorships. You'll make back my additional fee and double your revenue."

"You're suggesting we move the event to Moonlight Ridge?" Her tone was incredulous. "I mean… I know the place was glamorous in its heyday, but I've heard… I mean… I'm not sure it's right for the kind of event I'm trying to put on here."

Travis tried to relax the scowl that slid into place the moment he'd recognized Riley. His heart had thundered in his chest as he recalled the events that unfolded the night of the accident.

When he'd first shown an interest in Riley, Mack had warned him it wouldn't end well. His brother had been right. But Travis had never imagined it would cost his family…everything. It seemed only right that Riley would help them reclaim some of what they'd lost.

"I understand your reservations," Travis said calmly. "And that might've been true a few months ago. But Mack and Grey have made vast improvements to the place in the past several months. And I'm here now to continue those efforts."

"The three of you are working on this…*together*?"

Travis narrowed his gaze at her, then thanked the server who'd brought him another boulevardier, courtesy of Chef Henri.

Riley and Chef H had been discussing more than just gala themes and dinner menus. How else would she know things had been tense between him and his brothers? Was she keeping tabs on them?

He certainly hadn't been following her. In fact, he'd tried to scrub Riley George from his brain.

Clearly, he hadn't been successful.

"I have fond memories of Moonlight Ridge, and I'm thrilled that you and your brothers are restoring it. But—"

"Moving the event to Moonlight Ridge is a nonnegotiable part of this deal." Travis had the leverage here, and he was going to use it.

"You're hijacking my event by making a change of venue a *requirement*?" Riley's expression went from apologetic to indignant, her nostrils flaring. "That isn't fair."

"*Hijacking?* That's a bit dramatic." Travis calmly sipped his drink, enjoying Riley's sense of outrage a little more than he should.

"You're blackmailing me into moving my event to your… your…run-down shack of a hotel." Riley folded her arms.

Gloves off, huh? Okay, let's go.

"First, 'run-down shack of a hotel' is harsh and categorically untrue, in light of all the renovations we've already completed, *Princess*." Travis used the term of endearment often employed by Riley's father. Something he'd teased her with when they were kids. "Second, blackmail implies coercion. I'm not *coercing* you into this deal. Hell, I don't even want to do this. But if you want me for your little charity shindig, you'll have to pay to play. And this, RG, is the price of admission. Double the booking fee, which you'll easily recoup, and make Moonlight Ridge your new, *larger* venue." He ticked each item off on his fingers. "Take it or leave it. I don't really care either way. Personally, I'm hoping you pass on the deal."

There was a momentary crack in her cool demeanor. A flash of what seemed like genuine hurt. Not that *genuine* was a word he'd associate with any member of the George family.

Travis glanced at his watch, then stood and dropped a tip on the table for the server.

"Let me know what you decide, but keep in mind that with the new renovations and Mack's new brewery opening on-site, that date will book out soon." He made his way toward the exit to the parking lot.

"Travis… Wait!"

He halted in response to Riley's voice, strung tight with frustration. When he turned around, she was standing in front of him.

His eyes trailed down, involuntarily, to her legs, which looked a mile long in tall designer heels. Her silk blouse revealed a hint of cleavage between her full breasts. A slim skirt skimmed her curvy hips and a small slit rose a few inches above her knee, revealing the smooth brown skin of her lean thighs. All of which made his heart beat faster. Heat rose up his neck.

Riley folded her arms and glared at him.

Had she caught him checking her out? Or was she just pissed because someone other than a George was calling the shots? The latter gave him great pleasure. Giving her the impression he was still attracted to her did not. Especially since it was true.

Riley looked *incredible.*

"I'll need to see the event space before I decide." Her quiet control had returned.

He was just another vendor to her; not the boy she'd once claimed to love. The boy she'd sneaked out to meet by the pond. Who'd taught her to fish and skip stones across the water.

So he shouldn't let their past cloud his judgment, either.

"You can tour the place anytime you like." Travis handed her a business card. "Just call to make an appointment."

"This is the number to the front desk?" Riley seemed insulted.

"Ask for Molly Haskell-Holloway. She manages the resort. She'll show you the ballroom space, answer your questions and book the date, if you choose."

"Mack's girlfriend, Molly?"

"Mack's *wife*, Molly," Travis corrected.

"I'd need to work closely with the chef…with you…on this, especially since we're revamping the menu." Riley tucked her hair behind her ear. "I'm sure Mack's wife is a very nice person, but I'm making this deal with you, Travis. Not the hotel or your family."

Travis groaned, then pulled a different card from his wallet. He handed it to her. "That's my private business line. Call me when you're ready. I'll schedule a tour with me *and* Molly."

Riley accepted the card. "If the tour goes well, I'll also need to spend a night or two at the resort before I can recommend Moonlight Ridge for lodging."

"If you decide to move forward, Molly will see to it." Travis glanced at his watch again. He was trying to instill the need for order and discipline in the kitchen staff. Arriving late to his own meeting wouldn't be a good look. "I really have to go."

Travis left without waiting for a response. Because there was no one on the planet he was less interested in than Riley George.

He didn't blame her for the accident anymore. Still, he'd allowed his obsession with the hedge-fund princess to fuck up his life once. He wouldn't do it again.

Four

Riley pulled up to the familiar stone fence and wrought iron gate with its welcoming Moonlight Ridge sign in black script. She hadn't seen this beautiful, historic property in fifteen years. Yet, despite fond memories of the place, she was filled with a sense of dread.

The horrible mistake she'd made one summer night had poisoned those memories and ruined so many lives and relationships.

It was good to hear Travis and his brothers were working together on restoring Moonlight Ridge. Learning of its decline had broken her heart. But she'd been gutted to learn what had happened to Travis and that the tragedy had caused a rift between the brothers. According to Henri, they'd grown apart, each brother blaming himself for the accident and burdened by the guilt. Each of them struggling with the fallout of that horrible night.

Like Travis, Mack and Grey, she, too, blamed herself. But rehashing the past was useless. It wouldn't turn back time or change what had happened.

For months afterward, Riley had been plagued by nightmares, the events of that night replaying in her brain. Each time it ended exactly the same. With Mack's truck in a tangled, bloody mess.

Riley inhaled deeply and tried to forget the ugly past as she followed the winding drive that led to the main building. Moonlight Ridge was a fine estate, if a little dated and worse for wear. And despite her objections to Travis strong-arming her into moving the event here, Moonlight

Ridge had the potential to be a far better venue for her *Great Gatsby*–themed gala.

The event would raise money for one of her favorite charities. One of the many causes her family's foundation helped each year.

Once she'd handed her keys to the valet and followed the bellman inside, Riley glanced around at the old place. There was something so magical about the ornate desk with all its decorative details that were a throwback to the 1930s, when the home was built.

She could still remember Travis telling her the story of how the original owners had acquired the front desk from an abandoned hotel built in the same period. It'd been transported there in the 1950s, when they'd turned their family estate into a resort for their wealthy friends.

Riley had always been fascinated by the history and architecture of this old place with its original lighting fixtures; stunning, regal staircase; and countless other historic architectural details that made the art and history geek in her giddy with joy.

She'd liked that the building was lovingly worn, like a favorite pair of old shoes. But to Travis's credit, there had been many updates to the lobby and exterior that brought back some of Moonlight Ridge's old Hollywood charm.

But would it be enough to compete with the growing number of luxury hotels in the area?

"Ms. George." A beautiful young woman with messy blond curls and mesmerizing eyes somewhere between gray and green approached with her hand extended. "Welcome back to Moonlight Ridge. I'm the manager, Molly Haskell-Holloway."

"It's good to see you again, Molly." Riley shook the woman's hand warmly.

"I didn't think you'd remember me." Molly's smile

broadened, then she asked the bellman to take Riley's bags to her room.

"You remember me." Riley followed the woman as she walked in the direction of the ballrooms. "Why wouldn't I remember you?"

Molly tucked a few of her wayward blond curls behind her ear. "Because I was an insecure kid whose dad was the help, and you were the glamorous Riley George."

They stopped in front of the double doors that led to the ballroom.

"I know it seemed like I led a perfect, charmed life," Riley said. "But things aren't always as rosy as they seem from the outside."

The other woman's mouth fell open and she seemed to be at a loss for words.

Riley hadn't meant to make things uncomfortable; she was just being honest. Yes, she was from an ultrawealthy family, but they were emotionally distant, leaving her feeling isolated. She'd often wished her family was as close as Jameson and his sons were.

"I look forward to seeing the ballroom again," Riley said, eager to alleviate the sudden awkwardness.

"I've always loved this old ballroom, but wait until you see it now." Molly beamed.

Riley glanced around. "Will Travis be joining us?"

Molly tried to hide a knowing smile. "He'll join us later. Promise."

Riley's cheeks heated. *Great.* Now Travis's sister-in-law would think she still had a thing for him. Which she absolutely did not. Despite how enticing he'd looked in that pair of dark-wash jeans and a button-down dress shirt that fit snugly over his biceps and broad shoulders.

Not that she'd noticed.

"I just need to talk to him about the theme and menu," Riley said nonchalantly.

"Of course. Right this way." Molly opened the doors and turned on the lights.

"It's beautiful." Riley stared around the room, her eyes a little misty. She'd attended her first formal dance there as a tween.

"It is, isn't it?" Molly seemed as mesmerized by the enchanting space as Riley. "It's always been one of my favorite places in the building."

"Mine, too." Riley walked through the space set up with round tables covered in white tablecloths. "It looks smaller than it did when I was a kid."

Molly noted the temporary walls that had been installed to divide the room up into three separate spaces that could be rented out simultaneously.

"We're having a luncheon here tomorrow and only needed this center space. But for your event, we'll use the room at full capacity." Molly grinned. "So, if you're ready for your tour, I'll take you through the space, we'll look at a few of the cottages on the property then we'll come back here and meet with Travis."

"Sounds perfect." Riley tried to ignore the fluttering in her belly whenever Molly mentioned Travis's name.

Travis followed the sound of Molly's and Riley's voices to the conference room. He gritted his teeth and tried to tamp down his conflicting feelings for his ex. Feelings he'd tried to erase long ago.

He'd lived in a world where Riley George no longer existed, and it had suited him just fine. So if he hadn't been seated when Riley walked into that restaurant, seeing her again would've knocked him on his ass.

She was still stunningly gorgeous. In fact, she'd gotten more beautiful. And while she'd always had an enticing figure, her fuller curves were tantalizing.

Don't even think about it.

Travis shook his head, trying to jostle the vision of Riley in that little skirt from his brain.

Riley George was a potential client who could help accelerate their plans to rebrand Moonlight Ridge and make it relevant again. She was a means to an end, as he'd obviously been for her.

Travis stepped through the open door and Riley's gaze immediately met his. An unsettling warmth spread through his chest.

"Thanks for meeting with me, Travis. I realize you have a lot on your plate right now."

"I do, but Moonlight Ridge is a top priority. So I'll do everything in my power to ensure this event exceeds your expectations." He accepted a document from Molly that laid out the specifics of the event.

He froze when he saw the name of the charity.

"You said this was one of your favorite charities." Travis glanced up at her.

"It is. They do important work and the organization is well run."

The organization helped teenagers who'd aged out of the foster system transition to life as independent adults. It was a charity he often supported, too.

Travis was aware of how lucky he and his brothers had been. Countless older kids in the system never found families. And transitioning to adulthood without a support system wasn't easy, so the work this organization did was vitally important.

"How long have you been working with this charity?" It wasn't relevant to this meeting or his ability to plan the menu. Yet, he needed to know.

"I began volunteering for them as an undergrad. When I started working for our family's foundation, I insisted we make it one of our top-tier organizations," Riley said.

What kind of head game is she playing?

She'd known that he'd come to Jameson as a foster child. Was that why she'd chosen this nonprofit?

"It's an organization that's important to all of us here, too." Molly placed a gentle hand on Travis's arm, bringing him out of his temporary daze. "So rest assured that we'll all work hard to ensure that this event is spectacular and goes off without a hitch."

Travis gave his sister-in-law a discreet nod of gratitude for getting him back on track.

So Riley and the George Family Foundation had a charitable streak. That didn't mean they were nice people. And it certainly didn't mean he should let down his guard.

Five

Riley settled into her room, obviously one that had been recently renovated. The classic architecture was still there, but the bathroom was updated, the bedding, window treatments and carpeting were new and there was a large-screen television in the room.

The resort was a gorgeous space that fit with her *Great Gatsby* theme. Her parents wouldn't be happy about her moving the event to Moonlight Ridge, but when it came to the foundation, she had the final say. She was at least thankful to her grandfather for that.

Riley's phone buzzed. She checked the caller ID and sucked in a deep breath. She'd hired a team of expensive lawyers to contest her grandfather's will, and she'd been eagerly waiting to hear from them.

"Devon, tell me you have good news." Riley didn't bother with small talk. She was paying this man an obscene hourly fee. What she wanted was results. Pure and simple.

The older man drew in a long breath, and a stone formed in the pit of Riley's stomach.

"I'm sorry, Miss George. I wish I had better news. But your grandfather made his will ironclad. He was of sound mind at the time, so we have no grounds on which to contest it. And believe me, we've tried to come at this from every possible angle."

Riley's pulse throbbed and her head ached.

"This is a bunch of sexist bullshit," she muttered, more to herself than him.

"I couldn't agree more, Miss George," the man said. "But the bottom line is that it was your grandfather's money to distribute as he saw fit. Now, there is some room to interpret exactly what 'a man of independent means' entails, but unfortunately there's no way around the marriage requirement."

"So your best advice is there's nothing I can do?" She sank onto the bed.

"Officially? I'm afraid so."

"But *unofficially*?" she prompted.

"Unofficially, if it were me, I'd make an *arrangement* with a man of means. Draw up an airtight agreement of your own and get married for one year. He gets something out of the deal, and you get full access to your sizable trust. It's a win for both of you."

"A marriage of convenience? *That's* your best advice, Devon? I'm not living in a regency romance novel. Why should I have to jump through hoops to get *my* money?" she demanded.

"Because until you fulfill the requirements of your grandfather's will, it's still very much *his* money," Devon Myers reminded her. "I'm sorry, Miss George. I wish I had better news for you."

"So do I." Riley ended the call and stifled the scream building at the back of her throat.

"Make an arrangement with a man of means," Riley muttered as she paced the floor angrily, her heart racing. "Is he kidding?"

Devon better not bill me for that stupid-ass advice.

She wasn't involved with anyone right now, and because of her busy work life, she hadn't been for some time. So where was she supposed to get this wealthy fake husband?

Even if she was involved with someone, a deal like this would be the kiss of death for the relationship. Her money—or their lack of it—had been at the root of the disintegration of every romantic relationship that had ever really meant anything to her.

There was the longtime boyfriend turned fiancé who'd ended their engagement when she'd refused to cosign a terrible land deal for him. College boyfriends more interested in her last name and family's bank account than her. The guy she adored who was uncomfortable around her family and friends. And Travis—her first love whom she'd ended it with because her family hadn't approved of him.

She obviously wasn't winning at this whole relationship thing, despite how perfect and glamorous Molly Haskell-Holloway believed her life to be.

Riley stared out of the window at the extensive property. The Moonlight Ridge estate was still picturesque and serene with all of its lush green trees that would soon be turning lovely shades of orange, yellow and red.

As a teen, Riley had found solace in hiking the beautiful trail around the lake. Sometimes she'd ventured deeper into the property to a lovely little bench beside the small pond in the woods where she and Travis would eventually begin to meet. Their initials were carved underneath the bench.

There's nothing fresh air and a little exercise can't fix.

It was her grandmother's philosophy, and exactly what she needed right now.

She'd change out of her business clothes and take a brisk walk in the woods. Maybe the fresh air and exercise would rev up her brain cells. Then she'd fire Devon and that bunch of useless lawyers and find another law firm that would be more diligent about getting her out from under the archaic parameters of her grandfather's will.

Travis changed into his running shorts, shirt and shoes. He honestly hated jogging. But after the two years of recovery required for him to be able to run again, he'd learned not to take it for granted. Besides, it always helped clear his head, which was exactly what he needed. Because Riley George had commandeered premium space in his brain.

He was physically tired after a long day, but mentally exhausted. He'd spent the past two days working with the executive chef, Hallie Gregson; the events and catering manager, Ross Barnes; and the kitchen and catering staff.

As promised, Hallie was eager to learn new techniques. She'd nailed every single task he'd given her. She understood that this was about saving Moonlight Ridge. Ross, on the other hand, was less open to change.

Travis got it. Nobody liked the implication that they were shit at their job. And grown men who thought they knew it all were particularly resistant to guidance. But he'd dealt with plenty of overblown egos. He could handle a guy whose pride was hurt.

Ross would just have to get over himself.

After stretching, Travis stepped outside into the crisp mountain air. He was staying in the same cottage where he and Riley had sometimes met. Being at the very back of the property, it was the least desirable, and often the last to be booked. It seemed ironic when Harry at the front desk had assigned him to this cottage. But now that Riley had waltzed back into his life, it felt like a cruel cosmic joke.

The universe was fucking with him, and maybe he deserved it.

Travis secured the door and took the path that went toward the lake. Riley George's words still rang in his head.

So you're blackmailing me into moving my event to your run-down shack of a hotel.

Maybe he had. And he wasn't sorry about it, either. The George family—including Princess Riley—had been a collective ass to him. He was doing this event as a favor to Henri, but also because he'd do whatever it took to help make Moonlight Ridge successful again. If he got the chance to relish the sweet taste of a little payback while helping out the people he cared about, all the better.

Travis picked up the pace of his run, his heart pumping harder as he tried to outrun the vision of Riley George in that cleavage-bearing top and hip-hugging skirt. But he couldn't; the image was tattooed on his brain.

Travis followed the trail, pushing himself harder than he had in a long time. Hoping the exertion would take his mind off Riley George. Finally, he came to a little clearing by the lake where he'd often gone to sit and think while he was growing up here on the estate. His gaze swept the property.

Much of the main building had been renovated, and they'd made several landscaping upgrades. However, several of the outbuildings were in need of repair and a fresh coat of paint, including the old building on the lake that was once a little café. It'd been closed since Chef Henri's departure. Mack's brewery would be opening on the property in a few weeks. If it and their efforts with the resort were successful, maybe he could convert the old café into a signature Traverser restaurant. It was something he'd dreamed about since he'd first become a chef.

"Chef Henri made the best Belgian waffles there for Sunday brunch."

Travis turned quickly toward the voice behind him.

Riley Frickin' George.

Because of course it was. Evidently, seeing her twice in one day hadn't been enough.

Be nice. Right now, she's not your ex; she's a Moonlight Ridge client.

Travis silently assessed the hot-pink tank top and black leggings that highlighted Riley's finer assets. God, she looked amazing. Not that it mattered. Because he wasn't interested.

Been there. Done that. Got the scars, the shattered dreams and a metal screw in my leg to show for it.

"You aren't stalking me are you, RG?" He was only half joking.

"Don't flatter yourself, Holloway." Riley plunked down

on a large rock. "I needed some fresh air, and I just kind of ended up here."

"Same." Travis picked up a pebble and skipped it across the lake.

Riley's soft laugh pulled his attention to her. Her beauty was stunning, and her soft smile and warm laughter had always filled him with contentment. But that was then.

"Think you can do better?" he asked with an involuntary grin.

"I know I can." She hopped off the rock and dusted off her bottom, drawing his attention there.

His cock tightened in his shorts.

Riley stood beside him on the shore; her floral scent—honeysuckle maybe—tickled his nostrils. She stooped down to pick up a handful of stones, then opened her palm.

"Three for you. Three for me. Best two out of three wins," she said confidently.

Travis lifted a brow as he studied her. He picked three stones from her palm, careful his skin didn't touch hers. "You sure you want to go up against the master, Princess?"

Riley rolled her eyes. "If you're scared, maybe you should call your big brothers."

"Oh! And she's talking shit, too. Yeah, I'm definitely down for this." Travis weighed the stone in his hand. "Ladies first. But try not to take this ass-whipping I'm about to hand you personally."

"Duly noted." Riley stepped forward, positioned her body sideways—in a way that gave him a perfect view of her mouthwatering profile. Then she pitched her arm forward as the stone went skipping across the water.

"Not bad, Princess. We've got ourselves a ringer here. You've been practicing."

She lifted her bare shoulders. "Maybe you should've asked me that before our little bet."

"Oh, now it's a bet?" Travis turned to her. "And what exactly does the winner get?"

Riley frowned, her mouth twisting. "I haven't thought that far. How about we make it a favor to be named at a later date?"

"Sounds open-ended as hell and hella dangerous." Travis studied her for a moment before turning toward the water. "But you're on."

He pitched the stone, skipping it across the water. It went a few feet beyond where hers had sunk into the lake. "Point for me."

Riley bounced on her heels, shook out her shoulders and rolled her neck, her ponytail waving behind her. She looked like a prizefighter preparing to enter the ring.

Travis couldn't help chuckling. He honestly didn't want to be amused by Riley George. But she was cute as hell with her competitive self.

Obviously, that hadn't changed. Challenging him to a run was how she'd first gotten his attention when they were teens.

She'd beaten him handily.

Riley pitched her next stone. It skipped on the water three times before sinking.

Nice, but not unbeatable.

He stepped up and pitched his next stone. It skipped three times, too. But it sank just short of the ripple where hers had.

Shit.

"Point for me!" Riley squealed, gleefully. "So this one is for the win."

Riley pitched the next stone and it skipped four times before eventually sinking into the water some distance away.

Impressive. But still not unbeatable. He'd done better.

Travis rolled his right shoulder, which still ached sometimes from the crash. But it locked up as he pitched his arm forward, and the stone plunked and sank to the bottom rather than skipping across the water.

Don't be a sore loser. It's a stupid stone-skipping contest.

Travis turned to Riley, who was pumping her arm in the air and doing a little dance that made his dick twitch.

"Congrats, Princess. You won." He wiped his hands together to remove the sand. "Good for you. I'd hold on to that favor for when we start working on your event menu."

"I'll keep that in mind." Riley rubbed her hands on her thighs. "Speaking of which, do you think you'll have some time tomorrow to work on the menu?"

"I'm booked. Got meetings with the staff here and with the network production team."

"But I'm only booked for one night. I was hoping we could take care of this while I'm here."

"Look, I realize you're accustomed to people dropping everything and rearranging their schedules for you," Travis said calmly. "But I was pretty clear about how packed my schedule is. So if you need someone who's more readily available, I understand."

"No, I'll just stay another night." Riley stared out onto the water.

"Great. We can meet over breakfast on Friday morning. I'm free then."

"Perfect." Riley offered a weak smile.

"It's getting late. I'm headed to my dad's house, but I can walk you back to the resort." He hoped she'd pass on his offer.

"I'd appreciate that." Riley started back toward the trail and he walked beside her in silence. "By the way, congratulations on your success with Traverser and your cooking network shows. You've done some amazing things, Travis."

"Thanks." Her seemingly sincere compliment was unexpected.

"When did you know you wanted to be a chef?"

Travis halted, narrowing his gaze at her. Was she deliberately being obtuse? When did she think he *decided* that this was what he wanted to do with his life?

"Oh, I… I should've thought… I'm sorry." Riley's sweet expression crumpled. She seemed genuinely horrified by her misstep. "Of course, I know the accident changed your career prospects. But you've always loved to cook. I just wondered…never mind." She turned to walk again.

Travis fell into step beside her. The silence between them felt like a thick, choking cloud of smoke. Finally, he answered her. Mostly because he couldn't stand the weird silence.

"I spent the better part of a year in a wheelchair," he said. "So it became obvious that I'd need to find another line of work. Cooking was something I was good at and enjoyed, so Chef H encouraged me to pursue it as a career. Besides, it was a way to burn off my anger."

"I didn't know," Riley said softly. She stopped and turned toward him with a pained expression. "I knew your injuries were serious, but I didn't realize you'd been confined to…" The indomitable Riley George looked flustered. She tucked loose strands of hair behind her ear. "I'm sorry, Travis," she blurted suddenly, her big brown eyes going wide. "I've wanted to tell you that since that night, but I never got the chance. It's been eating away at me all this time."

His shoulders stiffened, but he didn't respond. He didn't need the princess's apology, and he sure as hell didn't want her pity. Not then. Not now.

He'd done just fine without either.

Travis continued toward the resort, and Riley fell into step, despite his faster pace.

"I understand why you didn't want to see me at the hospital and why you wouldn't take my calls," she said, slightly winded. "But I'm sorry about everything and… Travis, wait. *Please.*"

Riley grabbed his forearm, forcing him to stop. He dropped his unsmiling gaze to where her skin touched his. She immediately withdrew her hand.

"I know you're still angry with me and that maybe you'll never be able to forgive me for that night. I don't blame you. But I still needed to say I'm sorry for my role in what happened."

Travis wasn't interested in revisiting the past. He didn't blame Riley or anyone for what happened. It was just an accident. But she'd been awful to him that night, and he wasn't here to absolve her of any guilt she might still feel over it. That was her problem.

"The main building is just up ahead." He pointed. "You'll be fine from here, right?"

She nodded, the corners of her eyes wet. "Yes, thank you. I'll see you on Friday."

He grunted in acknowledgment, then jogged toward his dad's, running as fast as he could, his legs and lungs burning. Determined to get all thoughts of Riley George out of his head.

Six

Riley stood in front of the mirror in her room, fretting over the skirt and blouse she'd chosen. This was a business meeting, not a date. Yet, she'd changed twice this morning and had put in a little extra effort with her makeup. Because even though Travis Holloway clearly didn't want to spend a second more with her than necessary, she couldn't help wanting him to forgive her. Or at the least not to hate her.

Running into him at the lake had been unexpected, but it had been nice to do something as benign together as skipping stones on the lake. There was even a moment when he'd actually smiled at her. Albeit begrudgingly. But then she'd needed to absolve herself of some of the guilt she felt by apologizing to him.

Clearly, he hadn't wanted her apology. Rather than clearing the air between them, her words seemed to dig up all of the pain and the anger simmering below Travis's cool facade.

Riley raked her fingers through her tousled waves, grabbed her purse and portfolio and headed for the third floor, where the offices were located. When she got off the elevator, the smell of bacon led her to the small conference room where she was meeting Travis.

"This smells amazing." Riley's stomach rumbled in response to the delicious smell. After a walk on the trail that morning, she was starving.

Travis stood, his gaze trailing down her body appreciatively for a moment. But then he frowned and returned to his seat. His eyes were glued to the electronic pad on the table in front of him. "Grab a plate, then we'll get started.

Hopefully, we can knock this out in—" he glanced at his all-black Shinola chronograph watch "—an hour tops."

Riley set her things on the table and grabbed a plate, her skin tingling from his brief but heated gaze.

Travis typed out the last of his notes from their meeting. They'd quickly agreed on a new menu, based on the old one. Next, he'd conduct a tasting for her final approval the following week. Then, they wouldn't need to see each other again for a while.

He was thankful for that. The sooner Riley George was relegated to the past, the better.

"I guess that wraps things up." Travis stood.

"I suppose so." Riley stood, too, and gathered her things. "I passed by the old café on my walk this morning. Are there any plans for it?"

"One day, I hope to reopen it as a Traverser Southern fusion restaurant." He'd admitted that only to Chef Henri. "But our priority is continuing to update the main building, spa and cottages. Plus, the brewery will be opening soon."

"How much would you need to make the necessary updates *and* open the restaurant?"

Was she hoping they'd finish more renovations before her event?

"We probably need to put another half mil into this place. I'd spend about the same converting the old café into a state-of-the-art restaurant by expanding the footprint of the building and bringing everything up to date."

"Are you looking for investors?" Riley asked.

His gut tightened in response to her question. "I'm considering it, but my dad isn't on board with bringing in investors. I'm still trying to wear him down. Why?"

"I might know someone interested in the opportunity." Riley shrugged. "I'll keep you posted. See you next week."

Riley left the room, her sweet scent trailing in her wake.

Travis's wayward eyes followed the sway of her hips as she exited the room. He groaned. He'd have to deal with Riley for a few more weeks. Then he could go back to forgetting he'd ever met her.

Seven

Riley took another bite of the creamy, delicious cranberry crème brûlée dessert that was the final sample of the menu Travis had developed for her event at their meeting one week earlicr.

The entire presentation had been fantastic, and everything from the cranberry orange roast duck and filet mignon to the duchess potatoes and oysters Rockefeller was absolutely divine. She would never admit it to her beloved Chef Henri, but Travis's menu was definitely an upgrade. The guests were going to love the new selections.

They hadn't sent out formal notice that Travis was headlining the event, but the news had been leaked. The charity's office had been receiving daily calls inquiring if it was true. Without even making the formal announcement, ticket sales had increased.

Henri had been right. Making Travis Holloway the star of the event was a brilliant move. They'd easily sell out the larger venue. She glanced over to Travis a few feet away on a call.

"All right, Pops. I'll see you and Giada for dinner about seven." Travis held up a finger, indicating he'd be with her momentarily. "Thanks. Love you, too."

Travis ended the call and joined her at the table, looking as scrumptious as the food he'd prepared. The crisp white chef's jacket and hat gleamed against his satiny, dark brown skin.

"So what's the verdict?" Travis asked.

"Everything was phenomenal." Riley finished the last spoonful of her cranberry crème brûlée. She should be stuffed. Yet, she'd be willing to arm wrestle her own grandmother for another serving of that creamy deliciousness. "You certainly live up to the hype."

"You doubted it?" Travis chuckled. He removed his hat and stuffed it in his pocket. "Any changes?"

"No, I wouldn't change a thing."

"Excellent. My publicist has been creating some buzz for the event with some of the networks. She'll connect with your PR person to iron out the details. If you need me for anything else, you have my number." Travis stood again. "Enjoy your stay."

"Travis, wait." Riley grabbed his wrist. He tensed, and she released it. Which didn't bode well for the proposal she'd practiced on her drive up from Charlotte that morning.

"Is there something else?" His voice was tight.

"Yes. Could we take a walk? I'd like to show you something."

Travis checked his watch—something he did constantly around her. "I have half an hour before my meeting with the catering manager."

They made their way through the lobby, across the lawn and toward the lake.

"If this is about decorations or changes to the grounds, that's a conversation for Molly and our groundskeeper, Milo."

"It isn't." Riley's stomach knotted.

"Then what is this about?" Travis pressed as they made their way toward the lake.

"I need you to have an open mind about this."

"About what?" Travis was increasingly tense.

"I've been thinking about your dream of reinventing the old café as a signature Traverser restaurant." She gestured toward the building. "It's a brilliant idea, Travis. I'd love to see the place open by this time next year."

"So would I." He studied the building longingly.

The old place held lots of fond memories for Riley. She could only imagine how much it would mean to Travis to open one of his signature restaurants there.

"Like I said, our focus is on making updates to the property first." Travis turned back to her. "We're all already pretty heavily invested in the place, and in our own businesses. So short of one of us winning the lottery, it ain't happening. Not right now."

A slow smile spread across Riley's face. "I can help with that."

"You found an investor?"

"You could say that." Riley's heart beat rapidly, and her throat felt dry.

"Who?"

"Me."

His expression of anticipation crumpled, then transformed into a frown.

Not the reaction I was hoping for.

"Not a good idea, Princess," he said. "No, scratch that. It's an absolutely *terrible* idea."

"What difference does it make if it's me or some random investor whom you seemed perfectly happy to accept money from?"

His nostrils flared. "We both know the answer to that, Riley."

"You're not even going to listen to my offer before you reject it?"

"No," Travis said emphatically. He turned and walked back toward the main building as she scrambled to keep up with his long stride in her four-inch, black-and-silver, Italian-made Kendall Miles slingback Siren pumps. A wardrobe choice she currently regretted.

"You're not being fair," Riley huffed.

"To whom?" He stopped suddenly and swung around. She nearly slammed into him. "To *you*? Because the George family has always been so fair to everyone they've dealt with, I'm sure." His tone dripped with warranted sarcasm.

Riley cringed inwardly. There had definitely been times when her father and grandfather had been complete assholes to get what they wanted. And the way she'd treated Travis… She hadn't been much different.

"You're not being fair to your dad or to Mack and Grey. To the employees here at Moonlight Ridge. Because, though you've made some improvements, if things don't turn around quickly, we both know the future of the resort is in jeopardy." Riley stood taller when his expression softened. "Are you really going to risk everyone's future just to spite me?"

"I'll find other investors. I just need time."

"Why? When I'm right here offering to give you what you need to complete the renovations *and* open the restaurant."

That got his attention. He stared at her, as if considering it. But then seemed to think better of it.

"I'm not interested in going into business with the George family," Travis said coolly. "That clear enough for you?"

Before he could turn and walk away again, Riley grasped his arm. She stood in front of him, unintimidated by his scowl. "This deal would be strictly between you and me, Travis."

"I suppose you think that's more appealing." He laughed bitterly. "It isn't. I remember how this goes, Princess. And I won't risk you pulling the rug on this deal when you suddenly lose interest."

"I deserve that, and I can understand why you're hesitant to trust me, Travis. But I was a kid then. We both were." Riley's eyes searched his, her heart racing. "I can't fix what happened then. But I can help Moonlight Ridge now. Please, at least hear me out."

"Look, I appreciate that you want to make amends or

something, Rye." He used the affectionate nickname he'd called her when they were dating.

It gave her a little hope.

"But it would be better if we dealt with someone I don't have a rocky personal history with. Besides, I know you're saying this deal would be between us, and I hate to sound grim, but if something happened to you while you held a stake in the property, as part of your estate, that stake would go to your family. That's a risk I'm not willing to take."

"What if I didn't want a stake in the property?"

"I'm supposed to believe you'd hand over the cash expecting nothing in return?"

"I would need something in return. It just wouldn't be a stake in the property."

Travis stared at her through narrowed slits, his arms folded. "What do you want, Riley?"

She lifted her chin and met his gaze. "A husband."

He stared at her a moment, as if he couldn't possibly have heard her right. Then he broke into laughter that began as a quiet chuckle but escalated to a deep belly laugh that had him nearly doubled over. Travis laughed so hard he nearly went into a coughing fit.

"You've got jokes, I see, Princess." He wiped his eyes, still laughing. "For a hot second, I thought you might be serious."

"I *am* serious." Riley folded her arms. "You need a million dollars. I need a husband for one year."

"Rich people." Travis shook his head, as if he himself didn't fit that description. "You think the rules don't apply to you. That you can do whatever the hell you want. I'm not a mail-order husband, sweetheart. But I'm sure you can find yourself one for a lot less."

"I'm not trying to buy you. I need your help. We'd be helping each other. Just walk with me. I'll explain."

Travis stared at her for what felt like forever. Just when

she was sure he was going to tell her to go to hell, he sighed. "Let's sit on the bench there. Your feet must be killing you."

"They are." She was more aware of the pain now that he'd mentioned it. "Thank you."

They sat on the bench and Riley explained the parameters of her grandfather's will and why she needed a husband for one year to gain full control of her trust.

He listened carefully as he stared out onto the lake. "There has to be some loophole. Have you checked with a lawyer?"

"I had a team of *very* expensive, highly rated lawyers working on this for the past few months. Grandad's will is ironclad." She sighed. "It was one of those overpriced lawyers who recommended that I strike a mutually beneficial deal with 'a man of means.'"

Travis rubbed his stubbled chin as he stared out onto the placid water. "I can appreciate your dilemma. But why ask me?" He turned toward her. "I'm sure your rich playboy friends would be falling over themselves to strike up a deal like this."

"I'd rather forfeit my inheritance than spend the next year pretend-married to any of those self-centered jerks." Riley shuddered at the possibility.

"Sounds like you should choose better friends, Princess."

"That's what I'm *trying* to do."

"Oh, so you're not just trying to buy a pretend husband. You expect us to be friends, too?" He was mocking her and enjoying every moment of it.

But as long as he was actively involved in the conversation, he was considering it.

"I'm not trying to buy *you*, Travis. I'm buying your cooperation with a *mutually* beneficial deal. It's essentially free money. No other investor is going to hand you a deal as sweet as this."

Travis's dark eyes lingered on her mouth. "It's not exactly free, Princess. You're asking me to give up an entire year of my dating life."

"You'd just be my husband on paper," Riley countered. "I'd append your last name to mine, but we wouldn't be sleeping together. We wouldn't even need to live together necessarily. And I suppose, as long as you were discreet about it—"

"I don't fuck around with married women, so if I'm wearing a ring and claiming to be your husband, I'm not hooking up with anyone else. And since we wouldn't be sleeping together, what you're asking me to do is go a year without. That's a mighty big ask."

"I realize that," Riley said. "But it would be worth it. You'd get to do all of the additional improvements here without spending a dime of your own cash or giving up a stake in the place."

"You're talking a year from now. I need to continue the momentum Mack and Grey have built *now*." Travis stood abruptly, as if he'd heard enough. She sensed he'd lost whatever interest he might've had in the deal. "Thank you for your very generous but unusual offer. But I'll take my chances with a *traditional* investor."

"I'll give you half the money up front." Riley shot to her feet, too, and grasped his elbow. "That way you can keep moving forward with your improvements. You'd get the rest on our one-year anniversary."

"It's a tempting offer, RG. But—"

"You don't have to answer today. Just think about it. *Please.*" Riley hated sounding so desperate. "Talk it over with your dad and brothers. This involves them, too."

"They wouldn't be the ones giving up sex for a year, would they?"

"No, they wouldn't. But I'm sure they'd be eternally grateful to you for doing this."

"Too bad that won't keep me warm on a cold night." Travis's dark eyes glinted in the sunlight.

"I'll buy you a year's supply of Vaseline and a subscription to the adult cable channel of your choice," Riley teased.

"I already have both." Travis winked. "Tell me the truth. Are you asking me to do this just to piss off your parents?"

"I consider that icing on the cake." Riley shrugged.

She'd taken pleasure in anticipating her parents' reaction when she announced she'd be marrying Travis Holloway. It would be like their dismayed reaction when she'd told them Travis would be the featured chef at their charity gala…but times ten.

"While I'd get a kick out of playing *Guess Who's Coming to Dinner* with your parents, a year of that shit is not my idea of a good time. Thanks anyway, Princess. Now, unless you have any other indecent proposals, I have a meeting in about five minutes, and I don't want to be late for it. Good luck on your husband hunt," Travis called over his shoulder as he trotted back to the main building.

Riley palmed her forehead and groaned.

Well, that went well.

This was a long shot, she realized. Still, the fact that Travis Holloway had *zero* interest in her offer, despite her million-dollar bribe, had taken a sledgehammer to her ego. Especially since she was still mildly attracted to him.

Okay, that was a lie. She was *very* attracted to him.

Yes, there were lots of other possibilities who would happily accept her offer. But she didn't want or trust any of them.

Her grandfather's will hadn't left her any choice as to *how* she'd secure her inheritance. But at least she got to decide with whom. And Travis Holloway was the only man she could possibly imagine doing this with. So she wasn't prepared to take her ball and go home. Not yet.

Time to play hardball.

Eight

Travis ended a videoconference with a producer friend and a cooking network exec. Both had been excited about getting behind a limited run reality show that followed the revitalization of Moonlight Ridge. They'd discussed the next steps and would send a camera crew out the following week to begin capturing footage.

He stretched in his chair, his legs and back aching from a long, busy day—most of which he'd spent on his feet. Travis was pleased with Hallie's progress. He understood now why his father wouldn't give up on her. She had the potential to be a really good chef.

She was independent and yes, she could be a smart-ass, but he liked her. More important, she was self-aware enough to recognize her need for improvement. And she soaked up everything he taught her like a sponge.

"Ready to shut it down for the night?" Mack stood in the doorway suddenly.

"Just about." Travis kneaded the knot he sometimes got in his neck from looking down while he cooked. In LA he'd taken up hot yoga. It felt like torture, at first. But it eased the tension and the aches and pains he often experienced. Some of it was occupational. Some of it was lingering repercussions from his catastrophic injuries in the crash.

Maybe he'd find a yoga studio around town.

Mack sat in front of his desk. "How's everything going with Hallie and Ross?"

"Things are going great with Hallie. Ross is a little more resistant," Travis said.

"Will he be a problem?" Mack raised an eyebrow.

"Nah." Travis shook his head. "Ross just needs a minute to adjust. He'll be fine."

"And how are the plans for the new menu coming?"

"Great, actually. Also..." Travis leaned forward, his elbows on the desk "...I've been considering converting the old café into a Traverser restaurant."

"A signature Traverser restaurant plus the brewery? That could really put Moonlight Ridge on the map again. What kind of timeline are you looking at?"

"Not sure." Travis shrugged. "Our focus has to be completing renovations on the resort. What's the point in drawing people here if the amenities are outdated?"

"I'm sure Grey would agree," Mack said. "But then again, I jumped right into opening the brewery before the renovations were done."

"What would I agree with?" Grey popped his head into the doorway, his dark blue eyes twinkling with mischief.

"Still a nosy, eavesdropping busybody, huh?" Mack furrowed one brow.

Travis laughed. He missed moments like this with his brothers. Since he'd returned to Moonlight Ridge, the tension that had knotted his gut whenever he was around Mack or Grey had dissipated.

They'd even fallen back into the habit of giving each other shit without anyone taking offense. He and Grey more than Mack, who'd always been Mr. Serious. Still, Mack was making an effort to let down his guard, and Travis appreciated that.

"I heard my name while passing by." Grey sat beside Mack. "What are you two up to?"

"I'm waiting on Molly. She's finishing up a meeting with Ross about the charity event we're doing for Travis's girlfriend." Mack smirked.

"Riley isn't my girlfriend, and you know it." Travis organized the papers on his desk.

"I heard you were doing an event for your ex. How'd that happen? I thought you hated her." Grey scooted to the edge of his chair.

"I never hated her." Travis sighed. "Was I devastated by what she did? Hell yeah. Have I forgotten that shit? No. But I also don't blame her for what happened that night." Travis looked at Mack, who'd been driving the truck. "Nor you," he added before turning to Grey. "Or you."

His brothers stiffened slightly, then nodded. Both of them seemed relieved he'd finally said the thing he hadn't been able to say all those years ago. That he didn't blame either of them or Riley for what had happened to him.

Something he should've said long ago.

But back then, he'd been too angry to let any of them off the hook. He was in physical and mental agony. And he'd wanted them to feel a little of that pain, too.

"Maybe you don't blame her, but part of me does. I still can't believe she had the audacity to show up to the hospital afterward," Mack grumbled.

"It took guts for her to show up there." Grey ran a hand through his thick brown hair. "She could've walked away and not looked back or just sent flowers. But she came to the hospital, devastated and desperate to see Travis. When you refused to see her, she kept calling to check on you." Grey shrugged his narrow shoulders. "Seemed like genuine concern to me."

"Enough talk about Riley, okay?" Travis said. "First Chef H ambushes me with a request to headline her event, strongly hinting that we should move it here. Then I keep having to meet with her. And today she actually asked me to *marry* her." Travis still couldn't believe it.

Grey broke into laughter. Mack didn't.

His elder brother tilted his head, one eyebrow raised. "Please tell me you're kidding."

"I'm dead serious."

"Wait, I thought you were joking," Grey said midlaugh. "You're serious?"

"Yes!" Travis said again, irritated. "Is it that remarkable that a woman would ask me to marry her? I get at least three marriage proposals a week in my fan mail, you know."

"Yes, it's remarkable." Mack steepled his hands. "Especially when it's the George family heiress who proposed to you. Has she had a thing for you all this time?"

"This wasn't a romantic proposal. It was a business one." Travis explained Riley's situation and why she was looking for a temporary husband.

Grey whistled. "That's unbelievably sexist. Is it even legally binding?"

"According to the expensive lawyers she enlisted, it was the old man's money. He can distribute it however he sees fit. Even if it makes him a controlling misogynist from beyond the grave." Travis shrugged.

"So she needs this marriage to claim her inheritance." Mack rubbed his chin thoughtfully. "What is she offering in exchange?"

Travis tapped his thumb on the desk blotter. "To finance the remaining renovations at Moonlight Ridge, including enough to transform the old café into a state-of-the-art Traverser restaurant."

"Shit." Mack covered his open mouth. "That's one hell of an incentive."

"And you turned that down?" Grey asked incredulously. "You wanted to raise cash, Pops is against outside investors and we're all tapped out with our personal investments. But if you marry Riley, problem solved. We'd be keeping it in the family." Grey's dark blue eyes danced.

His brother was enjoying this way too much.

"You are so fucking unfunny." Travis tossed a balled-up piece of paper at Grey's head.

Grey swatted the paper missile down and disintegrated

into laughter. "Would you have to take her last name? I mean, it only seems fair since she asked you."

"I knew I shouldn't have told you two." Travis dragged a hand down his face.

"C'mon, T, I'm just kidding." Grey chuckled. "Don't be so sensitive."

"I'm not being sensitive," Travis shot back. "You're being an ass."

"You're awful quiet about this." Grey turned to Mack.

Their older brother grunted and rubbed his chin. "I don't like that she thinks she can just waltz in here and buy herself a husband. Besides, hasn't Riley done enough already?"

"I told you, I don't hold her or anyone responsible for what happened. We were all just kids." The tension was rising in Travis's neck again. "But I do think her lingering guilt is part of the reason she's offering such a favorable deal."

"Then I say let her do it." Grey wasn't joking.

"And give the Georges a stake in Moonlight Ridge?" Mack asked. "Over my dead body."

"I said the same thing," Travis told him. "But this deal would be strictly between her and me, and she doesn't want a stake in Moonlight Ridge."

Mack's eyes widened. He leaned forward with his elbows on his knees. "So she's just gonna hand over the money, no strings attached? No way." He answered his own question.

"It's true." Travis shrugged. "She's willing to draw up a contract explicitly stating as much. But it wouldn't exactly be *free* money. I'd have to stay married to her for an entire year."

"A year is a long time to be tethered to someone you don't even like." Grey tilted his head. "Or are you still into her?"

Heat traveled up Travis's neck and his throat suddenly felt dry.

How did he answer that?

"No, I'm not 'into' Riley."

"But you are attracted to her." Mack said the quiet part out loud. The part Travis thought he'd been clever enough to conceal.

"That's immaterial," Travis said. "The marriage would be in name only, so I'd be giving up sex and dating for a year. Because despite what she insinuated, I'm not telling the world she and I are together and then creeping all over town. Not my style."

"Good move." Mack nodded approvingly. "With your visibility, there's no way that wouldn't blow back on you. She'd come out looking like the sweet, angelic heiress who'd been done wrong, and you'd forever be the bad boy who cheated on her."

"Exactly." Travis turned to his computer when it dinged, indicating he'd received another email. He'd had his fill of those for the day.

"Also, Pops would never buy a marriage on paper," Grey said. "So if you're going to do this, it needs to be legit. That means living together, eating together, sleeping together. That's also the only way he'll accept Riley's money."

"Why are you talking like this is an actual thing he plans to do?" Mack asked.

"Because now that you two are locked down in relationships, he can't stand to see me happily unattached," Travis said. He checked his email. "Speak of the devil."

"An email from the future Mrs. Holloway?" Grey raised his eyebrows and smirked.

"Shut. Up." Travis gritted the words out between clenched teeth. This time Mack laughed, too. Travis opened Riley's message. "Wow."

"What is it?" Mack's voice was laced with concern. "Is she pressuring you?"

"You could say that." Travis fell back against the chair, one hand clamped over his mouth. "She's upping the deal."

"How much?" Grey asked.

"Another 100K, payable on the day of the wedding. And even if things blew up the very next day, I wouldn't have to return it." Travis scanned the bullet points in her concise email.

"She *really* wants this. With you," Mack added. "Because I'm sure she could find some guy who would've qualified and is willing. I'm not sure if that makes me feel better or worse about the deal."

"Now *you're* talking like this is something I should actually do," Travis said. "Both of you have lost it."

"Any other incentives to sweeten the pot? A Tesla for your favorite brother or a house at the beach, maybe?" Grey joked.

"Neither." Travis stared at the screen.

"But she is offering *something*," Mack said.

It wasn't a question, and Travis was equally comforted and annoyed that Mack still knew him so well.

"She respects that I'm not down with hooking up with someone else during our fake union, so she's offering to… *consummate* the marriage."

He felt ridiculous using that word instead of saying what it really meant: *sex*. Riley was willing to take the relationship where it hadn't gone before…to the bedroom.

"Wow. She really does want you." Grey echoed Mack's earlier sentiment.

The three of them sat together in silence. Finally, Mack said, "You should consider it."

"A minute ago, you were pissed she'd come in here and tried to buy herself a husband." He parroted Mack's earlier words, mimicking his voice and making Grey chuckle.

"I know. But this is a pretty damn good payday for spending a year in the company of a beautiful woman you're totally into anyway," Mack said.

"So now I've graduated from being a long-term male escort to a straight-up gigolo." Travis shook his head. "Well, at least I'm moving up in the world."

"It's not like that." Grey's voice was more serious now. "I hate how Riley ended things between you two and that it triggered an unfortunate chain of events. But the truth is that we've always liked Riley. She was a genuinely decent human being who was nothing like her stuck-up family. Her behavior that night was an anomaly."

It was true. Even before he'd shown an interest in Riley, he'd liked her. She was sweet, thoughtful, funny. And she'd never treated them or any of the staff as if they were beneath her. But sometimes people changed, and not always for the better.

"Or maybe she finally showed us who she really was." Travis frowned.

"You don't really believe that," Grey said.

"What I believe doesn't matter." Travis shut the lid to his laptop, sliding it into his bag. "Now, I'm getting out of here. I suggest you two do the same."

Travis said his goodbyes, then took a golf cart back to his cottage. But he couldn't get the photos Riley sent out of his head. She hadn't sent some racy photo to entice him. Instead, she'd attached old selfies she'd taken on her cell phone. One was a sweet shot of him kissing her cheek while she stared at the camera, her eyes and mouth widened in surprise.

The second photo was of him holding her in his arms as they stood by the lake at sunset. She gazed up at him lovingly as he leaned down to kiss her. It was a photo Grey had taken.

Travis hadn't told his brothers about the photos. And

he'd tried to hide the feelings they stirred in his chest. Those moments with Riley were branded into his memory. No matter how much he'd tried to forget them.

Travis was starving after his long day at work and running a few miles around the lake. He'd taken a hot shower, gotten dressed and made it over to his dad's place—the house where he, Mack and Grey had grown up. He was having dinner with his dad and his live-in caretaker, Giada, who'd once worked for Moonlight Ridge as a housekeeper before leaving to become a nurse. Maybe they'd play a few games of billiards. He might even let the old man win.

He made his way up the steps of the wide, wraparound porch. It was a lovely end-of-summer day in the Blue Ridge Mountains. The temperature was mild, and his father's front door was open to permit the fresh mountain breeze to blow in through the screen door.

There was laughter inside. Travis knocked and his father's two golden retrievers, Trouble and Nonsense, met him at the door, their tails wagging.

"It's open. Come on in, son," his father called out to him.

Travis opened the door and stooped to pet his father's companions. Then he followed the heavenly scent of Italian food. His belly rumbled. Giada was an excellent cook. Whatever she'd made would be delicious.

"Hey, Pops." Travis nodded toward his father, seated in his favorite chair. "Hey, Gi—"

Travis stopped in his tracks. His jaw dropped. "Riley? What are you… *Why* are you here?"

"That's no way to greet a young lady, son." Jameson eyed him.

"Sorry, I was just surprised to see Riley here." Travis ran a hand over his close-cropped hair. His eyes locked with hers. "Hey, Riley. Good to see you *again*."

"Hi, Travis." Riley gave him an innocent little finger wave that made him want to both scream and kiss her.

Kiss her? Where the hell did that come from?

What he wanted was for Riley George to get out of his spot on his dad's sofa and out of his father's house. But Jameson Holloway wasn't above grounding Travis and sending him to his old room if he said so.

So instead, he sucked in a deep breath, cleansing any ridiculous thoughts of kissing her from his brain. Then he released the breath and forced a polite smile as he stared her down.

Riley George, what the hell kind of game are you playing?

Nine

Riley watched Travis do what she was pretty sure was some yogic deep breathing, which meant he was probably pretty furious at her for crashing his dinner plans with his dad.

But desperate times called for desperate measures.

Riley didn't need access to her full trust for herself. She lived a comfortable life with her salary and the monthly stipend from her trust. Plus, she had a healthy savings. No, she needed that money because two of the organizations she supported personally had lost the government funding that was the linchpin of their very existence.

Neither organization met the established criteria to receive funding from her family's foundation. And both had maybe enough money in reserve to struggle through another year or so before going under. She needed to secure that money to help fund both organizations while they sought alternate, sustainable funding sources.

So here she sat on the cozy, well-worn sofa of Jameson Holloway, a man she admired and had always been very fond of, hoping to convince his son to marry her for money.

Wow. Even in my head that sounds pathetic.

Travis sank onto the opposite end of the sofa and studied her carefully. "What brings you here, Riley? Did we forget something in today's meeting?"

His father's deep baritone chuckle drew both of their attention.

"Riley isn't here to see you, son. She didn't even know you were coming until we invited her to stay for dinner.

She came here to see your old man." Jameson winked at him. "No need to be jealous."

"My bad, Pops." Travis grinned at his father, then gave her a knowing look.

"Riley was telling me about that cranberry crème brûlée you made for her today. Had my mouth watering." Jameson chuckled and climbed to his feet, ignoring the cane Giada had made a point of setting beside his chair before she'd gone to the kitchen to finish dinner.

"I'd planned to bring you some, but the kitchen staff crushed the leftovers." Travis watched his father shuffle toward the fireplace mantel.

"Sounds like it's a hit, son. Let's add it to the holiday menu."

"You've got it." When Travis pulled out his phone and opened it, the photo of their first kiss filled the screen.

He'd read her email, and that photo was the last thing he'd been looking at before he'd arrived.

Hope stirred in Riley's chest, and her heart beat faster. When she glanced up, Travis's eyes met hers.

He closed the photo and typed something into his phone before putting it back into his pocket. Travis turned toward his father, who was flipping through a photo album.

"Is there something I can help you find?" Travis walked over to his father.

"No, I'm just… Here they are," Jameson said gleefully. He lifted the plastic sheet and pulled out two photos. He handed one to Travis, then held the other out to Riley.

She walked over to him and took the photo from his hand.

"This is me." She turned to Jameson, who watched her with a warm grin that made her heart dance.

"Sure is." He chuckled, moving back toward his chair. He sat down with some effort. "And that's Travis standing right there next to you. I think at the time he might've been ten or eleven. You were a bit younger."

"This was one of the children's day events you all used to have here." Riley walked over to Travis and showed him the photo. In the picture, the two of them stood together with about twenty other kids of hotel guests and employees. "I hadn't seen this photo before."

Travis nodded to acknowledge the photo, then stared at the one in his hand.

"Is that from the same day?" Riley asked.

"No, that's a photo of you at one of the dances we had here," Jameson said. "More accurately, it's a photo of my son here mooning over you like some lost puppy." He chuckled. "The boy was head over heels for you from that moment on."

Travis glanced over at his father, then at her.

Her cheeks heated. Chef H had known about their clandestine relationship. But it seemed Jameson hadn't been oblivious to their feelings for each other, after all.

"I remember that night." Travis's voice was faint, his expression wistful.

Riley couldn't help wondering what Travis was thinking now and what he'd been thinking the night that photo had been snapped.

Travis handed the photo to her. "You never said what brought you here this evening."

"I couldn't come here two weekends in a row without stopping in to visit your dad."

"And she brought the loveliest bouquet of flowers and a warm apple pie." Giada's accented voice floated into the room ahead of her.

The older woman's long dark hair was swept up in a neat bun. She wore an apron over her dress. Her dark eyes shone as she grinned at Riley.

"Did she?" Travis studied her with one brow hiked. "Well, that certainly was thoughtful of her, wasn't it?"

"It was indeed." Giada squeezed Riley's arm.

"My most vivid memory of your dad is him rearranging the flowers in the front lobby." Riley shrugged. "I was driving past a florist, and I saw this arrangement. It reminded me of that. I'd planned to pop in to see your dad anyway, so it seemed like fate." She ignored the heat that crawled over her skin beneath his assessing gaze.

"Well, dinner is ready. I made my famous eggplant Parmesan, so I hope you're both hungry," Giada said.

"Sounds fabulous," Riley said. "May I use your restroom first?"

"Of course," Jameson said. "It's just down the hall there."

"Meet us in the dining room when you're done," Giada called after her.

Riley went to the restroom, as much to escape Travis's heated stare as to wash her hands for dinner. When she emerged from the bathroom, Travis was standing in the hallway.

"Did you follow me to the bathroom?"

"What are you doing here, Riley?" he asked again. "If this is about your crazy-ass marriage proposal, leave my father out of it."

Travis placed a hand on the wall above her and leaned closer. Her heart thumped in her chest as his clean, woodsy scent surrounded her. Suddenly, it was much harder to breathe.

"Was I not clear about that?" she asked flippantly. "I'm here to see your dad. You know how much I've always liked him."

"So much that you haven't been in contact in over fifteen years." Travis's nostrils flared.

"Before I started planning this gala, I hadn't been to

Asheville in fifteen years," Riley said. "Our events are usually held in Charlotte."

Travis glared at her. "So this has nothing to do with your offer or the fact that you heard me saying I'd be here tonight?"

"Maybe that, too," she admitted. "But I would've come to see your father regardless."

"Did you tell him about your offer?"

"Of course not. I think you should consult with him before rejecting my offer out of hand, but I wouldn't take thc proposal to him myself. I'm not that manipulative."

"But you are trying to manipulate me into accepting your deal?"

Riley held up her thumb and forefinger, peeking through them. "Maybe the *tiniest* bit."

Travis removed his hand from the wall and stepped back. He folded his arms and his sleeves pulled tight over his thick biceps.

Riley held back an involuntary whimper.

Lord, have mercy.

Travis looked good and smelled enticing. And when she'd put her hand on his arm earlier that day, his strong, muscled bicep had felt so solid. She couldn't help wondering how it would feel to have those strong arms circling her waist. Or to press her lips to his.

"I'm the one who'll decide whether or not I do this. Appealing to my dad is only gonna piss me off," he said. "Got it?"

Riley nodded, her heart thudding. "I just wanted to be here in case your dad had questions. To reassure him of—"

"Your intentions for his son?" Travis lifted a brow.

"Something like that." She shrugged, then asked, "Does this mean you're considering—"

"I don't know what I'm thinking right now." Travis seemed irritated. He drew in a slow breath. "But if we do this, and that's a huge, monumental-sized *if*, we can't tell my dad about this arrangement."

"You want me to lie to him?" Riley really liked Jameson. She wasn't comfortable misleading him.

"It won't be a lie." Travis's stare set her body on fire. His arms dropped to his sides. "My dad obviously knows how we felt about each other back then. Since he went through all the trouble of digging out those photos and asking you to stay for dinner... He probably thinks he's slick with his not-so-subtle matchmaking."

"So that's why he showed us those photos." She smiled. It was sweet that Jameson wanted to see them together.

"So we tell him that seeing each other again stirred up some old feelings," he said.

Riley shifted her weight from one foot to the other as Travis stepped closer in the narrow hallway. "Definitely true."

"Good," he said. "Then maybe we spend the next month or so getting to know each other. If we can make it through a couple of months without strangling each other, we'll see where things go from there."

"I'm grateful you're considering my offer," she said. "But could we accelerate the timeline? I was hoping we could elope to Vegas maybe. And soon."

"I appreciate your dilemma," Travis said coolly. "But surely you can appreciate mine. I'm not spending a year of my life tied to someone I can't stand being in the same room with. So before I'll agree to this deal, I need to know that we're compatible enough to make a long-term, *non-sexual* relationship work." He stressed the word and her heart deflated a little.

Was he not attracted to her? Riley was sure she'd seen him checking her out on more than one occasion. At Henri's. At the lake. And just now, she was sure that there'd been heat in his dark eyes as they'd taken her in. She'd offered a bona fide, *consummated* marriage.

So why was he insistent that sex was off the table?

"Just take a breath and—"

Travis was midsentence when Riley stepped forward, clutched the soft fabric of his button-down shirt and lifted onto her toes. She pressed her mouth to his and he stiffened.

She cradled his whiskered chin, kissing him again. And again.

After the third kiss, Travis's arms slipped around her waist. He backed her against the wall, his lips gliding over hers. Travis angled her head, deepening their kiss as his warm tongue slipped between her lips.

Riley sighed softly, her eyes closed as her fingertips drifted to his back.

"Ahem."

They were both startled as they turned toward the petite woman who stood there smiling.

"Sorry to interrupt your...reunion," Giada said. "But your father needs to eat, and we wouldn't think of starting without you."

"Of course. We're sorry." Riley's face flamed with heat as she stepped away from Travis and straightened her shirt.

Giada looked at Travis then circled her mouth, indicating the colored gloss all over his.

He nodded his thanks, then stepped inside the bathroom.

"See you two in a sec. Then after dinner...have at it." Giada grinned before heading back up the hall.

Riley sighed, her heart still racing from the kiss that had set her entire body on fire and left her wanting much more from the man she'd asked to be her fake husband.

Travis washed and dried his hands before stepping into the hall and looking around.

"Giada went back to the dining room," Riley assured him as she leaned against the wall.

The sensation of how it had felt to be pinned between Travis's hard body and the wall sent a fresh wave of electricity up her spine.

"Looks like the plan is in motion." Travis ran a hand over his head.

"Excellent. I'll have my lawyer draw up the agreement and get it to your lawyer by the end of next week."

"Fine." Travis nodded stiffly, then held out his open palm to her. "Showtime?"

"Showtime." Riley slipped her hand in his and they walked into the dining room, greeted by wide, knowing grins from Jameson and Giada.

Let the games begin.

Ten

Travis stood in the bedroom of his cottage and rummaged through his closet. Which tie worked best for a dinner date with one's soon-to-be in-laws?

"I'd go with the dark red one." Riley leaned against the doorway. A mischievous grin curved her sensuous mouth, which he'd found himself preoccupied with lately.

"You're supposed to be waiting for me downstairs." He picked up the dark red tie and looped it around his neck.

"We need to talk."

"I know. I haven't signed the papers yet." He knotted the tie.

It'd been two weeks since Riley had kissed him at his dad's house. Two weeks since they'd been pretend dating. But he hadn't agreed to the marriage. Only to think about it.

And it was still very much a *maybe*.

"That's not what I was going to say." Riley trained her dark brown eyes on his as she tightened the knot, straightened his tie then smoothed it down his chest. His skin danced with electricity beneath her touch, even through his clothing.

"We haven't discussed our living arrangements," she said.

Travis lifted his gray suit jacket from the bed. He hadn't permitted himself to think that far ahead. But it was a pretty damn important question. Especially since Grey had pointed out that the two of them needed to live together if they had any chance of making Jameson believe they were really a couple.

"I certainly can't help run Moonlight Ridge from your

place in Charlotte," he noted. "But I imagine you can't run the foundation from here, either. So where does that leave us?"

Riley took the jacket from him and held it up as he slipped one arm, then the other, inside.

"The situation isn't ideal, but I can create a satellite office and work virtually from here. I can drive into the office a couple of times a week from here or Atlanta," she said. "You're the one doing me a favor, so it only seems fair that I'm the one who has to make the sacrifice."

"Will your family go for that?"

"I run the foundation. Besides, as long as the work is getting done, what does it matter where I'm working from?" She seemed to bristle at the implication she needed her parents' approval to work remotely.

"You'd be willing to move in here with me?" Travis glanced around the cottage.

The twelve-hundred-square-foot shabby-chic bungalow was in need of renovation. Perfect for an unpretentious bachelor who used it to sleep and change clothing between activities. But a lot less appealing for an investment heiress who was accustomed to the best.

Riley followed his gaze around the room, but her mouth curved in a soft smile. "It's adorable," she said. "With a few tweaks here and there, the place will look great."

That hadn't been the reaction he expected at all. He'd expected her to insist they move into one of the renovated cottages or rent something nicer off the estate.

Point one for Riley.

Actually, that wasn't true. Riley had impressed him in a number of ways in the past few weeks. He wasn't surprised she was running the George Family Foundation. She'd always been kind and empathetic. She'd been the most relatable person in her family.

But in the past few weeks, he'd gotten to see her working with some of the charities up close. She hadn't shown up in an expensive suit and shoes, smiled for the camera and handed over a check. Riley had arrived in sweats, sneakers and an old T-shirt. She rolled up her sleeves and went to work.

He'd seen her dig in the dirt and shovel fertilizer while planting spinach, lettuce and greens in the winter garden at a homeless shelter. She'd helped unload a truck and washed dishes at a women's shelter. All of it had taken him by surprise. But he'd been most impressed with how truly genuine Riley was with the people she dealt with.

She'd been sweet and gregarious as she chatted with a group of homeless men who were absolutely charmed by her. She'd held babies and wiped their little noses so their mothers could have an uninterrupted meal and a little time to themselves at the women's shelter.

The employees and clients of those agencies adored Riley, and he was beginning to see why. But he wouldn't allow that to throw him. This thing between them wasn't real, no matter how hard they sold it. It was a means to an end for both of them.

"So it's settled?" Riley smoothed a hand down his lapels. Her crisp, sweet scent tickled his nostrils. "After the honeymoon, I'll move in here until you're ready to return to Atlanta."

"Honeymoon? Is that really necessary?"

She folded her arms. "Unless you want the entire world to know this is a business arrangement and not a marriage...*yes*."

"We wouldn't be the first busy couple to forgo their honeymoon," Travis complained.

"But it will look awfully suspicious to the world and to my family if we skip it. I wouldn't put it past my father to contest the validity of the marriage."

"Fine," Travis huffed. "Then we'll go on a honeymoon."

"Kind of you to be such a trouper through the hardship of spending a week in the Maldives with..." She smoothed her hands down the sides of her body and turned sideways, showing off her profile. *"...this."*

Travis chuckled. Riley made an excellent point. Most men would fall all over themselves to spend some alone time with the gorgeous heiress. She looked stunning in a dress that clung to her incredible curves. The royal blue fabric looked brilliant against her brown skin. And her legs looked magnificent in her designer heels.

"You do look...amazing."

"Thank you." She curtsied. "You look great, too. Nervous about seeing my parents?"

"It's kind of early in the relationship for the meet-the-parents stage."

"Not when you plan on getting married in a matter of weeks," she countered. "And you didn't answer my question."

"Were you nervous about seeing my dad?" He countered her question with his own.

"No. I was thrilled to see your dad. You know I've always been fond of him."

"That's because my father has always liked you." He didn't need to say the rest. Once her parents realized their little princess had an interest in him, they'd treated him like something they'd tracked into the house on the bottom of their riding boots.

Riley slipped her hand in his. Something she'd first done the night they'd had dinner with his father two weeks earlier.

"I know tonight won't be easy for you, Travis. So I appreciate you doing this for me."

He tugged his hand from hers and buttoned his suit jacket. "It's not a favor, Princess. I'm a husband for hire, remember?"

"Right." Her eyes were filled with disappointment. "Well, I'm grateful, still."

Okay, now he felt like a jerk.

"I haven't signed the agreement yet because I need to know exactly what I'm dealing with here. Personally, I'd get a kick out of pissing off your parents," he admitted. "But I have a brand and a growing empire to protect. I can't afford to get dragged into a contentious, public family squabble."

"My parents won't be happy, but they won't make this messy and public. That isn't their style. They smile on the outside while they quietly plot their revenge. So there's that to look forward to."

"Great."

This just keeps getting better.

Riley slipped her arm through Travis's as they entered the elegant restaurant not far from the Biltmore Estate. They followed the hostess to the table where her parents were seated.

"One more thing," she whispered to Travis. "They had no idea I was bringing you."

"That would explain the shocked look on their faces," he whispered back. "Thanks for the heads up, *Princess*."

"Mom. Dad." Riley tightened her grip on Travis's bicep as they stood in front of the table. "You remember Travis Holloway from our summers at Moonlight Ridge. Before he became a world-famous restaurateur." Riley smiled at Travis with genuine pride. "And Travis, you remember my parents, Ted and Regina George."

"Mr. and Mrs. George." Travis nodded at them. "Pleasure to see you again."

Riley wondered how painful it was for Travis to say those words to her parents. But he was doing it. For her. And a huge sack of money. But she preferred to focus on the former.

"Travis, you've become quite the culinary superstar," her mother said after a few moments of awkward silence. A thin smile spread across her lips. "How nice of you to join us. Please, have a seat." She gestured to the other side of the table.

Riley slipped into the seat across from her mother while Travis sat across from her father, who still hadn't greeted them.

"So, what brings the two of you to town?" Riley asked, knowing full well what had brought her parents to Asheville after all these years.

She'd spent most of the past two weeks staying at Moonlight Ridge, just up the road. And she'd been making a concerted effort to expand the reach of their foundation here in town.

Most of the organizations they worked with were based in Charlotte. But in the two weeks that she'd been here in town, she'd been laying the groundwork to begin funding a few agencies in the surrounding area, including a homeless shelter and a women and children's shelter. And since she'd gotten Travis to volunteer with her at those organizations as part of the PR for the upcoming gala, the news had undoubtedly gotten back to her mother that she was spending lots of time with her former beau. A relationship they hadn't approved of.

Her parents had come here to guilt her into doing what they felt was best for her. Their seating formation was a dead giveaway; they were seated on the same side of the table so they could team up on her and convince her to see things their way.

Travis and her father were still staring each other down in silence. Her father wore a smug look of displeasure while Travis's expression conveyed amused derision.

If she had to declare a winner of their staring contest, it would be Travis by a landslide.

"Ted, you're being ridiculous," her mother whispered loudly as she poked him with her elbow beneath the table. "Say hello to the young man."

"Travis." Her father uttered his name through clenched teeth. "We have some family business to discuss with our daughter, so we weren't expecting you this evening. Your presence took mc by surprise." Her father smoothed a hand over the thinning spot at the back of his head.

"Your daughter is full of surprises this evening." Travis narrowed his gaze at her.

"I wanted my three favorite people in the world to sit down together." Riley slipped her arm through Travis's, ignoring the look of alarm on her parents' faces. "I did what I had to do to make that happen."

"Things are certainly moving quickly," her mother noted. "Didn't you two just reconnect a few weeks ago, when Henri bowed out of the gala?"

"We did," Riley confirmed. "But it didn't take long for us to realize how much we still cared about each other. We've been practically inseparable since then."

Travis draped his arm across the back of her chair. "It's been wonderful getting to know Riley again. She's a truly impressive woman."

His words felt genuine. Her heart swelled as she leaned into him.

Gina George gestured for the server to refill her glass with whatever it was she was drinking. Likely a gin and tonic.

"We're both determined to make up for the time that was stolen from us." Riley glared at her parents, trying to tamp down the anger rising in her chest.

Her parents exchanged a look that was part guilt, part indignation.

"The time you've spent apart has worked out well for both of you." Her father sipped his drink, then set it down.

"You've made quite the name for yourself in the food industry, Travis. Between your restaurant business and reality show appearances, I'm surprised you have time to gallivant around Asheville with my daughter."

"My father had a serious health issue a few months ago. My brothers and I are seeing after him and the resort." Travis's body tensed. "So Asheville is my satellite base for now."

"Traverser." Her mother pronounced the word in perfect French, which she spoke fluently. "That's French for *traverse, cross, pass through*. And, I believe, it's the origin of your name." Her mother gauged Travis's reaction.

"That's right." He nodded. "I've gone through a lot in my life to get where I am now. So Traverser seemed like the perfect name for my restaurant group."

"Interesting that you chose to use your given name rather than your family name for your company." Her father shook the ice in his glass.

"Dad!" Riley was angry on Travis's behalf. They'd been there less than ten minutes and already her father had managed to highlight Travis's difficult family situation.

"It's fine, babe." Travis dropped his hand to her waist and tucked her against him as much as their chairs would permit. "I'm not ashamed of being adopted or going through the foster system. Not everyone has the perfect, charmed lives your family has been fortunate enough to enjoy. Some of us aren't just handed a fortune on our twenty-first birthdays, Mr. George. We actually have to hustle and work hard to make something of ourselves."

Touché.

A vein bulged in her father's neck, and his forehead and cheeks flushed.

Riley held back a snort. *Another win for Travis.*

"On that note, perhaps we should order." Her mother

glanced nervously between the two men who continued to stare at one another.

"Yes, let's." Riley picked up her menu and handed Travis his. If they had their faces buried in their menus, they couldn't stare each other down.

They ordered dinner and managed to have civil conversation. Mostly owing to her mother's diligent efforts, honed through years of hosting dinner parties, and Riley's continual prompting of Travis to talk about some of his latest accomplishments. It was the most painful hour of conversation Riley had ever endured. She was almost relieved when Travis had to leave the table to take an important call.

"What do you think you're doing, young lady?" her father seethed the moment Travis walked away.

"Trying to eat my dessert in peace," Riley replied sweetly, putting down her fork. "But I guess you're set on ruining that, too."

"What's that supposed to mean?" her father demanded.

"It means I'm thirty-two years old and I'm sick to death of you trying to dictate what I do and whom I do it with." Riley folded her arms on the table. "So if this is the part where you forbid me to see Travis again, save it, Dad. It won't work this time."

"Riley Anne George—"

"What your father means, sweetie," her mother cooed, halting him with a well-placed hand on his arm, "is that you have such a big heart. It's what makes you the perfect person to head up the foundation. But when it comes to matters of the heart, your propensity for seeing the good in everyone can sometimes be a liability."

"Mom, I appreciate your concern, but I'm not an impressionable teenage girl. I'm a grown woman." Riley's voice slowly elevated, her frustration rising.

Diners at two nearby tables looked over, but Riley didn't care. She'd had enough of her parents' meddling in her life.

"There's no need to cause a scene, missy," her mother whispered loudly, her cheeks crimson as her eyes shifted around the space.

That was the George family way. Perception was more important than reality.

"I didn't intend to make a scene, Mother. But I'm sick and tired of you two looking down on anyone who isn't a blue-blooded trust fund baby." Riley shifted her gaze from her mother to her father, who'd leaned back in his seat and folded his arms over his chest.

"Well, I'm sorry if you think wanting what's best for my only daughter makes me a terrible father."

"I didn't say you're a terrible father." Riley rubbed her throbbing temple. "But it's presumptuous of you to assume you know what's best for me at this stage in my life. I'm not a child, Dad."

"But you are *my* child." Her father reached across the table and squeezed her hand. "You will always be my baby girl, Riley. I'll never stop worrying about you and wanting you to have everything you deserve in life."

"Everything *except* my inheritance. Because apparently, as the only female heir, I couldn't possibly be trusted to handle my own financial affairs." Riley stared knowingly at her father, tugging her hand from his.

Regardless of his feigned ignorance, she firmly believed he'd had a hand in the strange clause in her grandfather's will that singled her out.

"I'm going to the restroom." Her father stood abruptly and left the table. It was his way of signaling that the conversation was over.

Riley's mother folded her hands on the table and smiled sweetly, employing her bona fide Southern belle tone of voice. "I know it isn't fair, honey. But you *will* get your inheritance just as soon as you've fulfilled the parameters of your grandfather's will."

"I shouldn't have to fulfill any sexist *additional* parameters," Riley noted. "It was just Grandad and Dad's way of trying to control me. But this is *my* life, not theirs. So if I choose to see Travis, that's my business."

"I realize he's handsome and charismatic. A celebrity. Dating a man like that is exciting. Believe me, I've had a few Travises in my past," her mother whispered conspiratorially. "But sweetheart, that isn't the kind of man you settle down with. You're so kind and nurturing. I know you're looking forward to becoming a wife and mother. But if you keep wasting your time with these eternal-bachelor types, you'll *never* get the husband and family you want."

Riley groaned quietly without reply. Because as much as she wanted to refute her mother's argument, she realized she wasn't completely wrong.

Eleven

Travis had taken the call from his agent because it must've been important for the woman to call him in the evening. But truthfully, he would've taken one of those spam calls trying to convince him his computer needed repair just to get away from that table.

Ted and Gina George were even more pretentious than he remembered. He honestly didn't know how someone as sweet and kind as Riley had come from that brood.

Is the money worth putting up with a year of dinner dates with Riley's parents?

If the money was strictly for him, his answer would be a resounding *hell no*. But he was doing this for his dad, for the legacy of Moonlight Ridge and for the employees who depended on it for their livelihood.

Travis went to the bar and ordered another boulevardier made with King's Finest bourbon. The bartender made his drink and Travis stuffed a five-dollar bill in the tip jar. He sipped his drink with a sense of relief.

"I'll have one of those," a familiar voice said.

Travis's spine stiffened. He sucked in a deep breath and turned to the man beside him. "I thought Cognac was your drink of choice, Mr. George."

"Good memory." Ted grinned. "But I find that trying another man's preferred drink offers insight into who he is."

"Is that right?" Travis eyed the older man who'd always reminded him of actor Laurence Fishburne. More so now that he'd gone all gray and put on a few pounds. "I'd love to hear what you come up with, but I should get back to the table. Riley will wonder where I've gone."

"Travis, can I be completely honest with you?" Ted asked before he could walk away.

"You mean you haven't been?" Travis raised an eyebrow. "Because you've been pretty clear that you don't think I'm good enough for your daughter."

"I know you must think Gina and I are some uppity Black folks who've forgotten who we are and where we come from. That we think we're better than you," Ted said. "Hell, I'd probably feel the same way if our roles were reversed. But son, I haven't forgotten where my family came from. I realize how fragile wealth and power can be. Like every other parent in the world, I want my children to have an even better life than I had. And out of all of my children, Riley is the one I have the highest hopes for. She's got a brilliant mind and a compassionate heart. I know she's going to do important things in her life—as long as she doesn't get thrown off track."

Travis finished his boulevardier and set the empty glass on the bar. "And you believe I'm going to derail your daughter from her destiny? Or rather, what you believe to be her destiny."

Ted took a healthy sip of the drink, then studied the glass. "Not bad."

"The boulevardier—that's what that drink is called, by the way—or my observation of why you think I'm not good enough for your daughter?"

"Both." Ted set the glass down. "Don't get me wrong, son, I'm not implying you're a bad person, and I don't believe you would intentionally harm my daughter. But when you live a certain kind of a life…things happen. Like that horrible accident you and your brothers were in. What if my daughter had been in that truck? She could've been seriously hurt. Maybe worse."

A knot tightened in Travis's gut. He'd gone to that restaurant to get an explanation from Riley, hoping she'd return to Moonlight Ridge with him. What if she had?

It had taken him more than a decade to admit that he needed to talk to a professional about the pent-up anger he had regarding the accident. To finally forgive himself for his immaturity that night that had put nearly everyone he'd loved in jeopardy. For him to stop laying blame at the feet of Riley and his brothers. But if something had happened to her or to Mack and Grey, he would never have forgiven himself.

"That was a long time ago, Mr. George," Travis said finally. "I'm not that hotheaded kid anymore. Believe me, if I was, our conversation earlier would've gone differently. I held my tongue because while it might've made me feel better to tell you what I think of your opinion of me and where you can stick it, it would've hurt Riley. And that's not something I want to do."

The man frowned. "I appreciate that you've settled down somewhat, but now, just as then, my daughter is in over her head with a man like you. I regret how I broke you two up back then. Threatening to destroy your family's livelihood and reputation… To be honest, I feel bad about that. But my reasons for doing so were—"

"Hold up. *You* broke us up?" Travis pointed an accusatory finger. "As in, it wasn't Riley's idea to break up with me? You put her up to it by threatening my family?"

Heat flooded Travis's face. His shoulders stiffened, and his hands clenched so tightly that his short nails stabbed his palms, threatening to break the skin.

"What kind of man would do something so awful to his teenage daughter?" Travis's voice trembled as he tried to maintain his cool. He wanted to punch this pretentious asshole and leave him sprawled out on his back. Maybe knock loose a few of those brilliant white teeth.

"I'm not proud of what I did, son." The man's skin

flushed as Travis's elevated voice drew the attention of the bartender and a few other patrons. "But I did what I did in the best interest of my daughter, so I won't apologize for it. If that's what I had to do to save her from a life of..." Ted's words trailed off. He ran a hand over his thinning hair. "Well, I'd do it again."

"I honestly don't know how your daughter managed to become such a decent, compassionate human being when she was raised by a heartless, self-centered egomaniac."

"It's what you do to protect your family. If you wouldn't go to the same lengths to protect yours, it only proves you're not the man I want for my daughter." Ted calmly finished his drink.

"People like to believe you can play nice and still get everything you want in life. It's a load of hippie bullshit," the older man continued. "A word of advice. Shit rolls downhill, son. If you're not willing to take what you want in this world and do whatever you have to do to defend it, then you'll never climb to the top of the heap. And if you do manage to somehow rise to the top, you won't stay there for long."

"Thanks, but no thanks, for your unsolicited advice. If I have to forgo human decency to claw my way to the top, I'm happy to stay where I am."

Despite Travis's celebrity status and business success, Ted George's net worth made him look like a pauper. And regardless of what he'd achieved in his life, Mr. George obviously still saw him as that abandoned foster kid Jameson Holloway had taken in. Maybe he always would. That was Ted's problem, not his. He wouldn't waste a moment trying to convince him otherwise.

"Have a good night, Mr. George." Travis leaned in, lowering his voice so only Ted could hear him. "And by that we both know I really mean go fuck yourself."

Travis turned and stalked toward their table. Riley's hopeful smile quickly turned into a tense frown as he approached. He felt bad for being the reason she suddenly looked stressed.

He forced a smile as he addressed her mother.

"Mrs. George, it was a pleasure to see you again, but I'm afraid another matter requires my attention." He turned toward Riley. "Are you leaving with me, babe, or would you prefer to stay and enjoy dessert with your parents? If so, I can send a driver back for you."

"No, I'm ready to go home." Riley stood, her eyes studying his as she grabbed her purse.

"Home?" Gina's eyes widened. "You two are living *together*?"

"Yes," they both proclaimed without hesitation, their eyes meeting.

"That's why I brought Travis tonight." Riley turned to her mother. "To tell you things are moving quickly between us. We've already lost so much time together."

"It was good seeing you again, Mrs. George." Travis dropped three crisp hundred-dollar bills on the table. Enough to cover the entire bill and leave their server a generous tip. He didn't want anything from Ted George. Not even dinner.

He took Riley's hand and they made their way to the valet outside without a word. When the valet left to retrieve Travis's car, she turned to face him.

"My father must've really pissed you off if you were willing to tell my parents we're living together." She looked up at him, her big brown eyes dripping with apology. "I'm sorry for what he said at the table and for whatever he said to make you so—"

"You don't need to apologize for your dad, Rye." His heart still thudded in his chest and his shoulders were tense. "And I'd rather not talk about what your father said right now."

"Whatever you want. I'm just glad that after tonight you're still considering my offer."

"We'll talk more about that later, too." He still hadn't decided what he planned to do. "How about we talk about it back at *our* place, since we're apparently living together now?"

He still couldn't believe he'd stepped into that one. But he was so pissed at Ted and annoyed with Gina that it had given him a perverse sense of joy to tell him off and shock her.

"I said *home* inadvertently. But when my mother questioned it, I couldn't help turning the knife a little. It was immature, and I'm sorry I dragged you into it."

"I get it. My reasons for going along with it were pretty much the same." He shrugged.

"It wasn't exactly a lie," she said, glancing around them fondly. "Being here in Asheville… I feel more at home than I've felt in a long time. It's different from when we were kids, but I love the laid-back vibe and the amazing art scene. The historic architecture at places like the Basilica, Moonlight Ridge and the Biltmore." She gestured toward the grand estate in the distance. "I've found this incredible joy here."

"Were you unhappy before?" Travis studied her warm brown eyes.

"I never thought of myself as being *unhappy*." Riley shrugged. "I have a good life. I'm doing important work. I'm in good health. I don't have cause to complain."

"That isn't an answer." Travis lifted a hand to her cheek.

"No, it isn't." She gave him a sad smile. "I've been happier here the past few weeks than I've been in a while. How's that?"

"Fair enough." He could relate to that.

Travis helped Riley inside the car when it arrived. He tried not to notice how the hem of her dress rose a few inches as she slid into her seat, but he couldn't help himself. Nor could he help noting that his feelings toward her had changed considerably.

This is just a business deal.

Travis repeated the words in his head again and again. It was a reality he couldn't afford to forget. Otherwise he might be in serious danger of falling for the princess who'd once captured his heart.

Twelve

Riley padded around the cottage barefoot while Travis was upstairs taking another call from his agent. She couldn't believe he was staying in the same cottage they'd made out in a few times as teens. At the time, she hadn't been ready to take things further. Travis had been the perfect gentleman, never pressuring her for anything more.

Riley often regretted that Travis hadn't been her first instead of the impatient, subpar oaf she'd given her virginity to in college.

Travis trotted down the stairs, barefoot, tugging his shirt down over his rather impressive abs. The imprint in his gray sweatpants offered a hint of what lay beneath.

A quiet sigh escaped her mouth and she sank her teeth into her lower lip.

Travis's food isn't the only thing about him that's mouthwatering.

"Sorry to keep you waiting." He went straight for the little bar in the corner of the room. "With the rising popularity of the gastropub in London, my agent is pushing me to do a guest spot on a cooking network in the UK."

"Sounds like a great opportunity." Riley watched as Travis made a rum and Coke.

"It is." He handed it to her, then started making another. "But I have a lot going on right now with the show, the resort and the business. And apparently I've acquired a fiancée."

Riley was sipping her drink and wondering if he'd take the UK op when his words finally registered. She put down her glass. "Does that mean you accept my proposal?"

He climbed on one of the barstools and patted the other.

She sat beside him, as he'd silently requested. Something in his dark eyes gave her pause.

Travis studied his glass. "Why didn't you tell me what really happened that night?"

Riley's pulse quickened. Travis didn't need to specify which night. She thought of everything in her life as happening either before or after *that* night.

"My dad told you?" She could strangle her father. No wonder Travis couldn't wait to get out of there. Her father had the audacity to gloat about his role in the events of that night.

"That he threatened to destroy my family if you didn't walk away?" Travis gripped his glass so tightly she feared he'd shatter it. Riley placed a gentle hand on his forearm, and he loosened his grasp. He sucked in a deep breath, then sighed. "I knew your dad didn't want us to see each other, but I never imagined he'd do something so underhanded."

Behind the scenes, Ted George did whatever it took to get what he wanted. But he carefully cultivated his image as a generous family man who was a pillar of the community. So Riley was surprised he'd admitted to blackmailing his own daughter. He'd evidently wanted Travis to know he wasn't above stooping so low again.

"Said he felt bad about it in one breath, then told me he'd do it again in a heartbeat with the next." Travis gulped his rum and Coke.

The pain in his voice made Riley's heart ache. Her father was an asshole, and she planned to tell him as much—in person—in the morning.

"I'm sorry I couldn't tell you the truth then, and I'm sorry my father was so horrible to you…then and now. I wouldn't blame you for hating my family. Nor would I blame you for deciding you don't want to do this."

He looked at her, his head cocked as if seeing her clearly

for the first time. Travis tugged Riley off her stool so that she stood between his widened legs. His eyes met hers.

"I should've known that note you wrote and the way you reacted at the restaurant… That wasn't the girl I'd fallen in love with." He cupped her cheek and offered a pained smile. "I'm sorry I believed the worst of you."

"Don't be." Tears stung her eyes as she recalled the horrible choice she'd been forced to make. What had hurt most was knowing she'd hurt him and he'd hate her for it. That all of the beautiful memories they'd created would be destroyed. "That's exactly what my father wanted you to believe. He wanted you to be hurt, and he wanted me to be the one to do it. He knew if I wounded your pride you wouldn't want anything else to do with me."

"I spent so many years blaming you for what happened," he said finally. "But the truth is it was all my fault."

"It was an accident, Travis. It could've happened to any one of us. We've spent enough time blaming ourselves. Time that would've been better spent helping each other recover. Physically, mentally, emotionally." The tears that burned her eyes spilled down her cheeks. Her face was hot with embarrassment. "I know your world was turned upside down that night, Travis. But so was mine."

He handed her a cocktail napkin and she dabbed her tears.

"Why was that night so devastating for you?" His expression was pained and his question sincere. "You got to go on with your life as if nothing had ever happened. You moved on."

"I didn't just move on," she protested, fresh tears welling in her eyes.

What right did the poor little rich girl whose asshole father had precipitated the entire mess have to shed tears over what she'd lost that night?

Yet, she'd been devastated.

Every rejection by Travis after the crash sank her deeper into depression. When she'd overheard her parents discussing whether they should send her away to a hospital facility, fearing she might harm herself, she'd realized how deeply she'd sunk into the abyss. She'd finally admitted that she'd needed to see a mental health professional. It was her only hope of climbing out of the dark hole she'd fallen into. But there was no need to burden him with any of that.

"I couldn't bear that our last conversation was me telling you I didn't want you in my life anymore." She dabbed the rapidly falling tears. "Nothing could've been further from the truth."

Travis stood, wrapping her in his strong arms. He held her, her tears wetting his shirt.

Riley felt foolish making a spectacle of herself. But she couldn't ever remember feeling safer than she felt in Travis's arms now.

He let her cry, his large hand rubbing slow circles on her back. Finally, he said, "So about this proposal of yours. I'll do it. But that additional 100K won't be a gift. Let's establish it as a line of credit. I'm not looking to take advantage of you here, Riley. This deal should be mutually beneficial to all parties."

Riley was stunned by his insistence on repaying the bonus. It was more than fair in light of the long-term commitment required. He was a busy celebrity, and his time was valuable. She realized that. Besides, that money was a small percentage of her sizable inheritance.

"Thank you, Travis. But you don't need to—"

"I know, and I appreciate it." Travis shoved his hands in his pockets, which inadvertently highlighted the impressive imprint in those otherwise innocuous gray sweatpants.

A chill ran down her spine and her nipples beaded in response.

"So how do we do this?" he asked.

Wow. Travis had actually agreed to her marriage-of-convenience scheme. She'd worked so hard to get to this point that she hadn't given much thought to what happened next.

"We…get engaged?" It was more of a question than a plan.

"Okay. When do we announce it?"

"My focus needs to be on the gala for the next few weeks. But soon after?"

"All right." Travis moved behind the bar and refreshed their drinks. "And since you told your mother we're living together, I assume you'll be moving in here right away."

Riley couldn't believe she'd said that to her mother or that Travis had been gracious enough to play along.

"I understand if you're not ready for that yet," she said. "Maybe I could rent a nearby cottage. We could just say I'm living here." She accepted the refreshed drink from Travis.

"My father would find out. We need to convince him this relationship is real, too," he reminded her. "So you'll need to move in here."

Travis stated it without emotion, as a simple fact.

"When you check out on Sunday, bring your bags here. As for sleeping arrangements… Only the master bedroom has a bed in it. The second bedroom only has a desk. You take the bed. I'll sleep on the couch until I can get another bed for the guest room."

Riley should be grateful for his gentlemanly offer. Instead, she was disappointed and couldn't help noticing the way his shirt clung to his well-developed chest. Nor could she help eyeing the dickprint in his sweatpants.

God, she was awful.

"I won't put you out of your own bed, Travis. Why can't we just share it?"

He assessed her wearily. "You're sure about this?"

"It's a California king-size bed," she said. "We could

both spread out like starfish and barely touch...if we didn't want to."

But I definitely want to.

She gulped some of her drink, hoping to drown out the too-honest voice in her head.

"All right," Travis agreed. "And I have a double master at my place in Atlanta."

"Then we'll only have to share a bed for a few months. And only when we're both in town at the same time." She forced a smile. "I'll have to make trips to Charlotte, plus I have a couple of business conferences scheduled soon. And you'll probably have to travel to LA and to some of your restaurants. This is going to be perfect. Thank you, Travis."

She bounced on her heels, excited that everything was falling into place.

His attention was drawn to her breasts, and his eyes drifted shut momentarily before he met her gaze again. Then they fleshed out their plan.

Travis would talk to Autumn and reserve a date so they could get married at Moonlight Ridge. And he noted that since it wasn't a real marriage, she should let Autumn plan everything so she could focus on her philanthropic efforts.

Riley realized this wouldn't be a *real* marriage. Still, it smarted when Travis said it.

She set her drink on the bar. "I have an early start tomorrow. You probably do, too. I'd better head back to my room."

"Or you could just stay here." Travis shrugged. "I can loan you a T-shirt to sleep in."

She nodded, her heart beating faster. "Sure. Thanks."

Then they both picked up their glasses and drained them.

Maybe she wasn't the only one who was nervous about sharing a bed.

Thirteen

It's a California king-size bed. We could both spread out like starfish and barely touch if we didn't want to.

The words replayed in Travis's head as his feet pounded the mulch that padded the scenic trail around the lake.

Perhaps their conscious minds realized that this would be far less complicated if they kept their hands to themselves. But their subconscious minds maintained a different opinion.

They'd gone to sleep, each of them clinging to their respective corners of the bed. But at some point, they'd both drifted toward the center. He awoke to Riley's soft, warm body nestled against his. She'd thrown one arm across his stomach and her leg over his. Her head rested against his shoulder as she slept soundly.

He hadn't wanted to wake her, so he hadn't attempted to uncoil her limbs from his. Later, he'd awakened to find himself holding her in his arms, his chin resting atop her head. As if they were a couple accustomed to sharing a bed.

Holding Riley in his arms as she slept was comforting. But it had also alarmed him. They'd sorted out their past, but neither of them had indicated any interest in exploring a future together. There were too many years and too many painful memories to wade through.

Besides, hadn't Riley presented him with this fake-marriage proposal because she wasn't interested in doing this with someone who'd mistake it for an actual relationship?

She wasn't interested in a romantic entanglement, and neither was he. They were both focused on their work. Anything else was an unwelcome distraction.

Snuggling—consciously or not—wasn't a good move. Waking up with a raging hard-on and thoughts of how amazing she'd looked in that body-hugging dress and those sexy high heels? That was a terrible, horrible, no-good, extremely insane idea.

He'd awakened at a little after 5:30 a.m. and managed to slide from beneath Riley without waking her. Then he'd gone downstairs and done push-ups and sit-ups until his chest and abs burned. Once it was light enough, he hit the trail around the lake a few times.

But it was getting late. He needed to return to the cottage, shower and get over to the main kitchen. This afternoon, they were serving their fabulous new menu to the staff—including Jameson, Giada, Mack, Molly, Grey and Autumn.

The tasting menu consisted of bananas foster French toast; espresso waffles with hazelnut drizzle; red velvet pancakes; blackberry lemon ricotta scones; Gruyère, Parmesan and chives soufflé; quiche Lorraine with delicious brown sugar caramelized bacon; and eggs Benedict. Each was a complete treat for the senses meant to ensure Moonlight Ridge would become a bona fide brunch destination. And on the brunch drink menu: peach Bellinis, kir royale and mimosas.

Still, he was nervous. Each restaurant he opened was more than just a business. It was a manifestation of himself. Part of a legacy he was building. But the menu they were rolling out for Moonlight Ridge felt even more personal. He wanted the resort to thrive again because nothing would make his father happier. And as kind and generous as Jameson Holloway had been to everyone in his life, he deserved that kind of happiness.

Travis jogged back to the cottage, cooled down and stretched before stepping inside.

"Hey." Riley emerged from the kitchen in her own

T-shirt and another pair of body-hugging leggings. "How was your run?"

"Great." He inhaled the scent of his preferred brand of Jamaican coffee. "You made coffee?"

"I did," she confirmed. "And I had my things brought over so I could shower and change. I hope you don't mind." She seemed to hold her breath in anticipation of his reaction.

"No, it's fine," Travis said. "I'm gonna hop into the shower first."

Travis jogged upstairs, got out of his sweaty clothing and climbed into the shower, trying not to think of how incredible Riley looked in those leggings.

He hadn't gone to the shower with the intention of relieving the tension that had been building low in his belly since he'd awakened to Riley's warm body all over his. Her hair was spread across the pillow and shielded her gorgeous face. And she'd looked unbelievably sexy wearing his Carolina Panthers T-shirt. Then, in the kitchen, those leggings showcased every morsel of that curvy ass.

Could he really be blamed for a little hand action?

He'd taken his painfully hard dick in one soapy hand, the other pressed against the wall. His fist glided up and down the slick skin, slowly at first. Then faster, as Technicolor-vivid visions of Riley filtered through his brain. Until he'd finally reached his pinnacle, shooting hot, sticky fluid against the shower wall.

Travis slumped against the cold tile of the back wall, his body spent, his heart racing as he caught his breath. If he and Riley George were going to live together platonically, it seemed his right hand was going to become his new best friend.

Riley rearranged the flowers she'd placed in a vase.

"Those are beautiful, Rye. What's the occasion?"

"My way of saying thank you." Riley grabbed a mug. "Coffee?"

"Please. Black with sugar." Travis sat at the table. "And you don't need to thank me."

"I do," she insisted. "You're going along with this whole thing. You didn't deck my father last night, though I'm sure you wanted to." She handed him his coffee. "And you're letting me move in here sooner than you'd hoped. Flowers don't even begin to express my gratitude."

"But helping us renovate this place does, so thank you."

They drank their coffee in relative silence, a million thoughts running through her head.

"Having second thoughts about the marriage?" Travis watched her carefully.

"No, I was just thinking…" Riley shrugged. "It's silly."

"I won't laugh." He raised a hand. "Promise."

Riley sighed. "I used to doodle our names in the back of my notebooks."

One corner of his mouth lifted. "Like 'Travis loves Riley'?"

They'd carved those very words in a tree in the woods. Was it still out there?

"More like Riley Anne George-Holloway," she said. "And you promised not to laugh."

"I'm not. It's adorable." His mouth pulled into a lopsided grin. "Must seem surreal that it's actually going to happen."

"Yes, but it's also kind of…sad, I guess. We were head over heels in love back then. I would never have imagined us getting married as part of some business agreement." She sipped her coffee.

"You'll get your fantasy wedding one day, Rye." Travis squeezed her hand.

"Maybe." Riley shrugged.

Their wedding would be simple and elegant. Efficient. She wouldn't waste a ton of time and resources on something that wasn't real. Still, not getting her dream wedding was monumentally disappointing. She hadn't expected that.

"You sure you're okay?" Travis took his coffee mug to the sink.

"Yes, of course." Riley forced a smile. "Like I said, it was silly."

Travis confirmed she'd be joining them for the tasting of the new Moonlight Ridge brunch menu at noon. Then he handed her a slip of paper with the key code to the cottage.

Riley thanked him again and lifted onto her toes and kissed his cheek.

Travis looked down at her, his dark eyes indecipherable. "See you at noon."

"Do *not* fall for Travis Holloway," she whispered under her breath as she watched him leave. But as her heart swelled and a cascade of emotions swirled around her, it was clear her heart and body weren't listening.

Fourteen

Riley surveyed Moonlight Ridge's grand ballroom. In a few hours, the room would be filled to capacity. They'd sold out the larger venue in record time—thanks to celebrity chef Travis Holloway being the main attraction—and the resort was completely booked. Molly, Ross, Milo and their teams had exceeded her expectations for the *Great Gatsby*–themed event. The decor was stunning.

Thanks to her assistant, Adele, members of the charity's staff, a team of volunteers and the resort employees, nearly everything was set for the event.

Riley reviewed the printed program to ensure she hadn't missed anything.

"You've been going like the Energizer Bunny since before the sun came up." Travis approached her, his expression filled with concern. "Have you eaten?"

"Not yet." Riley rearranged a place setting. "I need to make sure everything is perfect."

"Rye, take a breath. Everything is under control. You can spare a moment to eat."

His no-nonsense expression indicated he wasn't taking no for an answer.

Riley's stomach rumbled and she felt a bit faint. "Okay. But I have to get ready soon."

"I've got you." Travis's low, deep voice flowed over her like warm honey and sent a shiver down her spine.

Travis *had* been there for her these past few weeks.

He'd helped her with the preparations for the gala well beyond his obligations as the headline chef. His PR team had secured coverage on local and national news and talk shows. And Travis had appeared on many of those shows himself, despite his crazy schedule.

They shared a living space and frequently worked side by side after hours on the sofa or at the kitchen table. So Riley had seen firsthand how busy Travis was. But after sharing a bed those first few weeks, he'd ordered a bed for the guest room, and she'd been relegated there.

Riley missed their late nights together in bed, silently tapping away on their laptops. But at least they shared breakfast most days and dinner most nights. They even spent some evenings watching a movie together or playing the occasional board game. It was...*nice.* Very different from her solitary life in her pricey town house in Uptown Charlotte.

Her favorite day was Sunday, when Jameson gathered his sons and their significant others around his dining table over a delicious meal prepared by Giada or Travis. Riley loved the friendship she was building with Travis's family. She adored Molly and she was enjoying getting to know Autumn. Grey was sweet and easy to get along with. Funny. Mack had been a tough nut to crack, but he'd softened.

Then there was Travis.

They'd been rebuilding their friendship little by little, even as they presented themselves to the world as a couple. Yet, every time he held her hand or kissed her for the benefit of his family or hers, it felt a little less like a show and a lot more real. Because she genuinely felt the emotions they were putting on display: admiration, affection, desire.

Did Travis feel the same?

He'd given zero indication he felt anything more for her. So maybe that was her answer. But at least he'd signed the agreement and committed to marrying her sometime after the gala.

"Come with me." Travis guided her to a table in the corner of the room. He lifted the stainless-steel dome with a flourish, revealing his signature chicken salad—with walnuts, cranberries and thinly sliced grapes—served on a warm, freshly made croissant.

Her favorite.

She thanked him and cleaned her hands with a moist towelette. Then she took the first satisfying bite of her sandwich. The combination of savory flavors melded on her palate.

"So good," she muttered through a mouthful.

"I have to get back to the kitchen. I want tonight to be perfect, too." He winked at her, and she felt more at ease than she had all morning.

"Travis." Hallie jogged toward them with members of the reality show filming crew right behind her. "We've got a problem."

"What's wrong?"

"The filet mignon is gone," she huffed.

"What do you mean *gone*?" Despite Travis's calm facade, his voice was tense.

"What do you mean the filet mignon is gone?" Riley repeated, suddenly feeling nauseous. Donors had paid ten thousand dollars per table to be here tonight. And they'd preselected their meals.

Offering substitutions wasn't an option.

"Not all of it is gone," Hallie said. "But there isn't enough to meet the orders for the gala tonight. I don't know how this happened, I swear."

"And you're sure you didn't overlook it?" Travis walked briskly toward the elevator that led down to the kitchen. Hallie and Riley were both hot on his heels.

"Maybe the delivery was short, and we just didn't notice," Riley offered.

"I took inventory myself," Travis said. "It was there, and it sure as hell didn't grow legs and walk out of here on its own, so let's find it."

Riley joined Travis and Hallie on the elevator, her heart thumping. Her stomach dropped to her knees and her head spun. A blunder like this would leave their high-profile donors seething, regardless of how hot and charming their star chef was. She was grateful when Travis insisted the film crew take the stairs.

"We'll have to cancel the event tonight, won't we?" Riley asked. This was going to be a PR debacle.

"Babe, listen to me." Travis cradled her cheek. His voice was calm. "Everything will be fine. I'll do whatever I need to do to make this right. I promise."

The elevator door slid open and Hallie exited. Travis hit the button to close the door again. He turned to Riley and held on to her waist, her back pressed against the wall.

"I know this looks bad, Rye, but I've dealt with a lot worse and still managed to pull off the event without anyone noticing." Travis dropped a soft kiss to her cheek and another on her lips. For the briefest moment, Riley forgot that her world was crumbling around her.

Her father had vehemently objected to moving the event to Moonlight Ridge and having Travis headline it. So if tonight's event crashed and burned, she'd never hear the end of it.

"If I'm not panicking, you shouldn't, either. Go on and get all glammed up, beautiful. I've got this." His mouth curved in a soft grin.

Riley nodded, feeling numb as she watched him exit the elevator into the kitchen. She hit the button and watched the doors close, praying everything would be okay.

Fifteen

Travis joined Hallie in the walk-in refrigerator where there was considerably less filet mignon than there had been the day before. A knot tightened in his gut.

"I'm going to get fired, aren't I?" Hallie clutched her stomach, then answered her own question. "I'm *definitely* going to get fired."

"Relax, Hal. You're good. I know you didn't do this," Travis said calmly. "But someone certainly did. Ask Ross and every single person in this kitchen if they know anything about this. Meanwhile, I'm going to recheck every square inch of this fridge."

He'd rip the place apart if he needed to. If those premium cuts of meat were still in that fridge, he'd find them. Travis started a systematic search. Once Hallie finished questioning all of the staff about the missing meat, she returned and helped him look.

The meat wasn't there.

He enlisted Hallie and dishwashers Pauly and Ernesto to help them search the freezer.

Travis was on the verge of having his assistant call every reputable meat vendor in town—when he shifted a stack of frozen butter. The missing cuts of meat were there, frozen. This was no mistake. The filet mignon had been placed there intentionally.

"Who the hell would put them in here behind the butter?" Hallie asked.

"Someone who didn't want us to find them," Travis replied.

"Who'd do that?" Hallie rubbed her arms to warm them.

"Everyone here understands how important this event is to Moonlight Ridge."

"Maybe that was the point," Travis mused. "To sabotage tonight's event."

"Could the film crew have done this? Maybe they were trying to manufacture some drama for the show," Hallie whispered to Travis so the film crew couldn't hear her.

"They wouldn't have done this. But we'll worry about who did later," Travis said. "Right now, let's get this meat defrosted."

Thankfully, there was more than enough time to defrost the meat and get it prepped for dinner. But he needed to talk to Mack and Grey. Their elusive thief was likely behind this. If he hadn't found the thief's cache, he'd bet that filet mignon would've made its way onto the black market where disreputable restaurants and hotels sourced their goods.

A forensic accountant had combed over the books, and Mack and Grey had locked down Moonlight Ridge's expenditures, making it more difficult for theft to go undetected. Selling meat and other high-value goods on the black market was likely the thief's only option.

But for now, crisis averted.

He dialed Riley. "Hey, Rye. There was just a little mix-up. We're good to go."

"Thank you, Travis." She sounded relieved. "But I just stepped out of the shower, so I need to get dressed."

He was speaking to Riley *naked*? Travis shut his eyes against that visual. Something he found himself doing whenever he heard her shower running at the cottage because that vivid image had practically given him a hard-on.

"Should've placed a video call," he muttered, and she giggled.

They were flirting. Not as a pretense, but because he was wildly attracted to her and they genuinely enjoyed spending time together. So against his better judgment, they'd been teasing and flirting. A lot.

It was harmless, as long as they didn't cross the line. And he'd gotten dangerously close to doing just that.

"Sorry, I shouldn't have said that." Travis walked into the kitchen office and shut the door. He turned on the speaker-phone and rummaged through a file containing meat purchase orders. "Got a little carried away at the thought of you...well, you know."

"You're the one who put me out of your bed," she reminded him. "Tonight, you're going to regret that." The flirtatious lilt of Riley's voice made his pulse quicken. Electricity traveled the length of his spine.

"What's that supposed to mean?"

"That if we were sharing a bed, maybe I'd find a special way to thank you for saving the day."

His mouth fell open, but he was speechless as all the possibilities ran through his head.

When he didn't respond, Riley laughed. "Bye, Travis."

His heart thumped. For the past few weeks, he'd done his level best to ignore the way his body reacted to hers as she traipsed around the cottage in tiny sleep shorts and a midriff-baring top. But there was something particularly attractive about her moving about the cottage in his borrowed, oversize T-shirts.

It was ridiculous, and maybe even a little sexist... But he liked the idea of her body being draped in something that belonged to him. As if—by extension—it did, too.

"You kicked her out of your bed?" Grey stood in the doorway with his arms folded. "Seriously?"

"Still eavesdropping, I see. Is there something that actually is your business I can help you with?" Travis returned to digging through the files.

Grey fell into the chair beside the desk. "Autumn and Molly saw the three of you leaving the ballroom like you were in Jurassic Park and the dinosaurs got loose. They sent me down here to make sure everything is okay."

"Everything is fine. Now," Travis added.

"What happened?" Grey sat up straight in the chair.

Travis explained what had happened and shared his suspicions about the thief being a saboteur determined to see the place go down in flames.

"It must be someone in the kitchen." Grey rubbed his chin. "That narrows down the suspects. Maybe you were right about Hallie. We know she needs the money. When Pops met her, she was stealing meat from a grocery store. Maybe she's doing it again."

"She was a teenager shoplifting a ham and canned vegetables to feed her aged grandmother and younger siblings on Christmas," Travis pointed out. "I've been there. But I've gotten to know her, and I honestly don't believe she'd do anything to hurt Pops. She loves him like a father, and she feels like she owes him. He changed her life."

"Then do you have any theories on who it might be?"

"Nothing I can substantiate yet. But I am sure about who it *isn't.* And Hallie's at the top of that list." Travis pulled out the file folder, then slid into the chair. He shoved the file of meat purchase invoices toward his brother. "I'd start with these. Check to see if there have been other missing inventory items that caused Dad or the resort any kind of embarrassment."

"I'm on it." Grey flipped through the file. "Now, why on earth would you kick Riley out of your bed? I thought things were good between you two. And you're obviously still into her."

"Things are good between us, and I'd like to keep them that way. So I'm not trying to fuck with her head or mine."

"If you have feelings for her and she evidently has feelings for you—"

"I have no idea what this is, where it's going or if I

even want it." His voice was tinged with frustration over his constantly evolving feelings for Riley. "Yes, I was in love with her then. And yes, I like and respect her now. But our lives are on different trajectories. At some point, she'll need to return to Charlotte, and I need to return to Atlanta and then LA. If we move forward with plans for a Traverser restaurant in New York, I'll probably get a place there. What then?"

Grey shrugged. "Guess that depends on what you both want and how badly you want it."

His brother had gone to school and worked in New York, and he still had a green-building architecture firm based there. But like Mack, Grey had fallen in love with a woman who seemed to be his perfect match and with Moonlight Ridge again. Neither of his brothers had returned to their old lives.

Travis loved his family and this old place, but he had no intention of staying here.

He had a life to get back to, and so did Riley. There'd be no happy ending for them, and a meaningless fling for the next year felt like a monumentally bad idea. He was already in his feelings about her, so the stakes were just too high, and he didn't see that changing. It was better not to start something that would only hurt both of them.

"Now, I have much bigger issues to handle. I have a ballroom full of folks coming for this gala tonight, and someone has gone to great lengths to sabotage it. I doubt they'll stop there."

Grey stood. "I'll update Mack on what happened. We'll both be on the lookout. Call us if you need anything."

"Thanks, G." Travis bumped Grey's offered fist. "I'll keep that in mind."

"You'd better." Grey closed the door behind him.

He'd become accustomed to taking on everything himself, afraid of being let down. But it felt good to know he had his brothers there to back him up, and he'd missed that.

The Holloway brothers against the world.

Travis would make sure this event went off without a hitch. For Jameson. For Moonlight Ridge. And for Riley.

He opened the bottom desk drawer and looked at the item he'd hidden there earlier.

Yes, he had much bigger things to worry about tonight indeed.

Sixteen

It was nearly the end of the night and Riley was exhausted, but incredibly proud. The gala had gone flawlessly. The room was packed, and the guests were raving over their meals—especially the filet mignon.

The decorations were splendid. It felt like they'd been transported back to the Jazz Age. And everyone in attendance had really embraced the theme.

Most of the men wore suits that looked like something Leonardo DiCaprio would've worn in *The Great Gatsby.* Many had donned felt fedoras or classic homburg hats. Nearly all of them wore lapel collar vests that matched their suits and had the requisite pocket watch on a chain. And the two-tone oxfords were definitely a hit.

The ladies in attendance looked wonderful. There were lots of sparkling sequins and beaded dresses with flapper fringe, much like the jewel-green vintage dropped-waist dress she wore. Black fringe hung from the scalloped hem at her knees down to her ankles. She'd accessorized the dress with a black beaded headband with black feathers, and black fingerless gloves. T-strap pumps completed the outfit.

The live band had played classic jazz by all the greats: Duke Ellington, Miles Davis, Benny Goodman, Dizzy Gillespie, Ella Fitzgerald, Dave Brubeck and more. But they were currently playing "Sugar" by Maroon 5 and the dance floor was full.

"I have to give it to you, sweetheart. You've pulled off quite a feat," her father said as he and her mother approached, both of them smiling. "It seems Moonlight Ridge was the perfect choice."

"And we all love Chef Henri, but he couldn't have pulled the crowd and sponsorships Travis did. I hear you had a few hundred people wait-listed," her mother gushed.

"Thank you." Riley hated that she still wanted her parents' approval, despite their sharply different life philosophies. "It's big of you to admit you were wrong about this place and Travis."

"That's *not* what I said, Princess," her father objected. "And what your mother meant is it was a good *business* decision to replace Henri with the Holloway boy."

"He's no more a boy than you are, Dad." Riley folded her arms.

"You aren't actually comparing me to that—"

"Travis, dear, hello," her mother said loudly.

Riley and her father turned toward Travis. He'd changed out of the white chef's jacket and looked good enough to eat.

She sank her teeth into her lower lip as she scanned this incredibly sexy man. The white dinner jacket set off his dark brown skin. She envisioned taking Travis back to the cottage and stripping him out of the jacket and those slim black tuxedo pants. Totally inappropriate since they were fake-dating and she was standing with her parents, who noticed her reaction.

Of the four of them, only Travis seemed oblivious about how much she wanted him.

"Good evening, Mr. and Mrs. George." Travis addressed her parents, but his gaze was on her. "Hey there, Princess."

Her father huffed when Travis used his pet name for her.

"You clean up nice." She grinned. "The black-and-white combo looks good on you."

"And you look stunning." His eyes roamed down her

body before returning to her heated face. "You put on one hell of an event, Rye. You should be proud of yourself."

"I am." Her breathing became shallow when he leaned down and kissed her temple.

"I'm proud of you, too." He whispered the words meant only for her.

Her heart felt full and her eyes were misty. Why had Travis's sincere praise moved her to tears? Because he and his brothers were the reason she supported this charity. Many older children in the foster system didn't find forever homes as Travis, Mack and Grey had.

"Dance with me?" Travis extended his palm.

She hadn't danced all night, but she couldn't resist Travis's soft plea or the entrancing way he stared at her as if it was only the two of them in the room. She slid her hand into his.

"Excuse us," Travis said to her parents, whom she'd momentarily forgotten about. He led her onto the parquet dance floor in front of the stage.

The song ended, but no other song followed.

"Why'd they stop playing?" Riley glanced at the stage. "Everyone is sitting down."

"Maybe there's a good reason." Travis grinned.

"What reason could they possibly have for—"

"Thank you to each and every one of you for being here tonight and your generous contributions." The executive director of the charity took the stage. "Please give a special thank-you to the George Family Foundation and to Ms. Riley George for her tireless efforts tonight."

Suddenly, there was a spotlight on her. Her heart swelled as everyone stood and clapped. Riley nodded her thanks to the executive director and the applauding crowd.

"You knew about this?" She smiled at Travis, whose grin deepened. He joined the applause. His dark eyes were filled with affection. She blinked back tears.

Next, the executive director requested a round of applause for Chef Travis Holloway. The spotlight moved to him as she showed an enlarged version of the huge check Travis had written to the charity—it represented a sizable chunk of his appearance fee.

The woman had one more announcement.

"You may not know this, but Travis and Riley have a long history. They met right here, on the grounds of this hotel, as children."

The spotlight had moved onto both of them as the woman shared how they'd dated as teens and reconnected after he'd stepped in for Chef Henri.

Riley's face flushed and she was pretty sure the room was spinning.

She whispered to Travis, "What is happening right now?"

He squeezed her hand. "Wait and see."

"Travis would like to dedicate a special song to Riley. Travis and Riley, the floor is yours." The woman gestured toward the empty dance floor.

It was sweet. Also, totally embarrassing. Her cheeks burned, and the giant spotlight wasn't helping.

They walked to the middle of the floor and Travis slid an arm around her waist as the band started to play the opening chords of "A Fool for You." The lead singer belted out the lyrics about a deep, enduring, unconditional love.

She hadn't heard the song in years until it came on the radio a few weeks ago. She'd played it often in her room since then. Travis had evidently noticed.

Riley glanced over at her parents. Her father glared at them. Her mother regarded them with what felt like a mixture of envy and alarm.

She'd worry about her parents later. Right now, she would focus on Travis's thoughtful gesture. But before the song ended, Travis went down on one knee and pulled a black velvet box from inside his jacket.

He wasn't going to... *Oh my God. Yes, he is.*

"Riley, I fell in love with you when we were just teenagers. And after all this time, it feels like nothing between us has changed. We've wasted so much of our lives apart. I don't want to waste another second. Marry me, Rye. Please."

She stared at him, one hand covering her mouth. This was all an act for their parents and the TV crew. She realized that. But he'd given her the grand gesture she'd bemoaned missing out on. And everything he'd said and all of the emotions running through her head felt incredibly real.

Riley lowered her hand and held it out to him as tears slid down her face.

"Yes, Travis." She nodded. "Baby, I can't wait to marry you."

Travis slid the gorgeous diamond solitaire onto her finger and stood. He kissed her as the room exploded with thunderous applause. When Travis finally released her, they turned and waved to the crowd cheering them on. The cameras were rolling, but her parents were no longer there.

It wasn't a surprise, but that didn't stop it from hurting. Riley glanced to the other side of the room where Travis's family was seated. Everyone at the table was clapping. Giada and Molly wiped away tears. Even Mack and Grey, who were aware of their deal, seemed moved.

The table where her family had been seated was empty, and her heart felt empty, too.

"They'll come around, sweetheart. Until then, I've got enough family for both of us." Travis indicated his family smiling and applauding.

Riley blew them a kiss, her eyes filled with tears. For the

next year the Holloways would be her family, too. Just the thought of spending Sundays with them made her smile, and her heart felt full again.

Back at the cottage, Travis set down his car keys and removed his jacket.

After his proposal, they'd spent the remainder of the evening fielding congratulations from guests and hugs from the hotel staff.

Hallie—who felt like the little sister he'd never had—had hugged him and said, "I knew you were too smart to blow it with someone as perfect for you as Riley."

It was a sentiment nearly everyone at Moonlight Ridge seemed to share.

Riley sank onto the sofa. "It's official. We're *really* getting married."

"Looks that way." Travis loosened his black bow tie, but left it hanging around his neck. He stepped behind the bar and pulled out two highball glasses. "Rum and Coke?"

"Please." Riley unstrapped her shoes.

Travis made their drinks, then handed her one before sinking onto the sofa, leaving an empty cushion between them.

"Regrets?" He sipped his rum and Coke, wishing he'd gone a little heavier on the rum.

Holy shit. He and Riley were about to get married.

"None." There was no hesitation in her voice. "You?"

Did he have regrets?

The public declaration of love wasn't his usual style. Yet, the moment they'd shared on that dance floor felt right and maybe a little too real. Like he was beginning to buy into the story they were selling.

This relationship wasn't real, and he needed to keep reminding himself of that.

"No regrets." He took a healthy swig of his drink as he

watched her flex her feet, which were obviously in pain from the cute shoes she'd worn all night.

Travis set down his drink and reached for her foot, which she offered reluctantly. He gently massaged her arch.

Riley moaned softly, her eyes drifting shut.

He sucked in a deep breath and willed his body not to react to the sensual sound. He massaged the ball of her foot with his thumb, then gestured for her to switch.

"You all right?" he asked. "About your parents, I mean?"

"That's the reaction I expected." She shrugged.

"Expecting it and experiencing it are two different things," he said. "Don't beat yourself up for being affected. They're your parents. The fact that it hurts just means you're human."

"I thought they'd at least *pretend* to be pleased in public. Of course, I didn't expect you to propose, let alone so publicly." She smiled sheepishly.

"You deserve your big, romantic gesture." He grinned. "Hope I didn't embarrass you too much."

"It was perfect and so sweet. I'll never forget tonight." A soft smile curved her sensuous lips.

The same lips he'd kissed earlier that evening. The lips he'd caught himself staring at since they'd returned to the cottage where they were playing a high-stakes game of "house."

He removed her foot from his lap and stood abruptly, running a hand over his head. "Been a long day for both of us. I'm exhausted. You must be, too."

He glanced at his watch. It was nearly two in the morning.

"I am." She seemed disappointed. "In fact, I'm too tired to get up and go to bed."

He could relate. Right now, his bed seemed a million miles away.

"Let me help you." Travis pulled her to her feet.

Riley gazed up at him, her hand still in his. "You were a superstar tonight, Travis. The gala and your proposal were amazing. I couldn't have asked for anything more. Thank you." Riley lifted onto her toes and kissed his whiskered face.

But as she pulled away, Travis cradled her cheek, his heart racing as his eyes met hers.

He leaned down and covered her mouth with his. This kiss wasn't for the sake of anyone else. It was because he longed for another taste of her lips.

Riley tipped her chin, her lips parting. He swept his tongue inside the warm cavern of her mouth. The rum and cola mingled with the sweetness of the crème brûlée that lingered on her tongue. Her soft, warm body molded to his as he kissed her in the same room where he'd last kissed her all those years ago.

Riley made a delicious little murmuring sound that sent a jolt of electricity down his spine and he no longer remembered all the reasons he shouldn't do this.

They were two perfectly sensible, completely willing adults who'd be married for a year.

Why not give in to their desires?

Travis sank onto the sofa behind him, pulling Riley onto his lap. She hiked up the dress, giving herself room to straddle him, then wrapped her arms around his neck.

Their kiss grew hotter, more intense. Travis glided his hand up her outer thigh as Riley ground her hips against him. The warm space between her thick, brown thighs glided along his painfully hard length, both of them murmuring in response to the delicious sensation.

Travis glided the zipper down her back and kissed Riley's bare shoulder. She helped him shrug the garment down her arms, revealing a sheer black bra. He traced the stiff, brown peak with the rough pad of his thumb through the sheer fabric.

When he pinched the hardened nub, Riley gasped, then bit her lower lip. Her brown eyes reflected every bit of the lust that coursed through his veins.

"Upstairs?" she whispered roughly, her chest heaving.

"Upstairs." He trailed kisses along her shoulder.

Travis stood suddenly, his hands beneath her perfect, round bottom as he lifted her. When he released her, Riley slid down his body until her bare feet touched the floor.

"Give me ten minutes, then I'll see you in my room." Her teasing smile was part vixen, part girl next door.

"See you in ten." He adjusted himself as he watched her ascend the stairs, her curvy form on full display as she clutched the dress to keep it from falling off.

Travis groaned quietly. He put away their glasses and turned off the lights downstairs before hurrying up to his room. After a quick refresh, he rummaged through his luggage.

He hadn't planned tonight. But given the increasingly flirtatious nature of their relationship, it seemed wise to be prepared. He tore into the box of condoms and stuffed a few into his pants pocket. Then he made his way down the hall.

He hesitated as he stared at her partially open bedroom door. The scent of Riley's body wash filled the hallway between her bathroom and bedroom. He wanted this, and evidently, so did she. He only hoped it wouldn't ruin the deal and the friendship they'd been rebuilding.

Seventeen

Riley paced the chilly hardwood bedroom floor in her bare feet.

After several torturous weeks of living with the man and behaving in public as if they were head over heels in love, her entire body burned at the thought of his rough hands gliding over her bare skin.

Sleeping together could change the dynamics of their business deal and tentative friendship in unpredictable ways. Yet, she couldn't regret giving in to the growing attraction between them.

"Hey, beautiful." Travis rapped his knuckle on her slightly ajar bedroom door and she nearly jumped out of her skin.

"Hey." Riley opened the door and stepped aside.

"I like what you've done with the room." He glanced around at some of the shelving, wall art and knickknacks she'd added to the space.

"Thanks." Her stay at the cottage was temporary, but she wanted it to feel like home.

"Rye, if you're having second thoughts about this..." Travis shoved his hands inside his pockets and gave her a small, reassuring smile. "I understand. This thing between us is complicated enough as—"

No, no, no. Travis was talking himself out of this. Enumerating the reasons it wasn't the best idea. But her heart and her body were determined not to let her brain—or his—ruin tonight.

Riley gripped his white tuxedo shirt and tugged his mouth down until it crashed into hers.

She wouldn't let Travis talk her out of this. She wanted this deliciously handsome, incredibly brilliant and devastatingly sexy man on her, around her, inside her. It'd been all she could think about during the moments she lay awake tossing and turning in her bed at night, knowing Travis was asleep just down the hall.

Riley had spent her entire life being the sensible, good girl who did mostly what was expected of her. She thought of everyone else before herself, and she didn't regret that. But not tonight. Tonight, all she was thinking of was how her lips had tingled when Travis had given her that quick kiss in the elevator. And about how her entire body had burned with heat as Travis's mouth had slid across hers during their kiss in front of that crowded ballroom.

Travis wrapped his arms around her waist, tugging her closer. His hardened length pressed against her belly through the black lace nightgown she'd slipped on over a lacy thong after her quick shower. His hand glided down her back and cupped her bottom.

Their kiss began tentative and slow but quickly turned feverish. Her body ached with the need for his touch. Her nipples beaded and the space between her thighs pulsed. Soft, involuntary murmurs escaped her mouth as he deepened their kiss.

Riley shivered. Her skin felt as if it was on fire as his fingers dug into her flesh, pulling her into him with a sense of urgency that mirrored her own. She'd imagined this so many times.

Now, as his tongue glided against hers and they shared a hungry kiss, she couldn't wait to have Travis's hands on her heated skin. For him to touch her in the way she'd fantasized.

She unbuttoned his shirt and he helped her remove the garment. Travis tore his mouth from hers just long enough to tug his undershirt over his head and drop it onto the floor.

Then he gripped the hem of the black lace nightgown and lifted it over her head. He cursed beneath his breath. His gaze trailed down her body and lingered on the hardened tips of her breasts.

Riley folded her arms over her chest, suddenly self-conscious beneath his heated stare.

"Don't." He lifted her chin and leaned closer. His breath warmed her cheeks. "You look amazing, Rye. I can't wait to taste every inch of that gorgeous brown skin."

"*Every* inch?" she teased. Her belly fluttered and her knees trembled at the thought.

"Every. Fucking. Inch."

The lascivious grin that kissed his sensuous lips had her heart beating double time and made her breath hitch. Her brain was too preoccupied with the image of his mouth on her heated skin to respond.

Travis gripped her waist and lifted her onto the bed. His tongue danced with hers as his hands glided over her bare skin. Then he trailed slow kisses down her neck and down her chest. When his warm mouth covered one of the straining peaks, Riley whimpered softly. Her stomach tightened and her toes curled as her back arched. Her body demanded more of his kiss and his caress.

He willingly obliged.

Travis licked and sucked the sensitive peak as his free hand glided down her belly and into the space between her thighs that ached for his touch. He tugged aside the damp fabric, gliding his fingers over the sensitive nub. She shivered, as much in anticipation of what was to come as from the delicious sensation.

Riley clutched the bedding beneath her, her heart racing. Her heels dug into the mattress and her hips lifted. A silent plea for more.

He glanced up at her with a wicked grin that made her stomach flutter and set her skin on fire. Travis slipped one finger, then another, deep inside her, curling them. His fingers moved slowly at first, then more quickly, bringing her closer to the edge.

Her breath came faster, and her limbs felt heavy as Travis torturously teased one nipple, then the other. Then he kissed his way down her belly and over the black lace. Before her pleasure-addled brain could register what was happening, Travis pulled his fingers from inside her, replacing them with his warm tongue.

Riley gasped, her legs falling open wider and her hands resting on his head. His closely cropped hair tickled her palms. She rocked her hips and rode his tongue, greedy for more of the intense pleasure building low in her belly. Her knees shook, and her involuntary whimpers grew louder as Travis intensified his efforts.

She'd tried to hold it together. Held back the desire to scream his name loud enough to rattle the old windows and be heard by the guests in the neighboring cottage. But when he added his fingers again, the competing sensations were more than she could take. When he sucked on the distended bundle of nerves, she shattered into pieces as she called his name.

Riley lay there, breathing heavily, her muscles tense, her sex contracting. Liquid warmth spread up her torso. Her skin tingled all over. Travis lay next to her on his side, his large hand splayed on her belly. He sank his teeth into his lower lip as he studied her.

His stubbled cheek scratched her ultrasensitive skin when he leaned down and kissed her bare shoulder.

"Watching you fall apart is the hottest thing I have ever seen." There was a hint of reverence in his husky voice.

"I'll bet you say that to all the pretty girls you've been fake-engaged to." Riley stroked his cheek, then pressed her lips to his. He tasted of her. Something about that made her want to purr like a territorial feline who'd just staked her claim.

"I've never been engaged—fake or otherwise." He kissed her again. "You?"

Riley didn't respond right away. They often talked about their lives and careers, but they hadn't discussed past relationships.

"I was engaged several years ago. I wouldn't cosign a horrible land deal, so Patrick called off our engagement." Riley absently stroked Travis's stubbled cheek. "My father and grandfather were right. He'd only been in it for my family's money. That's what prompted my grandfather to add the 'man of means' marriage clause to his will."

Compassion filled Travis's dark eyes. "Sorry things didn't work out, Rye."

"I'm not. It hurt when Patrick ended it, but I'm grateful the marriage didn't happen. I'm better off without him in my life, and if things had worked out…" Riley paused, thinking better of what she was about to say.

"Then you wouldn't be here with me now," Travis said the words she'd been thinking. His lips curved in a sincere smile that warmed her chest. He dropped a soft kiss on her eager mouth. "Then I guess I should be glad things didn't work out between you and what's-his-face."

Riley stared up at Travis's dark eyes, trying to read them. Did tonight mean as much to him as it did to her? Would this change things between them for the better or worse?

Her brain was trying to ruin their perfect night, but she wouldn't let it. Instead, she pressed her mouth to his. Lost herself in his kiss. Luxuriated in the warmth of his brown skin beneath her palms as she glided her hands down his back and gripped his firm bottom.

Kissing this incredible woman was Travis's new obsession. He'd really tried his best to keep emotional distance between them and to keep his hands to himself whenever they were here alone in the cottage, away from prying eyes. After all, this was a business deal, not a relationship. That was what they'd agreed to. And yet… Here they were.

They'd steadily been building a friendship. But since the night they'd gone to dinner with her parents there had also been something more building in the background. Something deeper and more personal.

Tonight had been inevitable. Because for the past few weeks, their growing desire had been impossible to ignore, no matter how hard they tried. But despite all the reasons he knew he should, Travis could no longer hide his desire for Riley.

Maybe this relationship wasn't real or lasting, but tonight he would push all of those fears aside and allow himself to enjoy being with her.

Travis tore his mouth from hers, their chests heaving. He stripped off her lacy thong, then rolled off the bed and quickly shed his remaining clothing. He retrieved the strip of foil packets from his pocket and sheathed himself before joining her beneath the comforter on the chilly fall night.

He captured her mouth in a greedy, devouring kiss, his hands roaming over her soft skin and voluptuous curves. Her fingers dug into his low back and then traveled lower as she pulled him closer.

Travis gripped the base of his length, stretched tight and aching with need for this woman. He slowly pressed inside her wet heat, and Riley arched her back on a quiet gasp. Her nails dug into his biceps as she cursed beneath her breath.

Travis inched inside her as her body adjusted to his. Both of them murmured in response to the deliciously sweet sensation of their first connection. She held on to him, softly whimpering his name as her hips moved with his. Pleasure simmered low in his belly and rolled up his spine. His breath came faster, and his pulse raced as he moved inside her. Learning her body, as she learned his.

He circled his hips, supplying the friction she needed against her slick, engorged clit. Until her body went stiff and she called his name. Her sex pulsed, intensifying the already overwhelming sensations. His hips moved faster until pleasure erupted low in his belly and rocketed up his spine.

Travis tumbled onto his back and lay beside her, both of them spent. He gathered Riley in his arms, his heart still racing. "That was incredible, Rye."

"It was, wasn't it?" Riley's eyes gleamed in the low light cast from her bedside lamp.

Her cheek was pressed to his chest. Her hand was splayed on his stomach, inches from his cock, already stirring again from holding her in his arms like this, her velvety soft skin gliding over his.

"I thought it was just me because I've been fantasizing about this since I was sixteen," she admitted. "And then the fact that we're staying in *this* cottage—"

"I know," Travis said wistfully, not wanting her to say the words aloud.

Almost as if it was fate for us to cross paths again.

It was a thought that had danced around his head one day when she was sitting with him at his father's dining room table. Maybe their meeting had been serendipitous. But it wasn't fate. They still lived very different lives in opposite corners of the country. And there would be no happy ending for them. But they could enjoy their time together now.

He excused himself to clean up and discard the condom, taking longer than the task required as he thought about the awkward conversation they needed to have. About what this meant or didn't mean for them going forward.

Travis returned to the bedroom. "Riley, I think we should—"

She sat up suddenly, waving a hand to silence him. "Did you hear that?"

"Did I hear what?"

Suddenly, there was an urgent knock at the front door.

"Who would be here at this hour?" Riley whispered.

"Someone at the wrong cottage?"

There was another, more persistent knock.

"I'd better see who it is before they wake the guests next door." Travis slipped on his pants and undershirt. He kissed her forehead. "I'm sure everything is fine, but—"

"Be careful." Riley pulled the cover up over her chest and settled against the headboard.

Travis could see Hallie through the window at the top of the door.

Why would Hallie come to his cottage at this time of night? None of the reasons he could think of were good.

He called to Riley to let her know everything was fine. Then he opened the front door, his heart racing a little. "Hal, what's up?"

"Sorry to bother you, Travis, but it seems urgent." Hallie took a quick glance at his rumpled clothing and bare feet. "I would've called, but you left your phone in the office."

"What's the big emergency?" He stepped aside to let her in.

"You've gotten a bunch of calls and text messages from a Rosemary. That's your agent, right? She's been trying to reach you all night. When I saw the words *urgent* and *prospective investor*, I thought I'd better bring you the phone." Hallie handed it to him.

His lock screen showed the missed phone calls and text messages from his agent and an email from Autumn confirming the date for his and Riley's wedding there at Moonlight Ridge.

He thanked Hallie and said good-night before listening to the first of Rosemary's three voice mails.

A potential investor for the New York restaurant was flying in from Germany. He wanted to meet Travis at a few potential sites in New York in approximately twelve hours. Rosemary had already booked him on an early flight out of Charlotte, which gave him about an hour to throw together a suitcase and hit the road for the airport if he was going to make the flight.

The investor's timing couldn't be worse.

Travis traveled frequently, so he kept his overnight bag stocked, and he'd become an expert at packing in minutes. He went to his room, packed his bag and changed into jeans and a long-sleeve shirt. Then trekked to the other end of the hall.

Riley exited the bathroom in her short, hooded robe. She'd swept her spiral curls up into a topknot and she was wearing her cozy slippers. His mouth curved in an involuntary smile.

"Not the sexiest thing, I know." She secured the belt. "But you left and it's cold tonight."

"I happen to think you look incredibly sexy in those cat ears and bunny slippers." Travis slipped his hands around her waist and kissed her. "And I'm sorry I had to leave."

"And yet, that kiss felt more like goodbye than an invitation to round two." Riley raised one of her perfectly arched brows as she gazed up at him. "Let me guess… business calls."

"I'm headed for the airport. I'm meeting a potential investor in New York."

"How long will you be gone?"

"A day, maybe two." Travis traced a finger along her exposed collarbone. "Will you be here when I get back?"

"No, I'm spending a few days with a sorority sister in San Francisco ahead of my conference there. From there, I fly to Holland for an international conference where I'm a presenter. You obviously don't consult the shared calendar my assistant set up for us."

He didn't. But now wasn't the time to admit that.

"Autumn was able to book our wedding in three weeks. You cool with that?"

"Yes, and I'm taking your advice and letting her handle everything. Just ask her to keep it simple and elegant."

"I will." He kissed Riley again, reluctant to leave his new fiancée behind. "Then I guess I'll see you a few days before the wedding."

"Guess so." Her sad smile made Travis's chest ache. He grabbed his bag and headed downstairs, already missing the gorgeous woman who would soon be his wife.

Eighteen

Riley sat at the bathroom vanity in Moonlight Ridge's bridal suite. Her wedding was an hour away. She'd wanted to keep the ceremony city-hall simple, but Travis suggested that a small wedding party would make the wedding seem more legit.

Mack and Grey were Travis's two best men, but her two closest sorority sisters were both pregnant. One was on bed rest. The other was due to deliver any day now. Neither could attend. Autumn and Molly had been gracious enough to stand in as her maid and matron of honor. Which meant Autumn, her wedding planner, was doing double duty.

"Everything okay?" Autumn stood behind her in the mirror.

The other woman tried to sound upbeat, but Riley could hear the pity in her voice. Autumn felt sorry for her—alone on her wedding day.

"Everything is perfect." Riley felt the need to reassure Autumn she was fine without her family there.

But it wasn't true.

There was a hollow ache in her chest. This wasn't the fairy-tale wedding she'd always imagined, filled with family and friends. Instead, she was preparing for a hurried ceremony she'd barely had a hand in planning, and none of her family would be there.

Riley and her parents didn't see eye to eye on much, but it broke her heart that they weren't there with her.

Maybe this wedding had begun to feel too real because she had developed a deep, genuine attachment to Travis. Still, neither of them had defined what the relationship had morphed into. And the geographical distance between them the past few weeks had heightened the awkward tension.

"I wish every bride of mine was this calm on her wedding day," Autumn said.

Molly came into the bathroom, her curls glossy and perfect. Her smile was tentative. "Riley, you have a visitor."

"Who is it?"

"Me."

Riley's eyes flooded with tears when she heard the familiar voice.

"Nana?" She stood, squeezing the older woman's hand. "What are you doing here?"

Her grandmother cupped her cheek and smiled. "You didn't actually think I'd miss my only granddaughter's wedding, did you?"

Tears spilled down Riley's cheeks faster than she could blink them away. "Dad said none of you would be here."

"Last I checked, *I'm* still the matriarch of this family," Mariah George said firmly.

Riley hugged her grandmother. "Thanks, Nana. You being here means the world to me."

"I know, sweetheart," her grandmother said. "Can we talk alone for a moment?"

Autumn ushered Molly out of the room and closed the door behind them.

Riley guided her grandmother onto the stool in front of the vanity. "What is it, Nana?"

"This is about the money, isn't it?" Her grandmother squeezed her hand.

"You think Travis is marrying me because I'm an heiress?" Riley worded her question carefully.

"I think you're getting married to receive your inheritance, and you chose Mr. Holloway to antagonize your father." Nana chuckled.

Riley didn't want to lie to her grandmother. But could

she trust that she wouldn't report back to her father? Maybe this was her dad's last-ditch effort to stop the wedding.

"Why would you think that, Nana?"

"Because it's *exactly* what I'd do in your position. But I would've done it two years ago."

Her grandmother cackled when Riley's eyes widened with surprise. "Don't worry, we'll keep this between us. I hate that your grandfather put you in this position. I had no idea about this awful provision to your trust. I wouldn't have stood for it."

"I know." Riley patted her grandmother's hand, freckled with age spots.

"You're a sensible girl, so I'm sure you've thought of protecting your financial interests."

"We have a carefully constructed prenuptial agreement that protects both of our assets."

"Good girl." Nana George nodded proudly. "That proposal of his was quite romantic. A man like that can be trouble in an arrangement like this."

"It's not just *an arrangement*, Nana." Riley clasped her hands.

"What do you mean?" her grandmother asked.

"I'm in love with him." The admission surprised Riley. "I honestly hadn't realized that until just now."

"Does Travis feel the same?"

Riley's heart sank to her stomach. "I know there's something more between us."

"But neither of you are quite sure what that is." Her grandmother nodded knowingly. "Well, that *is* a dilemma."

Nana squeezed her hand. "Is Travis a good man?"

"Absolutely."

"Do you trust him?"

"I do."

"Then I must trust that he'll take care of my granddaughter's heart." Nana George pulled her phone from her purse. She pecked on the keyboard. "Now, let's see this wedding gown."

"Autumn and Molly were just about to help me get dressed." Riley dabbed beneath her eyes, hoping she hadn't ruined her makeup.

"Perfect." Her grandmother moved to open the door. "Because I'm not the only one eager to see you."

When Nana George opened the bathroom door, her mother, Gina, stood in the doorway. Her eyes were filled with tears.

"Hello, sweetheart." Her mother waved tentatively.

"Mom." Riley barely squeaked out the word before tears streamed down her face again. She stepped into her mother's embrace.

"Enough of that," Nana George said. "We need to fix that makeup. No granddaughter of mine is going to walk down the aisle with her makeup a hot, unholy mess."

Within minutes, Autumn brought the makeup artist back. Then her mother and Autumn helped Riley into her wedding dress. Once she was ready, the four other women wore huge smiles. Her grandmother's and mother's eyes were filled with tears.

"You look absolutely exquisite, sweetheart," her mother said. "Come see for yourself."

Riley stepped into the handmade Italian Kahmune nude pumps that flawlessly matched her dark brown skin, then stood in front of the full-length mirror. The skirt of the romantic lace ball gown swished around her. She slipped her hands in the pockets and admired the dress with its long illusion sleeves and deep, plunging illusion neckline. The detachable beaded belt cinched her waist. She turned around, looking over her shoulder at the full illusion back and covered buttons, before turning to face the mirror again.

"Not bad." Riley rearranged a few strands of her tousled beach waves.

"Sweetheart, you're stunning. And I'm not the only one who thinks so." Her mother handed her the phone. It was a video call with her father.

"You are so beautiful, Princess."

"Dad?" Riley walked to the other side of the room. "I thought you didn't approve of my marriage to Travis."

"I still say it's a mistake, but you're my only daughter. So if this is the man you choose to marry, I'd regret not walking my baby girl down the aisle."

"I won't allow you to make Travis or his family uncomfortable," Riley insisted.

"I promise to be on my best behavior." He winked. "Now c'mon. In this family, we aren't late for our own weddings."

Her father ended the call abruptly, but Molly opened the door and he was standing on the other side. He stepped inside the room and took her hands in his.

"Look at you." He drew in a shaky breath, the corners of his eyes damp. "You're the most beautiful bride I've ever seen." He kissed her cheek. "I hope that Holloway boy realizes what a gem he's getting."

"Dad, you promised."

"Okay, okay. You ready?"

"Almost." Autumn approached with an ivory comb set with pearls.

Riley recognized the comb as her grandmother's. It'd been a gift from her mother on her wedding day.

She thanked her grandmother as Autumn swept her hair back on one side and inserted the elegant comb. Then she slipped her arm through her father's and made her way down to the ballroom where she'd finally marry Travis Holloway—in real life, not just in her dreams.

Nineteen

Travis slipped on his gray Tom Ford tuxedo jacket and straightened his burgundy tie as he looked in the mirror on the wall of the conference room where he and his brothers waited.

He and Riley had negotiated this marriage and the guest list. They'd talked about the wedding, though they'd allowed Autumn to do most of the planning of it. Still, it felt surreal that in less than an hour, Riley George would become his wife.

Travis straightened the collar of his white shirt, then picked up the boutonniere—a pink mini orchid with a burgundy center—and inhaled the sweet, calming scent.

"Let me handle that." Mack took the boutonniere from his hands, which he now realized were trembling slightly. Mack pinned the flower to Travis's charcoal-gray trimmed lapel. "You all right, T?" Mack lowered his voice and frowned slightly. "Not too late to change your mind."

"I'm fine." Travis fiddled with his shirtsleeves.

Truthfully? He did feel uneasy. The past few weeks had flown past in a blur, and things between him and Riley were in an odd place.

The night he'd asked her to marry him at the gala had been perfect. Had they not been interrupted, he would've gladly spent the rest of the night making love to her. But despite countless phone and video calls, they'd spent very little time in the same room over the past few weeks. And when they'd spoken or spent time together, things felt… *awkward.*

Sex had changed the easy vibe between them.

Maybe the universe was warning him not to fall for Riley again. Because, he was, in fact, falling for her.

That would explain why his stomach was in knots and his head felt light. He was more nervous about this wedding than he'd been doing live demonstrations to packed convention halls or in front of a live audience of millions.

"You don't look fine." Grey's dark eyes twinkled. "You look a little woozy. Should I get you a drink from the bar?"

"I'm good." Real or no, Travis wasn't showing up at his own wedding lit.

Besides, he didn't need a drink. Everything was fine. He and Riley were friends with benefits who would soon become fake spouses.

Nope, not confusing at all.

"It's just nerves. He'll be all right," his father said. "Travis has got a gorgeous woman who is a total sweetheart waiting to marry him. Hell, he should be skipping down that aisle."

"Did Riley send you to ensure Travis didn't pull a runaway groom?" Grey asked.

"No, she did not." Jameson narrowed his gaze at Grey, giving him a silent reminder to behave, like when they were kids.

"I realize how lucky I am, Pops." Travis shoved his hands in his pockets.

"Good." Jameson patted his shoulder and smiled. But for a fleeting moment he looked sad. "I love you, son." The older man squeezed his shoulder, then turned to regard Mack and Grey, too. "The three of you mean *everything* to me. Don't ever forget that."

"We know, Pops." Travis hugged Jameson. Mack and Grey did the same.

"Well, c'mon. Let's do this. Can't keep my future daughter-in-law waiting."

"Yes, sir." Travis took a deep breath and followed his

brothers to the conservatory, where they were really getting married—despite what Riley had been told.

Travis stood at the front of the event space with Mack and Grey beside him. When "Arioso," by Johann Sebastian Bach, began to play and Riley entered the conservatory on the arm of Ted George, his heart leaped in his chest.

He'd called Riley's grandmother—Mariah George—and told her how disappointed her granddaughter would be if her family wasn't at her wedding.

They could hate him all they wanted. He really didn't care. But he couldn't bear to see Riley hurting because of her family's notable absence from the ceremony.

The sadness in Riley's voice had been evident when she'd mused about the possibility of this being her only wedding and her family not being there.

Riley presented a strong front, but her family's plan to snub their wedding cut her deeply. So he'd made the call to the George family matriarch, realizing it was a long shot. Despite his feelings about Riley's family, he was glad to see them there. The broad smile on his bride's face as she descended the aisle on her father's arm made Travis's heart swell.

Riley was stunning in her lace wedding dress with its plunging illusion neckline. Her hair fell to one shoulder in soft waves. The other side was swept back with a decorative hair comb.

His heart danced with joy at the wonder and surprise on Riley's face as she surveyed the space.

They were in the conservatory where they'd first laid eyes on each other as children. He'd been playing a game with his brothers and she and her mother were sitting on a bench beneath a sunny window reading.

There was something about her he'd instantly found mesmerizing. But he'd been a preadolescent boy who still thought girls were awful, annoying creatures who ruined everything. So he'd exchanged a polite smile and a nod with her—as he did with the children of all the guests—and continued playing Battleship with his brothers.

Years later, Riley told him she'd first fallen for him that day in the conservatory. He'd asked Autumn to plan a lovely, ethereal wedding there in the place where they'd first met. But they'd told Riley the wedding would be in one of the small ballrooms.

Travis wished he could've been there to see Riley's face the moment she realized they were getting married in this lush, green space. He followed her big brown eyes as they took in the conservatory. Sumptuous swaths of fabric hung overhead. Lush pink camellias, regal purple hyacinths and fragrant white orchids filled the place.

Autumn had outdone herself. And by the look on Riley's face, she felt the same.

Riley and her father now stood in front of him. Ted hugged his daughter, then kissed her cheek. He exchanged a stilted handshake and tense eye contact with Travis before stepping aside.

"You look gorgeous, Rye," Travis whispered as he extended his elbow to her.

Riley thanked him and slipped her arm through his as they stood in front of the officiant.

The ceremony was short and sweet. When it was time to exchange vows, his heart threatened to beat out of his chest. The corners of Riley's eyes were damp, and her voice trembled slightly when she spoke.

This wasn't the simple business transaction they'd agreed to. Nothing about their ceremony felt like an act. He had genuine feelings for Riley. Maybe not love, but something akin to it.

When they'd exchanged rings and the judge pronounced them husband and wife, Travis captured her mouth in a kiss. His lips glided over hers, and he wished they were standing alone in this beautiful space. That he could kiss her for as long as he pleased.

The officiant cleared his throat and chuckled.

Riley smiled, a slight look of embarrassment on her lovely face as she reached up to wipe the lipstick from his mouth with her thumb. Travis kissed her palm.

Her smile deepened and his heart felt…*full*. In a way it hadn't before.

Mack was right. He was definitely in trouble.

It was the end of the evening, and Travis watched as Riley chatted with her family. He was surprised the Georges had stayed to help them celebrate their wedding along with a room filled with family, friends, business associates and several of Moonlight Ridge's employees. Despite not practicing and winging a song choice, Riley even got her father-daughter dance.

Travis was happy for his new bride.

He and Ted had even declared a temporary truce. It'd nearly choked the man to say the words, but he'd shaken Travis's hand and congratulated them on their nuptials.

"Made nice with the in-laws, I see." Mack handed Travis a beer as they watched Riley saying goodbye to her family in the rotunda of the hotel, just outside the ballroom doors.

"Temporarily." Travis was under no illusion that he and Riley's dad would suddenly become friends. "But as long as Rye is happy on her wedding day, that's all that matters."

"You seem pretty damn happy yourself." Mack chuckled. "Who's that your wifey is talking to? I don't remember seeing her at the wedding."

Travis turned back to where his wife was standing. Her family was gone, and she stood in the center of the rotunda speaking with a woman who looked…familiar. He chugged some of his beer, before handing the bottle back to his brother.

"Excuse me, Mack. I need to take care of something."

"That woman looks a lot like the pictures of—"

"I've got this," Travis said, his voice tense. "See if you can get the DJ to play something that'll get the remaining guests on the dance floor."

"You've got it," Mack said. "Just don't do anything… you know…stupid." Mack put his large hand on Travis's shoulder. "And if you need me, I'm here."

Travis made his way across the rotunda.

"Here's my husband now." Riley's eyes lit up as he approached. "Travis Holloway, meet Lenora Nelson—your biggest fan."

Is that what she had convinced herself she was? His biggest fan?

Travis slipped a protective arm around Riley's waist as he regarded the woman cautiously. He surveyed her dark eyes and generous mouth, so similar to his own. His heart thumped in his chest and his temple throbbed.

Riley looked concerned when he didn't respond. She seemed to notice the tension in his muscles as he and the woman studied each other. Riley pressed one palm to his chest; the other rested on his back. A silent show of support, for which he was grateful.

"Travis." The woman's raspy voice was filled with emotion. "I can hardly believe it's you. It's been such a long time."

Travis stiffened his spine, and his fists clenched. He tried his best to convey zero emotion.

"It's been twenty-six years, *Ma*." He tried to strain the hurt and anger from his voice. She'd abandoned him without sending so much as a birthday card in all this time. She didn't deserve to know how deeply her abandonment had cut him. That it affected him still. "And you decide to show up today?"

Her eyes filled with tears. "I realize how hurt and angry you must be."

Travis looked through the woman. The ghost of a painful past. "I *was* hurt and angry. But now I'm over it."

Riley tightened her grip on him as she studied the other woman's face.

"Travis, sweetheart, I didn't leave because—"

"I'm not interested in your excuses anymore, Ma. You're two decades too late. You weren't there for me then, and I don't want you here now," he growled, lowering his voice. "This is a private family wedding. If you're still here in five minutes, you'll be escorted off the property."

Travis held on to his wife, as if she was his lifeline. He was embarrassed Riley had to witness his messy family issues. But he took comfort in her presence.

"I understand if you can't forgive me, Travis." Tears streamed down her cheeks. "But we need to talk."

"Please don't approach me or my wife again." He ignored her plea and turned to walk away, his arm still around Riley's waist.

His wife hesitated, pulling him aside. She slipped her hand into his.

"Baby, I'm sorry. I didn't know," Riley said.

"How could you?" He sighed. "Let's just go back and enjoy the rest of our night."

"Travis, you have every right to be upset. But you don't want to leave your mother out here making a scene in the lobby." Riley glanced around, likely looking for any members of the filming crew who might be lurking about. They'd gotten footage of the wedding and from earlier at the reception. But they would be back shortly to get footage of them saying good-night to their guests. "Nor do you want her to feel her only option to be heard is to go to the tabloids. They'd gladly run with a salacious story about a beloved celebrity chef *allegedly* mistreating his long-lost mother."

His heart rate slowed and the tension in his shoulders eased. Riley was beautiful and brilliant. A much-needed voice of reason.

He'd seen too many celebrities with asshole relatives determined to milk their fifteen minutes of fame for all it was worth. People who'd been shitty and absent their entire lives suddenly appearing on morning television shows and in tabloids, making it seem like they were the ones who'd been abandoned and mistreated.

Just months ago, Autumn's father—a sleazy Hollywood producer and general trash human being—had pulled a similar stunt on national TV. It had led to several wedding cancellations and jeopardized that side of the business. The last thing Travis wanted was to cause more negative publicity for Moonlight Ridge.

"What do you propose?" Travis swept her hair behind her ear.

"Let me talk to her. Maybe I can diffuse the situation," Riley offered.

Travis glanced at the woman he'd once loved more than anything. But her lack of response to his countless attempts to contact her over the years had made it clear he'd never really mattered to her.

It had been one more thing weighing on him as he'd lain in his hospital bed recovering from the accident. Feeling as if everything he'd ever wanted in his life was lost to him. Wondering if this had all happened to him because he wasn't worthy of love or happiness.

"I'm not leaving you alone with her."

"I appreciate your concern, but Nicky and Ricardo are right there behind the front desk and the valets are right outside. I'll be fine." She squeezed his hand.

Travis glanced at his mother again. "Don't go anywhere with her and don't believe a word she says."

He'd learned that the hard way as a kid. So many times his mother had promised tomorrow would be different. He'd believed her and been disappointed every time.

He'd never forget the last lie of Lenora's that he'd believed.

I'm just going to the store, baby. I'll be right back.

Travis had waited for his mother for two days before the social worker had arrived. He'd spent that two days trying to convince himself there was a reasonable explanation for her absence. And that she really did love him, even if she didn't show it in quite the same way other mothers did.

"Promise me." He needed Riley to understand how persuasive Lenora could be.

"I promise," Riley said. "Our marriage may not be traditional, but we're a team, Travis. The night of the gala, you told me that you've got me. That I can rely on you to have my back. Well, I feel the same, so let me handle this for you. *Please.*"

Her dark brown eyes were so sincere.

Travis checked his watch. "We give our parting speeches in half an hour. If you're not back in fifteen minutes, I'm coming to check on you."

He kissed his wife's cheek, then headed back inside the ballroom without sparing a glance at the woman who'd decided her life was better off without him in it.

Twenty

Travis climbed out of the back of the turquoise-and-white four-door 1959 Ford Galaxie 500 hardtop convertible that once belonged to the original owner of Moonlight Ridge, Tip O'Sullivan. Then he helped his new bride out of the car.

Riley looked beautiful but exhausted after their full day. The reconciliation with her family. The wedding. The reception. Then meeting her new mother-in-law. She'd put on a big smile and returned to the wedding reception in time to thank partygoers and wish them a good night. But something about her seemed heavier. Sadder than before when she'd been floating on a cloud and he had, too.

It had brought him immense joy to surprise Riley with a fairy-tale setting for their wedding and to ensure that her family would be there. And when he'd stood in front of that officiant and declared that he loved and was committed to her, it hadn't felt like he was pretending at all. Little by little, almost without him noticing, it'd become the truth.

Riley was the only woman he thought of now. He cared for her. Worried about her. Would defend her at all costs. Just as she'd once made a huge sacrifice to protect him and his family. Even when it meant breaking her heart and his.

Their driver, Manny, a longtime employee of the hotel, snapped video and pics of Travis carrying Riley across the threshold—at Jameson's request. Then they bid Manny a good night.

While Riley made a mad dash to the restroom, Travis transported their bags to their rooms. He removed his jacket, loosened his tie and sat on the edge of the bed.

Travis had worked hard to push every memory of his

mother from his brain. Because remembering even the good times reminded him of all the pain. For his own mental and emotional health, he'd chosen to forget Lenora Nelson ever existed. So, of course, she'd turned up again to churn up all of that pain on what should've been one of the happiest days of his life.

It was strange to see his mother again. To hear her say his name. He'd engaged an emotional force field the moment he'd recognized her. And he'd kept himself from telling her what he thought of her in excruciating detail.

Because Jameson Holloway had raised him better than that.

I know you're angry, Travis. But she's still your mother, son.

He could hear his father's words in his head. Travis was glad Giada had taken Jameson home by then. The idea of those two worlds colliding always made him uneasy. As a teenager, Travis hadn't told Jameson about his attempts to reach out to his mother. A part of him felt as if reaching out to Lenora was a betrayal of the man who'd given him everything: a home, a family, a future and unconditional love.

Jameson Holloway had always treated him and his brothers as if they were his own flesh and blood.

Travis fought back the memories of his mother. His anger was the lid that kept all of the pain those memories conjured at bay. His mother's rejection had shredded his heart to pieces. But eventually, his raw, bleeding heart had formed a callus. Maintaining his hardened feelings toward Lenora had become his coping mechanism. His way of protecting his heart.

Yet, part of him wanted to demand answers to the questions that'd plagued him for years: Why had she abandoned him? Had he been that awful a child? Did she just not want a kid?

Travis had gone to bed each night with those questions

burning a hole in his chest for much of his life. But the only thing more devastating than not knowing the truth was being told more lies. So he'd pass on whatever his mother had come there to say.

Still, her reappearance had reaggravated his old hurts. Torn loose the stitches that tenuously held together those jagged wounds.

"Sorry to bother you." Riley stood in the doorway. The light from the hallway glowed around her like a halo. "But it took two women to get me into this dress. I'm going to need a little help getting out of it. Would you mind?"

"No." Travis stood, sliding the tie from his neck. He tossed it on the chair with his suit jacket. "Come here."

Riley walked over to him, then maneuvered the large skirt as she turned around, giving him her back. She swept her hair over one shoulder as she glanced back at him. "Think you can handle it alone?"

He whistled, assessing what looked like one hundred covered buttons trailing down the sheer back of the dress. "They've got you strapped in here good."

"I know. If I'd sneezed, there's a good chance someone would've lost an eye tonight." She laughed, patting her stomach.

"Good thing you didn't." He chuckled, slowly working through the task obviously meant for someone with slimmer fingers. Meanwhile, an awkward silence descended over them again, like a heavy, wet shroud.

"There." He'd unfastened the last of the buttons on the back of her dress. "All done."

"Thanks." She held the top of the dress up with one hand and lifted the bottom with the other.

"You were beautiful in that dress, Rye. Excellent choice."

"Thank you." She stared at him a moment in the mostly dark room. "We need to talk about my conversation with your mom—"

"I don't want to talk about her." He cut her off abruptly.

The soft, gauzy moment between them was shattered by her mention of his mother. But it was Lenora he was angry with, not Riley.

"But she said—"

"I've heard all of the lies, all of the excuses. I don't want to play those tired games anymore. So whatever sad story she's told you to garner your sympathy, Riley, I don't want to hear it. All right?" He shoved his hands into his pockets.

"Okay." Riley agreed reluctantly. "And thank you for today. Having the ceremony in the conservatory was such a sweet surprise, and it meant a lot to have my family there. My grandmother told me about your stern lecture." She laughed. "You've certainly earned my Nana's respect. I can't thank you enough."

Travis's family had embraced Riley, and she seemed to appreciate that. But the sadness in her eyes whenever the topic of her family came up… It was something he could relate to. So he'd been prepared to do anything short of dragging Ted George's ass out of his house to ensure he was there to walk his daughter down that aisle.

Riley lifted onto her toes and kissed his cheek.

He studied her face. She was beautiful. Thoughtful and sweet. His family adored her, even if hers would just as soon see him dropped off the end of a pier.

And for at least the next year, they'd committed to being together.

When Riley had proposed this wild scheme, being married for a year to a woman he'd loathed sounded like being condemned to his personal hell. But after getting reacquainted and learning he'd been wrong about her, his feelings were completely different.

"What happened with your mom tonight is a lot to process. You'd probably like some time alone." Her tone indicated she hoped otherwise.

Maybe he did need time alone to process the pain and trauma Lenora Nelson's sudden appearance had revisited upon him. But that wasn't what he wanted.

Not tonight.

Tonight, he wanted to be with the woman who consumed his every thought.

"Don't go, Rye. Stay, *please*."

Riley stared at him wordlessly from beneath her thick lashes. She released the lacy garments, allowing them to pool around her bare feet.

She stood before him, naked from the waist up, wearing only a blinged-out scrap of fabric masquerading as panties. His cock twitched and his belly tensed.

Tonight, he fully intended to have Riley George-Holloway back in his bed, and there would be no interruptions.

Twenty-One

Riley's pulse raced as Travis's dark eyes locked with hers then slowly glided down her body. He held his hand out to her, and she took it, stepping out of the wedding dress. He helped her gather the frothy, lace confection and its underpinnings, draping them over the chair with his tuxedo jacket.

Travis closed the distance between them and pressed his mouth to hers. His hands moved to her bare back as he cradled her body to his. Her lips parted as she looped her arms around his neck. Travis accepted the invitation, his warm tongue gliding along hers. He held on to her tightly. Kissed her with a ravenous hunger that caused her sex to pulse.

He swallowed her quiet murmurs as he cradled her jaw. His kiss sent shivers down her spine that set her entire body on fire. The damp space between her thighs throbbed and her nipples beaded, scraping against his hard chest.

Travis's hooded gaze radiated abject desire. "Riley, you look absolutely amazing."

He captured her mouth in a kiss that made her feel that every kiss she'd received before this one had been amateur hour. He kissed her until she was breathless.

Travis's strong hands trailed down the sensitive skin of her bare back. He squeezed her bottom, pulling her flush against his hardened length pinned against her belly. He cursed beneath his breath in response.

When he lifted her, she instinctively wrapped her legs around him. Travis carried her to his bed and laid her down. He kissed her, his tongue searching hers as he teased one hardened nipple with his thumb.

Travis glided down her body, covering the nipple he'd been teasing with his warm tongue and grazing it with his teeth. The sensation went straight to her sex, already pulsing with her growing desire for him. When he trailed soft, slow kisses down her body, Riley's belly fluttered in anticipation.

Travis tugged off the sheer thong and kissed the space between her thighs, eliciting an involuntary gasp. She shuddered as electricity shot up her spine.

Travis's tongue glided over her swollen, aching flesh, bringing her to the edge. He stopped just short of her coming undone, giving her a small reprieve. Just as her heartbeat started to calm down, he went in for more. Travis repeated the cycle again and again. Each time, he drove her higher, the feeling more intense than before. Until she was trembling and cursing as she clutched the duvet. Begging him to let her come.

"All you had to do was ask." His eyes glinted with a wicked grin. His lips glistened with evidence of her pleasure.

Riley didn't just ask. She pleaded, begged and perhaps even threatened. She wasn't quite sure. Because at some point, she'd been on the edge of losing consciousness.

Travis slid two fingers inside her, his movements precise, as he continued to use his mouth to bring her the most incredible pleasure. Finally, her body tensed, and her inner walls pulsed as she called his name until her throat was hoarse.

He seemed to recognize when she'd reached her maximum threshold for pleasure. Travis eased off, finally removing his fingers and placing one last kiss on her slick, sensitive flesh. Then he trailed kisses up her belly before lying beside her. Travis wrapped her in his arms, flipping the duvet over them.

She laid her cheek on his chest, ruining his white shirt

with her makeup. She'd buy him another. Because right now, there was no place she'd rather be than in her husband's arms.

They lay together in silence, her pulse still racing, and her heart beating wildly. As amazing as Travis had made her feel, her body vibrated with need. She was quickly becoming shamelessly addicted to this man, her husband.

Riley kissed Travis slowly, unbuttoning his shirt as their kiss grew more heated. They worked together to strip Travis down to his underwear. When he stood and dropped those, Riley nibbled on her lower lip as she regarded the ridiculously sexy man she'd spent the past several weeks fantasizing about. She could recall with great detail every kiss and every touch from their memorable night together.

But this moment was about more than her growing desire for Travis. When they'd stood in front of their friends and family and repeated their vows, she'd meant them. She wouldn't be satisfied with a fake marriage. She wanted Travis in her bed and in her life. *Period.*

Now she only needed to make him see how good they could be together, too.

Travis gazed at his beautiful wife. Everything about Riley George-Holloway was soft and comforting. Her smiling face and open expression instantly warmed his chest.

It had taken cajoling, coaxing, a guilt trip and flat-out bribery to get him to agree to this marriage. But it had taken none of that to get him to stand in that conservatory today awaiting the beautiful woman who'd first captured his heart nearly two decades ago. Because he truly cared for Riley and he looked forward to their time together.

Travis sheathed himself beneath the appreciative gaze of his wife. They crawled beneath the covers and he kissed Riley, his tongue searching for hers. He loved the feel of her soft skin and the sensuous sounds she made as he trailed kisses along her shoulder. The way her back arched when he teased the hardened tips of her full breasts with his tongue.

Travis kissed his way down her stomach, to the valley between her thick thighs. He used his lips and tongue to bring her to the edge again. Until she was begging to feel him inside her.

He obliged, reveling in the delicious sensation of her body, soft and warm, opening to him as he inched inside her. Loving the sweet, torturous sensation of Riley dragging her perfectly manicured nails down his back. Marking him as hers.

She held on to him, her wide eyes filled with heat as they moved together. He wanted to hold on to this moment and to the passion building between them. But when Riley's body tensed, his name on her lips as her inner walls spasmed and she tumbled over the edge, he could barely hold on.

He quickly found his release, waves of pleasure overwhelming his senses as his heart hammered inside his chest.

Travis tumbled to the mattress beside his wife, gathering her to his chest. The room was silent, but the moment didn't feel awkward, as it had before. Instead, there was a feeling of quiet contentment.

He'd been living alone for so long, he'd forgotten what it was like to have someone to come home to. Someone to cook a special meal for: his language of love.

Travis kissed the top of Riley's head. "Sex won't make this weird, will it, Rye?"

"I'm fake-married to my childhood sweetheart." Riley raised her head and laughed. "I'm pretty sure it can't get any weirder than this."

"Guess you've got a point." He chuckled softly.

But the truth was nothing about today felt fake. Maybe that was the weirdest thing of all.

Twenty-Two

Jameson Holloway rocked on the back-porch swing. He studied the trees turning various shades of red, orange and gold. Autumn was always gorgeous there in the Blue Ridge Mountains. He never took for granted how fortunate he was to be here. He loved his work, and he was lucky to have become the father of three fine men.

Moonlight Ridge and his boys had kept him too busy to think of love or marriage. There had been dalliances over the years. But nothing serious enough to make him consider sharing his life with someone.

Of course, he wished he hadn't almost died. But he was grateful for everything that'd happened since then.

All three of his boys had come home. One by one, they'd found love with women who couldn't be more perfect for his sons if he'd handpicked them.

Mack and Molly were happily married, and Mack's new brewery was opening that night. Jameson expected Grey to propose to Autumn any day now. Travis and Riley were returning from their honeymoon later that afternoon—just in time for the grand opening of the brewery.

When the boys had gotten in that accident, he'd never been more frightened in his life.

Afterward, Travis had been so angry. At his brothers. At Riley. At the world.

Jameson had tried to be a good father to his sons. But he'd been so focused on Travis's recovery that he'd left Mack and Grey to struggle with the fallout on their own. The physical distance between the boys had increased their emotional distance. Travis was angry and bitter about losing his football career. Mack and Grey were scared of losing control and disappointing the people they loved. All three of them had focused on their careers and avoided close personal connections.

A chasm formed between his sons. For him, that had been the biggest tragedy of the accident. One he hadn't known how to fix.

So, if it had taken what had happened to him to reunite Mack, Grey and Travis and remind them how much they loved each other, he couldn't regret that.

"I brought you some hot chocolate." Giada appeared in the doorway, her eyes twinkling.

Giada was the other reason he couldn't regret his illness. It had brought this beautiful woman, whom he'd always adored, back into his life. And as she'd taken care of him these past months, they'd fallen in love. Something he had yet to admit to his sons.

"Sounds perfect, sweetheart." Her decadent, thick Italian hot chocolate was a rare treat. How could he possibly say no? Jameson patted the space beside him on the swing. "Join me?"

"I'm still working on the appetizers for the opening at the brewery tonight," she said in her lovely Italian accent. "But I did bring you some company. An old friend, Lenora Nelson."

Jameson's eyes widened and his gut tightened. He climbed to his feet. "She's here. *Now?*"

"Yes, she is waiting in the front room. I thought I would bring her out here to join you." Giada frowned, stepping onto the back porch and lowering her voice. "Is there a problem, *caro*? Should I send her away?"

"No. You did the right thing, sweetheart." Jameson kissed her cheek. "Please send her out. Thank you."

Giada looked at him strangely. *"Va tutto bene, amore mio?"*

"Yes, darling." He stroked her cheek. "Everything is just fine. I promise."

Giada pressed a kiss to his lips, something he would never tire of. Then she smoothed his shirt before turning to walk away.

Lenora Nelson.

That was a name he hadn't heard in years. The last few times he'd thought of her, he'd hoped and prayed she was out there and still alive. For Travis's sake. Because he realized that at some point in his life, Travis would want to reconcile with his mother.

His son had tried to keep it a secret, but Jameson knew he'd tried to reach out to his mother several times over the years without success. Lenora just hadn't been ready to meet with her son. Hadn't wanted him to see her the way she'd been the last time she'd shown up there to beg him to take Travis in and raise him.

The screen door opened and Giada ushered Lenora out onto the porch. She gave him a questioning look, but he nodded to indicate she needn't worry.

"Hello, Jameson," Lenora said once Giada was gone. "It's good to see you again."

He wished he could say the same. But his gut told him otherwise.

"You're looking well, Lenora." Jameson sat down. He gestured for her to sit in a padded wicker chair opposite the swing. "What can I do for you?"

"We need to talk about our son," she said.

Jameson glanced toward the kitchen window. Could Giada hear their conversation?

"What would you like to talk about?"

"I spoke with him." She sat down heavily.

"When?" Jameson scooted to the edge of his seat.

Travis and Riley had been away in the Maldives on their

honeymoon. The first week had gone so well they'd decided to stay a second week.

"The night of their wedding," Lenora said.

"You crashed their wedding?"

"He's *my son*, Jameson," Lenora said defensively. "Why should I be considered an intruder at my own son's wedding?"

Because you weren't invited.

"I realize it must've been upsetting to be an outsider at your own son's wedding, Lenni," Jameson said. "But *you* created these circumstances. What did you expect? You cut the boy out of your life and now...*what*? You thought he'd be okay with you popping in at his wedding?"

"You're right, I know." Lenni studied her hands, folded in her lap. "Travis should be upset. If he'd told me how angry he was, I would've gladly taken it. But the way he looked at me. It was so...cold. Like I meant nothing to him." Her eyes welled with tears.

Jameson handed Lenni one of the napkins Giada had set on the table, and she dabbed her face with it.

"What *exactly* did you say to him?" Jameson's gut tightened in a knot.

He'd been bone-tired the day of the wedding. Giada had made him leave before the reception ended. But the entire family had brunch together the following morning before Travis and Riley left for the airport.

He was hurt that his son hadn't mentioned his encounter with his mother.

"I tried to apologize and tell him I'm ready to rebuild our relationship." She sobbed, dabbing her cheeks. "But he wants nothing to do with me."

His heart ached for her, but his son was his primary concern. "You didn't tell Travis—"

"No." She shook her head. "But he needs to know."

"It was you who insisted that I not tell him," he reminded her.

"I know." Her dark eyes, a carbon copy of Travis's, were filled with agony and regret. "It was a mistake. You were right. I should've told him."

"Telling him now… Do you have any idea what that will do to him? He's finally gotten over all of the anger and blame related to the accident. Travis and Riley have just begun their new life. Don't disrupt his happiness, Lenni."

"Whatever time I have left on this earth, I plan to use it to reestablish a relationship with my son. But we can't build that relationship on a lie, Jameson. I *have* to tell him."

"Think of how this will impact him. It'll turn his entire world upside down. Please, just give it a little more thought, and I promise I'll try to get Travis to at least talk to you. All right?"

Lenora frowned, then she sighed.

"I only want what's best for Travis. So I promise to consider what you've said."

"That's all I ask." A little of the tension rolled off Jameson's shoulders, but the knot in his gut was still firmly in place.

Whatever happened, he only hoped that his son wouldn't withdraw to that same dark place he'd gone to after the accident. Not when he'd finally found love and rediscovered the importance of family.

Lenora took her leave, and a few minutes later, Giada returned. She slid onto the swing beside him and placed a comforting hand on his leg.

"What is wrong, Jameson?" she asked in her melodious accent.

Jameson didn't respond. Instead, he held her hand. He wanted to tell Giada everything. But if he was going to talk to anyone about this, Travis deserved to hear it first. So he couldn't tell Giada. Not yet. But he could tell her the other truth he'd been holding inside for weeks.

He turned toward her and stroked her cheek. "I wish I could tell you everything, sweetheart. But right now—"

"I understand," she said. Her warm assurance that everything would be okay made his heart feel lighter. "This woman… She is Travis's mother?"

Jameson sighed heavily and nodded.

Giada leaned into him, still holding his hand. "Then we do not need to talk about it."

"I'm so grateful to have you back in my life." Jameson studied the woman's face through the haze of emotion that filled his eyes. "And this time, I won't let you go without a fight. I love you, Giada."

Jameson cleared his throat, then cackled. "I'm too damn old to get down on one knee. And don't feel you have to answer me right now, but will you—"

"Yes!" Giada interrupted his rambling. "Before we get any older…*yes*, Jameson Holloway. I would most happily marry you. I love you, too."

Jameson kissed Giada. He held her in his arms as they watched the sun set over the mountains in the distance. His heart was filled with a deep sense of joy and happiness. The woman who'd become his best friend and constant companion these past few months had agreed to be his partner for the rest of their lives.

But beneath the joy and happiness was the unshakable feeling that a storm was brewing on the horizon.

Twenty-Three

Travis checked the three trays of mini crumb-topped berry pies he had baking in the oven at the women and children's shelter. He and Riley had returned from their honeymoon in the Maldives one week earlier.

They'd spent two weeks swimming, lying in the sun, exploring local foods and culture, spending quality time together and making love. If it hadn't been for work and community obligations, they might've stayed another week.

"Need help in here?" Riley poked her head into the kitchen.

"Actually, I do need something. Come here a sec?"

"Sure, babe. What is—"

He pulled her into his arms, taking her by surprise when he kissed her.

"Nice." Riley wiped her tinted gloss from his lips. "Save that energy for when we get back home."

"You better believe it." He winked.

"Chef Travis, I… Oh, I'm sorry. I didn't mean to interrupt." Joan, the director of the center, hurried into the kitchen. "But the volunteer manning the smoker thinks the meat might be ready and he's afraid of overcooking it."

"I'll be right there." Travis still held his wife in his arms. He kissed her forehead.

When Joan left the kitchen, Travis gave Riley a pat on the bottom, and she laughed. Then he followed Joan through the kitchen doors.

Travis checked on the meat and gave the volunteer in charge of the smoker additional instructions. He turned back toward the kitchen but halted when a familiar voice called his name.

He turned toward his mother, who was wearing a volunteer T-shirt. "What are you doing here, Ma?"

Travis glanced around, thankful the film crew was elsewhere, capturing B-roll for the show. Still, there were local news crews on-site.

"Volunteering." She stepped closer.

"Don't pretend you didn't know I'd be here."

"I did. But I'm also here because this place was here for me during a really tough time in my life. I like to give back whenever I can, however I can."

"You spent time here?" He hadn't wanted to engage her, but he couldn't help himself. He knew very little about her life after she'd disappeared from his.

"Yes. My life was a roller-coaster ride for a while. One I couldn't take you on. Because you deserved a happy, stable life. The kind of life Jameson Holloway was able to give you."

"You had no idea where I'd end up. I could've been placed with abusive foster parents or ended up on the streets." His shoulders tensed and his temple throbbed. All of the pain and anger came rushing back, making it difficult to breathe. "But you didn't care. All you cared about was yourself."

"That isn't true, sweetheart." His mother's dark eyes filled with tears. "I did what I did *because* I loved you. I wasn't in the right emotional state to care for you. I tried, baby. I really did. But I was in a downward spiral. I had to do right by you, so I placed you in foster care until I could get on my feet again."

"Then why didn't you come back for me?"

"It's complicated," she said. "But I never stopped thinking of you."

"If that were true, you wouldn't have gone ghost on

me." Travis rubbed at the gnawing pain in his chest. "But the real question is, why are you here now? What is it that you want?"

"I have so many regrets in my life. None more painful than how I hurt you. I want to make things right with you, Travis." She wiped at the tears spilling down her cheeks.

He'd fallen for her tearful promises that things would be different time and again as a kid. He wouldn't fall for the waterfalls and bullshit again.

"I have to get back to the kitchen." Travis turned abruptly to leave.

"Wait! There's something you need to know." Her voice was loud enough to garner attention from a few nearby volunteers.

Travis gritted his teeth, his wife's words echoing in his head. He didn't want his mother to make a scene. He turned around. "What is it that you just have to tell me after all this time?"

Uneasiness crept down Travis's spine in response to his mother's expression. It was the same tortured look he'd seen whenever she'd had to tell him a painful truth; the kind that would change everything. His father was terminally ill. Their home was being seized by the bank.

What horrible news would she deliver this time?

"Are you in some kind of trouble? Do you need money?"

"Jameson Holloway is your father," she said.

"Of course he is. You agreed to the adoption. It was the only time you responded to—"

"No, Travis." She pressed a hand to her forehead. "Jameson is your *biological* father."

There was one person in his life who'd *never* disappointed him. Whom he could always trust. And that was Jameson Holloway. So what she was saying *had* to be a lie.

"You stay out of my life for more than twenty years and

this is the kind of nonsense you come at me with? Why? What could you possibly hope to gain?"

"It's true, sweetheart." Lenora sighed. "I met Jameson at a concert in Atlanta one summer. We hit it off and shared one incredible weekend together. Then I returned to my life in Raleigh and he returned to his here. We never expected to see each other again."

She rubbed her arms. "A few months later, I realized I was pregnant. By then, I'd met your dad—Doug," she clarified. "We'd gone out a few times. When I learned I was pregnant, I tried to break it off with him. But when I explained why, Doug just smiled. He said he'd fallen in love with me the moment he'd laid eyes on me, and that he'd always wanted children but couldn't have them. So rather than breaking up with me, he asked me to marry him." A soft smile lit her dark eyes. "Best decision I ever made."

"To marry Dad?"

"And to have you," she said.

He couldn't accept what his mother was telling him. Not because he didn't want to be Jameson Holloway's biological son. But because it meant everything he believed about his life was a lie.

Still, the uneasy feeling in his gut told him it was true.

"Does Jameson know?" Travis's voice was faint.

"He didn't at the time, and if Doug had lived, he'd never have known," she admitted. "We were such a happy little family, you, me and Doug. I couldn't risk losing that."

"When did Jameson learn about me?" Travis's stomach was tied in knots.

Lenora sank onto a nearby bench. "At the time, we lived in Raleigh. Your father surprised us with a weekend trip to Asheville, and we stayed at Moonlight Ridge. That's when I saw Jameson again. I was in shock. I'd never expected to see him again. You weren't quite three. Jameson took one look at you and he just…knew," she said. "I was terrified he'd try to take you away from us, so I denied you were his son and lied about your age so he wouldn't put it together."

"Did Dad know Jameson was my father?"

"Yes, I never kept anything from Doug. He agreed we shouldn't take a chance on Jameson fighting for custody. But he was glad we knew where to find your biological father, in case you learned the truth as an adult and wanted to know him."

Travis dropped onto the bench, his legs collapsing under the weight of her confession. He felt hot and cold at the same time. His head spun and his mouth felt dry.

"He's known since I was three?"

"He *suspected* as much then. I didn't confirm the truth until after your father was gone. We were about to lose the house, and I was unable to cope with losing the love of my life." His mother wiped away the tears streaming down her face again. "I had nowhere else to turn, so I came to Asheville and told him the truth, and that his son needed his help. He found us a place here and paid the first six months of rent. He wanted to get to know you. I thought we should ease into the relationship, but never tell you Doug wasn't your real father."

"And he agreed to that?" Travis's jaw clenched.

"Only because I threatened to disappear with you if he didn't. Soon afterward, things began to spiral out of control for me. In a moment of clarity, I explained my situation to a social worker who lived in our building. She talked to Jameson. Helped him get qualified as a foster parent. We made arrangements for him to care for you, if ever I couldn't."

So Jameson had known he was Travis's father long before he'd arrived at Moonlight Ridge. He'd never indicated as much. Nor had he treated him any differently than Mack or Grey.

Travis was stunned. Inside his head he was howling like a wounded animal. Yet, he had to maintain a calm facade in this very public place with the television crew and members of the media roaming around.

"I need to talk to my dad."

"He already knows I planned to tell you. So does she." Lenora nodded toward Riley, who approached.

"There you are, babe. Joan sent me to look for you because—" Riley stopped abruptly when she saw the expression on his face. That's when she recognized his mother.

She looked like she'd seen a ghost.

Riley lowered her gaze, her chin dipping to her chest as she smoothed back her hair.

"Mrs. Nelson." Riley's smile faltered. "Lovely to see you again."

"You knew?" Travis stood, facing her.

The sound of his heart thumping in his chest filled his ears. When his mother dropped this bombshell in his lap, his first reaction was that he needed to talk to Riley. To seek the comfort and advice of the woman he adored. Yet, for the past three weeks she'd already known. And she'd never said a word.

"I had no idea that your mother was volunteering here today," she said quickly.

Travis lowered his voice so the curious group over by the grills wouldn't overhear them. "You knew that Jameson is my real father?"

Riley shifted her gaze to his mother, then back to him, leaning in closer so only he could hear her. "I knew your mother *claimed* Jameson was your real father, and I tried to tell you as much at the cottage that night. You refused to hear me out, and you insisted I shouldn't believe her. So I thought I should at least talk to your dad first."

"And did you talk to my dad?"

"No, I… I planned to but… I…" Riley stammered. "I was worried about how it might impact your relationship with Jameson."

"You mean you were worried I'd back out of this deal. That I wouldn't be willing to sacrifice a year of my life to help my father restore Moonlight Ridge if I knew he'd been lying to me since I was seven."

"You think I kept this from you for selfish reasons?" Riley looked hurt. "Travis, I'd never do anything to intentionally hurt you."

She reached out to him, but he stepped backward, sinking onto the bench again.

He closed his eyes, shutting out their competing voices. Both women were apologizing and insisting he should let them explain. But the reality was they'd both kept the truth from him and so had Jameson.

He'd spent much of his life struggling with an inability to trust people. The one person he'd *never* doubted had been Jameson Holloway. And he'd slowly begun to trust Riley again, too. But his trust had been misplaced. Neither of them had been honest with him.

Travis stood abruptly, angry with himself for forgetting the lesson he'd learned at seven. The only person he could consistently rely on was himself.

He lowered his voice to a harsh whisper.

"I have an obligation to fulfill here." He looked at his wife pointedly, making it clear their marriage was one of those obligations. "We'll talk about this later."

He offered his open palm to Riley, who reluctantly placed her hand in his.

They'd been behaving like newlyweds who were madly in love all morning. If any tension between them was detected, breakup rumors would be online before he'd served dessert.

So instead, he'd smile and behave as if nothing had changed—despite the fact that his entire world had just imploded, and it felt as if there was no one in his life he could truly trust.

Twenty-Four

"Travis, say something, *please*." Riley spoke over the roar of the Hellcat's engine. They were nearly back to the cottage, and he'd barely said two words to her.

"What do you want me to say, Riley? That I'm disappointed in my mother, Jameson and you for not telling me the truth?" He shrugged. "That seems pretty damn obvious."

Riley wished Travis would just get angry. Tell her what he was feeling. Then they could fight, make up and move forward *together*. Instead, Travis was punishing her with a silent disdain that indicated he'd written her off.

Her heart ached at the thought.

Lenora and Travis had put her in an awful position, leaving her with no good choice. Riley had handled the convoluted situation in the way she thought best. She hadn't done anything wrong. Yet, given Travis's past, she understood why he'd taken her silence as betrayal.

"I'm sorry. If there was even a sliver of a chance that what your mother said was true, you deserved to know."

"Then why didn't you tell me, Riley?" he demanded. "And don't say it's because I didn't want to know. I didn't want to hear your marriage proposal, either, but that didn't stop you."

Direct hit. Like when she'd watched Travis and his brothers playing Battleship when they were kids. She needed to be honest with her husband and herself.

"That night at the cottage... What happened between us was so perfect. After everything we've been through, we were finally together and happy. I was terrified of screwing that up. And I've put off talking to your dad because I adore Jameson. I didn't want to hurt or embarrass him."

Travis turned into the drive leading to Moonlight Ridge. "Well, there's no avoiding that, huh, Princess?"

No, it didn't seem there was.

Travis walked into the house where he'd grown up. A place that had represented love and family. For a time, he and his brothers had forgotten that. But since their father's illness, each of them had rediscovered the importance of family.

Yet, a single conversation with his mother threatened to shatter it again. Because right now, it felt as if he'd walked into the house of a stranger.

"Hey there, son. How'd the banquet at the women's center go?" Jameson grinned.

"The event went fine," Travis said curtly, ignoring Trouble and Nonsense, who'd gathered near his feet, waiting to be greeted. "But we need to talk."

There was a look of realization in his father's eyes. Suddenly, Jameson Holloway looked every bit of his sixty-five years.

Jameson settled onto his favorite chair in the den as Travis sat opposite him. "I'm guessing you've spoken with your mother again."

"So it's true?" Travis felt like he'd been run through with a spear.

"Yes. I'm your biological father. I have the DNA test that proves it."

"How could you keep this from me? And why would you pretend to take me in out of the kindness of your heart when I'm *actually* your son?"

"You're all my sons," Jameson said. "And yes, my blood runs through your veins, Travis. But I honestly couldn't love any of you more than I do."

"I appreciate that, Dad." The word hit differently now that he knew Jameson was his real father. "But I still don't understand why you'd allow me to believe I was another man's son."

"You *are* his son, Travis. Douglas loved you, as surely as I do. Your mother didn't want to ruin your memory of him, so she made me promise not to tell you. It was the only way she'd agree to let me see you. So I promised her, and I've kept my word. No matter how badly I wanted to tell you."

The last time Travis had heard this kind of pain in his father's voice was when he'd been fading in and out of consciousness after the accident. He didn't want to hurt Jameson, but this conversation couldn't be avoided. And Travis had every right to be upset.

It was honorable of Jameson to keep his word to his mother, but Travis had the right to know the truth.

"I won't pretend to understand why the three of you kept this from me or to be okay with it." Travis's head throbbed. He could only imagine the anxiety this conversation was causing his father, who was still recovering. Travis studied his father, who was clearly distressed. "How are you feeling, Pops? Physically, I mean?"

"I'm fine, son." Jameson sighed. "But I'm sorry. We should've told you long ago. I realize you're angry with your mother and me—"

"And Riley," Travis said.

"Why Riley?"

"My mother told her the night of the reception. Riley did try to tell me that night, but I didn't want to hear anything my mother had to say. So Riley backed off and never brought it up again. Not once in three weeks." Travis grew agitated thinking of all of the opportunities Riley had to tell him the truth.

"Son, I understand why you're miffed with me, your mother and Douglas. But if Riley tried to tell you and *you* insisted you didn't want to hear it… Son, that's on you," Jameson said matter-of-factly. "Don't use this as an excuse to blow up what you have with Riley. You two were meant to be together, Travis. Look how happy you've been the past few months. A love like that doesn't come around too often. When it does, you'd best grab hold of it. Don't let a pigheaded misunderstanding destroy what you two have."

Travis set back on the sofa and sighed. His father was right; he'd put Riley in an impossible situation. She'd done as he asked. Yet, he'd accused her of keeping the truth from him. No wonder she'd looked hurt and bewildered on their ride home.

Guilt roiled in Travis's chest. He'd been unfair to his wife. But as he stared at his father now, he realized he was being unfair to him, too. He was angry Jameson had kept him in the dark about his paternity. But he was just as wrong for concealing the true nature of his marriage to Riley from his father.

Travis swallowed hard and met Jameson's gaze. Then he told his father the truth about Riley's dilemma and the financial proposal that resulted in their marriage. Something she'd given him permission to share with Jameson from the outset.

After his initial shock, his father listened patiently. Then he asked about a few details of the arrangement as it pertained to Moonlight Ridge.

"Thank you for leveling with me, son. But I have to be honest, I'm not comfortable accepting help on those terms. Though I suspect you already knew that." Jameson sighed. "But I'll tell you what I do know. Riley is an amazing woman. When I met her as a kid, I hoped she wouldn't let her family's money and elitist attitude change her, and she hasn't. She's doing so much good in the world and in our community. And it's obvious she truly loves you. I believe you love her, too."

"I do," Travis admitted quietly. It was a realization that had slowly been building over the past two months.

"Then tying your relationship to a financial arrangement—"

"Is a recipe for disaster?" Travis rubbed his stubbled jaw. "I know. I've been thinking about that since we got married and I realized..."

"That this wasn't an act anymore?" His father chuckled quietly. "Coulda told you that way before then, son."

"I haven't touched her money. Nor have I made plans to move forward with the restaurant." Travis ran a hand over his head. "It just didn't feel right."

"Good." His father raised a triumphant fist. "I know you find it hard to trust people, Travis. I'm sorry if keeping your paternity a secret has added to that lack of trust. But please don't let an inauspicious start or a miscommunication ruin the love you two have built."

His trust issues were the reason he'd been quick to attribute a selfish motive to Riley. Travis had struggled with his lack of trust his entire life. He'd entered every friendship, relationship and business deal with an eye on the exit. Expecting the other party to disappoint him the way people in his life often had.

"You and your brothers mean the world to me, Travis. It brings me so much joy to see the three of you finding love and being a family again. Molly, Autumn and Riley are the daughters I never had. Seeing you build families of your own with such incredible women..." The corners of Jameson's eyes were wet. "*That* is the greatest accomplishment of my life."

There was so much love and pride in Jameson's misty eyes. His mother's revelation had been shocking. But in the end, both Jameson Holloway and Douglas Nelson were still his fathers. They were good men who'd loved and cared for him. And they'd done what they'd believed to be in his best interest. He was lucky to have had both men in his life.

"I should get home and talk to Rye." Travis stood. His father stood, too, and Travis hugged him tightly. "I love you, *Dad*."

Jameson patted his back. "I love you, too, *son*."

"I guess we should tell Mack and Grey."

"Only if you want to. Like I said, it doesn't change a thing. I'm still as much their father as I am yours."

"I know. But I don't want there to be any more secrets in this family."

"Good." Jameson scratched his gray beard, a slow smile spreading across his face. "And on that note, I need to tell you boys that I've asked Giada to marry me, and she said yes."

"I knew you two were getting close, but *wow*. I'm really happy for you, Pops." Travis smiled. "I'd say Giada will make a great addition to the family, but she's already become an important part of this family. And after all of the sacrifices you've made for the three of us, I'm glad you're finally getting your happy ending, too."

"Thank you, son." Jameson smiled, then rubbed his beard, in deep thought. "I know you're eager to get back to your wife, but I have an idea. Can you spare a few minutes?"

"Sure, Pops." Travis could see the wheels turning in his father's head. He returned to his spot on the sofa. "What's on your mind?"

Twenty-Five

Riley had spent the past two hours at the cottage making a few phone calls and replying to pressing emails. Beyond that, she couldn't concentrate enough to get any real work done.

She couldn't control what Travis thought or was feeling. So she focused on something she could control. Riley was cleaning and reorganizing her office—located in the guest room. If Travis's silent treatment on the way home was any indication, she may very well find herself sleeping there again.

But she couldn't control that, either.

What she would do is dig in her heels and stake her claim. Riley didn't want a loveless, fake marriage that made them both miserable. She wanted the love and friendship they'd been developing over the past few months—even if they'd both been too afraid to call it that. Fate had conspired to bring them together again after all this time. She wouldn't give up on this so easily.

Riley stopped what she was doing when she heard the distinct roar of the Hellcat pulling up to the cottage. She descended the stairs just as Travis entered the front door.

"Hey." He shoved his hands into his pockets.

She stood at the foot of the stairs, her arms folded. "Hey."

An awkward silence lingered between them, then they both tried to speak at once.

"Travis, I…"

"Riley…"

Travis gestured toward her. "You go first."

Riley sucked in a sharp breath and stepped forward. She

met his gaze. "I admit to having selfish reasons for not forcing the conversation. Our wedding night was like a fairy tale, and I didn't want to burst the bubble. I was terrified that if I did, we'd never get the magic of that night back. So I sat on the news, and for that, I'm sorry."

"Riley, I—"

"I'm *not* finished." She pointed.

He snapped his mouth shut and gestured for her to continue.

She had to get this off her chest before she lost her nerve.

"You are a fucking adult, Travis Holloway. You said... no, you *insisted* you didn't want to hear what your mother said. You were adamant that I shouldn't believe anything she told me. Now you're angry with me for doing *exactly* what you asked me to do. I'm your wife, Travis. Not your nursemaid. I'm not here to coddle you. And I may have a lot of talents but being a mind reader isn't one of them. You need to say what you mean and mean what you say."

Riley huffed, her words running together so quickly she was out of breath. When he didn't interrupt, she continued.

"The day we stood in front of everyone and said our vows... That never felt fake to me, Travis. Because what I feel for you is real. I'm in love with you." The words came out in a strangled whisper. "Not just because you were my first love. Because I love the man you've become. You're an ambitious entrepreneur. Yet, you were willing to make this huge sacrifice for your family. You've become so invested in the community since your return. You've unselfishly taken Hallie under your wing, and you treat her like a sister. You're kind and respectful to all of the hotel employees. And I love spending time with you and your family. I've never been happier, Travis. And it seems like us being together makes you happy, too."

"I definitely should've gone first." Travis rubbed the back of his neck.

"Why? What were you going to say?" She searched his unreadable expression.

"That I'm sorry for being an asshole. You're right. You did exactly as I asked." Travis stepped closer. "I've got some shit I'm still trying to work out, and it was wrong of me to take that out on you." Travis lifted her chin, then he kissed her, his calloused thumb grazing her cheekbone. "I love you, too, Rye."

Tears stung Riley's eyes, and a slow smile spread across her face.

"Forgive me?" He brushed his lips over the backs of her fingers.

"Of course." Riley stared up at her husband through the haze of unshed tears. "But if we're going to make this work, we have to be honest with each other about everything."

"I know." Travis took her by the hand and pulled her over to the sofa. "And if we want this to be a real marriage, I can't accept your money. That's why I haven't touched it or made plans for the restaurant. Also, I leveled with my dad about our marriage arrangement."

"Your dad." Riley pressed a hand to her chest. "I was so focused on what I needed to say that I forgot to ask how your talk with Jameson went. Are you two all right?"

"We're good," Travis said. "But he feels the same way. He won't take money from you as some kind of payment for our marriage."

She should be flattered her husband didn't want her money, but she loved Travis, and she loved Moonlight Ridge. The place felt like home, and Jameson felt like family.

Riley wanted to be a part of that.

"You need my investment to complete the renovations, and converting the old café into one of your signature restaurants is a longtime dream of yours." Riley squeezed her husband's hand. "I have the money. I adore Moonlight

Ridge. And I believe in the Holloway men. I want to see this place thrive again while your dad is still around to see it, Travis."

"We all want that." A warm smile slid across her husband's handsome face. "That's why my dad proposed that you be given a proper stake in Moonlight Ridge."

"Your father is letting me be an investor in the property?" Riley was stunned, knowing Jameson had been adamant that only family members should invest in the estate.

"Pops is making you a *partner* in the estate—just like every other member of this family who has invested in Moonlight Ridge. And I'm offering you the same in the restaurant." Travis's smile widened. His eyes shone with emotion as he kissed the back of her hand. "I want you as my partner, Riley. In life, in Moonlight Ridge and in my restaurant here on the estate. If that's what you want," he added.

"That's exactly what I want." She nodded enthusiastically, wiping away the tears of joy that wet her cheeks.

Riley was genuinely excited about partnering with Travis in his new restaurant. She wanted to be a part of this new venture—the intersection of two things that meant so much to her: Travis and Moonlight Ridge. The place where they'd met, gotten married and were currently living.

"In fact, I think we should celebrate." Riley slid onto her husband's lap, straddling him.

"Is that right?" Travis's large hands settled on her hips. His voice was gruff. He wet his lower lip with his tongue. "What did you have in mind, Mrs. Holloway?"

Hearing him call her that made her heart dance, so she didn't bother to remind him that her name was hyphenated. For tonight, she was perfectly content to be Mrs. Travis Holloway.

Riley teased him with a soft, playful kiss. But Travis tightened his grip on her bottom as his lips glided over hers. His tongue searched her mouth.

Her tight nipples grazed his hard chest and she moved against the growing ridge beneath his zipper as their kiss became more intense. The space between her thighs grew slick and ached for his touch. Her skin tingled and warmth swept up her neck and face as their kiss became more urgent.

Riley pulled her mouth from his. Her knees were shaky as she stood. "I'm taking a shower…in case anyone is interested."

She headed for the stairs, hoping her husband would be right behind her.

Travis watched his wife ascend the stairs looking like pure sex wrapped in a sweet, angelic bow. In no time flat, he was off the sofa and had joined her in the bathroom they now shared. They worked together to remove each other's clothing between frantic kisses.

He brushed his lips over the glowing brown skin of his wife's shoulder. Riley was a stunning woman with her delicious curves. The pebbled peaks of her soft, full breasts made his mouth water. She had a curvy ass that could stop traffic, tantalizingly thick thighs and hips made to hold on to. She had warm, expressive eyes and a mouth he simply couldn't get enough of.

Riley stepped into the running shower and crooked a finger in invitation. The sexiest smile lit her brown eyes.

Travis joined her, pressing his hands to the shower wall on either side of her. He gazed down at this amazing woman. He could still hardly believe she was his wife. That she'd be sharing his bed every night for the rest of their lives.

Riley made his days so much better with her brilliant mind, sweet disposition and teasing sense of humor. Her mere presence brought him a sense of contentment.

Travis captured Riley's mouth in a kiss that set his body

ablaze with desire. His already stiff cock grew harder pressed against her soft belly, and he couldn't wait to be inside her again. He slipped his fingers between them, gliding them over her slick folds and teasing her sensitive flesh as he avoided her clit. Her breath came in short pants, and he swallowed her moans of pleasure during their feverish kiss.

Her murmurs escalated as he increased the pace and pressure of his touch, taking her higher and driving her insane with pleasure. Finally, he caressed the taut bundle of nerves with his thumb as his fingers glided in and out of her.

Riley's eyes shot open. Her mouth formed a little O. His spine tingled with the visceral memories of all the amazing things that sexy little mouth could do. Riley rode his hand, her breathy pants indicating she was close.

There was nothing sexier than his wife on the brink of orgasm. He got off on watching her. On knowing he was the one bringing her such mind-blowing pleasure.

"Omigod, omigod, omigod...*yes*." Riley's legs shook and she leaned into him as she came hard, her inner walls gripping his fingers as she called his name.

Every last ounce of his control snapped. He whispered in her ear, "Baby, I need you."

Travis flattened Riley's palms against the tile wall, lifted her foot onto the shower bench and entered her from behind. Both of them moaned with pleasure when he slid inside her and hit bottom.

The feeling so deliciously intense, it took every ounce of control he could muster to glide in and out of her wet heat with a slow, steady rhythm. His fingers glided over her clit, bringing her to the edge again.

Riley's body tensed and her inner walls pulsated around his heated flesh as she called his name.

He thrust harder and faster, until his muscles tensed,

and he came hard, whispering his wife's name in her ear as he emptied himself inside her.

Travis's chest heaved, both of them panting as he dropped to the bench, pulling her onto his lap. He kissed her shoulder, his head still spinning. Travis had one clear thought running through his mind: he was thankful to have Riley in his life, and he'd never let her go.

Later, they lay in bed after making love again. They'd spent the evening opening up to each other in ways they hadn't before.

Riley explained why she wanted to get her hands on her inheritance. She hoped to help save two charities that didn't yet meet the criteria to receive funding from their family foundation. It affirmed what he already knew: Riley was a selfless, amazing woman and he was damn lucky to have her back in his life.

He revealed that there was an embezzler within the ranks of the Midnight Ridge employees, and they were closer to uncovering who it was. Riley was as outraged that someone had been stealing from Jameson as he and his brothers were.

"Tell me what you've done so far to catch this person." She went from her soft, dreamy, post-sex mood into business mode in two seconds flat.

He updated her on what they'd done thus far and shared their suspicions that it was someone connected to the kitchen or catering.

Riley scrolled through her phone, then she typed out a message. "I'm calling in a favor."

She told him about a guy named Edge who was a fixer her father sometimes used. His methods weren't always *traditional*, but according to Riley, his results were impeccable.

"You sure about this?" He twirled a lock of her hair, still damp from the shower, around his finger.

"It's what we do for family, right?" She stroked his stubbled cheek.

Travis's heart expanded. "Have I told you how much I love you, Rye?"

"Repeatedly." She grinned. "Especially while I was doing that thing you like with my—"

"Don't say it." He kissed her. "I'm getting hard again just thinking about it."

Seriously, the things this woman could do with her mouth.

Travis cleared his throat. "Okay. Do it."

"Are we talking about engaging Edge's services or—"

"Both." Travis sank his teeth into his bottom lip, his dick tenting the sheet.

Riley grinned. "*That*, sir, is the right answer."

Twenty-Six

Travis scrunched his six-foot-two frame behind the wheel of his Hellcat. He and his brothers were parked on a narrow street in a nondescript part of Spartanburg, South Carolina, a little more than an hour southeast of Asheville.

"We should've rented a fake laundry delivery truck," Grey piped from the back seat. "That's what they do on cop shows. Besides, it would've been more comfortable."

"One of us is cracking under the pressure of this mission," Mack said from the front passenger seat.

"We should've brought a coloring book and snacks to keep him occupied," Travis teased.

"I'm fine back here, thanks, *unfunny* guys," Grey muttered.

"You should be. You've got the whole damn back seat to yourself," Mack grumbled.

"Shh..." Travis held a finger up to his lips. "Shit's about to get real."

A tall man climbed out of his sedan and ran his hands through his thinning brown hair. Two other men approached and shook his hand. He led them to his trunk and opened it.

"I hope this works," Grey said.

"That bastard better pray the cops arrest him before I beat the shit out of him," Mack said.

"Ditto." Travis echoed his brother's sentiments.

It'd been killing them to watch this creep move about the hotel each day for the past week, knowing he'd been stealing from their father for years. But they'd agreed this was the best way. He'd be caught red-handed and have to pay for his crimes.

The two men looked inside the trunk, inspecting its contents. Finally, the taller man nodded his approval and the shorter man handed Ross Barnes—the catering manager at Moonlight Ridge—a thick wad of bills.

Ross grinned wolfishly and counted the bills before stuffing the wad inside his jacket. He shook the taller man's hand again. This time, the man wrenched Ross's hand behind his back and cuffed it while the shorter man held a gun on him. The undercover officers told Ross he was under arrest for theft and attempting to sell meat on the black market.

The camera crew suddenly emerged from their undercover van and captured Ross's arrest for the show.

Edge had unraveled the complicated money trail left by Ross and his girlfriend—a brilliant former accountant who'd done time for embezzlement. Ross had been purchasing silverware, linens and other items, then stealing them and selling them on the black market.

Mack, Grey and Travis stepped out of the car and ventured closer, eager for Ross to know who was responsible for his current dilemma.

"I'd like to punch him in his smug face." Mack stared Ross down.

"Do you think he knows he's fired?" Grey smirked at the man.

Ross dropped his head as a uniformed officer led him to a patrol car.

Travis and his brothers got back into the Hellcat. He texted his wife to let her know they'd caught their thief and were headed home. He couldn't help smiling at her response. He was head over heels in love with Riley and grateful to have her in his life. When he glanced up, his brothers stared at him with knowing grins.

"What?" Travis started the car and headed back to I-26W toward Asheville and Moonlight Ridge. Toward the place and the people that felt like home.

"Marriage looks good on you, Travis," Mack said.

"You too," Travis replied.

"We're three incredibly lucky guys." Grey's broad grin filled the rearview mirror.

Travis couldn't help but agree. They were all very lucky men indeed.

Travis had recounted the details of his stakeout with his brothers to Riley while she helped him make dinner. Now he handed her a slice of the butter pecan layer cake she'd been impatiently awaiting. He was considering adding it to the Traverser restaurant menu.

Riley eagerly scooped a forkful of the moist cake into her mouth and purred. "God, Travis. This is so good."

Travis felt the sensual sound deep in his gut. A flush of heat crawled up his neck. He sank onto the sofa beside Riley and she fed him a bite of the cake.

"It's amazing, right?"

Travis shrugged. He was trying out a new recipe. It was good, but not perfect. He'd keep working at it.

"Your dad is going to love this," Riley muttered through a mouthful of cake. "In fact, it's going to be a hit with the entire family."

"You think so?"

"I know so." Riley kissed his lips. Suddenly, her mood was less bubbly. She set her plate on the table. "Speaking of family, there's something I need to say about your mom."

"Okay." Travis put his plate down, too. They'd avoided the topic of his mother for the past two weeks, since Lenora had dropped the bomb about his true paternity. He turned to her. "Let's hear it."

Riley turned toward him. She folded her legs on the couch and placed her hands in his.

"I can't imagine how much it hurt to have gone through what you did as a kid. But when we were at the shelter, I realized that several of the women there have stories similar to Lenora's."

He grunted but didn't interrupt.

"Your mother was battling anxiety, depression and grief as she struggled with losing the love of her life. She self-medicated to numb the pain. Just like many of the women there that we've committed to helping." Riley squeezed his hand. "Baby, I'll support whatever decision you make. But I can't help thinking—"

"I should extend my mother the same grace," he finished her thought.

It was a fair point. One Jameson had already urged him to consider. How could he forge a future with Riley without dealing with his past trauma around trust and relationships?

This second chance they'd been given meant everything to him. He had no intention of blowing it.

"I'll think about it."

"That's all I ask." Riley kissed him.

"Mmm… That butter pecan cake does taste good on you." He pressed another kiss to her lips, and she giggled in response.

Travis pulled Riley onto his lap and nuzzled her neck. He resumed their kiss, fueling his insatiable hunger for this stunning, brilliant woman he was so lucky to have in his life.

Piece by piece, their clothing drifted to the floor. He made love to his wife. Something he would never tire of.

"I love you, Rye," he whispered, holding her close. "I don't ever want to lose you again."

"You won't," she assured him as they snuggled together on the sofa beneath a cashmere throw. "Because I love you, too, Travis. And I'm never, ever letting you go."

Travis had never been happier.

He finally had the love, friendship and family that had been missing from his life. So he would hold on to them, and to her, for as long as they lived.

Epilogue

December, One Year Later

Travis stood in the kitchen of Traverser at Moonlight Ridge—set to open in time for the holidays. He checked on the beef Bourguignon, a perennial favorite at his restaurants. Travis fanned the steam and inhaled the aroma from the Cognac, red wine, carrots, pearl onions and garlic. It smelled divine.

He nodded his approval to Lathan, his executive chef. Then he instructed his sous chef, Rosa, to remove the red fluted ramekins filled with cranberry orange crème brûlée from the fridge. Once the creamy custard confection reached room temperature, he'd pull out his butane torch and caramelize the crème brûlée himself, creating the perfect sugary crust.

As Travis glanced around the state-of-the-art kitchen, buzzing with his recently hired staff, he was filled with a sense of pride.

Little more than a year ago, Riley had mused about the café being converted to one of his restaurants by that time next year. Sure enough, the expansion of the building to its larger footprint had been completed by then. And in a few more days, Traverser at Moonlight Ridge would open to the public.

Tonight, he and Riley were hosting the annual Moonlight Ridge staff holiday party at Traverser. The event was doubling as a dry run for their grand opening later that week.

Travis slipped on his navy blue dinner jacket and returned to the dining room. The old café was completely renovated and decked out in festive holiday decor. The place buzzed with joyful conversation and laughter, and Travis couldn't help smiling.

Serving his first meal in the new space to the people who'd become his family filled his heart with immeasurable joy.

"Everything good, Dad?" Travis squeezed his father's shoulder.

Jameson was seated at one end of the long table, holding the hand of his wife, Giada, seated beside him. "Couldn't be better, son."

"The bacon-wrapped scallops and creamy cauliflower and bacon soup were *delizioso*," his stepmother said in her lilting Italian accent as she kissed her fingertips in a chef's kiss.

"Thank you, Giada." It was high praise from such a brilliant cook. His stepmother's abilities in the kitchen, coupled with his father's utter contentment, had contributed to the slight tire around the old man's waist and his ever-present grin.

Travis was grateful to have both of them in his life.

He turned to his brothers. "I hope you saved room for my beef Bourguignon and dessert."

"Absolutely." Molly's green-gray eyes sparkled as she rubbed her burgeoning belly. She leaned into Mack, whose arm was wrapped around her. In just a few months they'd welcome the first of the next generation of Holloways. A baby boy they'd already named Landis. "I am eating for two, after all."

Travis squeezed his brother's shoulder as he walked past, and Mack grinned proudly in response. It was good to see Mack so happy.

He glanced over at Grey, who gazed dreamily at his wife as they chatted. After a brief engagement, he and Autumn had gotten married over the summer in the rose garden at Moonlight Ridge.

Since the completion of the renovations, Moonlight Ridge had become a premier destination for weddings and for Sunday brunch—keeping both of his sisters-in-law and their expanded staff busy.

Travis surveyed the space. Three long tables were filled with his family, key members of the Moonlight Ridge staff and their loved ones. Without their dedicated team, Moonlight Ridge would never have made its incredible rebound during the past year.

Travis nodded at Hallie, seated between her grandmother and younger sister. He was incredibly proud of how she'd blossomed into her role as Moonlight Ridge's executive chef. And with the limited-run reality series about the hotel's renovation airing soon, he had no doubt Hallie's star would continue to rise.

Travis slid into his seat at the head of the table and squeezed his wife's hand. Riley George-Holloway was beautiful, as always. Her glamorous, red sequin dress popped against her dark brown skin, and her hair fell in silky waves over one bare shoulder. His love for Riley grew exponentially every single day of their lives together. He gave his wife a quick kiss on the cheek as the restaurant staff brought out the main course and began serving it.

"You've outdone yourself, son." Travis's mother, seated to his left, beamed. "And I'm so very proud of you."

"Thanks, Mom." Travis kissed her cheek. He and his mother had been getting reacquainted over the past year and slowly rebuilding their relationship. He'd been resistant, at first. But now he was grateful for his wife's encouragement and the second chance he and his mother had been given.

Riley's family was vacationing in Vienna. His relationship with his in-laws had improved but was far from perfect. He and Ted George had one thing in common: they both loved Riley and wanted her to be happy.

Fifteen months ago, Travis couldn't have imagined he'd be happily married and living in Asheville when he wasn't filming in LA. But now he couldn't imagine his life without the people in this room. Especially the incredible woman sitting to his right.

Riley's lovely face and warm smile were the first things he wanted to see each morning and the last things he wanted to see each night, for the rest of his life.

* * * * *

COMING SOON!

We really hope you enjoyed reading this book. If you're looking for more romance, be sure to head to the shops when new books are available on

Thursday 14th October

To see which titles are coming soon, please visit

millsandboon.co.uk/nextmonth

MILLS & BOON